A BALLAD OF BETRAYAL AND BEAUTY

Also by L.H. Blake

Carnal Sins Series

A Song of Sin and Salvation

A Duet of Darkness and Dreams

The Elements Series

Where the Lights Lead

Playlist

Cherry Bomb - The Runaways
Send Me An Angel - Scorpions
Against All Odds - Phil Collins
Here Comes the Sun - The Beatles
You're My Best Friend - Queen
Only the Lonely - The Motels
Waiting for a Girl Like You - Foreigner
Something in the Air - Thunderclap Newman
What I Like About You - The Romantics
A Kiss to Build a Dream On - Louis Armstrong
Bad Blood - Neil Sedaka
Causing a Commotion - Madonna
If You Leave - Chicago
The Name of the Game - ABBA
Running With the Night - Lionel Richie
She's Like the Wind - Patrick Swayze & Wendy Fraser
Suspicious Minds - Elvis Presley
Foolish Heart - Steve Perry
Young Love - Sonny James
Separate Ways - Journey

Maneater - Daryl Hall & John Oates
(It Looks Like) I'll Never Fall In Love Again - Tom Jones
Goodbye Stranger - Supertramp
Bad to the Bone - George Thorogood & The Destroyers
Battery - Metallica
Head Over Heels - Tears for Fears
Love is the Drug - Roxy Music
Do That to Me One More Time - Captain & Tennille
Every Rose Has It's Thorn - Poison
Love Bites - Def Leppard
Love Will Tear Us Apart - Joy Division
Baby Can I Hold You - Tracy Chapman
The Waiting - Tom Petty
Alone - Heart
Live to Tell - Madonna
I'll Be Loving You (Forever) - New Kids on the Block
This Woman's Work - Kate Bush
The Things We Do for Love - 10cc
The Search is Over - Survivor
Love to Love You Baby - Donna Summer
Time After Time - Cyndi Lauper
Under Pressure - David Bowie & Queen
Need You Tonight - INXS
Nasty Girl - Vanity 6
Sexual Healing - Marvin Gaye

CHAPTER 1

Cherry Bomb

DUSTY

The only reason men are worth putting up with is their money. If I didn't need it to survive, I'd turn around and walk out of this club in these impossible heels. But I can't. Rent is due and while I have enough money stashed away in my dresser at home to cover my share, I still need to eat. Besides, I'm no one's charity case. And I'll never let myself rely on the word of a man to save me ever again—no matter what.

My head pounds, each throb made all the more potent by the flashing lights. The good mood I brought with me to work tonight is gone, and I'm dreading my stage time, even if it's the best moneymaker around here. Hopefully security followed through because the thought of him here, watching me. Him *seeing* me . . . I don't need to see pity in anyone's eyes—especially his. It's too painful.

I'm not ashamed of being a stripper. The money is great and I've made friends, and while it's not as glamorous as it looks, it pays the bills. I survive here. But what he said crawls under my skin, and I just can't get it out of my head.

Let me save you.

I scoff. I don't need saving, never have. I'm twenty-three

years old and know how to take care of myself. How dare he? After everything? All types of guys come in here. The jerks who believe they can own you, for a few bucks. The lonely ones looking for a girlfriend for the night. The married guys who aren't getting it at home so they come here for a little release. And while they're rare, there are also the ones with the savior complex. The ones who think this job is the lowest of the low and that I'm just waiting for a knight in shining armor to appear in this godforsaken strobe-lit club.

Well, news flash. This isn't a fairy tale. I don't need some guy who thinks he understands me to walk in and make me feel like shit. Besides, Vegas is the best place to be for a stripper. The endless supply of men willing to throw all their money at you is staggering, and the nightlife never quits. Why would I want to leave?

Let me save you.

Ugh, I feel like punching something. I push through the swing door into the back to give myself a once-over and calm down before I head onstage. Nausea rolls in my stomach and my hands shake.

"You okay, Cherry?"

I look up at the sound of my stage name, my eyes locking on Mandy in the mirror, standing behind me. I shrug. "Just some entitled prick I let get to me. That's all."

She comes around to lean on the counter. "Want me to tell security to throw him out?"

My red curls tumble down my back as I shake my head. "No, I handled it. He wasn't—" *How do I even explain myself?* "He wasn't getting handsy or anything. Just said something that bothered me. That's all."

She turns to look over her shoulder at herself in the mirror and wipes some of the smudged lipstick from the corner of her lips. "Okay, well, you're up next, right?"

I plaster on a bright smile, fluffing up my hair as high as it'll go atop my head. "Yup."

She hip-checks me and heads back toward the door with a wink. "Break a leg."

My smile falls once she's gone, and I take a deep breath. I can do this. I shake out my limbs and stretch my neck from side to side before adjusting the neon green fishnet mini dress over my itty bitty string bikini top and thong. It barely covers my nipples and my bare butt cheeks rub against the mesh fabric of the dress in a satisfying way. I wipe away the mascara from my undereyes and reapply my red lipstick.

"Next up, gentlemen, please give it up for our fire engine bombshell, Cherry!" the announcer calls, and my stomach swoops.

I straighten my spine and give myself a hard look. "Get your money, girl." Then I turn around and push through the doors toward the stage.

As I swing my hips, the sound of the whistling from the crowd chases my nerves away a little. At least it's dark in here; if I focus on one face in the crowd, I won't have to envision *him*.

My eyes are fixed on the silver pole in the middle of the stage, and I climb the treacherous stairs in my sky-high heels. The lights are warm on my glittery skin as I wrap my fingers around the pole and stick out my left leg in a pose as I wait for the music.

One face . . . just one . . .

There's a man sitting at the very end of the long narrow stage, and I'm immediately struck by how gorgeous he is. His dark hair hangs long and thick past his shoulders, and his cheekbones are so sharp they could cut glass. I hope this guy's got cash to burn, because I think I just found my target for the night.

"Cherry Bomb" by The Runaways starts to blast through the speakers, and I wrap my leg around the pole, falling into a slow spin. I lean forward, my breasts hanging heavily as I smile at him.

He swallows hard, his dark eyes flitting over every square inch of me he can see. I run my hands up my thighs, over my breasts, and up into my hair as my inner thighs clench around the pole. I let my head fall, my back arching until I spot the man from my upside-down vantage point. He leans forward to rest his elbows on his knees, his eyes intense and ever-watchful as I dance for him.

I lift myself back up and allow the spinning pole to twist my body down onto the stage floor. Rolling over on my hips, I spread my legs right toward him as my body turns so he knows he's the chosen one. The other men lining the stage reach forward to tuck their bills into any exposed part of me they can reach, and while I take it all, I never break my gaze with him.

He grins as I crawl across the stage toward him. My god, that kind of smile breaks hearts, I know it—and I bet he does too. When I near the end of the stage, I turn to lie on my back, my hair falling over the edge of the stage into his lap. Lifting my legs, I watch his face as he follows the way my legs point to the ceiling. How they kick and roll, then spread, and I smirk as he goes a bit cross-eyed—like he's trying to assign an eye to each leg.

I watch him laugh at himself before he slides a twenty-dollar bill between my breasts.

His gaze finds mine, and I bite my lip. I wonder what kind of man this one is. Lonely? A jerk? Married? Hopefully, he's not another savior.

I pull myself up, chest first, then use the pole to stand. I do another sweep as the men hold out their money, stuffing it through the holes in my fishnet over my ass. Turning back to my gorgeous stranger, I wink at him so he knows he's special. That I'll be back for him when I'm done with these losers. Sure enough, as the song ends, I make sure to pose right in front of him, lay my body back in a long sultry pose.

There's an eruption of wolf whistles and applause as I stand, heading for the stairs. The man sits back in his chair as though inviting me over. Good, I was coming anyway. Walking toward him, I finally get a good look at what he's wearing. Okay, definitely not some douchey clown with a flipped-up collar and pushed-up blazer sleeves. No, this guy is into music. Metal music, from the graphic on his T-shirt and the ghoulish tattoos covering his arms and neck.

But before I can reach my mark, a man in an expensive suit with slicked-back hair blocks my path. "Cherry, baby," he says, "what's a guy gotta do to get that ass rubbing my dick?"

Can the mind vomit?

I blink and take care not to breathe too deeply as the amount of cologne wafting off this creep might choke me. I press my lips together in a pained smile and place a hand on my hip. "Oh darlin', I save that for my private dances, but afraid I have somewhere—"

"Let's go then," he says, then grasps my wrist and pulls me toward the black velvet door.

"Sir, you can't just grab me," I say, pulling against his tight grip. Looking over my shoulder, I spot my handsome stranger watching me, the smile on his face vanishing the longer I'm detained by this dickhead.

"Come on, Red, I'm good for the money," he argues, fanning a display of twenties like playing cards. My eyes latch on the bills, realizing that this guy alone could fill my nightly goal. But that cologne . . . It's cheap, which means he is too, and however much he has in his hand doesn't mean he'll hand it over willingly. Besides, he's a fucking scumbag.

I manage to wriggle free and step back. His face contorts, as though he can't possibly understand why I'm not running toward that door with him to "rub my ass" on his dick. "Sorry, but I have another date to see first."

Turning back, I sigh with relief when I see my long-haired

admirer still sitting in his chair, staring down the neck of his beer bottle. I stop when I'm standing between his spread knees, and he does a double take when he sees me.

"Hey, darlin'," I say over the blare of the next song. "How're ya doin' tonight?"

"Much better now that you're here," he says, his voice a rich baritone. "I, uh . . . thought maybe you were busy."

I scoff. "With who? Victor Von Douche?" I ask, tilting my head back to where I'm sure that lump of a man is staring after me, in shock that he couldn't buy my attention.

He grins, that smile lighting up his face. "He really is, isn't he?"

"May I sit with you?" I ask, raising an eyebrow.

"Hell yeah." He gestures at the next chair, but I turn, sitting down in his lap, propped up on his strong thigh. His eyes widen, a smile growing on his face.

I loop my arms around his neck and lean in, my lips grazing the shell of his ear. "Did ya like my dance?" I whisper.

He blinks slowly. "I like everything about you, princess. I could watch you dance all night."

I wiggle my hips on his lap and watch as the muscles in his jaw tense. It makes this gorgeous man even more beautiful.

"Maybe you'd like a private show."

"How much will that run me?" he asks.

I hum, then push him back in the chair, leaning forward so that my breasts are flush against his chest. His eyes bounce just enough to tell me he's hooked. "Five bucks a song. Or three for twelve."

"Right," he says, reaching down to his pocket. My eyes widen when he pulls out a stack of cash, and I have to bite my cheek to keep from squealing. "Guess that means I can have you all night then, Cherry."

Winner, winner, chicken dinner.

"Come with me then, darlin'." With one last roll of my hips, I stand and grab his hand, easing him off his chair. He follows along behind me as I head toward the private rooms, the heat of him blazing against my back.

"Wait, I should tell my friend . . ." He trails off, stopping to look around.

I follow his gaze. With two, I can make double. But after searching for a solid minute, my new date shakes his head.

"Ah, fuck it. Asshole's probably already found himself some entertainment."

Bummer. Oh well, this guy's got enough cash to make sure I can eat for a month. I wink at one of the bouncers as we approach, and he moves aside to let us through the velvet-adorned black door. Finding the first room free, I lead the man in behind me before shutting the door.

This room, like all the others, has tufted leather bench seats, a table in the middle, and a phone hanging on the wall to call to the bar—or, in rare circumstances, security if anyone gets out of hand. I don't think my handsome stranger will be a problem tonight, though.

"Have a seat," I say, slipping my hand from his and looking back over my shoulder. "Should I call for some drinks?"

He sinks into the leather bench, and I'm surprised when he shakes his head. "Maybe later. Got a pretty good buzz going on and don't want to fuck with that."

Right, because he plans to keep me for a while. I could think of worse ways to spend an evening. Besides, when guys get too drunk, they can be hard to manage.

He relaxes onto the couch and gestures me forward with his fingers. I step toward him slowly, my knees pressing into the leather as I straddle him. He groans as I sink my hips onto him, and he reaches forward to grab my thigh but stops.

"What are the rules in here?" he asks. "Can I touch you?"

I smile. Yeah, he won't be any problem. "Such a gentleman to ask."

"Trust me, there's nothing gentlemanly about the intention."

He grins, and I smile. Okay, so he's funny. Funny *and* good-looking. Damn.

"Yes, you can touch me. Everything but between my legs."

"What happens if I do? You got a bear trap hidden in there?"

I narrow my eyes. "They'd kick you out."

He snaps his fingers. "Damn. Okay. But just so you know," he says, looking me up and down, "I'd happily lose a finger for you."

A laugh bursts out of me, and he grins. "Just one?" I pout.

"I need the others for my extracurricular activities." As if to prove his point, he grabs my thighs, each finger pressing deliciously firm into my skin. Usually, these guys just grab enough skin to fill their fists while I dry hump them to a three-song time limit. But there's something about this guy. And while he doesn't seem to take life too seriously, there's something reverent about the way he looks at me. I grind my hips and feel his fingers tighten sharply. I gasp. He's stronger than he looks.

"Sorry," he mutters, relaxing his hands.

"It's fine," I say, and start to make deliberately slow circles, dragging my center against his thighs. "What's your name, sugar?"

He swallows. "Joel."

"Hmm, I love that name."

"You say that to everyone, don't you?" He cocks a brow.

Busted. "Of course, but I don't always mean it. I do today." That part is true.

"Why'd you blow off Von Douche for me?" he asks, catching me off guard.

I shrug. "Would you prefer I didn't?"

"Fuck no!" he insists. "I guess I'm just surprised. Most girls would look between the two of us and go for the clean-cut guy in a sharp suit over ripped jeans and leather cuffs."

I press my breasts against his chest and lean in toward his ear. "I like my men in leather."

He laughs. "I'm sure you do." He leans his head back on a sigh, and I can feel the hard length of him between my legs.

"Cherry . . . that your real name?"

I drag my fingers along the hard ridges of his chest and smirk. "Do you want it to be?"

"I'd rather know your real name."

My hips grind against him a little harder, and he groans. "Sorry, darlin'. No one here knows my real name."

"Occupational hazard?"

"Something like that."

"And the Texan accent? Is that real?"

Rising, I spin around and sit on his lap, leaning back against him. I take his hands and place them on my stomach, gently encouraging him to roam my body at his leisure.

"No."

"So where are you from then?" he asks.

"I can be from anywhere you like. Texas?" I ask in the accent I use 90 percent of the time. "Georgia?" I offer, adding a singsong lilt to my voice. "England?" I attempt a terrible English accent.

"Do you find it tiring? Never being yourself?"

My eyes fly open and I stare at the ceiling. *Why does he care?* I angle my face toward his. "This version of me is much more fun."

His lips touch my ear. "I doubt that." He cups my breast with one hand, and heat pools in my belly. I don't normally get turned on at work, but something about this guy . . . *Careful now, Dusty.*

"How'd you end up in Vegas?"

He softly pinches my nipple, and my eyes flutter closed as my head drops back onto his shoulder. "How most people end up here. I was down on my luck and wanted to change that."

"Hmm, and did you?"

Okay, what is with all the personal questions? This guy pays for my time then wants to grill me? Why can't he just accept the part I'm playing for him? Time to put him on the spot.

"What brings you to Sin City?" I ask.

His warm breath tickles my neck as whispers, "A wedding," in my ear.

I stiffen. Did this guy seriously come here to get married?

As though sensing the direction of my thoughts, he raises his left hand, showing off his ring-free finger. "Don't worry, not mine."

Exhaling, I soften back into his touch. Why do I care? He wouldn't be the first asshole to ditch his wife to be here. I strip for married guys all the time, but I have to admit it bothers me to think this guy might be just like the others. "So, what do you do for a living?"

"I'm a famous rockstar, princess." I can hear the smile in his voice, and I can't help but smile too. *There it is*. This isn't as deep as he made it seem. He wants to pretend too. I don't know why all the pretense . . . I'm happy to play into his fantasy. It's why I'm here.

"Your life must be so glamorous," I say, winding my hips again.

"It has its moments," he says, his fingers trailing down my stomach toward the top of my panties.

"So why come here when you have girls lining up backstage for a chance to be near you?"

He pauses, then retracts his hand. "Stand up."

Shit, did I insult him? Hesitating for just a moment, I do as instructed.

"Turn around."

His face is serious now. The semi-permanent smile that seems carved in his skin is gone. I shiver, goose bumps scattering across my collarbone in the absence of his warmth. His eyes travel all the way down my body before slowly rising to meet mine. And while the jokester appears to have gone, his gaze isn't menacing. Just . . . intense.

"I'm here," he says slowly, "because I love looking at beautiful things. And since being in Vegas, you are by far the most beautiful thing I've seen."

My heart races. Careful. *Careful.*

I drop my hip and smile nervously, trying to break the tension. "You don't have to woo me, Joel," I say, leaning forward. "Just say the word, and you can see everything. Touch *almost* everything."

He leans forward on his thighs so our noses are almost touching. "This version of me is much more fun."

Damn. Why did he have to turn the tables on me so quickly? This is dangerous. We're close enough now it wouldn't take much for him to kiss me. I wonder what that would be like. It's been a long time since I let anyone kiss me. His breath is warm and smells a little earthy, sour, from his beer. When he drops his eyes to my lips, I can't help but lick them, like simply tasting the air between us could satiate the aching heat inside me.

I shake my head, then pull back, forcing a smile. Something tells me a kiss from Joel would break me, and I can't afford to fall apart. "As long as you know that your efforts sadly won't end with you getting laid."

He shrugs. "I don't need to fuck the *Mona Lisa* to appreciate that it's a masterpiece."

My smile falters. *Is this guy for real?*

He reaches out slowly, fingers skimming the bottom of my fishnet dress. He raises his eyebrows, asking for permission, and I nod. He pulls it up and up and up, my heart racing in my chest as he tosses it down onto the seat next to us. Fingers digging into the flesh of my hips, he pulls me back down onto his lap, my core throbbing as it rubs against the bulge in his jeans. We're close again, and I'm suddenly on edge. Why is this so intimate? How did this stranger come in and knock down all of my defenses so quickly?

"I'm not a work of art," I say, and I hate that my voice trembles.

"Yes, you are."

I shake my head. "I just won the genetic lottery, that's all. Big tits and long legs don't exactly equal art."

"Then I don't think you're looking at yourself close enough."

His eyes hold mine as he pulls on the thin strings of my bikini top.

"This is gorgeous," he says, his calloused fingers tracing down my sides. My top falls to the floor and all that separates me from him now is my underwear. "But this," he says, his hand trailing back to circle over my heart. "This is too." My lips part and while I try to stop it, some of the ice that has crystalized around the organ melts at his words.

As I search his eyes, he gently taps the rhythm of my heart over my skin. "See?"

I squeeze my eyes shut, my chest tightening, and shake my head. When I open them again I stare into his. I thought they were brown before, but they're not. They're amber—like dark honey in a pool of moss.

Beautiful. He's beautiful. *He's* the art.

"Tell me something about you that's true," he whispers.

"My hair," I say, all hesitation gone. "The red is real."

"Knew it had to be," he says, twirling a strand around his finger. "The way the light hits it. It's like the sun."

My heart is not prepared for this tonight.

"It's funny," he says, almost to himself. "My mom told me

once that a redhead would steal my heart." My brow furrows, but then he wraps his arms around me, pulling me close until his face is buried in my chest. He squeezes me gently and I feel the inhale he takes, his nose gently gliding up my sternum. As he moans, I'm shocked to find myself daydreaming about some impossible future together. Where he really is a world-famous rockstar and I'm his muse—his leading lady. How he'd be a generous and attentive lover, and we'd live in some twelve-bedroom mansion with a household staff, and I'd never have to work again.

Let me save you.

This is too much. Why am I thinking about this? My life is fine. I don't need this man who's only interested in one night of my time. He's probably exactly like the one earlier, wanting to ride in on his white horse and save me. I don't *need* saving. And I don't need him. I just need his money. But the longer he touches me, the more we talk, the more I find myself desperate to take this somewhere I've never allowed myself to before.

I shake my head.

"I—you know, all this talking is really eating up your money."

"I like talking," he says, his palms moving over my ass. "It would be weird to do this silently."

"Most guys don't talk as much," I counter.

"I'm not like most guys."

No, he definitely is not.

"However," he continues, looking up at me. "Talking is what is keeping me from breaking the rules."

"Oh."

Break them. God, how I want him to touch me in the one place he can't.

He drops his hands onto the bench, his head falling back with his eyes closed, and sighs. I open my mouth, wondering if I've done something wrong. Do I keep moving? Finally, he opens his eyes and looks at me for a long moment. A shiver races up my scalp as he wraps a red curl around his finger, staring at it intently. Then with a smirk, he says, "How about we get out of here and have some real fun?"

"What? I'm—Joel, I'm working."

"Oh, right." He frowns. "Well, what time are you off?"

LIFE REALLY IS UNPREDICTABLE SOMETIMES. After a shitty start to my night, I've had the most fun since moving to Vegas. Joel handed me two hundred dollars for my time—an amount that was way overboard for the time we shared in the backrooms and had me melting into the floor, speechless—and said he'd come back when my shift ended. Imagine my surprise when, even after I stressed how that fun wouldn't include sex, he still seemed keen.

Walking down the Vegas strip this morning, with my arm tucked into his, I feel on top of the world. It's nice to be out. It feels like a date. Maybe that's what he wants. The girlfriend experience. And I make sure to lay it on thick. Agree with wherever he wants to go, accept what he wants to give me— which includes a snazzy new pair of shoes—and laugh at his jokes . . . Okay, this part's been easy because he's actually funny. I can't remember the last time I smiled so much.

But as the sun begins to rise over the tops of the buildings, the light chasing the stars away, this happy little balloon begins to deflate. Reality hits me when I remember that this is a guy who got lucky with some cash and wanted to have a great night out. After I leave, he'll go back to wherever he came from and years from now have a story to tell his buddies about that one time he went to Vegas.

My feet ache, and I'm exhausted and hungry as we walk toward a motel next to a wedding chapel. What I would give to simply fall into one of those beds and sleep the day away. Stomach twisting, we slow down our pace as we approach.

"This is . . . well," he stammers, "this is me."

I glance between him and the motel. "Oh, right."

He looks down and shuffles his feet. "You could . . ." He pauses, then sighs. "If you've changed your mind, you could come in with me."

The offer is so tempting, despite it being a cheap motel. Joel has been nothing but generous and fun, and the way he makes me feel . . . I haven't had sex in a long time, and I know based on the intimacy we've already shared that he could rock my world. But then he'd be gone, and the part of my heart that's already been captivated by him in a few short hours would shatter.

I glance down. "It's very tempting, Joel, but I'm going to have to say no."

He runs a hand down the back of his head. "Yeah, I figured." When he glances back up, his cheeks are pink. "Thought I'd ask again. Just in case."

"I really had a lot of fun tonight," I say softly. "More fun than I've had in a while. So, thank you for that."

He grins. "I don't think I'll ever forget it. Last night was insane. Here."

Holding out another small stack of bills, he pushes them toward me.

"What's this for?"

"For indulging me."

Part of me doesn't want to take it. I was happy enough to be around him. But then he'd wonder why a stripper didn't take cash from a paying customer. And if he starts poking holes in my refusal to join him in his motel room, I don't think I'll have the strength not to end up on my back.

"Well, I guess I'll be going then."

His lips press together in a hard line. "You, uh, should I call you a cab?"

"No, I'm . . . the bus is more my speed," I say, gesturing past him to the bus stop.

"Oh."

"Thank you." Shit, why am I getting so emotional? I step toward him and press up to my tiptoes, kissing him on the cheek. My lips linger a moment too long before I pull back, my hand instinctively brushing my mouth where that small, sweet touch tingles, and I avoid looking into that beautiful gaze.

"You know, I think my mom was right," he calls, taking a step forward like he's about to come after me. But he stops.

"What?"

"She was right. This gorgeous redhead," he says, placing a hand over his heart dramatically. "Think she stole a piece of my heart."

I shake my head, fighting a smile. "Goodbye, Joel."

I steel myself and walk away, heels clicking against the pavement of the parking lot. When I look over my shoulder, he's already walking toward the motel, and I let out a long breath. I see the bus stop and pause, changing course to grab something to eat at that diner first. As I head toward it and further from Joel, my fingers clutch at my chest and I blink up at the pastel morning sky. Everything looks different today.

And his mom was wrong. I didn't steal a piece of his heart. He stole mine the moment I saw him.

TWO YEARS LATER

CHAPTER 2

Send Me an Angel

JOEL

Some fucking bird is about to die. I open one eye against the sunlight and spot the noisy fucker on the branch outside the window. Maybe the better solution would be to cut that tree down. Then no more birds will show up to happily chirp away when I'm trying to sleep. Wait . . . since when has there been a tree outside of my bedroom?

There's a soft moan in my ear, and a warm arm wraps around me, long pink nails delicately scratching my chest. Right, I'm not in my room.

I scrub at both eyes and turn to find a shaggy mop of—blond hair? Why was I expecting red . . . ?

Something tumbles around in my stomach—a memory. Oh, that's why. I dreamt of her again. The girl who's been living in my head and not letting me know peace for two fucking years.

"Mmm," the blond murmurs.

Next to her, my best friend sits upright, the movement sending his chin-length brown curls swaying. His hair sticks out at odd angles, and as the sheets fall to pool around his naked waist, the sun tattoo etched into his back ripples with his muscles.

"Key," I groan. "I'm going to fucking kill that bird."

He yawns. "No, you won't. That's Gary."

I raise my eyebrow. "Gary? You named that menace *Gary*?"

"Yeah, Gary. I've grown accustomed to him now. He has a family."

As I cover my face with my hands, the woman between us stirs again. We glance at each other, and I point at myself before pointing to the door, letting him know I'm getting the fuck out of here. Key brought her home—he can deal with the aftermath.

I gently lift her hand off my chest, then slide out of bed and stand. Fuck, where are my clothes?

"Heh-hem."

I follow the sound to find Key pointing toward the window where my nemesis is happily hopping back and forth between branches. It's a cardinal. His bright red plumage reminds me of my dream, and I nearly stumble over a discarded high heel.

"Shit," I mutter, stooping down to grab my boxers, jeans, and the shirt I was wearing when Key invited me in on the culmination of his date last night.

I step into my boxers and flip him off on my way out the door, slamming it intentionally too hard behind me, then pause.

"What the fuck was that?" the woman's voice asks.

"Asshole," Key says, loud enough that I can hear him through the door. I laugh, then head back toward my own bedroom at the opposite end of the house, the rest of my clothes thrown over my shoulder.

It feels empty now that James and Dave have moved into their own places with their ladies. I kind of miss those early days of the band in San Francisco, when it was all of us together playing whatever gigs our manager, Al, could get us. Wondering when we were going to afford studio time. That first album release party. It all feels like such a blur now.

In the shower, I rinse away any fluids that might remain on my body after last night's adventure. It's not like I'm ashamed of it, and I definitely didn't run out of there because I regret it. But I've found when Key and I go to bed with one woman, she's the one who wakes up feeling embarrassed. So, better that one of us disappears before they get the chance to question all of their life choices.

When I step into the kitchen twenty minutes later, Key is standing behind the counter in a pair of sweatpants and flip-flops, drinking a beer.

"Hey," I say. "Bit early for drinking, don't you think?"

He shakes his head. "Not early enough."

I raise my eyebrows as he chugs the beer down, then turns to the fridge and pulls out another. "Dude, you all right?"

"Just a hard day, that's all."

I flip through the calendar in my head. No dates jump out at me. As far as I know, it's no one's anniversary or birthday. No one's died, so . . . is this about the girl who just left?

"If you wanted me to deal with the chick, you could've just said so," I hedge.

"No, no, it's . . . never mind."

Fuck. Is he regretting last night? "Listen, I know it doesn't happen that much, but if you're not cool with it anymore, we can stop."

He looks up at me with an odd expression. "I—what?"

"Is that why you're drinking yourself to death on a Friday morning?"

He looks down at his beer. "Oh! No, it's . . . nothing about that. We're cool."

"Then what the fuck is wrong?"

His head tilts back, and he sighs. "It's been eight years to the day since I last spoke to . . . my family. Since they dropped me off at that place."

"Oh." So it's going to be that kind of day. "Right, yeah. Sorry, man."

With a shrug, he takes a long sip of his beer. "It's fine."

I slump into the bar stool opposite him. "We could do something today. Go see a movie? Or there's that new go-cart place we saw a few weeks ago. I could embarrass your ass on the track to distract you."

Key smiles but avoids looking at me. "Thanks, but I think I'm just going to go back to bed. Didn't get much sleep last night."

His eyes meet mine for a second, then he takes his beer and slips down the hall. After a few quiet moments, I hear the door shut, and I let out a breath. I hate his shitty family. Bunch of holy rollers who won't talk to him anymore because of the music he loves and plays. But they're his family. Even though 99 percent of the time it doesn't bother him, the one percent it does is rough.

I tap my fingers on the counter. Maybe I'll get him something to take his mind off it anyway. Distraction is my specialty, but considering he's still in a bad mood after last night . . . This might call for some big guns.

I grab the keys off the end of the counter along with my wallet, then head out the door.

"RISE AND SUNSHINE, MOTHER FUCKER."

Key's eyes snap open and widen as he looks up at me.

"Joel, what the fuck are you doing?"

I grin, finding my balance as my feet sink into his mattress, then fire the paintball gun at his belly.

"Fuck!" he cries, hand clutching at his paint-covered stomach. Rolling over, he sees the other gun locked and loaded and ready for him. He grabs it and looks up at me. "Oh, you're dead!"

I run from the room, nearly eating shit as I topple off the bed. Paint splattering off the door frame as I run through it, and I cackle loudly. One ear trained on Key's mad scramble out of bed, complete with a string of curses, I duck into the kitchen and hide behind the counter.

"Where are you, asshole?" he whispers, and I hold my breath as he approaches. His bare feet pad across the tile floor, and when I think he's on the other side of the counter, I pop up, shooting him between the shoulders before taking off down the hallway.

"Joel!"

I feel a sharp pain on my ass, so I dive over the couch in a last-ditch effort to take shelter. But Key comes from the other side of the living room, pelting me in the chest, then the thigh as I scramble to get away—blindly firing my gun at him.

"Do you yield?" he yells.

"Never!" I cry, rolling under the coffee table and army crawling out the other side.

He chases me back to the kitchen, and I open the fridge door to narrowly avoid being shot again. I'm breathing hard and sweating, my heart hammering in my chest. Then it's quiet—the only sound coming from the fridge motor and that constantly chirping bird, Gary. Slowly, I close the door, but Key's gone.

"Where did you go?" I mumble under my breath.

There's a squeak in the floorboards, and I turn just in time to feel the sharp smack of a paint ball hitting me dead in the chest. The gun falls from my hands with a clatter, and I reach up to rub away the sting.

"Ow! What the fuck? Not that close," I say.

"Oh, come on, you failed to negotiate any rules before you shot me in the gut in my own bed."

I squint to find Key twirling his gun in victory, wiping the paint from his stomach, and *smiling*. Mission accomplished.

"What are these anyway?" he asks.

"Gotcha paintball guns. They're new. Had to beat up a ten-year-old for these."

He laughs, and I snatch the fallen gun off the floor and set it on the counter. "Wicked. So what do I win then?"

My smile drops. "Awesome new toy guns that shoot paint isn't enough?"

He crosses his arms.

"Okay, fine. Winner chooses the loser's punishment."

Key scratches the tip of the plastic gun to his forehead. "Hmm . . . I think," he says with a devilish smirk, "you're on laundry duty."

I blink. "Laundry?"

"Yup," he says, slapping me hard on the shoulder. "Make sure to do my sheets first. Need to get rid of your rank drool stains, along with paint splatter and any other bodily fluids."

I press my tongue into my bottom lip and fist my hands at my hips. "Fine. Fine. Laundry it is."

I'm slinking away, head hung low, when Key calls after me. "Hey, Joel?"

"Yeah?"

"Make sure to separate my colors."

He smiles at me, and I know what he's really saying: *thanks for the distraction, however momentary it was.*

After I've changed and collected every piece of dirty laundry lying around the house, I'm up to my knees in clothes, towels, and bedsheets, facing our washer and dryer. There's a piece of paper taped to the top of the washer with instructions for different cycle instructions from when Becks lived here. Funny how neither of us has had the heart to remove it. That being said, I disregard her suggestions for whites and just shove enough clothing into the washer that will fit, topping it off with a scoop of detergent.

The lid snaps shut with a *clang*, and I turn the dial to start it. But instead of the expected rushing water, there's a stuttering bang and a loud gurgle, and then I'm being sprayed in the face by a freezing jet of water.

"What the fuck!" I cry, reaching forward to turn off the valves through what's now a steady geyser exploding from the hose behind the washing machine. Trying to grip the handles while simultaneously shielding my eyes from the onslaught, I twist and twist until the spray finally subsides.

There's a flurry of footsteps amidst the drips on the tile when Key bursts into the room.

"What happened?"

"What the hell do you think happened, genius?" I mutter, blinking the water from my eyes and gesturing to my soaked shirt. "Water line burst."

Key sucks his teeth. "Damn."

I sigh, looking around at the soaked laundry piles on the floor. "I'm uh . . . I'm going to try to get this cleaned up. Can you call a plumber?"

"Sure, man. Yeah," he says, disappearing out the door.

"Just great," I say to no one in particular.

When Key returns fifteen minutes later, his expression is grim. "Good news. I got hold of a plumber," he says.

"Why does it look like that is accompanied by bad news?"

"He can't get here for another week."

My eyes widen, and I drop the sodden pile of laundry to the floor with a splat. "A week?"

He shrugs. "Says they're super busy, and since we still have water to the rest of the house, it's not classified as an emergency."

"What do we do now?"

Key claps me on the shoulder. "Well, considering you managed to get every single piece of laundry soaked, it needs to get washed before it starts to smell like asscrack."

"That's very helpful."

"There's a laundromat a few blocks away," he says.

I hang my head. "A laundromat? Seriously?"

Key rolls his eyes. "Oh, come on, you used laundromats for years."

"Yeah," I counter. "But that was before I was making shit tons of money playing bass."

"Come on, I'll help you load this mess into the car."

He picks up one of the baskets and starts toward the door. I follow along behind, muttering to myself. It's not like I loved doing laundry in the first place, and now I'll have to sit for hours with a bunch of strangers so our shit doesn't get stolen.

"You could come with me," I say.

Key grins. "Yeah, no way, man. You lost. Time to pay up."

He shuts the trunk and drops the keys into my hand. I roll my eyes. "I really wonder why I ever bother with you."

"Aww, you love me," he says, ruffling the top of my hair as I try to bat him away.

"I think you're confusing love with my wanting to smother you with a pillow."

"Nah, sounds about the same to me."

I shove him in the shoulder before getting in the car and slamming the door, ignoring his mocking wave through the window. I make sure to flip him off one last time for good measure as I back out of the driveway, and head toward the laundromat.

"GREAT, just great. Great, great, fucking *great*."

This is the second laundromat that's closed for repairs. For fuck's sake, it's 1988. Are there no working laundry machines in San Francisco? I'm seriously starting to consider whether clothes are that necessary to my life. As the sun begins to set, I spot a neon blue and red sign in the distance that reads *The Sudsy*

Dream. I scoff. Lame, much? Might as well come right out and call it *The Wet Dream*. But it looks open, with the handful of people I see inside and the rotating dryer drums. Perfect.

I pull up curbside and peer around. I've never been to this area of town before but it's pretty rundown. Looking up at the sign, I notice now that there are missing bricks at the corners of the building and most of the awnings are torn and rusted. There's a cat sitting in the smudged window of the second floor, which must be an apartment.

I blow out a breath. Well, as long as their machines are in service, I suppose it doesn't really matter. I open the trunk and struggle to get the four waterlogged bags of clothes inside the front door. A bell jingles overhead, and the sudden smell of laundry detergent and bleach overwhelms my senses, my eyes watering and throat stinging. The few people sitting on chairs in front of the window glance up at me, then return to their books and crosswords, but they don't seem to give me a second thought.

There's an older woman smoking behind a counter with a register, and I set down the bags by the door before heading over. She doesn't even glance up as I approach and I find myself standing awkwardly right in front of her. I clear my throat, but still she continues to read her magazine.

Finally, my patience wears thin after the day I've had, and I tap the bell on the counter by her arm. She looks up at me and raises an unimpressed eyebrow.

"Change?" she asks in a voice more akin to Oscar the Grouch than a woman in a furry green cardigan and grey-streaked black hair.

"Huh?"

She tilts her head at the machines. "You need quarters for the machines."

Oh shit, right. "Yeah, sorry, can you change a ten?"

Reaching forward with alligator green–tipped nails, she

snatches the ten-dollar bill from my fingers, then hands me a cup of quarters. I don't even know if she counted them.

"Don't leave your laundry unattended. Carts are at the back." Then she returns to her magazine, holding it up in front of her like a shield.

I blink. "Thanks, I guess."

As I grab a cart from the back of the store, the doorbell chimes again. My heart jumps into my throat the moment I look over my shoulder, my stomach turning over on itself when I see her. It's as if the sun has lit her hair, a ring of orange and gold like a blazing sunset around her pale face. Her red lips part in a smile, and the other patrons who ignored me greet her like an old friend—even the old bat behind the register.

Before I know it, I'm moving toward her. Remembering the way her skin felt under my fingertips, the way her blue eyes shone brighter than any crystal. The way she sparked something in me that's made it impossible to forget her, made it so even my dreams have been filled with visions of her.

"Cherry?"

I'm so focused on reaching her I miss the dryer door swinging out in front of me and slam into it hard, the sound ricocheting around the room as I fall to the floor. My ears ring and my vision blurs, every muscle in my back tensing as I try to blink up at the fluorescent lights of the ceiling. Did I walk right into that door? Or did I die?

Because there appears to be an angel looking down at me.

CHAPTER 3

Against All Odds

DUSTY

"**O**h my god, are you okay?"

Looking down at the man on the floor, my chest squeezes. I know this man. I know his hair, his cheekbones, the smile that seems to linger on his face even after hitting his head on a dryer door.

"Joel?"

I fall to my knees and crouch next to him, my hand flitting over his head to see if he's injured. My hair falls forward, and he reaches out to grasp a strand of it between his fingers. He shakes his head and rubs at the back of his scalp before squinting at me again.

"Cherry? What's a place like you, doing in a girl like this?" he mumbles.

He looks almost exactly the same. His hair might be a bit longer—is that *paint?*—but he's still every bit the non-conformist he was two years ago, with his tattoos, metal rings and anarchist clothing choices—and still so, *so* handsome.

I wrap my fingers around his arm and pull him into a sitting position. His face is close to mine now, and those feelings I've buried for two years suddenly come rushing back to the surface.

"What—what are you doing here?" I ask.

"Well, I was planning on doing laundry, but apparently I went back in time."

My smile spreads before I can even try to stop it. "You really went down hard. Are you okay?"

He nods, but as he does he grasps at his temple and flinches.

"Maybe I should call an ambulance and have you checked out."

"No! No, it's fine," he says. "I just—" He blinks up at me and my legs turn to jelly as I gaze into his beautiful amber eyes. Heat rushes into my cheeks, and I look away. "I can't believe you're here." It comes out too soft, too reverent, too . . . lovestruck. *Not again, Dusty. Be cool.* "I thought I'd never see you again. I thought— What about Vegas?"

I shrug. "I left about a year ago. Vegas wasn't dealing me the best hands anymore."

He lets me help him up and we notice everyone watching. "Guess I'm finally interesting enough for them," he remarks. "Not every day they get to see an idiot smash his head off a dryer."

I step back to put some distance between us. The way he *still* makes me feel is simply too intense. "In all fairness," I say, "they're a hard bunch to crack."

He looks past me to where I'm sure the crowd is hanging on his every word. "They're fans of yours, though."

"I've managed to wear them down."

I walk over to where I abandoned my empty basket and carry it over to my favorite dryer.

"You come here often, then?" he asks, following along behind me.

"No more often than necessary."

"Right."

He rubs the back of his neck under his straight black hair and

I take in the four sodden bags of laundry by the door. "You new to the area?"

"Huh?"

I jut my chin at the bags. "I haven't seen you around here before."

"Oh!" he says, as if remembering why he's here at all. "Oh, no, I . . . my washing machine at home is busted."

"That's too bad."

"Is it? I mean, if it hadn't, I wouldn't have been lucky enough to run into you."

I glance at him out of the corner of my eye, annoyed by the thrill his words spark in my heart. "I don't really believe in luck."

"What about fate? I mean, this is kind of unreal. I even had a dream about you last night."

I raise my eyebrows. My lips part, at a loss for words. As though he realizes what he said too late, his cheeks darken. He massages his temple again, looking lost.

"Did I say that out loud?" he whispers to himself.

Fighting against the flutters that have erupted in my stomach, I look up at him. "Are you okay? Are you sure you don't want me to call an ambulance?"

He shakes his head. "No, I'm okay. Look . . ." He turns and heads toward his bags of laundry, dragging them back across the room. "Motor skills are still functioning. That's good, right?"

I smile gently and nod as he opens the lids across from my machine and dumps what looks like every piece of clothing he owns inside. While I pull my clean clothes from the dryer, he meticulously fills the coin slots with his quarters, then stops. For a long moment, I watch as he stares at the machines, his eyes bouncing between them all.

"Fuck," he says quietly.

I lean forward over my basket. "Problem?"

He looks up, his cheeks flushing. "Yeah, I ah . . . forgot to bring detergent."

"Oh."

"You don't suppose that old reptile over there will sell me some, do you?" he asks, tilting his head Doris's way.

I press my lips together to smother a smile. Reptile is definitely the right descriptor. "No, definitely not."

He closes his eyes and sighs. "Great."

Don't offer, Dusty. Don't do it. He'll think you're flirting. "You can borrow some of mine." *Damn it.*

"Really?"

I shrug and close the door on the now empty dryer, bringing my full basket of warm clothes over to the folding table. "Of course." I grab a cart and, after looking around and making sure no one is watching other than Joel, push back a loose piece of paneling to grab my stashed detergent box.

"Smart," he says, grinning as I start to scoop the detergent into his open machines, acutely aware that his eyes never leave my skin.

I shrug. "I have my moments."

"I really appreciate this."

Flipping the lids down, I smile at him. "Everything in there?" I ask.

He nods, and we both start pushing the coins in to start the machines.

Over the noisy gurgling, I hear him exhale. "Thanks."

"No problem."

"I guess now I have to wait."

He glances at my basket of laundry and his smile dampens. He's just put it together that I'm done with my laundry and won't be here to keep him company.

"Do you want some help folding?" he asks.

"Oh, no, I think I'm okay."

He leans over and splays both palms on the table. "You sure? I've got time to kill and I happen to be an excellent folder."

I shouldn't let this continue. I should head straight upstairs and never look back. But that damn smile. Maybe a stronger woman would say no. Say that she can fold her own damn laundry. But what could it possibly hurt to hang around him for a few more minutes?

"Well, okay. But if you're not as good a folder as you say you are—"

"Then I'm gone," he says, holding up his hands.

He moves to stand beside me and grabs one of my bedsheets. I watch in amazement as he effortlessly folds a perfect square with my flat sheet. When he places it on the table, he cocks an eyebrow at me.

"Wow, you weren't kidding," I muse, impressed. "Where'd you learn to do that?"

He grabs the fitted sheet and starts doing some elaborate origami with it while I grab a pair of jeans. "Military school."

"You're in the military?"

He scoffs. "Oh, fuck no. But I was a little shit in high school and my parents didn't know what to do with me anymore. So they shipped me off to this radical Christian military school to learn my place."

I pause, my jaw dropping. "That sounds awful."

"It was. But it wasn't my parents' fault," he adds. "They didn't realize what the place was really like. I don't think most parents did. They've apologized to me for years."

I frown, wondering what an apology from a parent must feel like. "And you forgave them?"

He turns to me. "Of course. I was out of control—they loved me and didn't want me to end up in jail someday. I don't blame them for sending me there."

"I'm sorry," I say, before picking up a shirt from the pile.

"Don't be," he says with that winning grin. "It was hell, but I did learn a few tricks. And it helped me appreciate just how good I had it at home. But if you ask my parents," he says, lowering his voice, "I'm still a little shit."

I laugh and he places another crisp square down with my fitted sheet.

"I have to admit, I don't think I've ever managed to make those sheets look like anything but a lumpy potato."

"I can teach you if you want," he offers.

When I look over, we lock eyes for a moment. Why does this feel like a date? It's not. And it can't be. A guy like him doesn't want a girl like me for anything other than what's between my legs, even if he really was dreaming about me. "Maybe I *like* lumpy potatoes."

He nods. "Well, the offer stands."

A few minutes pass in silence. His precisely folded pile growing next to my rumpled, lopsided one until there's nothing left. I take the two piles and place them in the basket, holding it under one arm on my hip. "Thanks for the help," I say.

"Any time."

We stand a little awkwardly by the machines as they spin and whirl. His fingers tap compulsively against the metal and I'm starting to wonder if I should just turn and go.

"So what do you do now? For work, I mean," he adds. "Unless, wait—are you still dancing?"

I lean back on the washer behind me. "Oh, no. Had to hang up my dancing shoes after I broke my ankle one night at the club. I work at a call center now."

He nods. "That's cool. Not the ankle, of course. I'm sure that was rough. So, a call center, huh? Like customer support?"

Not quite. People can be so judgmental of what I do for work and chances are he'd be the same way. It's not that much different than stripping. But . . . it's different enough. "Sort of."

"Is that why you moved here?"

"Yeah. I started at a call center in Vegas, but the manager . . . Let's just say he wasn't the best. So a few girls told me there was another one here in San Francisco, and . . . the rest is history."

"That's amazing."

I raise my eyebrows. "It is?"

His cheeks color and he looks away. "I just mean, I never thought I would see you again. I mean I hoped—" He glances up at me and this time he doesn't blush as much. Does he want me to know just how much he's thought of me since that night? "And now, here you are, doing laundry of all things."

No, don't do that. Don't let yourself hope. God, how I wish I could tell him everything about me, but I don't want to scare him away. He'll just leave like everyone else.

"Right. Well, I'm done, so I better get going."

"Oh."

I take another few steps back and watch his smile slip away. "It was really nice to see you again."

"Yeah, you too."

Then, with all the strength I have, I turn and head for the door. I feel claustrophobic. I need to get outside into the air. His presence is overwhelming, reminiscent of that night two years ago. The door is ahead of me. I can almost breathe.

"Wait," I hear him call from behind me, but I'm outside and can finally take a breath in. I hear the bell go off and Doris yelling out in her raspy voice not to leave laundry unattended. "Yeah, yeah, I'm not going anywhere," he assures her before the door closes once more.

I turn to face him, keeping my basket between us for some distance.

"That's it?" he asks.

"What's it?"

"'It was really nice to see you again'? That's all?"

I open my mouth but close it again when it's clear everyone inside the laundromat is watching us. "I mean . . . yeah? Isn't it?"

"What if I didn't want that to be all there is?" he asks, taking a step toward me.

My heart races but I shake my head. "Joel, you . . . you don't even know me. I'm just that stripper from Vegas you paid to hang out with one night. We can't just be friends."

"Who said anything about being just friends?"

My eyes close and I let out a long breath. "I don't think that's a good idea."

"Why not? You got a boyfriend?"

"No, but I—"

"You're not attracted to me, then?" he asks with a knowing smirk.

I bite my lip. *Damn him*. "It's not that. I just—I don't really have the time to date anyone right now."

"Surely you must have some days off from the dreaded call center," he teases. "Let me take you out on a date."

Stomach flipping, I tilt my head. "A date?"

"Yeah," he continues. "Preferably one where I don't get a concussion."

Yes. *Yes.* It would be so easy to say yes, but how do I know he'll be different from the others? *Why can't I just make up my fucking mind?* "That's very sweet of you, but I can't."

I turn again to leave but he calls after me. "Come on, I have to see you again."

I point up at the sign. "Maybe if you ever need to do laundry again we'll run into each other."

"At least tell me your name," he begs. "I know it's not really Cherry."

"I guess you'll just have to wonder."

He smiles and pushes his hand through his hair. "Wait. I don't have any dryer sheets."

With a laugh and a shake of my head, I reach into my basket and pull out a box of Snuggle fabric softener.

He takes it, his hand lingering on mine for what feels like an eternity. "Thanks. I'll just have to call you *Snuggle* for now, I guess," he says.

I cross my arms and scoff, but he just flashes that mild-melting grin again.

"You know, because you're soft and smell great."

A laugh bursts out of me. "Wow, that was something," I say, backing away.

"Come on, not even after that line?"

I turn, my cheeks hot and my heart galloping in my chest. "See you around, Joel."

"You're breaking my heart," he calls, and I peek over my shoulder at his electric smile and twinkling eyes one last time before I turn the corner and flatten myself against the brick wall, out of sight.

IT TOOK ten whole minutes for me to conjure up enough courage to peel myself off the bricks and sneak back down the alley next to the laundromat. I couldn't very well let Joel know where I live. Not that I think he's a stalker, but because if he found himself on my doorstep, I don't think I'd have the strength not to pull him inside and let him lay that gorgeous body on top of me. I collapse against the door, drop my basket of clean clothes onto my messy bed, and duck into the kitchen, opening up a can of tuna for Stella.

"Hi, pretty girl," I say as she rubs herself between my legs and purrs. She's really come out of her shell since I rescued her from the alley a few months back. "You'll never guess who I ran into today."

She meows as I plate her tuna and put it on the floor by my feet, and I take it as a sign that she wants me to elaborate. I settle down on the kitchen floor next to her, bending my legs and folding my arms around them.

"Remember how I told you about that man? The one from Vegas?"

She sniffs then starts nibbling on the tuna.

"No? Maybe you don't remember. Well, he was downstairs today. Can you believe it?"

Another mournful meow.

"*No*, it wasn't a dream this time. And . . ." I pause for dramatic effect. "He wanted to take me out on a date."

She stops chewing and looks up at me with what I would classify as a surprised face.

"I said no, of course," I add, dropping my forehead to my knees.

She meows again and paws at me, ignoring her food.

"How could I say yes?" I say, scratching her ears. "You know they never stay long."

There's a gentle purr and she rubs her nose into my palm. I sigh. "I don't mean you. You've stuck around. But then again, I'm the one who feeds you."

She returns to her food and I wave my hand at her. "Since when are you a romantic anyway? Huh?"

I stand, brush off my behind, then make a beeline for my fresh laundry. I grab an old Sonny and Cher shirt, my comfiest pair of jeans, and some clean underwear. Ducking into the bathroom, I pile my hair up into a blue velvet scrunchie and shower, dress, then pinch a few slices of bologna from the fridge before I'm pulling on my shoes at the door.

Stella has since abandoned her empty plate on the kitchen floor and is snoozing on the windowsill, under the hanging planter next to my bed. "Okay, pretty girl, try not to stay up too late. You know how cranky you get when you don't get your twenty-two hours of sleep."

She lifts her head to look at me, meows, then promptly falls back asleep.

"See you in the morning," I say, and lock the door behind me.

THE SUN IS SETTING as I walk toward the bus stop at the end of my block, its proximity a big part of the reason I snapped up an apartment in such a bad area. Well, besides the cheap rent. One thing's for sure, my feet are a lot happier with my change in career. I don't need to wear sky-high heels for hours on end, and with my bad ankle, not having to walk very far is a blessing.

One ten-minute bus ride and three whistles from strangers later, I push through the door of the unassuming building and head up the stairs. The sound of a dozen phones ringing and the quiet chatter of the other workers greet me the moment I step inside. A few people look my way when I come in, but it appears things are busy earlier than usual tonight, and I quickly spot Anita heading toward me, looking frantic.

"Cherry, great, you're here early. Can you jump on? The lines have been lighting up for the past twenty minutes and we just don't have the staff on yet."

"Sure," I say, stopping at the punch clock. "Let me just grab a glass of water and I'll get—"

"No time, I'll grab you an entire jug of water. Just start taking calls, okay?" she rushes out the moment my time card is punched, ushering me over to my cubicle.

I groan internally but nod anyway, then sit down and pick up the phone, clicking on the first blinking red light I see. There's a ding through the line, then an automated voice says, "Horny college girls are waiting to speak to you now.

They're excited to hear from you. So excited that we're going to give you three free minutes on this call. Enter your credit card information now or at any time during this message."

So this guy's into college girls, then. Fairly simple request for a first call of the night. After all, working as a phone sex operator? These guys can get off on some weird shit. I hear numbers quickly being punched in on the line. Seems like this one is eager to get things started.

When I hear the ding again, that's my cue. "Hi, this is Cherry, who do I have the pleasure of speaking with tonight?"

There's a hint of static and the line connects. "Hello?"

I pitch my voice just a touch higher to sound younger. "Hey baby, what's your name?"

A deep breath. "You can just call me Baby, I guess."

His voice is deep. Rough, with a hint of raspiness that digs its way into your bones and grips you tight. This should be fun. Besides, I don't need his real name. "Baby, I'm so glad you called."

There's muffled laughter through the line and I frown. This better not be a prank call from some horny teenager who stole his dad's credit card.

"Baby?" I ask when he doesn't reply.

"I . . . sorry," he says, a smile evident in his tone. "I just—this is stupid, I shouldn't have called."

I roll my eyes. "Then why did you?"

"I don't know," he says.

"Baby, you called me."

"But I didn't have to," he argues. "I could easily have gone out and taken whichever girl I wanted home with me. Given her the time of her life then sent her packing in the morning."

Someone thinks highly of himself. I roll my finger through the phone cord. "Then why didn't you?"

There's a long stretch of silence. I double check that we're still connected, and a thought occurs to me.

"Maybe you don't want that," I say slowly. "Maybe you want more but want the safety of the phone line between us."

Another pause. "Maybe."

"I need that too sometimes. Connection," I say, "and not just a physical one. When was the last time you felt a connection with a woman?"

"A long time ago," he admits, his voice softer. "And today . . . today is a hard day."

Hmmm . . . okay, maybe it's not an ego thing. "That can feel really lonely."

Something rustles in the background. Maybe he's in bed. "Yeah, it can be."

"Baby?" I ask.

"Yeah?"

I pout my lips for extra effect. "I'm so lonely."

"Are you?"

"Yes, I moved very far away to go to college and my boyfriend just broke up with me. I just don't know what to do with myself."

He sighs into the phone. "You poor thing. All alone and away from home."

I smirk. Okay, now he's got the hang of it, he just needed a little coaching. "Maybe we could be a little less lonely together?"

"That sounds nice. Don't worry, I'll take care of you."

I giggle. "You will?"

"Of course. A gorgeous girl like you needs someone to look after her. Tend to her."

With a sigh, I lean back in my chair. "No one ever pays any attention to me, Baby. But you will, right?"

"Oh sweetheart, I'll give you all my attention."

I coil the phone cord around my finger absently. "Hmm, that sounds nice."

"What were you doing when I called? I'm not interrupting anything, am I?"

"No, I was just getting out of the shower."

He sighs into the speaker. "Must be nice to feel so clean."

"Can I tell you a secret?" I whisper.

"Of course."

"It feels better getting dirty."

CHAPTER 4

Here Comes the Sun

FOURTEEN YEARS AGO

I t's so hot I can barely breathe, and singing this hymn right now might actually cause me to pass out. No one would listen to the complaints of a church choir boy, though. They would simply praise the ability to suffer. I wonder if anyone would notice an eleven-year-old passing out? Probably not . . . at least not until the next hymn went unsung.

Sweat drips down my temples and back, my undershirt clinging to me under the suffocating gown. What I wouldn't give to be able to go to the local pool and jump in with all the other school kids. Maybe if I survive this, I can sneak out later and go without telling my parents.

The hymn concludes and I take a deep breath before the heavy doors of the church are thrown open with a *bang*.

"Can't believe you're dragging me out of bed for this bullshit, Rhonda," a surly man's voice calls loudly.

Every head turns to look at the commotion, half of their mouths dropping open at the obscene language. No one's ever spoken that way inside of these walls before.

"For Christ's sake, Ellis, just sit down and shut up," a woman in a flowered dress says as she pushes him forward. "Come on, girl, keep up."

Then I see her. Maybe I *did* pass out. Or maybe I died from heat stroke, because I'm clearly in the presence of something ethereal. Her hair glows like the sun, lit from behind like a fiery halo. As the doors shut, her pale skin comes into focus, the freckles that dance across her skin like the heavens above. Blue eyes like sapphires glance around as the girl and her parents head for a seat in the last pew.

I think my heart just started singing.

The girl sits down in her ruffled pink dress, then is promptly bumped to the side by her father, who seems to collapse with as much drama as possible next to her. He yawns loudly, burps, then lifts his dirty boots up onto the back of the pew in front.

The mother, who has similar copper hair to her daughter, seems unaware of the attention they've drawn and sits next to her husband before pulling out a compact mirror to reapply her lipstick. The girl, whose pale cheeks have turned the shade of a tomato, glances sideways at her parents and sinks into her seat.

As the reverend continues his sermon, the congregation refocuses on the front, but not without the scattered whispers that are no doubt because of the newcomers. It's not until close to the end of the sermon that the girl finally meet my eyes and it's as if life finally blooms. Her eyelashes flutter, and her cheeks turn almost the same pink as her dress. I grip the hem of my sleeves and sigh. Why couldn't I be dressed cooler? Will she think I'm a total weirdo?

When the reverend clears his throat and raises his eyebrows at me, I shake my head, realizing I've missed my cue for the closing song of the sermon. I squint down at my sheet music— the words are jumbled and nonsensical, but I've memorized the entire book by now and can recognize the pattern of the notes.

When I glance back up, the girl is smiling at me, her bright eyes sparkling.

I sing for her and think wildly that I would compose symphonies if only for her to speak to me.

When the sermon is over, I regret ever joining the choir, as I have to follow everyone back into the vestibule to change out of the ceremonial gowns. What if she's gone by the time I get back out front? What if they were only passing through and I never see her again? I don't even know her name.

Thankfully, no one interrupts me, and soon enough I'm bursting through the doors into the hall for the church social. All the adults stand around, gossiping and sipping coffee and tea, munching on cakes. I'm looking for golden copper hair and the most beautiful face I've ever seen. But . . . she's nowhere to be found.

My face twitches. Did I imagine her? I thought I changed quickly enough. Maybe her parents were just super determined to leave right away.

There's some chatter to my left, and I spot the girl's parents over by the coffee cart. Her father seems to be adding something to his Styrofoam cup that isn't cream or sugar, and I spot the mother stuffing her purse with muffins. If her parents are still here, she must be too . . . somewhere. But where?

The front doors are open, and a gentle breeze blows through. Despite the sweat still gathering on my skin, I head out into the blistering heat, the sound of cicadas and twittering birds leading me. And there she is. Sitting against a tree trunk in the shade, her legs stretched out in front of her and her head tilted back against the rough bark.

I roll back my shoulders and head over with a confidence I'm not sure I possess. When I approach and she doesn't open her eyes, I clear my throat.

"Hi."

She squints up at me with one eye. "Oh, hi."

"Too hot in there?" I ask.

"Yeah. Too hot. Too stuffy. Too noisy."

Her voice is like music.

She raises her eyebrows and I realize I haven't said anything for a while. "Would you like to sit with me?"

I grin and nearly trip over myself as I sit next to her, our backs leaning up against the tree. Glancing sideways at her, I watch as her eyes close and she breathes deeply.

"It's so much better out here, don't you think?" she says with a sigh. "You'd think God wouldn't want us to be cooped up inside when there's so much beauty to enjoy out here."

My eyes dart around, making sure no one is within earshot. "Careful who you say that to. Suggesting church outside is something I'd get the belt for."

She turns to look at me. "That seems silly."

I shrug. "Silly or not, it doesn't make it hurt less."

She nods seriously. "I know what you mean."

Something sinks in my stomach. Does she get hit too? Before I can ask, she's speaking again, and I'd never dare interrupt her.

"You won't tell on me for my wild ideas, will you?" she asks.

I shake my head like it's a rattle in the hand of a toddler. "No! No, of course not."

She smiles wide, her bottom teeth slightly crooked. Perfectly imperfect.

"So," I continue, "why haven't I seen you here before?"

Please say you're staying.

"Mama got a job here."

Yes!

"Oh. What does she do?"

"She's working over at that new canning factory just outside of town."

I grin. "My dad works there."

"Really?"

"Yeah, he's one of the managers. Are you going to be at school tomorrow?" I ask hopefully.

Her face falls. "Oh, no. Daddy doesn't believe in schools. Says the government's trying to make commies out of us."

My excitement plummets. "Oh. So how do you learn, then?"

She shrugs. "My dad teaches me."

"Huh." I can't help but look back toward the church. That rude, obnoxious man teaching in front of a blackboard in a suit and tie like Mr. Hardman? It doesn't seem possible.

"But you'll be coming back here next Sunday?" I can barely keep the hope out of my voice.

She picks up a fluffy dandelion. "Most likely." The two of us watch it, and the way the seeds fly off as she twirls the stem back and forth until there's a single seed left.

"Mama says you can make a wish on these," she says solemnly. "What would you wish for if you could have anything?" she asks.

Before I can stop it, I'm smiling. "To sing in front of hundreds of people."

She smiles back. "You could do it, you know. You're a great singer."

I feel a flush of heat spread across my cheeks. "Nah."

She shoves my shoulder and gives a knowing nod. "You could! I heard you. You could be the next Johnny Cash."

My face on fire, I look down at my fidgeting hands. "Thanks." I swallow hard. "What would you wish for?"

She throws away the dandelion, then fingers the gold pendant hanging around her neck I didn't notice before. The thin gold chain wraps around her delicate fingers and I realize it's a golden sun. When I glance back up, she sighs. "To feel loved."

My brows pinch, not understanding. "You don't feel loved? But—but what about your parents? They love you, right?"

She half chuckles then looks away before pulling her knees up under her chin. "No. No, I don't think they do."

"Oh," I say, then fall silent. What can I say after that?

We're quiet for a while. The adults and kids begin to pour out the front doors of the church toward the parking lot. I spot my little brother with my parents and realize my time with this girl is about to end. Standing, I look down into her blue eyes, my heart beating quicker than if I'd just run a mile.

"Maybe I'll see you next Sunday?" I ask.

She grins and nods. "I hope so. I'm Dusty Connors, by the way."

The breeze rustles her copper hair and those eyes sparkle like a blazing comet through the night. "I'm Keith. Keith Prentiss."

CHAPTER 5

You're My Best Friend

JOEL

"**K**ey. *Key.* Keith motherfucking Prentiss!"

Key looks up at me from where he sits on the old couch in the green room, fiddling with his guitar. "You say something?"

I roll my eyes. "Yeah, dipshit, we're about to start and you're daydreaming over here."

He jumps up. "Sorry. I was—never mind."

Dave and James are talking to each other as they head out but I hang back. "Are you okay, man?"

Key blinks and shrugs. "Yeah. Why wouldn't I be?"

He tries to walk past me but I clasp a hand on his shoulder, stopping him in his place. "Seriously. The past couple days . . . you've been in a funk."

His eyebrows rise under his wavy mop of brown hair. "A funk?"

I roll my eyes. "Yes, a fucking funk. Mopey as shit, wandering around the house like Droopy Dog."

He shakes his head. "I'm fine."

I hold my arm out straight and give him a hard stare.

"I said I'm fine, Joel. Back off."

"It's cool if you're not, you know. We could do something. Anything. Or you could tell me what's bothering you."

He pushes my hand away and rolls his eyes. "What's bothering me right now is some asshat blocking the way to the stage."

I raise my hands in surrender. "Fine. Fine. But, if you say no to going out for chicken wings after the show tonight, I'm calling 911."

His mouth drops open in mock-outrage. "I would never turn down chicken wings. If I ever say no to that, your concern is valid and I've obviously been body swapped by aliens." He grins at me, and I think maybe this has all been in my head.

I smile back. "Right. Okay, then."

We head down the hall, the dark corridors muffling the chanting from the crowd.

"By the way," he says, "sorry about ditching you with all that laundry. I bet that sucked balls."

I shrug, a wide grin stretching across my face. "I have no regrets."

He narrows his eyes at me. "What's that look?"

"What look?"

"That 'I just got to stuff my face in the biggest pair of tits' look."

"Jesus, Key, you really do have a way with words."

Now *he* stops *me*, and I have to bite the inside of my cheek to tone down the smile. "No, really. What aren't you telling me?"

"Hey, fuckheads, you ready or what?" Dave yells, standing next to James, who cracks his knuckles methodically.

"We're ready," I say, moving to meet them. Then, to Key, "Listen, I'll tell you later while we're stuffing our faces with hot wings."

He pushes his tongue into his cheek but nods, and a moment later, the four of us are stepping out into the blinding lights to a thunderous crowd. I head for my bass guitar on a stand at the far side of the stage, while Dave settles behind the drums and James slings his guitar over his shoulder. Key is the last to take position and I watch as he adjusts his guitar strap before stepping toward the microphone.

"Oakland!" he shouts. "Are you ready to repent for your Carnal Sins?"

There's an explosion of noise from the crowd, and I watch out of the corner of my eye as Dave taps his drumsticks together. We're off with our first song of the night—the first song on our debut album that went gold—and the crowd is insane. I don't know if I'll ever tire of this. The adrenaline rush of being on stage playing the music I helped write. That the four of us brought into existence with nothing but willpower and luck.

And I can't believe I get to do it with my best friend.

Don't get me wrong. We're all a family, the girls too. Becks and Izzy? I'd do anything for them. But Key is like my brother. The other half of me. And while I know we give each other a hard time, that's only because we know how much to push. That it's all in good fun, and even though we disagree on a lot of things, I'll never forget the way everything changed when he walked into my life.

FOUR POUNDS of superhot wings later, it's two in the morning and I'm only just starting to come down from the high of performing. I might also be another type of high after smoking a joint with James in the alley behind the bar. But my whole family is here and happy. James sits with his arm around Becks, whose head is nuzzled into his neck, her eyes droopy from the late hour. Izzy and Dave are in their own little world, her knees propped up over his thigh like they're the only two people in the room.

It makes me think of Cherry. Or Snuggle. Or whatever her real name is. I wonder briefly if she's working tonight. What kind of call center does she work for? And what place requires her to work at night? I briefly imagine her dealing with irate customers over their faulty VCR equipment and have to stifle a laugh.

"Hey," Key says as he wipes his face with a napkin. "What's funny?"

"Just thinking of how much you're going to regret that hot sauce in a few hours. At least our toilets are still working."

Izzy scrunches her face. "Ew."

But Dave narrows his eyes. "Why wouldn't the toilets be working?"

James is staring at me now too, and I shrug. "Just a little problem with the plumbing, that's all."

"What kind of problem?"

Key licks his fingers and wipes them on a napkin. "Washing machine exploded."

"Exploded?" James says a little too loudly, jolting Becks awake.

"Shut up. You're so dramatic," I say. "It didn't explode. The hose burst."

Dave rubs his forehead. "For fuck's sake. Are you getting it fixed? You know my name is still on the lease for another three months."

I wave my hand. "Yeah yeah, don't worry about it. We've got it under control."

"A plumber is coming out later in the week to fix it," Key explains.

"Please tell me you took any wet clothes out so they aren't rotting in the washing machine," Becks asks, cringing now.

"Yes, Becks, the clothes are fine," I drone. "I took them to a laundromat."

"Really?" she asks.

Again, a grin pulls at my cheeks and I can't stop myself. Key crosses his arms, but Becks looks concerned.

"Yeah, really. Don't look so surprised. I am capable of being an adult sometimes."

"Only when he needs clean underwear," James chimes in.

"Are you all out?" Dave asks. "Is that why you guys didn't bring any girls out tonight?"

I think about Cherry and suddenly realize I haven't thought about any other girl since a certain beautiful redhead came back into my life. But it is unusual for Key, that liar. I *knew* he was in a funk.

"Bit worn out from the last one," Key says casually and flicks me a knowing stare.

"Okay, I know that look," Dave says, sliding out of the booth. "We're out of here before I hurl up a pound of wings listening to the details of your . . . escapades."

He pulls Izzy by the hands and wraps his arms around her waist from behind.

"It would serve you right after all the nights we've had to listen to you two going at it," Key volleys back. "And you two aren't any better," Key interrupts James as he opens his mouth, who promptly shuts it and turns to Becks. But his face softens when he looks at her, and they share some silent communication through their eyes.

"Well, on that note," James says, "Becks and I are heading home. We'll see you guys tomorrow."

We all exchange some goodbyes, and the couples head home.

Key shakes his head. "Thank god that isn't us," he mumbles.

I turn to him. "What do you mean?"

"Dave and Izzy. James and Becks. They're all about their couple shit." He looks up at me and smiles. "Good for them, but I'm glad it's us. You and me. Girls only when we want them, you know?"

My stomach sinks. The only girl I want right now is Cherry. I've wanted her for two years, and if I ever manage to convince her to give me a chance . . . I don't think a single night would be enough, which means we'd be dating. The prospect is terrifying, but this thing Key and I have going on can't last forever. Key must know that too, right? "I don't know. You don't think it would be nice to love someone that much?"

He scoffs. "Love? Love is a delusion. A chemical reaction in the brain that eventually wears off. It's not the fairytale romantic notion everyone says it is."

My eyes widen. "Jesus. Who the fuck broke your heart?"

"No one," he says a bit too quickly. "But that doesn't mean I'm wrong."

I lean forward. "Come on, you don't think what those four have is love?"

Key grabs the last wing from the basket and tears off a strip with his teeth. "What they have is a mutually beneficial relationship labeled by society as love. They get companionship and sex, so they fulfill their hormonal and emotional needs. But if either of those weren't being met? You can bet the 'love' would die out pretty fast."

My jaw is almost on the table. I stare at my best friend of almost eight years while he finishes his chicken. Finally, he looks up at me.

"What?"

I pull at my napkin and shrug. "Nothing man, just—I guess I never realized you felt that way about relationships."

He stalls. "Joel?"

I look up and he gives me an expression I don't see often. Softness.

"If love really is real, I think how I feel about you is the closest I've ever gotten."

My chest tightens and it makes me swallow down the urge to

tell him that I like a girl. That I plan to visit that laundromat every day until I see her again. "Thanks." I clear my throat, unsure what else to say, and reply, "Ditto."

I mean it. I really do. I love him. He's my best friend. My brother. My bandmate. But that doesn't mean I don't want a woman in my life. He's my favorite person in the world, but what if I want a relationship? A girlfriend? A wife and a family? Will Key be left on his own, resentful of me?

"So," Key says, wiping his face and sipping his beer. "What were you so smiley about earlier?"

Shit. "Oh, uh . . . I forgot to tell you something that happened at the laundromat."

"Oh?"

I swallow, then grin. "Some idiot walked right into an open dryer door. Knocked him right down on his ass."

"No shit?"

"Poor guy probably concussed himself. It was hilarious. I can't stop thinking about it."

Chuckling, he nods. "Yeah, I'd probably be laughing about that for days too." He drains the last of his beer, setting it down on the table between us. "And sorry, by the way."

"For what?"

"For being weird lately. I've been a moody bastard and I know that's tough to live with."

"Yeah, it is," I say dramatically. "Keep it up and I'll have to divorce you."

CHAPTER 6

Only the Lonely

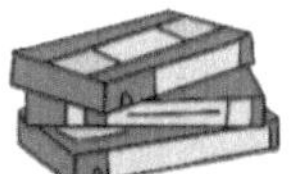

"**N**aughty girls are waiting to speak to you now. They're excited to hear from you. So excited that we're going to give you three free minutes on this call. Enter your credit card information now or at any time during this message."

I pick at a hangnail while I hear the person on the other line enter their credit card information, then clear my throat at the sound of the *ding*.

"Hey, sweetheart, how are you doing?" I ask without much enthusiasm. It's been a long night and it's almost four in the morning.

"Better if you call me *Baby* again," the caller says, and my stomach jolts. The gravelly, smooth cadence of his voice. It's the same guy who called last week. He's back.

"Baby! Oh, how I've missed you." I perk up in my chair.

"Have you? I . . . this is going to sound really lame but—I kind of missed you too."

"Now, now," I tsk. "Why would that be a lame thing to say? Especially if it's honest."

He sighs. "You're right. It's . . . I guess it's just something that's hard to admit."

"I can understand that," I say. "So what prompted you to give me another call? Feeling lonely again?"

"I was out with my friends—couples—they're so fucking happy . . ."

My eyebrow quirks. "You sound mad at them for being happy."

He scoffs.

"Or maybe you're jealous?"

A long pause stretches over the line. "I told my friend I don't believe in love. That it's not real. But I don't really think that."

"No? You don't believe love is just some made up feeling by the Hallmark company?"

A breathy laugh comes through the phone. "No, I know it's real. I had it once."

My heart thuds extra hard. Ah, so here's the real reason he calls me instead of running out to pick up any girl he wants. He loved someone and it didn't work out and he can't get over it. It's all starting to make sense.

"Well, I'm here now," I encourage. "And I've been ever so bored until you called."

"Bored, huh?"

"Mm-hmm, I've been so bored I could almost fall asleep."

"You won't fall asleep on *me*, will you?"

I lean forward, placing my elbows on the desk. "I guess that depends."

"On?"

"Will you entertain me, Baby?"

His voice rumbles through the speaker and it's like adrenaline shoots down my spine. "No."

I blink. Wait, what? "No?"

"No."

I pull at a split end, trying to figure out what to say. Maybe that connection we shared a moment ago isn't what I thought.

Maybe it's backfiring. They've never really covered this in the handbook. I've never had to pull it out of a guy before.

"Well, I . . . what do you plan to do with me, then?"

There's a long pause where I hear him take a deep breath in and out. "You," he begins, his voice dropping deeper. "*You* are going to entertain *me*."

Well, this is new. "Am I?"

"Do you want to please me?" he asks.

I take a deep breath. "Yes."

"Yes, what?"

Oh, so it's like that. "Yes, Baby."

He chuckles, and I can almost see a smile. An unidentified chiseled jaw, full lips hiding gleaming white teeth, a grin like a predator who caught me in his trap.

"Get on your knees," he says.

While I'm under no obligation to actually play out the scenarios I voice, something throbs inside of me, wanting to obey. But I blink and shake my head. *Don't be stupid, Dusty. This is all pretend. Never forget that.*

I lick my lips. "You like seeing me on my knees, Baby?"

"Such a gorgeous little slut you are."

My mouth drops open and my breath hitches.

"But you're so far away. I want to see those tits up close."

"Baby?"

"Riddle me this," he says, and I hear him moving, something like blankets rustling in the background. He must be lying in his bed. "How does a filthy whore get from one end of the room to the cock at the other?"

I swallow hard. "She crawls."

Another chuckle, darker this time, with an edge to it. "Tell me."

"I place my hands in front of me, my breasts are heavy as they hang. Then I crawl, one hand and knee moving at a time."

He groans.

"My nipples are so sensitive. Every time my breasts swing, they tingle until they're hard."

"Is it painful?" he asks.

I shake my head even though he can't see it. "Yes. But I'll be your good little whore. I won't complain. I don't want to be punished."

"Something else is getting hard and painful," he says with a hitch to his voice.

My eyes close and I picture the faceless man standing over me, hand wrapped around his hard length.

"I can see you're hard. Let me help you. I don't want you to be in pain, Baby."

He hums. "How does someone like you plan to take away my pain?"

My core throbs and my heart is pounding. "I—let me touch you. Please."

"Look at you. Dripping wet already," he says. "Do I have that much of an effect on you, or are you just so fucking needy for my cock that your pussy weeps to be filled?"

I gasp and my thighs clench. "I . . . I—" *You're at work, Dusty. Get a hold of yourself.*

"Use your words," he whispers.

"I need your cock, Baby. Please. Please, let me touch it. *Please.*"

He clicks his tongue and every hair on my body stands on end. "You sound so pathetic and weak when you beg."

"Can I touch you now?" I ask.

"Yes."

I sigh into the speaker but he continues.

"You can touch me, but not with your hands."

"Not with—oh."

His rasping chuckle vibrates my bones. "That's it. Open that filthy mouth for me."

Goddamn, who is this guy? "I can't wait to taste you."

I moan into the phone, my eyes closing and head falling back and I hear him groan as well, his heavy breathing mirroring my own.

"Fuck, your mouth feels so good. Such a good fucking slut."

With a hum, I moan again. "You taste so sweet, Baby. I can't get enough."

"Don't you dare fucking touch yourself. You're here for me."

"Oh god, *yes*. I just want you to use me."

He laughs darkly. "I wish everyone could see you the way I do. Desperate and needy for what only I can give you."

My pussy clenches and I gasp into the phone. "Fuck my mouth. Take what you want from me."

"I'm going to paint your face with my cum." He groans and something animalistic bursts out of my throat. "You don't get to swallow. You haven't earned that yet, but I'll mark you so you never forget you're mine."

Shit, I'm so turned on that I'm sweating. My hair is damp at the temples and my shirt clings to my back. "I'm yours," I whisper. A door slamming in the background startles me and I become acutely aware of where I am. The ringing of the phones in the attached cubicles. The sound of my coworkers acting out their roles. *Acting, Dusty. Remember?*

He groans loudly and my fingers clench in the phone cord as I listen to his climax. That sound pierces right through me like liquid heat. My teeth dig into my bottom lip and I'm panting like a dog in heat. What just came over me? This wasn't acting. I've never had such a visceral reaction to a call before. There's just something about his voice . . .

He clears his throat on the other end of the line and there's some shuffling around that I try to distinguish while getting my bearings.

"You okay?" he asks.

I open my eyes and sink down into my chair as I'm overcome with embarrassment. "Yes, I . . . I—"

"Seems I got you so worked up you lost your accent."

My hand covers my mouth with a dull slap and my eyes widen. *Shit!*

He chuckles into the receiver, and shivers cover my body from the sound, as though his breath is on my skin. "Thanks, sweetheart. Until next time."

The line goes dead and I'm left sitting here wondering what the hell just happened.

MY APARTMENT DOOR clicks shut behind me, and I collapse against it. Stella emerges from around the corner, winding her way through my legs.

"Hey, pretty girl," I say, squatting down to pet her. "How was your night?"

She meows again, then sticks her face into the plastic grocery bag searching for her breakfast. Sniffing the cat food, she purrs like a tiny motorbike before skipping off into the kitchen. I sigh then stand, pushing off my shoes, my toes cracking as I press them into the carpet.

I quickly put away the few groceries I picked up on my way home while I fight off yawn after yawn. Putting a scoop of dry cat kibble into Stella's bowl, I grab the microwavable lasagna meal from the bag and pop it in the microwave. My eyes close and I roll my neck and shoulders as I wait for my dinner to heat up. I'm desperate to crawl into bed, but my stomach growls angrily and I just need to eat something before disappearing under the covers.

When it beeps, I grab a fork and the tray then sit on my bed with my back against the wall. The radio is still playing from earlier—I figure Stella might feel less alone with it on, so it's become our new routine. But the soothing music I usually listen to has changed to rock.

"Were you trying to change the station?" I ask Stella around a mouthful, standing and walking over to the radio.

She meows from where she's curled up on my bed waiting for me to return, and I pause with my fingers on the dial. The song that's playing is hard and fast—aggressive. Not exactly something I want to fall asleep to. But there's also something catchy about it. The beat is invigorating and the singer . . . His voice seems familiar. I shake my head. What is wrong with me and men's voices lately? The song winds down with a dramatic crash of drums and screaming guitars.

"That was Carnal Sins with their latest single," the radio announcer says, and I startle. The band's name strikes a nerve—reminds me of countless awful days being dragged to church. "I don't know about you, but I can't wait for their next album if it sounds like more of this." The radio announcer continues with an introduction of the next song, but I continue to stare at the radio, my fingers tapping along the top. I wonder if the men in that band also have a strange relationship with sin and church. I've never heard of them before; they must be new.

Stella meows loudly and I sigh. "Sorry, I'll turn it back," I say, adjusting the station until an Aretha Franklin song begins to play. I sit back down in bed to finish my lasagna. Stella nuzzles into my side, and I pet her head between bites.

"Did you enjoy the heavy metal, pretty girl?" I ask.

She blinks up at me as I take the last bite then set my plate on the dresser. I wonder if Carnal Sins is the kind of music Joel listens to. He's obviously a metal music lover. He dresses like he's a part of that scene. In fact, didn't he joke that he was a famous rock star in Vegas? I bet that's his biggest fantasy—to rock out on stage like Metallica or Iron Maiden.

A head of floppy brown curls and bright hazel eyes swim out of the depths of my memory. Key wanted that life. Wanted to sing for millions of people with his unbelievable talent. My fingers twist into the necklace at my throat as my eyes squeeze shut against the painful memory. I hope he made it. At least then, all this—the hurt—would be worth it.

I unhook my bra and shimmy out of my jeans before sliding under the covers. Stella fits herself into the crook of my stomach, her warmth radiating through the bedsheets.

"I could be in the mood for some heavy metal myself, if the right person persuaded me," I mutter as I stroke her fur. "I think you'd like Joel," I say, offhandedly. But then I remember what my reality is. How I behaved at work. How I *felt*.

I was turned on.

I made the right decision turning him down. How can I possibly date someone like Joel? He'll never accept what I do for a living. No nice guy wants a woman who helps men get off over the phone for hours on end. And the way that one caller made me feel today? My own body betrayed me. After a year of being a fantasy phone girl I've never once gotten so worked up that I almost touched myself at work.

I want to hate him. Hate the way he made me feel. Hate the way he made me forget that it was just pretend. Hate that he might call me again.

"Being lonely sucks," I mutter. Stella nips on my hand sharply and I let out a yelp before she takes off to her perch on the window. "Ow! Okay, okay, miss judgmental."

I could quit my job. I think about it a lot. Usually on days when I feel lonely and especially unloved. But what would I do? I knew what I wanted all those years ago and look where that got me.

I roll over in bed and tuck my pillow under my chin. I shouldn't be ungrateful . . . at least I have a job. Besides, men have never taken me seriously. They've only ever cared about my body or how I can get them off—that's what's always paid the bills. So why should I let myself be shamed?

Then there's Joel.

I have to admit that for a few hours it felt nice to be desired by someone real. Not just a voice who pays for it over the phone, or someone from the club with money to burn. I haven't felt that way since Key.

Not that any of it matters. Joel will never accept me—not really. Besides, the first impression he ever got of me is Cherry the stripper. That's why he wants to date me. He thinks I'll be this wild girl in bed and he'll be able to cross *fuck a stripper* off his bucket list. We aren't compatible. It's the cold hard truth. And my cat can judge me all she wants, but I'm meant to be alone. The love I want will always be just out of my reach.

It's such a shame, because my heart is so big it could love as wide as the whole sky.

CHAPTER 7

Waiting for a Girl Like You

KEY

FOURTEEN YEARS AGO

"Dusty, there you are," I say, rushing up the balcony stairs to find her in the back row. It's been a month since I saw her last. A month of sitting in school and wondering where she is and when I would see her again. "Why are you all the way up here?"

Her face lifts and she smiles when she sees me. Butterflies escape in my belly and I nearly trip over the last step. "Hey, Keith. I just wanted to be alone."

"Oh." I stop. "Do you want me to go?"

She shakes her head. "No, I was hoping you'd find me."

I dip my chin and take the seat in the pew next to her. She's wearing a blue dress today, and it makes her eyes shine brighter than I remember. I think of what my mom said on the ride home the day I met her. How her hair was unruly and wild. That she was glad Dusty wasn't enrolled at my school, because she'd probably give lice to all the kids. But that's not what I see at all.

I see an angel. But . . . something's wrong.

"Hey," I say pointing to her face. "What happened to you?"

She pulls her hair forward to cover the side of her face and the bruise on her temple. "Oh, nothing. I just . . . I tripped and hit my head on the edge of the counter. I'm fine."

"Are you sure? That looks bad—"

"I'm fine, Keith." Her voice is hard, but she doesn't yell.

I nod, swallowing down what I was going to say next. "I missed you the last few weeks. I thought maybe you were never coming back."

She shrugs. "Mama left that night. After church that day."

"I . . . what?"

"I-I think she knew she was leaving and wanted to talk to god or . . . ask forgiveness, maybe. But she's gone," she says, staring through the floor.

"Well, when is she coming back?" I ask, outraged.

She scoffs and shakes her head. "She's not coming back."

We're quiet for a really long time. The truth is I have no idea what to say. There have been times when I've wished with all my heart my parents would disappear, but I can't imagine them actually leaving me. Finally, Dusty sighs and blinks quickly.

"He feels guilty today. My dad," she adds at my confusion. "He's the reason she left. He's the one who . . ." She almost touches her temple but stops herself. I understand enough, though. That her dad did that to her. That he hurt her. I could kill him. "Anyway," she continues, "he *must* feel guilty because how else could I have gotten him to agree to church when he hates it so much?"

"Yeah," I offer. What else can I possibly say?

"I heard you sing today," she says suddenly, and I sit up in surprise. "You're really a very good singer."

Heat creeps into my cheeks. "Yeah?"

She nods and smiles, the first real smile she's given me since I sat down. "It was my favorite part of today, listening to you sing."

I rub the back on my neck at the compliment. "I write music

sometimes. In my head, or on the piano at home. It's not church music though, so they'd never let me sing it here."

Her eyebrows lift and I catch the flinch as her bruise contorts. "Really? What kind of music?"

I shrug. "I don't really know. Just melodies and some lyrics. My parents won't let me practice anything that isn't a hymn in the house."

At this her eyes seem to light up. "Oh, is it a secret?"

"Yeah, I guess it is," I say, smiling at her enthusiasm.

"I love secrets. Will you sing something you wrote for me?" she asks.

Those fluttering butterflies in my stomach turn into a full-blown tornado. "Oh, I uh . . . I don't know—"

"Come on, please?" She pouts and bats her long eyelashes. "For me?"

I don't think I could deny her anything—even if she asked for the cross on the top of the roof, I'd find a way to get it for her. And if it'll help keep that smile on her face after all she's gone through . . . "Okay," I say, grabbing the notebook from my back pocket and flipping it open. "But remember, these are just rough ideas."

She turns and crosses her legs under her skirt on the pew next to me as her finger twists in the gold chain around her neck. Her hands come up under her chin, giving me her full attention, and I take a deep breath. My hands shake as I try to hold the paper still, but after two attempts to sing, my voice finally works. I have to be quiet. The congregation echoes below us for the after service social and the ceilings are too vaulted and might carry the sound. So I half sing, half whisper the melody that's been churning in my head for months.

The words that seemed like poetry when I wrote them down suddenly feel juvenile and stupid on my tongue, but I push on anyway because Dusty is watching me, waiting. I wish I had my piano. It would be so much better if I could play the notes at the same time. When I finish, I let the notepad fall into my lap and my face scrunches as I wait for her verdict.

"Wow," she says breathlessly. "You wrote that?"

The muscles in my face relax. "Yeah, I guess I did."

"Are you sure? It sounds like a grown up wrote it."

Heat flares in my cheeks. "I wrote it. I swear."

She examines me carefully. "Well, it's amazing."

Something sticks in my throat. "You really think so?"

She nods. "Absolutely. Totally groovy. People should call you Key. Like piano keys."

I grin so wide my cheeks pinch. I've never had a nickname before. "I like it. Don't think my parents will though."

"We can use it just between us then."

"Okay."

"I think if you had some guitar and drums," she continues, "it could be on the radio someday."

I tear the page from my notebook and hand it to her. "Here."

Her smile fades. "What?"

"I want you to have this," I say, holding the paper out to her.

"But, you need it. To turn it into a real song."

I shake my head. "No need. I've got it locked tight up here," I say, tapping at my forehead. "Come on, I want you to have it. You're the first person I've ever told about it."

"Me?"

Nodding, I take her hand and press the paper into her palm. She stares at it for a long moment, and I start to think maybe she doesn't want it. That she's just being nice. That she's just spying on me, and will end up telling my parents about what I've been doing in secret.

"Why are some of these letters mixed up?"

My stomach drops like a lead balloon, hurtles through the floor to drag me down under the earth. What was I thinking?

Giving her something I wrote? I'm such an idiot. Now she's going to think I'm stupid just like everyone else does. She'll never want to talk to me again. I reach for the page and try to take it back.

"Actually, I need that back—"

But she holds it out of my reach. "And some of these words are . . ." She looks at me and tilts her head. "But your songs. They sound—"

I lower my head into my hands and sigh. "I swear I wrote them."

"I believe you," she insists. "You sometimes talk like a grown up. You sound smart."

"No one else thinks I am. All they see is this . . ."

She twists her lips. "It's not so bad. Yeah, some of the letters are in the wrong places, but it's still—"

"It's terrible! I know, trust me, I know!" I blurt out. "And I try so hard but I don't know why, my brain just gets jumbled up sometimes. I don't even realize I'm doing it. I tried to explain to my parents. I study every day but my marks are always so bad they don't believe me, and then . . ." I hold out my hands and turn them over, showing her my palms. The red scars criss-cross my skin. "My dad, he—well . . . he says this will help me learn."

She lowers her outstretched arm and places the page on her lap. Her hand takes one of mine, her finger gently brushing over the jagged lines. I flinch away as she traces a particularly rough ridge.

"Don't be ashamed," she tells me, low.

I shake my head. "They're ugly."

"No, they're part of you. That makes them beautiful. Also," she says, looking at me through her long eyelashes, "no one who composes songs like that can be stupid."

Her words are like ice cream on a hot day. Sweet and soothing. No one's ever made me feel good about myself before.

"I listen to the radio a lot," I admit. "*The National Radio Theater*, *NPR* and stuff. It's easier for me to learn when I can listen."

She smiles. "Maybe I need to start listening to the radio too. I don't want to fall behind you."

Our hands linger for as long as I dare until I awkwardly pull mine away, my palm suddenly sweaty. She picks up the page and holds it out for me.

"Here. You can have it back if you really want it."

I bite my lip and make a choice. "No. No, you can have it."

"I can?" She holds it to her chest and smiles. "Thank you. I'll keep it safe." She tucks it into her pocket and it feels as if she's tucked away a piece of my heart too.

"Okay," I start. "Your turn now."

Her eyes widen. "What?"

"I told you my secret. Now you need to tell me one of yours. It has to be even."

"I don't have any secrets."

As my head tilts, I pull my legs up, my toes pointing toward her. "Come on, you must have one."

A pretty blush spreads across her cheeks. "Well, there *is* something."

I clap my hands. "Tell me."

"But you have to promise you won't tell anyone, okay?"

Holding out her hand, her pinky finger lifts and she waits, eyes serious. I hook my pinky with hers and nod. "I swear to never tell another living soul."

She sighs. "I want to be an actress."

"An actress?"

"Like Grace Kelly. She's so beautiful and talented. Do you know she married a prince? She's like a real life Cinderella."

I stare at her beautiful face. Her freckles and her button nose. Her red hair that seems as untamable as the wind.

"Actually," she adds. "Just anything to do with movies. They're my favorite thing in the world."

"You could do it," I say.

She shakes her head. "No, I couldn't."

"Why not?"

"Daddy would never let me. He hates Hollywood."

I shrug. "Maybe when you're older you can go."

"Go where?"

"To Hollywood! Run away and be an actress and marry a prince."

She grins. "Would you come with me?"

My eyebrows lift. "Me?"

"You can sing your music and I'll be in movies and we can live happily ever after."

I can almost see it. The two of us running away and hopping on a bus to California. We'd be celebrities and kids everywhere would hope they could be us. But then I think of how far away that is. She grabs my hand and my fingers slip through hers.

"Promise we'll do it someday," she whispers. "Promise we'll do everything we want to do." Her necklace swings forward and I can see the little golden sun. It sparkles as it catches the light from a nearby window and reminds me of the first time I ever saw her. How her hair was like a glowing halo of sunlight.

I realize then and there that I would wait an eternity to make her dreams come true. I squeeze her hand. "I promise."

CHAPTER 8

Something in the Air

JOEL

It's the fourth time this week I've sat outside of The Sudsy Dream hoping Cherry might appear, but she doesn't. I might have missed her. I can't possibly sit here all day. Key is already suspicious enough, and there's only so many gallons of milk I can drink to excuse these trips. He's still in his funk, and one of the perks is that he seems to readily accept my excuses, but the more I think about it, the more I'm worried for him.

I had no idea he felt that way about romantic love. I thought he was just super happy being single. A young up-and-coming rockstar taking advantage of our newfound fame to take home any girl he wants without the hassle of a relationship. But what he said about the others—about love—he sounds bitter, and it makes me all the more nervous to mention I might have fallen for a girl who still hasn't even agreed to go on a date with me.

There's a flash of red out of the corner of my eye, but when I turn to look, it's an elderly woman in a red head scarf who walks quickly past the laundromat windows. I press my fists against my temples and sigh. I'm going fucking insane. I'm such an idiot. Why did I think this was a good idea? The woman won't even give me her real name. I know she's attracted to me, but that doesn't mean she *likes* me. Our connection in Vegas must just have been an alcohol-induced fever dream that I've spent the last two years obsessing over. I should go home.

Another flash of red, this time from inside the laundromat, and I'm out of the car and walking through the door, searching for fiery hair before I can convince myself to leave. Glancing around, my chest deflates when I confirm that the red I saw was someone's football jersey in a dryer.

"This is stupid. I'm stupid. Everything is stupid," I mutter. "Just go home, Joel." Turning for the door, I grasp the handle.

"Back again?" asks a voice that sounds like sandpaper.

I whip around only to find the old lady at the counter staring at me over her magazine. Her nails are purple polka dots this week, I notice as I walk toward her. "So it would seem."

She tilts her head and glances up at my forehead. "Nasty bruise you've got under all that hair."

"You're very observant," I mutter, wondering why she bothered speaking to me at all.

There's a pause, and I glance over my shoulder to where Cherry and I folded laundry together less than a week ago.

"Don't even think about it."

I turn back to the woman who's watching me shrewdly. "Huh?"

"You and her. Ain't no way that's gonna happen."

"What? Why not?" I ask indignantly.

"She's too good for you."

I scoff. "You don't even *know* me."

She looks me up and down. "I know you couldn't take care of her the way she needs."

I cross my arms. "Oh really? And how's that?"

"That girl needs a strong man. One who can provide for her and keep her safe. Not some little boy who's charmed by long legs and a pretty face, hanging around to have fun."

"I'm not just hanging around to have fun," I argue, but as the words leave my mouth, I really think about what that means. What this woman is trying to tell me in her own crabby way is that I shouldn't be coming around if I don't want something serious. A relationship. And now that the word is floating around in my head, do I even want one? What exactly is my plan here?

The woman leans forward, folding her fingers together so that her nails click. "My advice? Forget about The Sudsy Dream and forget about her."

My mouth twists. I wish I could argue with her, but how can I when I don't even really know what I want? So instead, I say, "I'll be back tomorrow," and leave the sloshing machines and tumbling symphony behind me.

THE SOUNDS of a large crowd are still thrilling even years into this music journey. The chanting of our band name, the adrenaline that seems to explode through my veins as we get hyped up for a show. I've never known anything that's matched the thrill and as I peer out from the wings of the curtains on stage, I don't know if I ever will.

"Joel?"

I look up to find Becks with her short blond hair and bright green eyes. "Oh, hey, what's up?"

"The others are in the green room. Al's here. He has some news," she says with a grin.

I narrow my eyes at her. "You know what the news is, don't you?"

She tilts her head back and forth, trying to suppress a huge grin. "Maybe. Now hurry up."

Standing, I wrap my arm around her shoulder and we head back down the hall. When we enter, she takes her place on

James's knee and I sit down next to Key on the sofa, whose attention is fixed on our curly-haired, pot-bellied manager.

"Right," Al begins, "so I have some big news. Granted, I don't have exact dates nailed down yet, but when I got off the phone earlier, they were really insistent. I tried to tell them that—"

"For fuck's sake, Al," Dave mutters, "spit it out, we have a show to do."

Al shakes his head. "Sure, sure. Well, a producer at MTV has requested that you guys make a music video."

There's a pause as we all process what the fuck he just said.

"Did you just say a music video?" James asks.

"Like an actual music video?" Key reiterates next to me. "Like, for the television?"

Al rolls his eyes. "Yes, Fucknuts, for the *television*. What kind of music video do you think I mean?"

"Holy shit. That's . . . that's—" I start.

"This is fucking awesome!" Dave shouts, jumping out of his seat to rush Al in a ginormous hug.

The next thing I know, I'm plummeting against Al too. All of us are, and I can see it in my mind. The four of us, playing our music on the biggest stage of all, and the ideas already start spinning in my head. What song do they want us to do? Will it just be us playing or do they want a concept video? What will I wear? Holy shit, my mom will see this and be able to show her friends that I'm not just a small time fuckup.

When we finally release Al, his glasses are askew and one of the buttons over his large belly has popped, but he's smiling.

"What song are we going to do?" Key asks.

Al straightens himself out. "They want to release a video for 'Neon Crush,' since it's the official first single off the full album."

"Really?"

I turn, and Key has paled. In fact, he looks like he might be sick.

"Are you sure?" Key asks, a stammer creeping into his voice. "I mean . . . that song isn't exactly our most hardcore."

I frown. What is he so worried about? He's always been confident about his lyrics.

Dave shoves his shoulder. "What are you talking about? That song is killer. Definitely one of the best you've ever written."

"Yeah," James interjects. "And maybe it's good it's not as hardcore. It'll appeal more to the masses. Rope them in."

Al nods. "That's exactly the plan. We don't want to scare off the public by going straight to 'Futility.'"

"Fuck, I love that song," James muses.

Becks places her hand on his knee and squeezes. "It's kind of a downer though," she adds.

James tilts his head in agreement. "Yeah, but it's a big fuck-you to the man. Fuck-you to the bullies, fuck-you to the government, f—"

Becks places her hand on James's cheek and the color that had begun to appear in his face during his rant recedes at her touch. I can see the way he visibly relaxes. How she centers him after so much of his young life was spent in turmoil. Maybe I *do* want that. Maybe I want that with my own woman.

"Yeah, okay, you're probably right. At least there's a rad solo in 'Neon Crush,'" he concedes. "Just make sure you get my good side on camera."

I grin then glance over at Key again, who's cracking his knuckles and looking at the floor. What the hell is up with him now?

"When does production get underway?" Dave asks.

Al holds up his hands. "I'm still ironing out the details, I just wanted to let you know. Now"—he glances at his watch—"you're on in fifteen, so blow the fucking roof off this place."

They all give a resounding whoop before finishing their beers and heading for the stage, but I haul Key back by the shoulder. "You okay, man? You looked like you might be sick for a second there."

He nods. "Oh, yeah. Fine. Just . . . 'Neon Crush' is—well, it's a lot of pressure. It's one of the only songs on the record where I'm the sole writer. I guess I'm just worried that if it bombs . . ."

"You'll think it's because of you and not us," I finish for him.

He nods. "Yeah. Exactly."

I twist my lips and sniff. "I wouldn't worry. If it bombs it'll be because your ugly mug is on the TV, not because of your songwriting."

He rolls his eyes. "Oh, fuck off."

"No seriously," I continue with a shit-eating grin, following the others out the door. "Your hideous face on TV? We'll be lucky if people don't think we've started a zombie invasion."

"He really is an ugly mother fucker."

The two of us stop, our path to the stage blocked by a figure in the dark corridor. His voice is familiar, and it's as if the floor has just disappeared beneath me. I can feel the tension taking over Key's whole body as the man steps into the light in front of us. Someone neither of us has seen in almost eight years.

"One-Punch Logan?" I mutter, followed by a swift elbow to the ribs from Key.

But he seems to ignore the offensive nickname, and instead, smiles even brighter. "Hey, guys."

"Uh, hey, man. How are you doing? How'd you, uh . . . get back here?" Key asks.

Logan Samuels steps closer, his hands sliding into the front pockets of his jeans. He looks exactly the same, right down to the braid tucked into the brown ponytail that trails down his back. The same smug smile on his lips, like he thinks he knows more than everyone else in the room. The only thing different is his nose and, well, I guess I'm to blame for that.

He raises his arm where a blue rubber bracelet with the name "Carnal Sins" is visible.

"Fuck," Key mutters.

While we haven't used the bracelets to hand out to groupies in a few months, I guess they're still out there circling. Did Logan find one by accident? Or did he seek out a fan and steal it from her? Either way, this guy is as loony as I remember.

"Well, it was nice to see you again but we have a show to do," I say, trying to get Key to push ahead. "Enjoy the show."

"Oh, I will," he says. "And you guys enjoy being out there. Must be awesome to have everyone screaming and cheering for you."

I frown. "Yeah, it's fucking unicorns and rainbows all day." Rolling my eyes, I shove past him with my shoulder. "See you around, Samuels."

"You never know which performance might be your last."

We both stop and turn around to find this prick grinning like he won the lottery.

"What the fuck is that supposed to mean?" Key asks, stepping forward.

He shrugs. "Nothing. You just never know when your luck will change, right?"

Key moves but I grab his arm. "Forget about him. He's just being a massive cunt."

"Guys, they're waiting for you—oh!"

Becks appears in the hallway behind us, her lips parted in surprise to find us with a stranger. Her eyes dart between us, clearly sensing something is amiss with the way her gaze lingers on my hand holding Key back.

"Sorry, Becks, we're coming right now," I say.

"Oh, so *you're* Becks," Logan says, his eyes sweeping up and down over her, and my blood begins to boil as I see the way she cringes back. "Sorry, I didn't recognize you with your clothes on. That album cover photo you did is positively scandalous. I'd recognize those tits anywhere."

Becks's face turns beet red, but I barely register it. My fist flies before I can even think but at the last second I'm yanked back, my knuckles missing Logan's nose by an inch.

"The fuck—" I shout out, feeling James's arms wrap me from behind and seeing Dave pin Key in a hold. Becks is off to the side, squeezing herself against the wall to avoid any flying limbs.

"Joel, what the hell is wrong with you?" James asks as I pry him off me.

"This fucker—" I start, but I catch sight of Becks, and she subtly shakes her head, her wide eyes darting between me and James. I understand that look. She's worried if I tell James the reason I almost punched this asshole, he won't hesitate to commit murder. I take a deep breath and look at James. As his grip loosens, I shrug him off me then take one last look at Logan.

"It's nothing. This guy was just hoping I might straighten out his crooked nose."

Logan's smug smile drops for an instant, and I can see the rage brewing underneath, but he knows better than to take on four guys in a narrow hallway with security within reach. So I back away toward the stage, pulling Key along with me.

"See you around, One-Punch Logan," I call over my shoulder, motioning for security to escort him out. "Enjoy the show." Then without a glance back, I walk out onto the blinding stage to calamitous applause.

What I Like About You

DUSTY

I haven't heard from my mystery caller, and I'm grateful. His last call was intense, and I'm not sure what the next one might be like. Plus, I gave part of myself away. Forgetting my accent? That's never happened before. I suppose now there's no point in using it with him if he ever calls back. Now that it's Tuesday, I'm grateful for my first day off in over a week. Even though my job isn't physically taxing, it can be hard emotionally. There are days where everything is great and golden, then there are days like today where I hate myself. Not necessarily hate my job, but hate the way others feel about it, because all it does is change how they feel about me. It's the reason I wish I could just find a normal job like any other woman in her twenties.

But I've been in this life now for so many years that it's really all I know. Or rather, it's all I know how to do well. Plus, the thought of working a nine-to-five terrifies me. I don't have a high school diploma and thanks to my fuckup parents, I don't have many useful skills for the workforce. I can't type fast enough for a secretarial job, I'm not strong enough for manual labor, and anything to do with math? Forget it . . . they might as well just toss my résumé in the garbage.

My voice is rough from talking for hours on end, so I make myself a mug of boiling water, add lemon and honey, grab my Walkman and laundry basket, and head downstairs to the laundromat. When I step through the back door, I scan the room, and I know it's silly, but I can't help but hope, for one brief moment, that Joel might be here. He's not. Of course he's not. Why would he be? I basically told him to go away and never come back. In fact, I didn't even tell him my real name. It should come as a relief that he's not here. It's what I wanted, but I'll admit, now that I'm here, it hurts. Like a bruise deep, down under the skin.

Shaking my head, I walk over to my usual machine, thankfully free, and open the lid. I pull on my headphones and can already feel the comforting sound of Frank Sinatra calming my soul. Before I can reach for my hidden stash of detergent, there's a tap on my shoulder. I turn around and Doris is standing next to me.

Her body is hunched over from her sciatica, and she gestures with one long polka dotted nail for me to lean in.

"Is something wrong?" I ask, slipping off the headphones.

"Do me a favor, love, and tell that young man to find another laundromat."

I narrow my eyes. "Tell who?"

She waves her hand. "The one who's been here every day looking for you," she says, her voice like gravel.

In an instant my heart is in my throat. "Someone's been here looking for me?" I ask.

"The man with the long dark hair," she continues. "Told him to stop coming around unless he has actual laundry to do. This is a business, not a bar."

I open my mouth to respond but nothing comes out, and with a huff, Doris turns and shuffles off back to her desk by the windows. I turn to stare at my clothes in the drum. Joel came back for me? And not just once but every day? Why would he do that?

He likes you!

There's a rising heat in my cheeks as I try to reason with myself. Does he really?

The bell above the door jingles, and I freeze, terrified to look, but it seems I don't even need to. I can feel him. Feel the heavy presence of his gaze on me, and my knees wobble as I continue to methodically toss my clothes into the washing machine.

His heavy footsteps travel across the room, and a shiver shoots down my spine as he stops right behind me. There's a tap on my shoulder, and the rest of body breaks out into goose bumps.

"Excuse me, is this machine taken?"

I turn, and there he is. Smile radiating happiness as he stands across from me with a laundry basket tucked under one arm.

"It's you again," I say.

"Me again."

After staring at his face for a little longer than is probably considered normal, I clear my throat. "I, uh . . . I didn't think you'd be back. With the amount of laundry you did last week I was sure you'd have enough clean clothes to last a month."

His eyes sparkle. "Yeah, well, it would seem you underestimate just how many clothes I go through in a week." He hikes up the basket on his hip and my eyebrows rise when I catch its contents.

"One sock?"

He nods, then settles at the machine next to me. "As I said, the need to get to the laundromat was dire."

I can't seem to stop it. A smile blooms across my face so wide my muscles hurt, or maybe it's just that I don't use them much. He came all the way here to see me with his one sock. My chest aches with the desire to trust him. That this isn't just a game he's playing. Can he really be genuine? With a short laugh, his eyes crinkle.

"Yes, I suppose 'dire' is the appropriate word for your laundry situation."

For a long time we just stand, goofily staring at each other, but I've never felt more comfortable. Finally he blinks and dumps his soiled item into the machine.

"Oh, I uh—" He clears his throat. Is he nervous? "I brought you something."

"You did?"

"Yeah." He reaches into the pocket of his baggy jeans, and something in me freezes. I've never accepted gifts well, what if it's something important or valuable? What if—

My thoughts are cut off when he pulls out a small box tied with a red ribbon.

"Laundry detergent?" I ask.

Now it's his turn for his cheeks to turn pink. "I thought, you know . . . because you let me borrow some of yours last week." At my silence he fidgets and licks his lips. "Sorry, it's stupid, I—"

Don't give too much away. Be careful. I look sideways at him and allow my smile to pull at the side of my mouth. "Cute," I say, taking the box and putting it in my basket even though I just want to hold it to my chest like it's made of gold. Guys have tried to buy my affection before, and it's never meant anything, but this? This is worth more than any of that.

His shoulders relax. "I'm glad you like it."

"Thank you," I say. "That's very sweet of you."

A throat clears behind us and there's Doris, glaring at Joel. He leans in toward me and says, "I don't think she likes me very much."

I whisper back, "To be fair, she doesn't like anyone much."

"She seems to like you though," he offers. "Practically ran me out of here the last time I dropped by to see you."

Feigning ignorance, I arch an eyebrow. "You stopped by to see me?"

"Well, I'd hoped to see you, but she really has a thing against loitering so I made sure I came with laundry today."

I grin. "Hence the single sock?"

"Single sock for a single man."

Suppressing my smile, I cross my arms over my chest. "Is this your not-so-subtle way of reminding me you're single?"

He shrugs. "Just wanted to make sure you didn't forget."

I bite my lip and look away, opening the new box of detergent and filling my machine before placing the coins in the slot. After a few moments, Joel does the same, silently gesturing to me for some powder. We make quick work of shutting our respective lids, the water whooshing through the hoses with a loud gurgle, and head toward the window seats.

Doris is still glaring at Joel, but when I give her a look, she returns to hiding behind her magazine. *The Price is Right* is on the TV in the background, and I'm overtly aware of the heat from Joel's body as he sits close to me. I try to keep my eyes on the screen, but I'm acutely aware that Joel is staring at me. Finally, I turn to him.

"Why are you looking at me like that?" I ask.

"Because you're beautiful," he responds without missing a beat. The bluntness of it has my cheeks scorching hot in a moment.

"You're very direct."

"Considering you hardly gave me the time of day last week, I want to be clear about my intentions."

"And what are those?"

He steeples his fingers and props his chin on them. "Well, I'd like to take you on a date. Preferably somewhere with pizza and music but if you like fancy shit, I'm okay with that too. Then maybe to the arcade or bowling. After I've wildly impressed you with my skills, we'd come back here and we'd pretend like all of our clothes went missing from the laundromat so our only option under the terrible circumstances would be to get naked."

I can't help but laugh. "And then what? Naked twister?"

His mouth twists. "Naked twister? Now *there's* a sport I would participate in. Great idea."

I kick at his boots with my trainers.

"Okay," he continues, "but after you beat my ass at naked twister—even though, let's be real, I'm still winning—I'd probably move on to trying to impress you with my random animal fact knowledge. For example, did you know that polar bears actually have black skin underneath all that fur?"

My eyebrows lift. "Really?"

"And penguins mate for life."

I press my lips together and stare at my lap. "Hmm, I wonder what that's like."

"What? Being a penguin?"

I shake my head. "No. Someone loving you permanently."

It's been quiet for a long time. I shouldn't have said anything. What a pathetic thing to say—my god, he's going to think I'm some unlovable maniac.

Looking up, I blink furiously. "Sorry, that—I didn't mean it that way."

"Do you do that a lot?"

I rear back. "Do what?"

"Say something vulnerable and immediately try and take it back?"

I squeeze my thigh, and let out a long breath. I could try to deny it but where would that get me? "Not often. I've made a living acting the part."

He raises an eyebrow. "And what part is that?"

"Whatever part I need to."

Again, silence, and this time I know I've said too much.

"You don't have to pretend with me," he says quietly.

Our eyes meet again, and waves crash and swirl inside me, igniting my nerves. It makes me want to just pour myself out onto the floor and show him all the battered and bruised pieces of me.

"I only ever wanted to know the real you. Remember? The woman who turned down Victor Von Douche and his guaranteed cash to give the outcast a chance."

This is too much. No one is really this nice. Who the hell does he think he is? What is he playing at? I stand abruptly. "I need a smoke." I turn and head out the door into the fresh air. Twisting my bag around, I fish out my pack of cigarettes and place one between my lips. Furiously, I dig for a lighter, my heart racing. When I find it, I click and click and click but the damn thing just won't light.

"God damnit," I mutter.

"Need a light?" Joel asks, placing his own cigarette between his teeth and holding up his lighter.

I sigh, then nod. "Yes, thanks."

He sparks it, covering the flame with his palm against the wind, and holds it out for me. He doesn't invade my space, but rather lets me come to him. It's a subtle thing. I don't even know if he's doing it on purpose, but I appreciate it.

"Sorry, I just—" I inhale when the cigarette lights and step back. "I needed some air. Didn't mean to be so abrupt before."

He waves me away. "It's fine. I needed some air too. That bleach smell was starting to give me a headache."

I hum. "I guess I'm used to it by now."

"How so? You don't work customer support for a bleach company, do you?" he asks.

"No, I uh—" *Shit.* "I live upstairs."

His mouth drops open as he backs away from the wall to look

above the neon sign for The Sudsy Dream. "You—you live right up there?"

I take another drag and nod.

"That little—" he mutters, spinning around, taking a moment to glare into the laundromat. "All week I came here and she knew—"

"Joel, why are you here?"

"What?"

"Why are you *here*?"

His brows soften. "I told you. Laundry."

"Your one sock?"

"It really needed washing."

I flick my cigarette away and make for the door, but as I go he gently grasps my wrist and stops me.

"No, wait. Come on. Listen, I really just wanted to see you again. I figured that was obvious."

I watch his face. He seems sincere, his amber eyes dancing over my face. Can I trust things might be different with him? "Why would you want to waste your time with me? You don't even know me."

"I'm trying to change that but, if you haven't noticed, you're making it really hard."

I suppose I am.

He steps toward me slowly, a gentle smile on his face. "I just want to spend time with you. It's why I'm here, across town with a single sock and a pocket full of quarters instead of at home with my fully repaired washing machine."

My mouth drops open. He's so honest. "Joel—"

"If you're not attracted to me—if what I felt between us in Vegas . . . what I felt between us last week—what I feel *today* . . . was all just one-sided, tell me now. I'll take my soggy sock and never darken the doorstep of The Sudsy Dream again."

My heart spins in circles as his eyes trail over to my lips, lingering there.

"But if it wasn't, all I'm asking is for one chance. You're right, we don't know each other, but isn't finding out ninety percent of the fun?"

Half of me wants to take the risk and the other half is too terrified to believe life is presenting me with this opportunity again. If only there was a sign, a message . . . something to show me how to trust again.

"Hey," Joel says, looking past me, "do you hear that?"

"I—what?"

He touches my shoulder and moves past me down the alley. "I can hear something. Hold on—"

"Joel?" But he's gone, and I'm left panicking about my decision. Worried I won't choose right.

"Hey!" I hear, then Joel emerges from around the corner with something small bundled in his arms. "Look what I found."

He jogs over to me with that bright smile.

"Check it out."

Leaning in, he shows me what he went down the alley for.

"Oh my god," I gasp, rushing toward him and the rumpled orange fluff ball. "Stella? How the hell did you get outside?"

Joel passes her to me, and my panic is instantly soothed by the fact he found her. I look up at the window she normally occupies and see that the screen has popped off at the corner. "Shit!" I brush leaves out of her long fur. "Oh, Stella, what were you thinking?"

"Seems like she didn't want to go far. She must really love you."

Joel looks up at me then, and I know this is it. If I let him leave, he won't come back. He'll move on and I'll forever regret that I wasn't brave enough to give him a chance.

You can do this. You can trust—one more time.

"Joel?" I ask.

"Yeah?"

I pull Stella tighter toward me for strength. "I-I . . ." *Just say it.* "Could you help me upstairs? The screen needs to be fixed so she doesn't escape again."

He raises his eyebrows. "Upstairs?"

"To my apartment."

"Oh, uh . . . okay."

I nod, tilting back on my heels. "Come on."

There's a small alcove tucked into the side of the building that leads to a staircase, and I lead Joel up past the front door to the laundromat. I pull my keys from my bag and open the door before heading up.

"Must be nice to only have to go downstairs to do your laundry," Joel admits when we reach my apartment.

"Why do you think I picked this place?"

He smiles, and I can't help but mirror it back.

I open the door, and Stella immediately jumps from my arms and shakes out her fur, dust and dirt scattering onto the floor. She meows loudly, then looks at me, as if to say *I thought you weren't going to bring this boy home, you hypocrite.*

"This is Stella," I say, shutting the door behind me. "I found her in the same alley six months ago."

Joel chuckles. "Hey, naughty girl, it's nice to meet you. I love that name, by the way."

I raise my eyebrow. "Stella?"

He chuckles. "Yeah. It's one of my favorite movie lines. You know—" He dramatically reaches out his arm with a pained expression. "Stella . . . *Stella!*"

Be still my heart. "You've seen *A Streetcar Named Desire?*"

"Yeah, of course."

A wide grin takes over my face. "It's one of my favorite movies."

He smirks. Damn him and that smirk. "The, uh . . . the window is just over there," I say, pointing toward my bed, because *of course* the window I need fixing is right beside my bed.

Okay, just keep yourself together. He's just here to help me fix the screen.

He shucks off his leather jacket and . . . okay, this just got a whole lot harder. The arms on this man? Black and grey tattoos cover his skin—bats and devils and all manner of hellish beasts. The juxtaposition of his skin and personality is unbelievable. Heat spreads between my legs, and I press my thighs together while remembering to close my mouth. He examines the window for a few seconds. "Doesn't seem too bad. Looks like a screw came loose. You got a screwdriver around here?"

"Uh . . . no," I admit. "Not exactly very handy."

He turns to me and smiles. "No problem. I think I have an idea."

He walks past me into my kitchen and I watch as he so confidently opens the cutlery drawer and pulls out a butterknife. He looks so good in my space, as if he's lived here the whole time. "So, you like movies?"

I watch him, amused, as he slides back past me in his socks. "Correction. I love movies."

"What's your top favorite movie?" he asks, kneeling on my bed now, twisting the butterknife in his capable hands.

"*To Catch a Thief.*"

He inspects his work and hums. "Never seen that one."

"Really? You're missing out."

"I'll have to check it out." He's standing in front of me now, placing the butterknife in my palm. "All fixed."

I peek past him at the repaired screen where Stella has already taken up her loafing position in the sun. "Thanks. I owe you one."

He gently shakes his head. "Nah. I'm happy to help."

I take a deep breath as we stare at each other, not five feet from my bed. I sneak a glance at my wrinkled sheets, the fantasy of the two of us tangled up in them too much to fight against. Our eyes meet and I realize that he was looking at them too.

"I should go—"

"So about that date—"

His eyes widen as we both stop talking at the same time. Why is my heart beating so fast?

"Wait . . ." he says. "What did you say?"

I tuck some hair behind my ear and stand up straight. "That date you asked me on. What if I said yes?"

His brilliant white teeth shine from his wide smile. "Really?"

"Yes. I'll give this a shot."

My heart flutters as his eyes crinkle with joy. "You will?"

"I can't possibly say no now," I say with a smirk. "You saved my cat."

Joel chuckles. "Oh, I get it. It's a pity date. It's okay, it's okay," he says when I try to correct him. "I'll take it. And no, Stella and I were definitely *not* in cahoots to get you to agree."

I laugh. "What can I say? She's a great wingwoman."

There's a pause, then we slowly make our way back toward my door. "So, how about Wednesday, then?" he asks.

I pretend to mull it over. "Wednesday could work. It'll give Stella time to do her nails . . . have a bath. You know, make herself look pretty."

"It's a date then," Joel asserts.

He heads for the door, and I follow behind him, feeling lightheaded and warm.

"So I'll see you here on Wednesday," he confirms.

I nod. "Yes. You will. Wednesday."

Standing in the open doorway, I wonder briefly if he'll try to kiss me. I want to kiss him. It's been two years of dreaming of his lips against mine, and now that I've agreed to give this a chance, I don't know if I can wait anymore.

"You wanted to know my name," I say, feeling exposed and nervous. "It's—"

But Joel shakes his head. He reaches forward with one hand to push back a stray curl from my face, and my body comes alive from his touch. "It's okay," he whispers. "I have our whole date to figure it out."

CHAPTER 10

A Kiss to Build a Dream On

KEY

TWELVE YEARS AGO

The heat is malicious today. Every pedal of my bike feels like torture as the sun radiates down on the back of my neck. I can't wait to get to the pool. At least I'll have some relief there. I think the heat even got to my parents because I was shocked they agreed to let me go. But I'm thirteen now, hardly a little kid in need of constant supervision. Even if they think the pool is the devil's playground.

Sweat trickles down my face and back, but finally I hear the noise from the public pool. I'm only a block away, and I feel cooler already, as if the water nearby hangs in the air. There's the sound of children screaming, splashing, and laughter as I round the corner and spot the massive fenced pool deck.

It's super busy, but I'm hardly surprised. On a day like today? There isn't anything better to do. The bike racks are practically full, but I find one last empty slot, grabbing my towel and swim trunks and heading around the pool house to the change rooms.

The soles of my feet burn as I tiptoe across the concrete five minutes later. I look around, wondering if any of my friends from school are here or if they went to the other one across town. Standing by the pool, I curl my toes around the edge, breathing in the sour smell of chlorine.

Making sure no one is in the way, I don't hesitate any longer and cannonball into the deep end. The water isn't overly warm, but every muscle relaxes as I sink below the surface, feeling that sweet relief I've been craving all day. My butt hits the bottom of the pool, but I wait before kicking back up to the top. How long can I stay here until I need to take a breath?

Something prickles up my spine and I open my eyes to find the blurry figures of swimmers around me, and . . . *there*. Sitting at the bottom of the pool across from me, a watery halo of hair the color of fire.

Air escapes my mouth, bubbles floating away from me, and I'm suddenly desperate to breathe. At the top, I wipe the water out of my eyes as I tread, searching for her, but she's not there. Am I so desperate to see her again that I'm hallucinating, or is it that I finally have heat stroke?

I spin around when someone taps on my shoulder, and blue eyes the color of the pool look back at me. "Hey, Key."

She's here. I haven't seen her in over a year, but she's actually here. A wave hits me in the face and I swallow too much water, my eyes squinting shut as I cough and splutter.

She giggles and I shake my head, finally spitting out the last of the pool water. "Dusty? What—what are you doing here?"

She grins. "Same as you, dummy. It's hot as hell today."

I blink. Did she just swear?

"I—right. Yeah. It's hot as—yeah."

She smirks, knowing as well as I do that no one cusses around here, not even the adults.

"You . . . haven't been coming to church."

Her face scrunches. "I know. I wanted to, but after Mama left, Daddy had to find an actual job and we moved out of town."

"Oh."

She tilts her head, the wet strands of her hair falling over one side of her face. "It didn't work out though."

"No?"

"No, so we're back while he tries to find something else. Daddy was real mad he got fired, but they didn't take too kindly to him drinking at work."

"Will you be coming back to church, then?" I ask, then blush when I hear how hopeful my voice sounds.

"Why? You miss me?"

I've missed her more than she'll ever know. "I just mean, it would be nice to talk to someone about music again."

Her eyes brighten. "Are you still writing songs?"

I nod. "Yeah! Well, trying to."

"Key, that's amazing. You'll have to sing them for me."

I look around. "What . . . here?"

She rolls her eyes. "No, dummy. Come on."

She turns and swims toward the ladder. I watch, stuck in place as she climbs out of the water in the tiniest bathing suit I've ever seen.

The blue polka dot fabric clings to hips I never noticed before. She stands, glittering in the sunshine as she turns back to me, and while her smile has never failed to draw my attention to her face, I can't help but stare at her chest hidden under the triangles of her bikini top.

"Are you coming?" she asks.

My throat is dry, but before I can move to follow her, I panic and sink a little deeper in the water. I reach down to the front of my swim trunks and feel a bulge. *No no no no.* What am I going to do now?

"Key?"

I look up and she stands with her hand on her hip. "Uh," I

start. "Yeah. I just—I forgot something over there. I'll meet you by the lifeguard tower."

"Oh, okay!" She smiles easily and disappears into the crowd, her hips swinging.

"Oh man," I groan. It's only happened a few times before. What did I do then? Right . . . think of gross things. That'll do it. But as hard as I try, it's impossible not to think of Dusty in that bikini. I try not to watch her as she walks across the pool deck, but it's impossible. She's hot.

I don't know if I've ever seen anyone hotter than her. And, as I glance around, it seems I'm not the only one who thinks so. A dozen men, some even as old as my father, are staring at her like they've never seen a girl before. She doesn't seem to notice as she flips her hair over her shoulder to wring it out, the water dripping down between the polka dot fabric on her chest and glinting off the golden pendant hanging there.

Okay, this isn't helping.

What *does* help me is a man in a tiny pair of shorts walking along the pool deck. He's eating a hot dog and he's got mustard dripping down his chin. He stops and drags his towel off his shoulder, rubbing it all over and smearing the yellow sauce and hot dog juice into his hairy chest. Taking my opportunity, I swim across to the other ladder and climb up, moving to wrap my towel around my waist, then head for the lifeguard tower.

I find her leaning against it like the statue of a goddess. She's so much more than hot. She's pretty. *Beautiful.* Long gone is the babyish quality of her voice or the roundness in her cheeks. She grew up, and I guess . . . so did I. I just wish we could've grown up together.

"Want to get out of here?" she asks me once I join her.

"Where would we go?" What I'm thinking, though, is *why would anyone want to leave the pool in this heat?*

But all thoughts of the pool disappear when she leans forward to whisper in my ear. "It's a secret."

Dusty winks at me and my knees nearly buckle. Next thing I know, we're on our bikes and I'm following her down a street I've never been on before. Dusty's bike is a bit rusty, and it squeaks like crazy when she brakes, but the white shirt she threw over her bikini top has gotten soaked through and nothing else but that seems to matter.

Soon enough, she turns down a narrow, overgrown driveway and for a moment I think she's taking me to her house, but then she cuts through some dense trees on the right. I slow down, amazed at how she so effortlessly darts down the dirt path through the woods. I'm about to ask her how far till we're there when the trees part and a small wooden cabin appears before us.

She stops by the front staircase and looks back at me, her red hair dry and wind blown out around her face.

"This is it," she says, her eyes wild. She looks . . . excited. *Happy*.

I push off my bike. "Is this your—?"

"My house?" she answers. "No way. It's no one's house. It's abandoned, but I fixed up the inside. Come on, I want to show you."

She grabs my hand, and I follow along after her as she opens the creaking door and pulls me inside. *Woah*. From the outside, it looked like the place was about to fall down, and maybe it still is, but the inside is clean. There's a sofa with blankets and cushions without a speck of dust on them, a table with candles in the middle that look like they're only a few hours from being completely burned out. It's small—one main room, and there's a wood stove in the corner next to the sofa.

"What do you think?" she asks, staring at me.

"It's . . . amazing," I whisper.

She squeals, dropping my hand to clap and bounce on her

toes. "I knew you'd like it. I cleaned the place up myself. I even figured out how to get the old generator going out back."

I blink in surprise. "A generator? What for?"

She leans forward until our noses are almost touching. "That's the best part!" Dusty skips over across from the sofa and throws both arms out wide. "Ta-da!"

My mouth drops open when I notice the TV. I step toward the large square box, bunny ears poking up, and slide my fingers along the thin metal rods. "Wow, and it works?"

She shrugs. "It doesn't get cable, we're too far into the woods." She flops down on the sofa and grins. "But look underneath."

My eyes trail down to where—

"A VCR?"

She grins and shimmies in her seat. "That's right! Now I can watch whatever movies I can get my hands on."

I glance around the place again. It's cool in here, the tree canopy cutting at least a few degrees off the top. But part of me wonders . . .

"Aren't you worried someone will find you in here? What if they arrest you for trespassing?"

She stands up and grabs my hand again before pulling me to the couch. "You worry too much. Who the hell is going to come back here? Besides, I've been coming here for two months now and never seen so much as a hint that someone else has been on the property."

With a sharp tug, she pulls me down onto the couch next to her, our bodies press into each other's sides, and all worries about being caught in someone else's home fly out of my mind. All I can think of is the feel of her damp shirt against my arm, the skin of her knee touching my thigh, and the fact that her hand is still clasped in mine.

"So," she starts, her face turning serious. "Sing."

"Wait . . . what?"

"You told me you had new songs. Sing them for me."

An odd squeak comes out of my throat. "I-I don't—"

She rolls her eyes. "Come on! How are you ever going to become a super famous singer if you don't practice in front of anyone?"

Because she's not just anyone. She's everything.

"Yeah, but I . . ."

She leans back, pulling her hand away to cross them over her chest, blue polka dots taunting me.

"I—okay. But they're not practiced or anything and I don't have a guitar—"

"Oh! I have one back here."

In a flurry of red curls, she's gone across the room to a closet and pulling out an old electric guitar. "It's nothing fancy but it'll do, right?"

She hands it to me, and I grasp the neck of the guitar gentler than I've ever handled an object before. She hurries around, sitting back down on the couch and pulling her knees into her chest to watch me. I look down at the guitar, which is chipped and missing a few frets near the bottom as well as the E string. But it's something.

"Sorry, I don't have an amp to plug it into—"

"It's great," I interrupt, flashing her a nervous smile. I've never played an electric guitar before. Actually, I've never even held one, until now. My fingers curl around the neck and I strum the strings. Immediately both Dusty and I scrunch our faces against the terrible noise, and I have to spend a few minutes tuning it before it sounds even remotely decent. Without an amp it's a bit pitchy and nasal sounding, but I couldn't be more excited.

"That sounds better," I say, and take a deep breath. "Okay. Ready?"

She nods, and her eyes seem alight with wonder as I start to strum the strings in the basic chord patterns that I want. When my parents said I could learn the guitar, they strictly meant classical guitar and fingerpicking hymns, but I couldn't help myself from stealing over to the public library and learning a handful of chord combinations. I feel like a real rebel now. Playing in a secret place on a forbidden electric guitar? I'll be in so much trouble if I ever get caught.

But soon I forget all about that and am simply carried away by the freedom to play something my parents don't approve of. Freedom to improvise and be creative. My eyes close, and my fingertips start to sting from the thin nickel strings as I press them into the board, but I don't care, and before I can chicken out, I'm singing.

Singing a song I wrote inside my head, sure, but who cares. Because it sounds . . . good. There's something missing, maybe the missing E string, but the words flow out of me, the dynamics of my voice following the intensity of the guitar. Before I know it, I strum one last time, the sound echoing around the room and I'm breathing hard and fast as the adrenaline rushes through my veins.

I open my eyes slowly to find Dusty staring at me wide-eyed, her dark pink lips open.

"Sorry, I'm still working on it—"

"That was amazing," she whispers.

"Re—really?"

"Key, I . . . wow. I had no idea how good you are."

A blush spreads across my cheeks. "No, I'm not."

"No, really," she says seriously, leaning toward me. "I'm kind of in awe of you right now."

"I—thanks, I guess."

She frowns and sits back against the sofa.

"What's wrong?"

"Nothing, I just—Key, you could really be something, you know?"

I shake my head. "No . . . I don't know—"

"You could!"

We look at each other for a long moment.

"When we said we could run away to Hollywood together," she starts, "it was just a dream . . . but you—you could really do it."

I place the guitar next to me and reach forward to grasp her hand. "You can too! Come on, show me some of your acting."

She shakes her head and wipes a tear from her eye. "No, I'm terrible at it. You'll just laugh at me."

"No, I won't." She scoffs but I press on. "Come on! You didn't laugh at me—"

"Because you were good!"

"And you will be too!"

She tucks her bottom lip behind her teeth and it turns my insides to marshmallow.

"Please?" I beg. "For me?" This seems to win her over. "What's your favorite movie? Show me a scene."

A smile peeks out from the corner of her lips. "Promise you won't laugh?"

I cross my heart with my finger then hold up my hand. "I would never."

She grins widely then, and bounces up from the couch to stand next to the TV.

"Have you ever seen *To Catch a Thief*?"

I shake my head. "No . . . my parents, they don't really let us watch anything unless they're there."

"Okay, perfect. Picture this then. A big fancy room with fancy furniture, fireworks shooting into the sky in the background as a beautiful woman with a diamond necklace stands across from the most handsome jewel thief."

My eyes widen. "Jewel thief?"

"Yes, hush!" She closes her eyes. When she speaks next, she takes on an accent that suggests it's decades earlier. That she is the grown-up woman in the diamond necklace. She walks about the room with the air of someone with royal blood, like she's been trained her whole life to look down on those beneath her, but somehow keeps her kind eyes and friendly smile. Her acting is subtle, each movement purposeful. It makes me wonder if she's rehearsed this a million times.

Her fingers skim across her bare neck, and I let myself imagine a diamond necklace. Her chest heaves, and I can't even hear what she's saying as her breasts pull at her see-through shirt. Before I know it, she's moving toward me, her hips swaying in a pair of high-cut shorts until she's sitting right next to me.

I freeze. She takes my hand and places it where a necklace might be if she was wearing one, but my brain breaks and the earlier problem I had in the pool comes back with a vengeance. She leans toward me and I can't breathe anymore. Her head tips forward and her eyes close and like a speeding train there's no stopping it. Her lips touch mine and I can *feel* and *see* the scene she described.

Then, all too quickly, her lips are gone, and I take in a sharp breath, blink her back into focus. The only sound is our breathing and the cicadas chirping in the tall grass outside.

"How . . . how was that?" she asks, her voice barely above a whisper, no hint of that accent she had only minutes ago.

My mouth bobs open and closed for a few seconds. *She's just acting.* I remind myself she didn't kiss me because she likes me, but because it was part of the scene. Why does that make me so sad?

"That was the best acting I've ever seen." I finally say.

The worry on her face softens. "Really?"

I nod and swallow. "Really. We're going to get out of here, Dusty. Everyone will know who we are someday. Both of us."

Bad Blood

I don't step inside the house until after dark, with a paper bag full of groceries we don't need. Key comes into the kitchen from the living room a few seconds later, his hair standing on end and a beer in his hand.

"Joel, where the fuck have you been?"

"I had to get some things," I say, setting down the bag on the counter.

He pulls out a jar of sauerkraut and cough medicine. "This? This is why you've been gone for hours?"

I shrug. "They didn't have it at Fred's. I had to go across town for the good stuff."

"'The good stuff'?" Key blusters. "Since when are you a sauerkraut connoisseur?"

"Since always!" I insist, sure he can see right through the lie.

I put away the rest of the items while Key watches me intently. When I close the fridge, he sighs and shakes his head. "Whatever, dude." He grabs his beer off the coffee table. "This came today while you were out." He slides a letter to me across the table. It's opened and handwritten, so it's not a bill.

"What is it?" I ask.

"Just read it."

Picking up the paper, I unfold it and read.

JOEL AND KEY,

I WAS DISAPPOINTED TO HAVE OUR REUNION LAST WEEK TAINTED BY SUCH ANIMOSITY AND VIOLENCE. PERHAPS IT WAS TOO MUCH TO HOPE THAT EITHER OF YOU HAVE GROWN UP AND WE COULD HAVE A CIVILIZED CONVERSATION. I SEE NOW THAT I WAS WRONG. I'M SORRY THAT YOU BOTH STILL FEEL SUCH HATRED TOWARD ME AND OUR PAST FRIENDSHIP, ESPECIALLY WHEN YOU CONSIDER HOW CLOSE WE ONCE WERE. YOU THINK YOU KNOW PEOPLE, THEN THEY STAB YOU IN THE BACK. I DIDN'T WANT IT TO COME TO THIS, AND I HOPE YOU REMEMBER THAT GOING FORWARD I'M JUST TRYING TO DO WHAT'S RIGHT.

LOGAN SAMUELS

"What in the actual fuck?" I shout. Key seats himself at one of the barstools and downs the rest of his beer. "No, seriously, what the fuck is this?"

"Apparently One-Punch Logan is more delusional than we thought," he says, sounding exhausted.

"*'I'm just trying to do what's right?'*" I ask, scanning the letter again. "What the hell does that mean?"

"Beats me. The guy's an idiot with an ego the size of the moon. Always has been, always will be. I knew when he showed up at the show it was a bad omen. Things have been going too well around here."

"Should we call Al? Let him know?"

Key frowns and twists his lips. "Let him know what? That a guy who was never officially part of the band showed up after eight years and sent us a vaguely threatening letter?" He shakes his head. "Look, he's probably just bluffing. Trying to scare us into giving him some money. Once he realizes we're not playing around, he'll go away."

But something churns in the pit of my stomach. Something uneasy and sour that ferments like rotting meat. Perhaps it's because there was a time when Logan and Key were friends before I showed up. There's a whole history between them that I was never invited in on. Then there was that day . . .

"Hey," I start cautiously. "What was it that you two got into that fight about, anyway? I can't remember."

It's not that I can't remember, it's that I literally have no idea. I just remember walking in on the two of them. Key, holding Logan up by his collar against the wall of the barracks. Key had seemed to come to his senses for a moment, and when his back was turned, Logan was ready to swing at him from behind. So I clocked him in the face. I never liked the guy and didn't particularly like that he was a part of our little makeshift band at Samson Academy. I was thrilled when Key started to pull away from him. Then when I saw them fighting, I didn't even need to ask whose side I should be on. Key is my brother. I'd do anything for him.

"Who remembers?" Key says quietly. "It was so long ago."

"Seriously? It must have been bad. You two were really going at it. I was worried you were going to kill him."

Key sighs, his head falling back on his shoulders. "From what I remember, which isn't a lot . . . I think he'd gone through my personal effects."

I raise my eyebrows. "He went through your shit?"

He nods slowly and smacks his lips. "Yeah."

"But . . . why?"

His gaze locks on some memory in the distance. "He went through my mail. Letters and shit I had in my trunk. Took something from me that—something important that I can never get back."

Key's cheeks turn red and there's an ache that begins to spread in my chest. "Dude, I'm sorry. I didn't know—"

"It's fine." Key brushes his hands off on his lap and stands, but his eyes are wet. Whatever it was that Logan took from him . . . it still hurts him.

"Why didn't you tell me?" I ask.

Key grins even though his lip quivers. "I didn't feel like I needed to. You were exactly who I needed at that moment. I didn't even need to ask or explain . . . you just had my back."

I nod. "I always will."

He claps me on the shoulder and squeezes. "Right, well, now that I've been thoroughly drowned in bad memories, what say you to us hitting up the titty bar?"

My muscles tense. Shit . . . I wasn't expecting this tonight. "Uh, really? Tonight?"

Key rubs his hand down his face. "Yeah, I could really use the distraction. Maybe bring home a friend?"

I can't go there with him. Not after finally getting Dusty to agree to a date. I mean, she used to be a stripper, but I doubt she wants to date a guy who is out and gawking at other women. Not to mention, it'll be more difficult to convince Key that I can't bring someone home once I'm out.

"Actually, I can't."

"What?" he blusters. "Why not?"

I grab the cough medicine from the counter. "I think I might be coming down with something." I fake a cough. "Don't want to screw up our performance schedule by getting some nasty bug. I'm just going to take this and go to bed."

Key groans. "Come on, seriously?"

I shrug. "We can go some other time."

"*Fine.* I'll see you in the morning."

Key huffs before turning toward his room. Feeling like an absolute asshole, I call after him. "Hey, Key?"

"Yeah?"

"Everything will be okay."

He nods. "Yeah, I know."

Then, with one last smile, he disappears down the hallway, and I stand with my feet glued to the floor wondering if the friendship we have is strong enough to welcome another person into our lives.

CHAPTER 12

Causing a Commotion

DUSTY

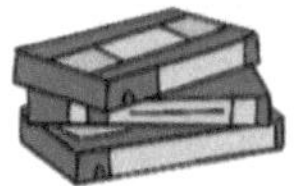

"Yeah, I want to ride your cock so bad, sugar. Ooh, just like that. It feels so—"

From the other side of the phone line comes the unmistakable sound of a man ejaculating. I roll my eyes. This call barely lasted five minutes and three of those were free.

"I, uh—I just . . ." says the man. His voice sounds like he's experiencing the phenomenon after coming where the horny haze dissipates and finally gives way to embarrassment. He feels ashamed of himself and now is dreading the awkward post-coital conversation. I take a deep breath and shush into the line. "Don't worry, sugar. You did so good. That was amazing."

He clears his throat. "Right, you were great. Uh, thanks."

"Can't wait to hear from you again, darlin'," I say in my Texan accent.

"'Kay. Bye."

The phone disconnects and after hanging up the receiver, I drop my head forward into my hands. A heaviness weighs on my chest and I roll my shoulders, trying to lessen the discomfort. I wish I could be anywhere but here right now. I'm tired and my throat is dry, and after hearing the first twenty callers from the night come with embarrassing quickness, I start to wonder just how much longer I can do this.

I lean back in my chair, a few strands of hair falling in my face, and I blow them up toward the fluorescent lights of the drop ceiling.

What happened to me? How did everything go so very differently than how I dreamed it would when I was thirteen? I mean, it's no mystery—I know how I ended up here. What I really mean is why did it have to happen to *me* this way? Did I do something wrong? Was I a terrible person in another life and so I need to be punished in this one?

"Cherry? Do you need a break?"

I glance up at my supervisor, Claudia, and shake my head. "No, no . . . I can keep going for a bit. It's only been a few hours, I'd rather take my break later."

She nods. "Right, well, line twelve is waiting."

My stomach lurches, an uncomfortable sensation sweeping over me as I push myself to continue. But I do my best to sit up straight and smile. "Sure, I'm on it."

Offering me an encouraging thumbs-up, she pats the top of my cubicle then disappears before I turn to the ominous blinking red light. Maybe I should've taken her up on that break. I glance around at the bare-walled cubicles, unable to see anyone sitting at their desks. I know it's intentional. That it's easier to talk on the phone like this when we aren't staring at our colleagues, but it's lonely. When I hear Claudia's heels approaching again, I adjust my headset, shake out my hand, and press the button.

Come on, girl. Make your money.

"Well hey there, darlin'," I purr into the phone. "How are you doin' tonight?"

"Better now that I'm talking to you."

A shiver races down my spine. Is it really him? Again? "Baby?"

"Hi there, sweetheart."

I close my eyes as my thighs clench together at the sound of his voice. That damn voice. "I didn't think I'd hear from you again. I've missed you," I whisper into the phone.

He chuckles, and the sound scatters goose bumps over my bare thighs. "Is that so? I thought after last time I might have scared you off."

My teeth snag on my lip at the memory of our last encounter. Fuck, it was hot. "I don't scare so easily," I tease.

"Do you touch yourself when you think of our last conversation?"

My cheeks burn as I whisper, "Yes."

He chuckles again. "You don't have to be embarrassed, sweetheart. Nothing to be ashamed of."

"You ought to be ashamed of that mouth of yours," I tease. "You kiss your mother with it?"

"I wouldn't. Even *if* my mother ever chose to speak to me."

I pause. Does he not speak to his mother? I'm not a therapist but maybe he has mommy issues. Is that why he's so into degradation? There's a whole lot to unpack there, but I can't make assumptions based off one phone call confession. Besides, I'm not one to judge.

"Do you talk to your parents?" he asks.

"I don't speak to either of them."

"Why not?"

I sigh. "A lot of reasons. None of them nice."

"Yeah . . . me too."

"I'm sorry," I say softly.

"Don't be. Some people just can't see past their own prejudice."

"That's hard. Are you happy, at least?"

He hums into the phone. "Sometimes. I am right now."

"Any particular reason?"

"A certain sexy lady on the phone answered my call for the third time. I'm starting to think the universe is trying to tell me something."

I suck in a quiet breath. "You haven't spoken to anyone else?"

"You're three for three, sweetheart."

I don't understand it, but the tight knots in my shoulders seem to loosen knowing he's only ever spoken to me. "We never agreed to be exclusive," I tease again, trying to lighten the mood. "If you speak to other girls on the phone . . . it's okay."

"Maybe I don't want to talk to other girls."

Heat creeps into my cheeks. "I'm flattered."

"God, your voice is so fucking sexy," he groans into the phone. "I feel like I've known you forever. Just hearing you gets me hard."

"Can I tell you a secret?"

"Of course."

"I had to clench my thighs together when I heard your voice on the phone," I admit. "Your voice . . . it does things to me."

I can practically see him smile. I really try to picture it this time. Try to imagine it's Joel's smile, but like a dream, the more I concentrate on it, the faster it fades away. Then that guilty feeling crawls back in. "Oh really? Does hearing me call you a dirty slut make you wet?"

Nodding, I swallow and answer, "Yes."

"What else?"

"My nipples get so hard," I continue, my breaths getting shallower, "it's almost painful."

"If I was there with you, I'd strip you down piece by piece until you're naked, nipples standing at attention for me to do with as I please."

As if they can hear him, my nipples rub uncomfortably against the inside of my bra. I check behind me and look around to make sure no one in the office is watching my cubicle then take a moment to adjust my breasts. The touch of my fingers against the sensitive peaks nearly rockets me out of my chair. "What would you do to them?"

"Oh sweetheart, you know I like things a little rough. You're hoping for it, aren't you?"

"I might be."

"So, if I attached some clamps to those perky little tits, it would make you wetter, wouldn't it?"

My eyelids flutter closed. "Mmm, yes."

"How long do you think you could stand it? Waiting naked for me. Waiting for me to touch you. Waiting with nothing but the sensation of pressure on your nipples."

"You wouldn't torture me like that, would you?"

"It wouldn't be torture. Maybe I'd sit and watch you try not to squirm. Maybe I'd have a drink while I watched you."

"Don't leave me too long. I'm desperate to be touched."

The sound of his bed rustling comes through the speaker. "You know what I want from you before I touch you, right?"

My skin is flushed and tight, and like a runaway train, I can't stop from falling down into this rabbit hole with him. "I'll do anything you want me to do, Baby."

"I want you to beg."

Heat pulses between my legs and an involuntary gasp drags past my lips. "Yes. I'll beg for it. I need to be touched so badly. Please touch me."

He tsks through the phone. "Hmm, no I don't think I will. I'm not convinced you really want me to."

My fingers clench on the arm rest of my chair, sweat trickling down my back. "Please, Baby. I've been so good for you."

A sigh. "What would you let me do to you?"

"Anything."

"Would you let me use your mouth again?"

I breathe. "Yes."

"Would you let me fuck you up against the wall?"

"Yes. *Yes*."

"What if I wanted to tie you up? Play with you all night until you're an incoherent mess?"

My clit pulses and my back arches in my chair.

"Please, Baby. Please! I can't take it anymore."

Shit, I'm being so loud. I glance around, terrified someone will look over and find me face flushed and gripping the phone like my life depends on it.

"I'd go slow, you know," he rasps. "Starting at your ankles, my touch light against that gorgeous skin. Could you stand still, sweetheart?"

"It's so hard to stay still. Your touch is so good."

"Fuck, your thighs are soaked. What a desperate little whore."

"I am. I am desperate. Please just touch my pussy."

"What are you?" he growls.

My lips part and I throw my head back as my stomach clenches. "I'm your whore, Baby. Your filthy, desperate whore. Now please, touch me!"

"What a good slut. I'll fuck you with my fingers for being so good."

I can't see Joel but I can visualize a tall, hard body kneeling before me with dark brown hair, his hand parting my dripping thighs, and as if he's really here I shudder at the thought of him sliding his fingers inside of me. "Oh, god!"

"So sensitive," he coos. "Fuck my fingers, sweetheart. Show me how desperate you are for it."

That tension builds between my legs and I squeeze my thighs together more, but I can't help it. Before I know it, my hips softly thrust against nothing. Wishing desperately that he were really here. It feels like he already is.

"You're making me feel so good," I cry. "I-I think I'm going to come."

"Me too, sweetheart. Me too, I want us to come together."

"Yes, *yes.*" And even though there's nothing touching me, I come hard, my toes going numb in my sneakers as I cry out in the middle of the office.

The sound of his orgasm follows and I sink down into my chair, the muscles that have been tense for hours all releasing at the same time and the throbbing ache between my legs begins to dissipate.

Then all too quickly, I realize where I am. What just happened? I bolt upright in my chair, pushing the sweaty hair away from my forehead. My hand grips the phone as my eyes widen and I glance around me at the walls of my cubicle. Now my heart rate spikes because of an entirely different reason.

I just had a real orgasm over the phone with a complete stranger.

This is too personal. I've never let myself get this carried away. Never been so caught up in the act that it turned real. I feel dirty, and not in a good way. A horrible taste fills my mouth as I think about Joel. How he's been so kind and romantic in his funny way. How he wants to date me, get to know me. How he's crazy, but what the fuck am I doing where I have a man like that and let another get me off over the phone?

"You okay?"

"I . . . I don't—" I think I might start hyperventilating. A single tear slips down my cheek. "I'm not sure."

I expect him to hang up. To say *until next time, sweetheart* like he did before and leave me to sit here in my self-hatred and spiral.

"That was pretty intense," he says softly. "I don't want to leave until I know you're okay."

"Yeah . . ." I breathe. "Intense. Yes."

"Just take some deep breaths," he continues. "If I were there, I'd wrap my arms around you and stroke your hair."

I almost chuckle as I realize I'm mindlessly stroking a thick strand of my hair for comfort. "That would feel nice."

"*You've got a very strong grip. The kind a burglar needs.*"

My heart stutters as I recognize that line. "Hey, is that—are you watching *To Catch a Thief*?"

There's a pause as the music from my favorite movie swells in the background. "Oh, yeah. It was on the TV when I called. I can turn it off . . ."

"No!" I cry, then wince. If my moaning didn't draw attention, shouting certainly will. "Sorry, I just mean . . . it doesn't bother me."

"Have you seen it before?"

"It's one of my favorites."

There's a pause before the dialogue and music of the movie becomes louder, like he's turned up the volume just for me.

"Can you hear it?" he asks.

I smile. "Yes."

"Good. We can watch it together if you like."

My lips part. "Wait . . . what? Like through the phone?"

"Sure, why not?"

I glance up to the clock above me, it's three fifty in the morning. "I know it's not your first time but . . . usually once guys get what they called for—you know . . ."

"They hang up?"

"I mean, you are paying by the minute."

"Maybe I want to pay to watch a movie with you."

I scoff. "Usually that's a date."

"Consider it a tip for a job well done. Besides, there's something about your voice. It makes me feel better knowing you're on the other side of the line."

Oh no. *Oh no, oh no, oh no.* Not him too. What the fuck is wrong with me? I cannot fall for two guys at once. Especially not some random faceless man on the phone.

"It would be nice to just listen to you breathing. It's like you're here," he whispers.

Another tear falls down my face and I sniff. "Okay," I whisper back. The truth is I don't think I could take another call right now. I might just fall apart emotionally if I don't get this break. So I pull my feet up under me, wipe my cheeks, and say, "Do you think you could turn it up a bit more?"

He chuckles softly and the volume increases, so I can hear it as if there's a TV right in front of me. I've seen the movie so many times that when I close my eyes, I can envision it before me. See the scenes as I hear them play out. And every so often, I hear him move, the sheets of his bed rustling, or the sound of him breathing. It feels so nice.

Sooner than I'd like, the credits roll, the outro plays, and I've nearly fallen asleep at my desk while listening to my favorite movie after having one of the strangest yet most intense orgasms of my life.

"Movie's over," he says.

"I guess this means goodbye then."

"Just for now."

"Okay," I whisper.

"Until next time, sweetheart."

CHAPTER 13

If You Leave

KEY

Twelve Years Ago

"You have to go to the hospital," I say insistently.

Dusty shakes her head. "Don't be stupid. I'm fine."

But the bruising on her stomach disappearing up under her shirt is dark and angry and my blood boils at the sight of it. "You can't even catch your breath. What happened?"

Pushing me away weakly, her nostrils flare. "I said I'm fine, Key!"

My fists clench, and I have to take a deep breath to keep myself from shouting and slamming my fist through the wall. "Did your dad do—"

"For fuck's sake," she shouts, pulling at her hair. "Why can't you just let it go? You don't always have to be the big hero."

I blink. "I wasn't—" My jaw swings open like a broken door, unable to figure out how to respond as I watch her stumble and collapse onto the worn couch. A cloud of dust flies up into the air as she drops, the particles glittering around her head in the sunlight. "I'm not trying to be a hero."

Her eyes softly close and her head falls back on the couch. "I didn't mean . . . I'm sorry." She turns her head toward me and tugs her lips up into a small smile. "I promise, I'm fine. Okay?"

Even though her legs are still covered in yellowing bruises from the past few weeks, and she takes short quick breaths to avoid expanding her lungs too much because it hurts, I don't want to upset her any more than I already have. So I nod. "Okay."

She smiles for real and pats the couch seat next to her. "Come on, then. You promised me more songs."

I pull at the back of my neck and mumble, "I wrote a few down for you."

"You did?"

"Yeah." I grab the pile of papers from my backpack and the guitar from the side of the couch before sitting down. "They'll be hard to read," I blurt.

With a shake of her head, she rests her hand on my knee. "It's never hard to read the things you write."

If only everyone thought that way. If only everyone didn't think I was stupid because I struggle to read and write. If only someone had an explanation for why my brain works the way it does. But she's always understood me. It's the only thing that keeps me going.

"It's the craziest thing, but I just can't stop writing," I admit. "The songs just roll out of me."

"It's this place," she says reverently, looking around. "This is where we can be the real us. We don't have to hide."

I look around and realize just how true that is. The past six weeks here with her have been some of the greatest of my life. And while I've had to get more creative in telling my parents where I'm spending my time, every lie I've told to be with her has been worth it.

Handing her the papers, I place the guitar across my lap and adjust the pitch of the strings until they're perfect. My stomach does somersaults while she looks through them, wondering if she'll think what I've written is lame. But at least I know for sure she won't laugh at me. She would never do that.

"Sing me this one," she says, holding up a page with a water stain on it.

My cheeks heat when I see the title on the page.

"Uh . . . maybe not that one."

"Why not?" she asks, reading through the lyrics. "'Neon Crush' . . . ooh, does Key have a crush on someone?"

"I—no! I don't have a—"

"Is she a girl from school?" she teases.

My collar tightens around my neck. "No, she's not—"

"Oh, so there is a girl!" She punches her fist into the air.

I snatch for the page but she holds it out of reach. "That's not what I meant."

"Does she know you like her?" she asks. "Why haven't you told me about her?"

I shake my head. "No! She's not—I haven't—I . . ." I let out a shuddering breath and bury my face behind the body of the guitar to calm myself down. I can hardly breathe, my blood pulsing in my ears. Just breathe . . . in and out.

I flinch as I feel the subtle pressure of her hand on my shoulder. "Hey," she says softly, "I didn't mean to upset you. I was just teasing."

I nod against the guitar, not daring to look up yet. "I know."

"It's cool if you like someone," she continues. "It's also cool if you don't. I'll still be your friend."

With one eye open, I look up under my arm to where she peers over at me. If only I could tell her that the reason songs have been pouring out of me lately is because of her. How she's all I can think about when we're apart. How, since she kissed me all those weeks ago, I've hoped every day she might do it again.

"Dusty, I . . ." But the words won't come, and suddenly there's a clamor in my head of every awful thing that my parents have said about Dusty and her family. And that I'm lying to them just so I can spend time with her. How I shouldn't be kissing any girl without her parents' permission. Bile rises in my throat. God is watching everything I'm doing and knows everything I'm thinking, and I'm abruptly overcome with such shame that my throat tightens. "There's no girl," I mutter.

"Oh," she says, eyes widening. "Oh!" At my lack of understanding she waves her hand. "I'm sorry, I thought you were . . . but if you're into boys, that's cool. I won't tell."

My mouth drops open. "Wait, what?"

"I mean, I can understand why you're so panicked about it. I doubt your parents would let you live if you ever told them you're gay."

Horror strikes me through the chest. "I'm not gay!"

"It's okay if you are," she continues.

My fists clench. "Dusty, I'm definitely not gay."

"You're very good at hiding it. I never would have guessed." She frowns. "Oh god, and I kissed you. I'm so sorry, if I had known it would make you uncomfortable—"

"Dusty?" I interrupt.

"Yeah?"

Before I can stop myself, I'm grasping her face between my palms and pressing my lips to hers. She freezes, and I quickly peek at her face, thinking that maybe she's horrified. But her eyes are closed, her long lashes resting against her freckled cheeks, and I feel like I've just won the Olympic gold medal when she relaxes, my jeans tightening alarmingly fast as she breathes a sigh against my lips.

I pull away and watch in fascination as her eyelids flutter open. Her lips are cherry red, and all I can think about is pressing them back to mine.

"Key?"

"I'm definitely not gay," I insist breathlessly.

Her eyes scan my face before they drop to my mouth and I swallow hard.

"I believe you," she whispers.

I back up, taking a deep breath. "Good."

She looks away, her teeth sinking into her bottom lip, and I turn while I attempt to deflate the blood-hungry bulge in my pants. After a few painfully awkward moments of silence, she rolls back her shoulders, pouts her lips, and bats her eyelashes. "So, about those songs . . ."

How can I possibly say no? "Okay, but just one."

She grins, and the tightness in my throat eases. "It doesn't have to be 'Neon Crush'."

I huff out a breath and place the guitar over my lap again. "Yes, it does."

I start to strum the guitar, and her head sways a little to the tune. I don't need the paper to know every word, every chord, every key change. When it comes to her and music, my mind is like a vault. Memorizing every detail of her face and the songs she inspires. Her narrow, freckled nose, the subtle shimmer to her pale skin, the tiny flecks of silver in her blue eyes. And that smell —her strawberry hair. I start to sing and over the course of the song, watching from the corner of my eye as her face changes from happily watching to intense focus.

Maybe this is for the best. Summer's almost over and I never know when she might disappear. She's like a beautiful tornado. Touching down throughout my life with no warning and only for a brief time. Stirring up chaos and unrest but also the most excitement I've ever felt. Maybe I'm a tornado chaser. Maybe I always will be for her.

I never know if the time I have with her will be the last. At least this way . . . she'll know.

My heart is pounding by the time I strum the last chord, and the two of us sit silently in the cabin after the music fades out. I peek up at her to find her eyes downcast and her hands wringing in her lap.

"Dusty?"

"It's beautiful," she whispers.

I frown when I see the tear trickle down her cheek.

"She must be an amazing girl," she continues. "The one you wrote that about."

I may never know where my bravery comes from, but I reach forward to wipe the tear from her cheek, her wet eyes looking up into mine. "She is."

She shakes her head. "You think that . . . but it's not true."

"It's true to me."

A breathy laugh rushes out of her. "She should feel very lucky to have you care about her this way."

"She's the most important person in the whole world to me."

Dusty's blue eyes dart over my face. "Really?"

I nod. "Really."

She smiles and her face glows. "You are too."

This time, she leans forward and kisses me. This time, I don't have to peek. Her kiss is gentle yet insistent and she tastes like butterscotch candy. My heart is beating so fast I wonder if it's fatal. If I'll die here attached to her lips, then fall down to hell. But her kiss is by far the greatest happiness of my life, so I stifle down every awful thought and kiss her back until I'm lightheaded. She's not acting this time. She's kissing me for real. Because she wants to, not because she's a character in a movie or because I need to prove I'm not gay.

After what feels like an instant and forever, she pulls back, her eyes fluttering in that gorgeous way they do as she looks at me. A smile grows on her face and I can't help but smile back.

"I've wanted to do that for weeks," she admits.

My eyes widen. "You have?"

"I'm not gay either," she teases. "If we're clarifying things."

I grin as she twirls a strand of her red hair around her finger. She sits back against the couch but winces.

"Are you okay?"

Gingerly, she touches her side. "Yeah, I'm fine."

"I really wish—"

"Key." A warning in one word.

With a sigh, I nod. "I'm not trying to save you or be a hero," I start, "but if you ever need me to . . . I'll fight for you."

She smirks. "With these noodle arms?"

Poking me in the bicep, I laugh but grab her hands. "Seriously. I never know when I'll see you again. What if I don't see you because . . ." The words get caught in my throat. "Because something bad has happened to you."

She touches my cheek. "Nothing bad is going to happen to me."

I raise my eyebrows and glance at the spot under her shirt where the bruise is. She shakes her head.

"He doesn't mean to," she admits. "Sometimes I just get in the way, or mouth off. He doesn't always know his own strength when he's been drinking."

"Dusty—"

"And yesterday, his friend from work was over. I guess he thought I was flirting with him or something, because he tried to —" She stops. "Anyway, when I told my dad, he said I shouldn't have been wearing that skirt."

"He *what*?" I cry.

"Then I shouted back, and he didn't like that—"

"Dusty!"

"If it'll make you feel better, I'll keep my attitude to a minimum, okay? I won't give him any reason to punish me."

I cover my face with my hands. "None of those things should have ever happened. It's not your fault. You know that right?"

She shrugs. "I know guys look. I know what they say. Can

guess what they're thinking." She glances at me for just a second. "My mom always told me I should feel lucky. That at least I have a pretty face because I wouldn't amount to much else."

"That's . . . awful."

"It's the truth," she says.

"No, listen. Dusty, look at me," I say, grabbing her hands and pulling her to face me. "You *are* beautiful. But you're also so much more. You can be anything—*do* anything you want. Promise me you'll remember that, even if you're gone."

She nods. "Promise."

But even with her word, some dark feeling creeps its way up the back of my neck. Ominous and terrifying. "What should I do if you disappear again?"

She sighs and rests her head on my shoulder, her hand clasping mine in my lap. "Just know that I'll always come back for you. As soon as I can. However long it takes. I won't forget about you."

My stomach twists. She doesn't even try to convince me she won't disappear.

"Would you ever forget about me?" she asks, lifting her head to glance at me with those diamond blue eyes.

I smile softly. "Of course not. Nobody could forget the girl with the red hair."

I OPEN my eyes in the darkness to a tapping sound on my window. I'm disoriented. What time is it? The crickets still chirp, but it's too dark to read my clock. There's more tapping, then . . .

I sit up in bed, focusing intently on my bedroom window where a mane of red curls frames a bloodied and bruised face. In a flash, I'm ripping back the covers and running to the window.

Dusty winces while I fumble desperately with the locks until the window slides open.

"What happened?" I whisper as she climbs in. "How did you—"

But I'm stopped in my inquiry when she wraps her hands around my neck and falls into me. I pull her gently toward me. She cries into my shoulder, and I have no idea what to do as she shakes, so I simply stroke her hair until she finally calms down enough to talk.

Leaning back, I take in her face as clearly as I can in my dark bedroom. Her left eye is bloodied and nearly swollen shut, blood dripping from her temple, and her cheek bones are bruised and scratched. There's some marks at the top of her forehead, like someone tried to rip out her hair.

"Dusty—"

"I'm okay, Key," she starts. "I know it looks bad, but I'm alive."

"No! Look at you—"

"He's gone," she states.

I raise my eyebrows. "Your dad?"

"I finally called the cops," she continues. "They took him away, Key. He's finally out of my life."

"What happened?"

She closes her eyes and presses her lips together. "He . . . he found out about the cabin."

My blood runs cold. "What?"

She shrugs. "He must have been following me. I don't know how it happened, but . . . he saw you leaving before me and—"

I feel sick. Is this my fault?

"I think he thought we were . . ." Even under the bruising, her cheeks flush.

"Thought we were what?"

She chuckles darkly. "Doing what a teenage boy and girl might do if they're both alone and totally not gay?"

What is she . . . "Oh—but we weren't!"

Taking a step back, she wraps her arms around herself. "I know. But he wouldn't listen and . . . well, he trashed the place. Dragged me home by my hair and—" She motions to her face.

My guts cramp. "If I had known, I would've—"

"I know, Key. I know."

I nod my head and rub the back of my neck. "But he's gone now, and you're safe. Hey, maybe you can even enroll in school," I say, circling her wrists. "We can start high school together and maybe even be—what's wrong?"

Even through my excitement, I notice the tears welling in her eyes. "I'm leaving."

"What?" No. No, she can't. My throat is dry. I'm choking. I can't swallow because she's leaving. *Again.* "Leaving?" I squeeze my hands, harder than I probably should, because I never want to let her go. "What are you talking about?"

She takes a deep breath. "They can't locate my mom. And with my dad gone now . . . I'm going to move in with my aunt for a while."

"Oh, well—"

"In Nebraska."

My knees buckle from under me. "Nebraska? You're moving to Nebraska?"

My parents' bed squeaks from down the hall and my heart gallops in my chest. I need to be careful and quiet. But she's leaving me. What if it's forever?

"I'm so sorry," she whispers through tears.

"But I don't understand. Why do you have to leave?"

"I think it'll be good, actually. A fresh start. You know?"

"Right . . . a fresh start. Without me."

"No!" she says, her hair swaying as she shakes her head. "No.

This has nothing to do with you. Believe me, the only reason I'm upset about leaving *is* because of you. You're my best friend."

Now it's my turn to fail at holding back tears. "You're mine."

A horn honks in the distance, and for the first time, I glance out the window to see a car idling in the distance. "I have to go," she says, pulling her hands away from mine as fresh tears spill down her cheeks.

"What if I just kidnapped you?" I joke, but I know it doesn't come out sounding like one. "Kept you locked up in my closet. I'd make it comfy, of course."

She smiles. "Just remember what I told you." At the tilt of my head, she continues. "I'll always come back to you. I'll never forget you."

I pull her against me. She gasps, and maybe I handled her too hard considering her bruised body, but if this is the last time I'm going to see her, I want her to feel the way I'll miss her.

"Come back to me," I whisper into her hair. "I'll wait for you."

The horn honks again, and I squeeze her just a little longer before letting go. When I do, I can't even move as she walks toward the window, her fingers grasping mine for as long as they can before she's climbing back out. My heart feels like lead, heavy and aching in my chest. Why is life so unfair?

"Psst."

I turn and scrunch my face, willing the tears not to spill over in front of her.

"I almost forgot," Dusty says, then ducks down below the sill before reappearing with—

"My guitar?"

Her smile beams in the darkness. "Amazingly, it was one of the only things he didn't break. Keep playing, okay? I want to hear all the new amazing songs you've written when I come back."

She offers me one last smile, then runs off into the night.

For hours, I sit on the edge of my bed, cradling the guitar in my arms. My mind races, but nothing makes sense. She's safe. She's gone, but she's safe, and after fighting against my own selfishness, wishing she really could come back to live in my closet, I need to hold up my end of the bargain. When she comes back, and she will, I need to be ready to run away to Hollywood with her so we can both make our dreams come true. Together.

CHAPTER 14

The Name of the Game

JOEL

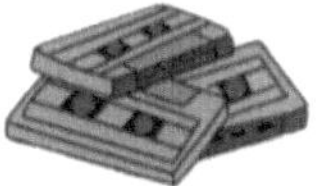

I'm nervous. *Really* nervous. And not the good kind of nervous, like right before a show. More like the kind of nervous where I might barf up my breakfast in the bushes over there. What if she doesn't want to see me again after all? Her voice on the phone when I called to arrange this date was strange. Happy but also not?

What the fuck is happening to me? Just as I begin to spiral, the door opens and the breath is knocked out of me. She stands there in a pair of skintight white jeans and a white cherry-covered shirt cinched at her impossibly tiny waist by a bright red belt. Her lips match and she's got her wild curls piled on top of her head with a white-and-red polka dot bandana. And those shoes. Those fucking red heels almost kill me. The freckles that grace her face are also on her arms, her ankles, and I bet they're all over her.

I could strip her naked and play connect the dots for hours with them.

"Hi," she says, pulling at her shirt slightly. Could she be . . . *nervous*? I shake the thought away.

"Wow," I exhale. "You—hot damn, you look out of this world."

Her cheeks darken almost to the shade of her lipstick. "Really?"

I grasp at my chest. "Think I almost had a heart attack."

She grins and moves back, letting me into her apartment. Her eyes flick next to me for a moment. "And what's that?"

From under my arm I procure the rolled paper and present it to her with a smile. "A gift."

"For me?"

"No, for Stella, but something tells me she'd probably destroy it."

She laughs and the sound rings clear through the small space. "You're right, she loves to chew on paper. What is it?"

"Open it."

She rolls the elastics off the paper, then glances at me one last time before unfurling the gift. I watch as she takes in the picture, the smile falling away from her face.

"The poster for *To Catch a Thief*?" she whispers.

"Yeah," I say, suddenly regretting my decision. "I remember you said it's your favorite movie. Thought this would be better than flowers."

She smiles, but it's short lived, and something heavy drops in my stomach. Maybe I really fucked up on this. Sitting down on the edge of her bed with the poster in her hands, she looks up at me. "Joel, I—"

My heart sinks. "If I misheard you and it's actually your least favorite movie, I've got a lighter. We could go downstairs and set that sucker on fire."

She breathes out a laugh and shakes her head. "No, it's just . . . before we go—I need to tell you something."

My eyebrows lift. "Oh?"

"And it's something that…" She fidgets with her other hand, plucking at her fingernails. "After you hear it, you might not want to see me anymore."

That's surprising. "Oh."

She presses her hand to her forehead. "I should've told you right from the start. But I didn't think you were serious, and to be honest?" She looks up at me with the most heartbreaking smile. "I didn't want to scare you off."

I walk over and sit down next to her on the bed. "Well, what is it? Are you a hitman for hire?"

The corner of her mouth twitches. "No."

"You're a mermaid like Daryl Hannah in *Splash*? I have to say, I'm kind of hoping that's true, because mermaids are hot—"

"Joel, focus," she reminds me gently.

"What is it?"

She sits up straight and takes a long deep breath. "You know how I told you I work nights for a call center?"

My brow furrows. "Yeah?"

"It's . . . well, it's not exactly customer support."

"So what is it?" I ask.

She bites down into that cherry red lower lip. "I'm a fantasy phone girl."

I don't know exactly what I was expecting, but it wasn't that. "Oh . . . okay."

Her eyes widen. "Okay?"

I shrug. "Yeah, okay. When we first met you were a stripper and I wanted to date you then. This isn't much different."

"You—really?" she asks.

I smile. "Really."

"But you realize that I help men get off over the phone. Like . . . intimately."

"You've got to make a living, right?" I ask.

She blinks. "I mean, yeah, it pays good, and it's actually safer than stripping. But it's still sex work and I—"

"Did you really think I'd have a problem with this?"

"Most guys would."

I reach out and place my hand on her bouncing knee. "Look, I'm not a jealous guy. Like . . . at all. And as someone who frequents strip clubs? It would be pretty hypocritical of me not to support sex workers since they're some of my favorite people."

"But could you date one?"

"I'd date you."

She closes her eyes for a long moment then looks up at me. "But the stuff I have to say, the way I have to act—how can that not bother you?"

I try to think of a reason but nothing forms in my brain. "Do you have feelings for those people?"

She shakes her head. "Well, no—"

"And you kind of sort of have feelings for me or you wouldn't have agreed to go out with me, right?"

A pretty pink blush paints her chest. "Yes."

I shrug. "Then nope, it doesn't bother me. Actually, it kind of intrigues me. Does this mean that you're a professional dirty talker?" I wiggle my eyebrows at her and she laughs.

"Hey, just because I'm a fantasy phone girl doesn't mean I dirty-talk on the first date."

I raise my hand to my chest in mock disbelief. "I would never suggest it m'lady. A perfect gentleman is what I shall be this fine afternoon."

Placing her hands in mine, I pull her up. "Okay." She smirks again. "But maybe not too gentlemanly."

"Perfect, because I don't know if I've ever been called a gentleman in my whole life. Let's go. And Stella?" I turn and look at the fluffy orange cat watching me from the window sill. "Be good, there's a lot riding on this date."

"Bowling?" she asks as we exit the car.

"You don't like bowling?" I ask.

She taps a finger to her mouth. "I don't know. I've never been."

"You've *never*—Jesus Christ. Okay, this should be an experience for you, then."

"You'll teach me?" she asks, an adorable wrinkle of worry creasing her forehead.

"Of course."

I grab her hand and entwine our fingers. She grins at me, and we walk through the double doors into the noisy bowling hall. The bang of bowling balls shooting down the lanes followed by the clatter of pins being knocked down is something I've been familiar with my whole life. It's somewhere I feel comfortable and confident, and I hope that comes across during this date.

"It's loud!" she says when we get to the shoe rental counter.

"Is that okay?" I ask over the noise.

She nods. "I'm used to loud."

"What size are your feet?" I ask.

She looks down and back up. "What? Why?"

"Because I was hoping I could try on those heels."

She blinks, but then I smirk and she playfully pushes my shoulder. "Ha-ha, very funny."

"When you bowl, you have to wear special shoes. No fancy heels on the lanes, I'm afraid," I say, jerking my head toward the other patrons.

Her lips part. "Oh. Umm . . . well, I usually wear a size nine."

I hold up a finger to signal the bored teenager behind the counter. "Ladies size nine and men's size twelve."

After paying for the shoes and the lane, I tuck my wallet back into my back pocket to find her staring at me with a smile. "What?" I ask.

"Size twelve, huh?"

I grin widely and grab the shoes off the counter. "It bodes well for me that that impresses you."

"Well, you know what they say about guys with big feet."

"Big bowling shoes?" I ask.

She chuckles. "Something like that."

"They may not be stylish," she says after she's slipped her feet in, "but at least I'm less likely to have a wipe-out in these."

"If you were allowed to wear them, I'm sure you'd crush in heels."

I pull up the screen for score keeping and make a sudden discovery.

"What's wrong?" she asks, sensing the change on my face.

"Moment of truth," I say with mock seriousness. "I'm going to need to know your name."

She tucks her chin to her shoulder. "I thought you were going to guess it."

She wants to play, huh? I can do that. "All right then, Red," I say, punching in the three letters as a placeholder. "Ten questions to guess your name."

Her mouth twists. "And what do I get if you guess wrong?"

"What do you want?"

After tipping her head back and forth for a few seconds, she says, "Pizza."

"And what do I get?" I ask.

"You get to know my name."

"A rose by any other name would smell as sweet," I counter.

"Okay," she says, leaning over the console between us. "I'll sweeten the deal. You guess my name right after ten questions and . . ." She turns to make sure no one's listening in and curls her finger to pull me in closer. "I'll give you a preview of what I do at my job."

I swallow hard as her breathy voice tickles my ear and causes shivers to race down my spine, hitting me right in the groin. Fuck, she's sexy. I can see why guys would pay to listen to her on the phone for hours at a time. Unbelievable.

She pulls back with a sly smirk, and I can't help but appreciate the way her arms squeeze her tits together, the line of her generous cleavage disappearing beneath her white shirt.

"Deal," I say, my voice deeper than normal. Fuck, what this girl does to me.

Straightening up, she bounces over to the ball return. "Okay, so how does this work? Do I just pick any ball?"

"Yup. You want me to go first?" I ask. "Show you how it's done?"

"Yes, please."

I push off my thighs to stand and walk over to the ball rack. After carefully inspecting half a dozen, I find a brown-and-red ball that lives up to my expectations. Then, I pull out the gloves from my pocket and pull them on.

"Whoa whoa whoa," she says, holding up a hand. "Gloves? I didn't know we needed to wear gloves."

"You don't."

She frowns. "Oh no. You're one of those serious bowlers, aren't you?"

"Unfortunately, yes."

Grabbing the ball, I line myself up on our lane, centering my shoulders, then let it rip. The ball rockets perfectly straight down the middle. *Strike.* Turning around, I dust off my shoulder and slide back over to where she's sitting, visibly shocked.

"You didn't tell me you're a ringer."

I shake my head. "I'm hardly a professional."

She raises her eyebrows.

"Okay, I may have come in second place during a state championship when I was twelve."

"Fascinating."

I wave her forward. "Come on, grab that green ball."

She scoops up the ball with a strangled "Oof, these are heavy," and walks in my direction.

"Yeah, fair warning, your shoulder might be sore tomorrow."

"A reminder of how you defeated me on our first date then," she teases.

I laugh and turn us both toward the lane. "Okay, feet like this," I say, kicking her left foot forward. "And these three fingers through the holes."

She glances at me out of the corner of her eye and I try very hard not to make contact because I'm thinking exactly what she is and damn, I'd like to fit my three fingers in her holes.

"Now you're going to swing back and as it rolls forward? Release."

I feel her intake of breath against my chest, my hand ever so gently atop of hers, guiding it back, then forward, then . . .

"Oh my god! I hit one!" she cries.

"Damn right you did."

"This is *fun*," she says.

Something in the way her voice breaks makes me realize that maybe she hasn't done anything fun in a long time. "Good. You get another turn, since you didn't knock them all down on the first try."

"Oh!" She turns around to find her green ball again and shuffles back to the center of the lane. I watch while she places her feet, her brows sewn together in concentration. She winds her arm back, releases, and hits all but two pins down.

"Holy shit!" she says, spinning around. "Joel, did you see that?"

I grin. "Knew you were a natural."

The pins reset, and she sits down at the console while I grab my ball. "So, first question," I say. "Is your name popular?"

She rests her cheeks in her hands. "Nope. Not at all."

I groan. "Damn . . . so this is going to be a tough one, huh?" Another strike.

She stands and passes me to grab her ball. "Is that your second question?"

I bite my lip. "No. Is it a name that could be for a boy or a girl?"

After she rolls her ball into the gutter, she waits for it to return and answers. "Umm . . . yeah, I suppose it could be."

"Hmm, interesting," I say, my eyes glued to her backside as she rolls the ball again to knock down half of her pins.

I step forward and take my turn. Another strike. "Does it end with a *Y*?"

"Yes. Yes, it does."

"Okay, now we're getting somewhere."

"Can I ask questions too?" she asks, standing up to take her turn.

"Of course."

She positions herself and throws the ball, knocking down all but one. With a shout, she jumps and claps her hands. "I almost did the strike thing!"

"Try throwing the ball with a bit of spin, it'll knock down that last pin if it goes straight down the middle."

With a tilt of her head she takes my direction, but maybe with too much spin because it ends up in the gutter. She turns around with her hands on her hips. "You trying to make me lose?"

I shake my head and pass her. "Of course not, I'm already whooping your ass."

While I take my turn, she sits. "How'd you get to be such a good bowler, anyhow?"

"My grandparents owned an alley back home in Wisconsin."

She nods. "Ah, now it all makes sense."

There's a loud crash as the pins drop. "My parents would leave me with them all the time, so I got my run of the alley. Then when

I was in junior high, I started working there. Resetting the pins and sanitizing shoes. It was something to keep me out of trouble."

"Sounds like you had a fun childhood," she says, standing up to face me, the timbre of her voice giving away that maybe she didn't. I would ask her, but I need to keep these questions about her name for now.

"Does your name start with a vowel or a consonant?" I ask.

"A consonant."

"Damn," I say. "Was really hoping to only have to pick through five letters."

She grins and takes her turn.

"Does your family still own the bowling alley?" she asks.

I shake my head. "No. When my grandad died, my parents couldn't afford to keep the place up and running. Plus, they had their own careers."

"Oh, Joel," she says. "I'm sorry."

I shrug. "It's fine. It was years ago."

"So you worked at a bowling alley, then were in military school . . ." She counts on her fingers. "Exactly what did you end up doing for work?"

This time I miss, a single pin still standing at the end of the lane. "I'm a musician."

Her eyebrows rise for a moment before dawning sets in. "Wait, but you said—"

"You really didn't believe me, huh?" I tease.

She shakes her head. "Wait, so you're actually in a band?"

I smile. "Yeah. And a pretty damn successful one at that."

Her mouth drops but I hold up my finger. "Uh-uh, my turn." Her lips press together, but there's tension in her step now. "Does your name have less than ten letters?"

"Yes." She's standing in front of me now. "So you're—you're really a rockstar?"

I frown. "Don't tell me you're disappointed."

"I'm not!" she insists. "I'm just—wow, that's . . . amazing. You know, I knew a musician once."

"Really?"

She shrugs. "Yeah, we, uh . . . we grew up together. On and off."

"What happened to her? Or him?" But she doesn't answer. Instead, she looks away, the color leeching from her cheeks. "Hey, you okay?"

With a deep breath, she picks up her ball and shoots it right into the gutter. "My name starts with the letter *D.*"

I blink in surprise. "Oh." Okay, I think I hit a nerve there. Does she have a problem with all musicians, or just one? Was it a guy? An ex? A friend? She's trying to distract me, and that's okay. I don't want to make her upset. "Starts with a *D* and ends with a *Y,* is unusual, can be for a boy or a girl and has less than ten letters. Okay, I'm feeling good about my odds."

I bowl another strike, getting back in my groove, while she taps her finger to her chin.

"What instrument do you play?" she asks.

Pretending to play air guitar for a minute, I wink at her and say, "Bass."

A smile tugs on her lips. "A bass player, huh? You must have good rhythm."

"The best," I say, puffing out my chest. "Your name . . . did your parents pick it for a specific reason?"

She sits on the bench, her fingers wrapping over the edge and looks at her shoes. "Yeah. Or rather my mom did. It has a bit of a biblical meaning."

This surprises me. "Now *that* I wouldn't have guessed."

She shrugs. "I was raised fairly religious, but for all the wrong reasons. Mama wanted to be just like the church families who had nice things and loved each other. My dad, he just wanted a way to control us."

My heart aches. I think about Key and Becks and how much religion has played a part in the difficult parts of their lives. "I'm sorry."

"It's okay. I'm not religious. Never was . . . but going to church felt normal when a lot of my childhood wasn't." She frowns and swings her feet back and forth. "Sorry, I'm kind of— let's change the subject. I'm being a huge bummer."

"Sure." I bite my lip. "But just for the record, you're not bumming me out. Getting to know you is the fun part, remember?"

She clears her throat. "So, your band. They're popular?"

I nod. "Yeah, we're even on the radio. You heard of Carnal Sins?"

Her eyes widen and she drops the bowling ball on the floor with a loud *crack*. "Holy shit, really?"

I smile. "You've heard us?"

She nods vigorously. "Only recently, but yeah! Oh my god, I can't believe it's you I've been hearing on the radio."

"That's me."

Staring in awe, she places her hand under her chin. "Wow. That's incredible."

"Maybe you could come to a show one night."

"You'll have to tell me in advance, you know I work nights."

I nod. "Of course. You can come backstage and meet the band and everything."

"That sounds incredible."

I bowl next, taking home a spare. "Okay, so I think I'm getting close to your name. Is it a name that has to do with nature?"

She bites her lip. "Hmm . . . that's a tough one. I suppose, yes, but not in a traditional sense."

I scratch my head. "Huh, okay."

"I really don't think you're going to get it," she teases.

"Oh, ye of little faith."

She grins and steps forward to the ball return. "How did you learn to play bass?"

"Probably the same way most people do when they learn an instrument. Showed up to music class in junior high one day and the only instrument left was the bass. The only time being late for class worked out for me. Turns out, I'm really good at it."

"Wow."

"What about you? You ever learn an instrument at school?"

"I wasn't really allowed to go to school." She bites the inside of her cheek. "It wasn't until high school that I ever attended a real school. My dad was convinced it would turn his baby girl into a commie."

I blink. "Yikes."

"Yeah."

"He still thinks that way?" I ask.

She shrugs her shoulders. "No idea. Haven't seen him since I was thirteen."

"I'm sorry."

"No, don't be. Being rid of him was the best thing for me."

I want to ask her about her mom. Are they close or are they estranged now too? But I have my priorities. "Is your name strictly a name? Or can it also be used in another way?"

"It's a name that can also be a word," she says, tucking a flyaway hair behind her ear.

This girl. "Is the first vowel an *A* or an *E*?"

Rolling her ball, she hits seven pins and does a little dance. "Nope."

I press my lips together and roll another strike.

"You're kicking my ass," she teases from behind me. "I have to admit, it's pretty hot."

Grinning, I walk toward her and gently place my hand on her hip. "If you could please go back in time and tell that to my twelve-year-old self, I'd really appreciate it."

She pushes my hair behind my ear. "Not so popular with the ladies in your youth?"

I scoff. "Definitely not."

"I bet they line up for you now. Successful, good-looking rockstar? Makes why you're here with me all the more confusing," she admits.

"I'm not confused," I say. "Actually, I've never been more certain that I'm in the right place."

Her blue eyes scan my face, once again looking for the lie, but she won't find one.

"Does your name have anything to do with flowers?" I ask, pulling her in closer, snaking my hand around her waist.

The corner of her mouth twitches. "No."

Goose bumps scatter over my skin as her hands rest on my arms.

"That's ten questions. Now you have to guess."

"I think I know what your name is," I say, pulling her close so her chest brushes against mine. The smell of her hair is making my head swim.

She swallows, her lovely throat bobbing with the movement. "Then I guess you're in for a show," she winks with a sultry tone. "A deal's a deal."

My eyes trace the shape of her lips, and the only thing that is clear in my head right now is how badly I want to kiss her—even here amongst the arcade noises and screaming children.

"Your name is . . ."

Her eyebrows rise in anticipation, her fingers pressing into my skin.

"Divinity."

Immediately her face falls, and she bows her back to cross her arms over her chest. "Divinity?"

"Am I wrong?"

"Very wrong, Joel. Not even close." She swats my arm and I laugh. "Divinity . . ." she mutters under her breath. "Who the hell is named Divinity?"

I grin. "Apparently not you."

She pushes away to take her last turn with the bowling ball, knocking down every single pin. "Looks like you owe me pizza."

"That's right, a deal's a deal," I admit, but I grab her around the waist from behind and lower my voice to whisper in her ear. "Dusty."

CHAPTER 15

Running With the Night

DUSTY

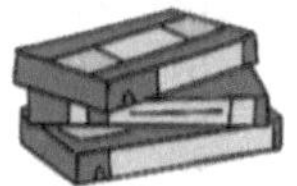

I stop, freezing on the spot. "Wait . . . you—you guessed it right?"

He's smiling, that permanent look of joy etched all over his face. "I told you I would."

"Then why did you say Divinity?" I ask bewildered. "You could've won the bet."

He shrugs. "Buying you pizza seemed like a better prize."

My mouth opens, my head spinning a million miles a minute. Not only did he manage to guess my name but he guessed wrong on purpose? What kind of guy does that? He gave up a sexy reward so he could buy me pizza?

He leans toward me and grasps my hand in his. "I can see you spiraling. Don't get caught up in overthinking it. I like you, Dusty, and I want you to know that spending time with you is more important to me than what you do for work."

My eyes dart over his face. Never has a guy passed up an opportunity for me to be sexual for them, and now here's Joel wanting to spend time with me—the real me—real name and all.

"Are you okay?" he asks in my silence.

"Yeah . . . yeah, I—of course."

"Come on, pizza's on me, but I have to warn you . . . if you tell me pineapple on pizza is delightful, I might be devastated."

I breathe out a laugh. "Who would say something so ludicrous?"

"A psychopath, clearly."

He steers me over to the booths in the back, where we sit and order a large pepperoni and mushroom pizza and two Cokes. I lean on my hand while we wait for our food, studying him closely.

"What?"

"How did you guess my name?" I ask.

He shrugs. "I'm super smart, can't you tell? Practically Sherlock Holmes."

I roll my eyes, and he sighs.

"Okay, fine. I cheated. I saw a piece of mail on your kitchen counter when I was fixing the window."

My mouth drops open. "What? You've known my name since then? Why didn't you tell me?"

"Because I wanted *you* to tell me, or at least be comfortable enough where I'd learn it and you wouldn't get freaked out."

"Joel—"

"I'm sorry. I didn't mean to . . . it was just there."

I grasp his hand across the table. "No, it's fine. Thank you."

"For what?"

"For respecting my privacy—or at least trying to."

He grins again, his eyes crinkling at the corners beautifully. "You're welcome. Besides, I learned a lot about you from that little game. I have no regrets."

Heat rushes into my cheeks, but I hide it behind my soda can. Am I going crazy? Is this really happening? Is this guy actually trying to win over my heart instead of just taking me to bed? And after everything I've told him?

But the way he's looking at me now, head resting on his fist, his free hand wrapped around mine. The subtle stroke of his thumb on my skin. Maybe this is *real*.

"What are you thinking?" he asks.

I take a deep breath. "After pizza, do you think I could take you somewhere?"

He sits up a little straighter in the booth. "Oh, yeah. Sure. Is it far?"

I shake my head. "No, it's actually close to the laundromat, but . . . it's a tiny bit . . . illegal."

"That settles it. I'm definitely intrigued."

A bored-looking server sets down our pizza, grease from the pepperoni oozing off the plate. It looks incredible. I smile and grab a slice, waiting on him before taking a bite. He holds his slice out to me and we cheers the cheesy goodness together.

"To hopefully *not* getting arrested."

"WHERE ARE WE?" Joel asks, his hand in mine as I pull him down a deserted alley a few blocks from The Sudsy Dream. "You're not going to murder me, are you?"

I smirk and make eye contact while walking backward. "I have considered it. But Stella knows we're out together. She'd turn me in for sure if you ended up missing."

"At least someone's looking out for me."

"It's just through here," I say, stepping toward a metal door at the back of a dilapidated brick building. I drop Joel's hand in order to pull two pins out of my hair, then insert them into the lock.

"Whoa whoa whoa," Joel says, coming to stand next to me. "When you said illegal . . . I didn't expect to add breaking and entering to our date itinerary."

Worry lines crease his forehead. It's sweet. "You scared?" I tease.

A pink flush rises in his cheeks, but he relaxes back against the brick with an air of indifference. "Of the cops? Hardly. Of you taking advantage of me in a dark abandoned building? Absolutely."

I laugh, then return to picking the lock. "Don't worry, darlin', you'll leave with your honor intact."

He grins. "Bummer."

The lock clicks open, and the door pulls free of the frame with a loud, rusty squeak. Stuffing the pins back into my hair, I grab Joel's hand and draw him into the darkness. The door slams shut behind us, and it's silent except for our breathing and the feel of his warm hand in mine. The pulse of his heart beats through his palm as he squeezes me tighter, dependent on me to keep from floating into the dark unknown.

"Wait here," I whisper.

"What?" he whispers back in a panic as my fingers slip away from his. "You're coming back, right?"

I chuckle as I walk across the floorboards, my heels clicking in the quiet. "Maybe. Now, cover your eyes."

"My eyes?"

Hand reaching along the brick wall, I find the heavy lever and push upward, the lights bursting to life.

"Ah!" Joel cries, and I spot him on the opposite side of the stage with his fists in his eyes.

"I told you to cover your eyes," I say.

He shakes his head. "I'm terrible at following directions." His head swivels as he takes in the surroundings. "Is this . . . a theater?"

My eyes scan the area before us. "It's an old movie theater— The Sapphire. They closed down years ago, but I guess they forgot to turn off the electricity." I look around at the red velvet curtains hanging down the proscenium of the stage where we stand. There's a massive screen behind us and out ahead are rows and rows of gold and red velvet chairs. The ceiling is vaulted, crown moldings with such ornate detail they look like they should be in a museum. But the best part is the chandelier that illuminates the seating area.

"Wow," he whispers. "This is incredible."

"Yes, it is. Want to know the best part?"

He nods.

"They also left their movie collection and projector."

"Oh?"

I walk toward the front of the stage toward the stairs and out into the audience. "I come here sometimes to watch old movies."

He shoves his hands into his pockets. "If you want to go on a movie date, I have money. Remember? Rockstar?"

I swat him playfully. "Where's the fun in that?"

With a shake of his head and a bite of his lip, he opens his hands to me. "Let's watch one then."

It's hard to contain my smile. "What do you want to watch?"

"*To Catch a Thief.*"

I blink. "Really?"

"Yeah, I got you that poster. I should see it in context."

A warmth spreads through my chest. It's been so long since a guy has taken interest in me and my passions. But Joel? No one has ever made me feel this way since . . .

"Okay," I say, blinking back tears I won't let fall. "Pick a seat and I'll be right back."

I'm like a teenager again, giddy and bouncing around. Peeking through the projector window, I watch as Joel weaves his way through the rows, his hand gliding along the velvet seats. His long dark hair shines like silk in the light from the chandelier. He's so beautiful. I can't wait to hear him play the guitar. My stomach flips. I suppose I have a subconscious thing for musicians. What are the odds that he's a guitarist in a famous rock band? How will it feel if he plays for me? Will it be liberating? Or will the déjà vu be too painful to bear?

With the movie reel on the projector, I dim the lights and start the machines, then make my way back down to him. There's a crackling from the speakers coming to life, then a beam of light as the projector lights up the screen. The opening overture of the film sings through the air and I'm greeted by the title sequence. The names *Cary Grant* and *Grace Kelly* appear on the screen followed by the title *To Catch a Thief*.

A moment later, I'm sliding into the seat next to Joel, and his hand finds mine instantly.

"I can't believe you haven't seen this before," I whisper.

He leans toward me. "I'm more of a horror guy myself. Met one of my bandmates at a showing of *Evil Dead*. But I'll try anything once."

Satisfied, I turn back to face the front. "I think I've seen this movie a hundred times."

He tilts his head. "Why so many?"

"I like the mystery, the action . . . the romance." I watch from my periphery as his eyes briefly flick to mine. "Besides, it's one of the only movies I could get my hands on as a kid. My parents . . . they didn't let me watch movies in the house."

"At all?" he asks.

I shake my head. "My dad—he didn't just hate the public school system, he also hated Hollywood."

"I'm sorry."

I lean a little closer. "Don't be. I still found a way, just needed to be a bit sneakier."

He smiles. "Hence knowing how to break into abandoned theaters?"

"Exactly."

We watch in silence for a while as Cary Grant's character,

who's a retired cat burglar, has to escape a group of thugs who believe he's behind a new slew of burglaries. He's helped in his escape by Grace Kelly.

Even though it's my favorite film, I admit that it's hard to pay attention when Joel's eyes continuously watch me. His calloused thumb brushes the palm of my hand, and I find myself leaning into him, relaxing into his body as the movie goes on.

"It's too bad this place is abandoned," Joel whispers. "It's a gorgeous theatre."

I nod. "I know, right? I can't help but think of all the things I would do if I bought it."

"What would you do?"

"Host movie nights. Feature concerts for local talent. Maybe even have acting and art classes for kids," I say thoughtfully.

"That sounds amazing," he replies.

I sigh longingly. "If only I could win the lottery, huh?"

He doesn't respond, and we spend the next several minutes watching the movie in silence.

"So do you bring all of your adoring fans here?" he whispers.

"Fans?"

"You know, the other poor saps who see you while they're washing their underwear and fall head over heels."

I scoff. "Hardly. I don't . . . I don't really date much."

"Why not? Surely it's not for lack of attention. Since we've been on our date I've seen no less than ten guys I wanted to pummel because they were looking at you like their next meal."

"I guess I'm just not one for relationships," I say, crossing and uncrossing my legs. "It's my job," I admit. "Not many guys are willing to date a sex worker. I mean, they all think it's great at first. The fact that I was a stripper and got naked for money means I'm super keen to fuck all the time, right? And now the phone sex thing? I must be a goddess in bed if all I do day and night is talk dirty. But then they quickly realize that I'm not the fantasy they thought I was."

Joel is quiet for a long moment, then his free hand reaches out toward me. His finger traces the shape of my jaw, then the backs of his fingers brush along my cheek. The gentle touch of his hand on my skin electrifies every cell in my body. Finally, his fingers gently grasp my chin and tilt my face up to look at him. His eyes are serious, even though his mouth still holds that faint trace of humor.

"Then those guys are idiots," he says. "Anyone who bothered to get to know you would know that this version of you is the best."

My eyes begin to sting with emotion, and his gaze drops to my mouth, the slow-motion feeling of him leaning toward me shredding down my walls with such ease.

"Hey, you! You two can't be in here!"

We whip around to find a police officer with a flashlight pointed right at us.

"Oh, shit," I say, and before I can even think, I'm on my feet and grabbing Joel's hand—pulling him down the aisle then up toward the stage.

"Stop! Stop right there!" the officer calls, his flashlight bouncing around the dark space as he chases us.

"Come on," I say with a laugh, "I don't feel like getting arrested today."

"Me neither." He chuckles breathily behind me.

The officer continues to yell after us, and before I know it we're bursting through the back door and out into the alley.

"This way," I say, pulling on his arm, the two of us laughing as we run.

My heart races, adrenaline pumping through my veins. This guy must think I'm crazy. Or maybe his crazy matches my own. Maybe that's why he's laughing with me and not running away.

"Where are we going?" he asks.

"Anywhere that isn't here," I heave out.

His fingers tighten around mine, and with a renewed sense of confidence we run, laughing at the way the officer shouts for us to stop.

When we turn another corner, I stop, Joel knocking right into me. "What are you—"

"Quick, in here," I say, jerking my chin over my shoulder. There's a small raised alcove of bricks that has just enough space to hide two people, and with the sound of the officer catching up, I rush to pull myself up into it. Joel grins widely then follows, and we fall back into the shadow of our hiding place.

The sound of clunky footsteps approach and I hold my breath, squeezing farther into the darkness and realizing for the first time that Joel's arm is wrapped around my waist. He seems to realize too, his lips parting. "Dusty—"

My other hand clamps down on his mouth to keep him from saying anything more. His eyes widen but he stills.

"Where did those assholes go?" we hear, and I see the way Joel's eyes look in the direction of the police in alarm. But I can't stop from staring at his face. His tanned skin and laugh lines. The warm amber of his eyes and his silky black hair.

I lower my hand from his mouth. "Sorry," I whisper.

He blinks. "It's fine."

The footsteps are gone now, but I can't let him go. He smells like expensive cologne, and I'm reminded of our first encounter in Vegas. How it felt to have his body so close to mine. How desperate I was for him to touch me where he wasn't allowed. How even now the spot between my legs throbs wantonly for it.

"I know you think you have to hide your real self from me," he whispers, "but you don't."

My lips part, and he sweeps his thumb along my bottom lip. I inhale sharply, and his fingers tighten their grip on my waist just like they did two years ago, the memory of those beautiful bruises flooding my mind.

"I saw you. I've seen you. And I still want more."

He drops his gaze to my lips, his hand gripping the nape of my neck before pulling me into a devastating kiss. We crash and roll and rumble—like the merging of two seas. Rough and fierce, soft and exquisite, all at the same time. He holds me to him, my body melting into his as though he's the missing piece to my complicated jigsaw puzzle.

Then it becomes so real for just a moment, and I see our future: a big house, and friends, and children, and my cat growing old . . . and the breath rushes out of my lungs so fast I need to push him away to breathe. He doesn't let go, but I feel him take a breath as I gulp down air, trying not to panic as I let myself think of a future I haven't dared dream of in a decade.

"You're going to see something you don't like," I whisper. "Everyone always does."

He presses his lips together then tucks back a stray curl that falls across my forehead. "Then they were blinded by the moon when there was an entire sky of stars."

He kisses me again and as our lips dance, euphoria washes away all of the doubt.

She's Like the Wind

KEY

NINE YEARS AGO

Spring break sucks. My hands still ache from the lashings my father dished out when he discovered a page of lyrics I had foolishly tried to write down. This is why I keep everything in my head. But the lyrics were about her, and for some reason, I wanted to see them on paper. Written out like maybe they might, just by existing, bring her back to me. It's been almost three years, and every day, it grows harder to think I might never see her again.

Every time I dove into the pool at the community center I hoped I would see those red curls at the bottom waiting for me. Or when I would sneak away to sit in the abandoned cabin we used to spend so much time together. I fixed it up. After it had been trashed by her dad, I cleaned the place. It's not the same, but at least it's somewhere I can keep the guitar she gave me without worrying my parents will find it.

And I can play music. Anything I want. Experiment for hours with rock and roll and my new obsession: heavy metal. Maybe it's because I'm angry at how she was taken away from me. Maybe it's anger at myself that I couldn't do more for her. But whatever the reason, the music comes out of me like poetry.

Something hard knocks into my shoulder as I walk toward first period.

"Watch it, spaz." I look up to see Emory Radcliffe sneering at me over the shoulder of his letterman jacket. His football buddies all snicker and jeer, but I just roll my eyes and continue on down the hall. Juniors in high school and they still act like we're in the third grade. It's pathetic. And while I have to dress the part of a good little church boy at school, it's not like I enjoy hanging out with the other kids at the Teens for Christ meetings.

I only go because if I don't, I'll get the strap again, and each time I do it takes days to recover before I can play the guitar again. So it's fine. I'll pretend. Pretend like I have friends when there's literally no one at school who I can even imagine having anything in common with. Pretend like I'm the god-fearing boy my parents so desperately need me to be. Pretend I'm happy.

The bell rings overhead, and I hoist my bag further up on my shoulder before ducking into homeroom. I smile politely at Mr. Ward, our English teacher, then head toward my desk at the back of the room, but before I can take another step, my heart stops.

There she is.

I blink wildly, then pinch my arm, thinking maybe I fell asleep in the library listening to Cynthia or Matthew preach about finding their godly identity. But no . . . she's really here.

Our eyes are locked on each other, and she smiles. The kind of smile that shows off the dimple in her cheek. The one that makes her freckles shine and her face glow, and if there really is a god, heaven must be made in her image.

"Mr. Prentiss, please find your seat."

I nod and quickly head to my seat across the row from where Dusty sits. I can't take my eyes off of her. I'm worried that if I do, she'll disappear again, and that is not happening. It's as if I'm having an out of body experience, sitting in this chair and staring at her. How is she here? She's enrolled in my school? She's in a real school? I have so many questions.

And as my mind races, her eyes never leave mine, her lips mouthing the word *hi* to me as though we only said goodbye yesterday.

"Dusty, I—"

"Mr. Prentiss, are you speaking out of turn?"

Every head in the classroom swivels to me, and I realize with horror that I'm halfway out of my seat. Dusty is looking at her desk, and there is so much energy racing through my veins I might actually rocket through the ceiling.

"Uh, sorry . . . I—the desk," I mutter, swiping my finger along the top. "It's dusty."

There's a muffled snort from where she sits and, after brushing off the imaginary dust on my desk, I sit back down—my heels bouncing against the tile floor. She won't look at me, maybe because she knows I'll get out of my seat to try talking to her again. As my eyes trace over her, my throat goes dry.

Dusty is stunning.

Her hair is longer, curlier, the red streaked with gold and sparkling from the morning sun filtering through the window. She's wearing a cream-colored shirt with a design on the front in different shades of brown that matches her geometric mini skirt.

Heat rushes up my spine. Her breasts have grown considerably since I last saw her, and I need to swallow hard to avoid thinking about her in a bikini all those years ago. Her chest isn't the only thing that's different. Her hips are wider, her stomach cinched at the waist by a brown belt, and beneath her suede skirt are mile-long freckled legs. My palms sweat at the realization that my best friend has turned into a goddess.

There's chatter scattered throughout the room as the teacher hands out work for everyone. Grateful for some time to breathe, I can't help but hear the conversation of two girls in front of me.

"That must be the new girl," one says loud enough for me and a few others to hear. "Heard her dad's in jail."

"I heard that she's been expelled from two other school districts for drugs," the other says.

"And her mother abandoned her as a kid. I hate it when other schools send us their white trash."

"Better keep a close eye on your boyfriend. I bet she puts out for a pack of smokes."

Snap.

The girls swivel in their seats, their gazes latching on me, then to the broken pencil between my fingers. I look up, their sneers piercing through me as I fumble with shards of wood and mutter a quiet "sorry."

After giving me twin looks of revulsion, they turn back around and begin whispering quietly to each other—probably about me now. My hand drops the broken pencil, and it's shaking. I don't know if I've ever felt anger like that. Not in a long time. Who do they think they are? They don't know anything about Dusty . . . but then again, do I?

I look across at her again, and she's watching me, her brow creased. She's worried. I try to smile but can't. I haven't spoken to or seen this girl in almost three years. Maybe she's changed. Maybe she *does* do drugs and has been expelled for it. Maybe she —I swallow, and it feels like barbed wire—sleeps around with guys.

But one thing I know for sure. She's still my best friend. I still love her.

There's a clatter, and I look over where a pencil lands by her brown suede platform shoes. Dusty bends over to pick it up and begins writing on her paper, and I—

I can see right up her skirt. Her legs are slightly parted, the mini skirt pulled higher from the movement, and . . . there are little black bows on her white cotton panties.

I'm sweating—panicking—shaking. And she seems totally clueless that I can see. I'm hard, and I've never been more grateful to be sitting in this wooden desk. If the teacher asked me to stand, that would be the end of me.

Nervously, I look around, wondering if anyone else is also looking where they shouldn't be, and when I confirm they aren't, my eyes are back and latched to that spot. I'm a pervert. What is wrong with me? I shouldn't be doing this, but even as I convince myself it's wrong, I can't tear my eyes away.

"Ahem."

Blue eyes are fixed on me when I look up, and her legs snap shut. I turn away, hitting my knee on the metal of my desk, embarrassed and horrified that she caught me looking at her underwear. She definitely knows what I was doing. There's no way she doesn't. I just got her back. What if she never wants to speak to me again after this? What if she tells the teacher? The principal? The school? Oh no, what if they call my parents?

The bell rings, knocking me out of my spiral, but I can't move as she leaves the room. After all this time, she didn't even speak to me. Why would she, after catching me looking up her skirt? I really blew it. Defeated and finally deflated, I grab my things and my broken pencil and stuff them into my bag. When I get out into the hallway, I see her red curls bouncing their way out the exit doors toward the football field.

I should apologize. Explain I hadn't meant to look. Tell her I was simply struck stupid by seeing her again. I'll get on my knees and beg her every day to forgive me.

I push through the doors into the morning sunlight. Squinting, I scan the area for her, finally finding her at the far end of the bleachers, a plume of smoke drifting up from where she stands.

When I'm two feet away, I clear my throat. "Uh . . . Dusty?"

She turns and looks me up and down, a cigarette held daintily between her fingers.

"Dusty, I'm so sorry. I didn't mean to look—I was so surprised and—I can't believe you're here. I've thought about you nonstop for three years and I—"

She flicks her cigarette and pushes me back against the bleachers, kissing me hard. For a moment I'm frozen. Is this a test? Is she punishing me? But how could this possibly be a punishment when it's the most amazing thing I've ever felt?

My hands reach up to grasp her face as her tongue swipes against my bottom lip. I jolt back, my hand reaching up to touch my mouth as a wide grin spreads across her cheeks.

"Hi, Key."

The sound of her voice is like coming home. "Hi."

"You sure grew up," she says, her hand pushing through my hair.

"So did you," I admit.

"No more noodle arms," she says, gently tracing her fingers down my bicep.

"And you . . ." *Oh no, don't say her boobs are bigger. Don't say it.* ". . . you're taller."

As if she knew exactly what I was trying not to say, she steps closer to me—she could always read my mind that way. "Did you like what you saw?"

I blink. "Huh?"

She glances around, then with a smirk, she lifts one side of her skirt to show me the little black bows again.

Blood rushes south for the second time this morning. Charmed by my panic, she leans closer. "Any requests for which ones I should wear tomorrow?"

My eyes nearly bulge from my head. "Wh-what?"

"My panties," she whispers. "You enjoyed looking at them, so I thought I'd ask if you had any requests."

I squeeze my eyes shut. "Look, I—that was a mistake. I didn't mean to—"

"I'm not mad."

"You're not?"

"Guys look at me all the time, and I hate it, but you?" She smirks. "I like *you* looking."

With that, she pushes me back against the bleachers again. She fists the collar of my shirt and presses up onto her toes as her lips nearly touch mine.

"I've always liked you looking," she whispers, then kisses me again. This time I can't contain it. My hands are all over her, because she's here, and I can't get enough. She likes me looking at her *and* she's kissing me. Her tongue begs for entrance and I give in, forgetting for a few moments everything I've been told in church. She tastes like smoke and butterscotch candy and it's the best drug I could ever hope to try.

When the bell rings in the distance, I'm breathless and floating, unsure whether it's been five minutes or an hour. Pulling back, we look at each other, her lips swollen and her hair a little messy from where my hands have been, but she smiles so brightly it's as if I'm looking at the sun itself.

"I promised I'd come back for you."

CHAPTER 17

Suspicious Minds

I don't think I can remember the last time I smiled so much. My cheeks hurt. Is that normal? Do I have lockjaw? But as I pull into the driveway I glance in the rearview mirror and my grin pulls even wider.

Oh man. I'm such a fucking goner.

One makeout session with this woman and she has me eating out of the palm of her hand. I rest my head back against the seat. What the hell am I going to tell Key? He wants everything to stay the same, but life isn't like that. What if he hates me for dating someone? What if he thinks I'm leaving him behind? Oh fuck, what if it breaks up the band?

"Fuck a duck . . ." I mutter, grabbing a cigarette and stepping out of my Honda Accord. I glance up at the stars above me, imagining they're Dusty's freckles across the bridge of her narrow nose. It's so dark now, the lit cherry of my cigarette the only light. I fumble with my keys, taking far too long in the dark to find the right one. Finally, the door opens and I'm assaulted by the lights and noise.

Key's not alone.

Panic floods through me. What if Key brought home a girl?

What if he wants us both to take her to bed? I don't want anyone else. In fact, I haven't thought about any other girl since Dusty reappeared in my life. I'm locked in. Hook, line, and sinker. *Jesus Christ.* Is this how Dave and James felt?

I close the door behind me and see Becks standing in the kitchen pouring coffee. With the noise of the door slamming, she looks up and her green eyes meet mine. "Oh good, Joel, you're home."

"Uh, yeah. What's—what's going on?"

Her mouth is turned down and a sinking feeling settles in the pit of my stomach. "You should come into the living room."

I turn the corner to find the guys sitting around Al wearing worried expressions. Becks passes out coffee, but it's not until I sit down in the seat next to Key that anyone notices I'm here.

"Joel," Al says. "Good, I think it's best that we do this with everyone here. Less confusion, I think."

"I don't understand," I say. "What's going on?"

"Something has . . . happened," Al starts.

I wait, but when he doesn't elaborate I look around the room. James and Dave don't meet my eyes, and Key has slumped forward, head heavy in his hands. Everyone seems to know but me.

I look back at Al to find him already watching me. "What happened?"

But Al can't speak and I'm starting to get really annoyed. "Will someone tell me what the hell is going on?"

"We're being sued," Dave says.

Of all the things that could have been said, that was not something I had even contemplated. I thought someone died. "Sued?"

Thankfully, Al seems to have found his voice. "Yes, uh . . . a man named"—he pulls out a piece of paper from his jacket pocket

—"Logan Samuels? He has filed a copyright infringement lawsuit against the band."

"But I thought—" It hits me then and it's as if I've been punched in the gut. The air is knocked out of me, and I turn to look at Key, whose hands are balled up tighter than Fort Knox in his shaggy hair. "Wait, One-Punch Logan is fucking suing us?"

James and Dave look at each other. "One-Punch Logan?" James asks.

I shoot out of my seat. "Yeah, this absolute fucknut we were in military school with," I say, gesturing to Key. "He was always hanging around us, following us around. He played mediocre guitar . . . the three of us, well, we sort of formed a band."

"Well, he's claiming that most of your songs . . ." Al sighs. "He's saying he was the one who wrote them."

Fire burns through my veins. "He what?" I spit.

"Joel, you can back this up, right?" Dave says, trying to stay calm. "Key says he was the sole writer on 'Neon Crush' and 'Firebird' and—"

But there's a scraping of wood against flooring and Key is halfway across the room.

"You fucking think I'm lying about writing those goddamn songs?" he yells.

Dave is on his feet, his hands up. "Of course not!"

"Then knock off the shit about 'oh, well, Key *says*.'" His eyes are red as he looks around, his face a little puffy. "Here's what Key says right now and will *forever* say: Those are *my* songs. I wrote them. *Me*. For fuck's sake, I wrote some of them as a kid!"

James is on his feet next. "We believe you, man," he says. "But there's one huge problem."

I frown. "Which is?"

Dave runs a hand down his face. "He says he has proof *he* wrote them."

"Proof?" Key says. "*Proof*? I'll shove his proof up his fucking urethra."

I place my hand on Key's shoulder. He's shaking, the tension in his muscles as hard as a rock.

"I don't know what kind of proof he's claiming," Al admits. "But Key, please tell me you have something. Anything to prove you wrote those songs."

"They're mine! I don't need to prove anything to anyone!"

James steps forward. "No one is denying you wrote them, but if this thing goes to court—"

"Oh, for fuck's sake," Key shouts, louder still. "You know what?" He shrugs my hand off his shoulder then stomps away to the edge of the living room. "Fuck all of you. I don't need this bullshit."

The sound of his footsteps retreating to his room echo off the walls, then a door slams, then silence. I turn toward the others. Becks sits ramrod-straight in her seat, her green eyes wide and unblinking.

"Well," James says with a sigh. "I think that went well."

I close my eyes and rub my forehead. "Look, I'll talk to him. He's . . . he hasn't been having a good go of it lately, and then this? I'm sure we can come up with something."

Al mops at his sweaty forehead as the front door slams shut. Izzy appears, holding a stack of newspapers under her arm. When Dave sees her, he's immediately wrapping her up in his arms.

"I thought you were going to Memphis?" he asks, holding her out at arm's length and scanning her face.

"I rescheduled that interview."

"What? Why?"

She holds out the newspapers. "Because of this."

Dave takes one in his hands but I can't bear to look. His expression is enough for me to understand whatever it is, it's not good.

"'Carnal Lies? The metal band's rise to stardom could be the worst sin of all.'" James reads softly, the paper crunching in his hands.

"This story isn't out yet," Izzy explains. "My friend from college—you know Henry? He works for the *East Bay Chronicle* now and called to give me the heads up. But this paper will be everywhere first thing tomorrow."

"How can they print something that hasn't even been proven true yet?" Becks asks.

Izzy rolls her eyes. "It's the *Chronicle.* You know all they print is trash. But because they don't come right out and use accusatory language, they can get away with it. It's bullshit."

Al grabs a copy of the paper, then pulls his car keys from his pocket. "I need to head back to the office to try and deal with this. See if they can pull the article before it hits the streets." He stops when he reaches me. "Joel, please see what you can get out of Key. I wish it was as easy as taking his word for it, but if this goes to court they're going to want some kind of proof and . . . so will the public."

I stand, shell-shocked, as he leaves through the front door.

"What the fuck are we going to do?" Dave whispers.

"You don't think this guy could be telling the truth, do you?" Becks asks.

James shakes his head. "No. No, there's no way. We've all been in a studio with him. Key knows how to compose songs. I've watched him do it."

"But what if he has no way to prove he wrote them?" Dave adds.

James turns to Dave with a frown. "Wait, you're not actually thinking—"

"No, definitely not," Dave admits. "But in all that studio time, all those rehearsals . . . have you ever seen Key bring a piece of paper with him? Has he ever written down a song? Who does that?"

"*He* does."

I don't even realize I said the words until the four of them turn to me.

"I know him," I say. "Key's brain works differently. You're right though, I don't think I've ever seen him write down a composition."

Dave steps toward me. "We need proof. If this Logan guy has something and we don't? How will we ever be able to clear Key's name?"

"I'll talk to him," I say. "It'll all be okay, you'll see."

Four pairs of eyes watch me as I back out of the living room, and when I reach Key's door, my legs are heavy.

How is this happening? There's no way that bastard has proof and if he does, it's obviously fake. There isn't a lot that I'm certain of in this world, but one thing I know one hundred percent? It's that Key is the furthest thing from a liar or a thief. It's impossible. So I stretch out my hand and knock on the door.

"Key?"

"Fuck off, Thanger," he shouts.

My guts turn. He never calls me by my last name. He must really be pissed. I grip the handle and turn it, thankful he didn't lock me out. When I step inside, I spot him laid out on the bed, his face buried in the pillows.

"Hey man," I start.

"I thought I told you to fuck off," he mumbles into his sheets.

"You ought to know by now that I'm terrible at following instructions."

"I have nothing to say that I haven't already said."

I cross the room and stand next to the bed. "You could talk to me. Like you always do." There's a grunt, and I roll my eyes before perching on his bed. "Or, you know, I could just beat the shit out of you until you spill it."

He's quiet for a moment before he turns, his eyes obscured by his hair. "How am I supposed to prove I wrote those songs, Joel?" he whispers.

I take a deep breath. "We'll figure it out. You wrote some of them before you left home. Maybe you just have to bite the bullet and go back there. Go through your old stuff for anything you might have written down."

"I didn't . . . I mean, I did, but—"

A spark of hope flickers in my chest. Could Key have the songs written in a journal back home? "But what?"

"They're gone, Joel."

"Gone? What do you mean?"

He sits up and rubs at his jaw.

"I only ever wrote them down once, and I-I just always kept them up here, you know?" he says, pointing to his head. "And the paper copies? Trust me, they're probably nothing but ash now."

"Surely your parents wouldn't—"

"Joel!" His hands fly up into the air. "Can you just . . ." He covers his face. "Just get out."

"Key—"

"I said, get out!" he yells.

He lies back down and turns onto his side. I frown. I guess that's the only thing I can manage for the night. My hands flex and tighten into fists. That article will come out tomorrow and people all over San Francisco will think Key is a thief. It makes me sick.

"I'll be here, when you're ready," I say. "Whatever happens, I'm not going anywhere."

He turns his head to face the opposite wall and, with a sinking feeling, I leave the room.

CHAPTER 18

Sleep Like a Baby Tonight

DUSTY

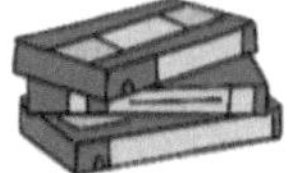

"Cherry, thank god," Monique says as I head back to my desk from the breakroom.

My brow furrows and I look around. "What?"

"There's a man on line three for you. Said he wouldn't pay for anyone else," she says.

A sharp pull tugs at my navel. For a fleeting moment I think maybe it's Joel. That he just wants to talk to me or maybe that he's regretting ending our date with just a kiss. But then another thought hits me like a train. Is it . . . *him*?

"Bastard is taking up an entire line. So hurry up and deal with him, please."

She stalks away, and I'm left bewildered and holding my steaming mug of coffee. I glance at my desk, where the light flashes on and off, on and off. Somewhere on the surface, I panic. Things went amazing today with Joel. When he kissed me it was electric. Then he left me horny and with no time to take care of it myself, so I wound up at work with an outlet that led to me describing certain scenarios I'd like to be involved in with him and no relief. But if Baby is on the line, I don't trust myself enough not to do something stupid . . .

I sit at my desk, sip my coffee, and pick up line three.

"Hello, this is Cherry speaking."

"Fuck, sweetheart, I thought you'd never pick up the phone."

I grip the desk. "I'm so sorry, Baby."

"I've missed you," he says.

There's something in the way he says it. Something that breaks along the edge of the words. Is he sad? I glance at the clock.

"You must really be missing me if you're calling at two thirty in the morning. I hope I didn't keep you waiting too long."

He sighs into the speaker. "I'd wait days for you."

"You probably say that to all the girls," I tease.

"Nuh-uh," he says, "you're the only one I call."

I pause. Normally I wouldn't believe him, but . . . this is the second time he's mentioned it and the sincerity in his voice is too pure not to take his word for it.

"I missed you too. What's got you down?"

"Nothing."

"Come on, I can tell when my Baby is upset. Tell me, and I'll make you feel better."

"I don't know if that's possible."

Hmm . . . something must really be bothering him. Normally, he's raring to go, dick hard in his hand and wanting to do vile things to me with hardly a how-do-you-do.

"If I were there with you, I'd wrap my arms around you. We'd lie in bed and I would stroke your hair."

He moans, and the sound zings through me. "Have you ever been so mad but so exhausted at the same time?"

I squeeze the phone in my hand. "I—yes, yes I have."

"I want to destroy everything. Break everything. Run through the streets swinging a bat. But I also just can't get out of bed."

"I'm sorry," I whisper.

"It's not your fault."

I shake my head. "No, but I'm sorry something has made you feel so terrible."

I hear a deep breath through the line then a long silence.

"Is there anything I can do to help?" I ask tentatively.

"No one can help me," he admits. "Unless you have a time machine."

I chuckle. "If I had a time machine, I wouldn't be hanging around here." I freeze. The number-one rule of sex work? Never interrupt the fantasy. This man has called me hoping for sympathy —comfort. To admit I'd rather be somewhere else? Not cool. "Sorry, I—I didn't mean that."

"It's okay," he says, and I can almost hear a smile in his voice. "I'm not an idiot. I know you're only listening because I'm paying you to."

Guilt racks me and for once, he's wrong. "That's not true. I've thought about you . . . even after the phone line goes dead."

"You have?"

I take a deep breath. "Yes. And more often than I care to admit."

A breathy laugh echoes through the speaker. "I don't know why, but it feels like I know you."

"Maybe we met in another life," I suggest.

"Star-crossed lovers, perhaps," he adds.

"Didn't work out so great for Romeo and Juliet," I tease.

"True, but it seems all of my relationships are doomed for tragedy."

I blink and think of Joel. Did I doom our relationship before it's even begun? Will it all end in sorrow?

"I worry the same thing for myself," I whisper. "People like me—we don't get happy endings. I'm not even sure they really exist."

"They do," he says suddenly. "My friends . . . they have it.

The happily ever after. I watch them sometimes and think how lucky they are to have found each other. I tell myself it isn't real but it is—I'm just jealous of what they have. They're soulmates. Meanwhile, I just sabotage everything that comes my way because I can't get over my own heartbreak."

Tears begin to sting my eyes. His words hit really close to home. "That sounds really lonely."

He sniffs, and I close my eyes as the first tear falls. "Not always. I have my best friend."

"That's good that you have each other."

"I think he's lonely too though, and while we have each other, we can't be everything for the other. There'll always be something missing."

"Is that what you're mad about?" I ask. "Do you think he's found someone?"

He takes a long deep breath. "I don't know. It could be nothing. I thought that maybe he seems a little different lately . . . but maybe it's all in my head."

I wrap the phone cord around my finger. "You could *ask* him."

Another long pause.

"I know that guys aren't always *super* comfortable sharing, but—"

A laugh.

"I—I'm sorry, did I say something funny?"

"Oh! No . . . no just—never mind."

Another phone girl walks past my cubicle on her way to the breakroom and I pull myself closer to my desk. "So, what are you going to do?"

He sighs. "I think I need to take a trip."

"Like a holiday?"

He clicks his tongue. "No. More like I need to go home."

I frown. From what he's told me about his parents, I have a

feeling home isn't a great place. "Are you sure that's a good idea?"

"Probably not, but there's some things and possibly . . . some*one* I need to find, so I should start there."

I nod. "I hope you find them."

"Me too." He yawns. "I think I'm going to try sleeping now, sweetheart. Do you . . . do you think you could do me a favor?"

"I'll try."

"Could you stay on the line with me until I fall asleep?"

I glance around. What will my boss think if she walks by and I'm not even speaking? She'll think I'm wasting company time is what.

"Please?" he begs, and the sound steals my breath away. My heart aches, and a prickling heat rushes into my face.

"Of course I will. I'll even be decent and hang up so we don't charge you for hours and hours."

He chuckles. "It would be worth it."

My cheek turns up at the side. "I hope you have a good sleep."

"Good night, sweetheart."

I listen as his bed sheets rustle, and after a few minutes of tossing and turning, it sounds like he finally falls asleep.

"Baby?" I say through the speaker. When he doesn't answer I whisper, "Good night."

Then I hang up the phone with a soft click.

By FIVE THIRTY in the morning, my feet drag across the sidewalk as I head home from the bus. I'm exhausted. And not the normal *I worked all night and live the life of a cave dweller* exhausted. No, right now? I'm *emotionally* exhausted.

This week has been a lot. My first date with Joel left me giddy and vulnerable. Then Baby was hurting, and he called *me* to make him feel better. Did he call me because he simply has no one else? Or did he call because everyone he knows is sleeping at two in the morning? What happened to make him so sad? He didn't even try to make the conversation sexual, even though that's what I get paid for. But the way he just sounded so defeated—it hurts my heart.

The neon sign for The Sudsy Dream comes into view, and I stop to stare at the alleyway beside the building. Nausea rolls around in my stomach. Oh god, I've spent the last few hours obsessing over a man's voice and feelings when I was kissing Joel in that alley less than twenty-four hours ago. I blink rapidly, trying to keep my emotions at bay. I know he said he's not the jealous type, and he doesn't seem to need any reassurances from me, but I'm starting to develop real feelings for this faceless voice.

What the fuck am I going to do? Everything is such a mess.

I duck up the stairs and slam the door shut. Stella attempts to weave through my legs, but I rush over to the bed and throw myself down onto it. My life hasn't felt this out of control in years. Not since—not since the hell I clawed myself out of. That feeling of hopelessness, desperation, betrayal, and, at the core of it all, the confusion . . . it's all rushing back to me, unwelcome. How stupid I was to have so gravely misunderstood his feelings for me. That any moment he was going to show up. That he would be the hero he always tried to be and save me. But then he didn't. So, once again, it was up to me to save myself. And it damn near killed me.

But I don't think Joel would do that. I don't think he would throw me away so carelessly. Sure, he might not want to marry me, but as far as relationships go, I believe he's genuine about liking me. Then again, I thought Key was too.

I'm too caught up in this phone stranger. It's scary and wrong, but also . . . intoxicating. The next time he calls? I'll just have to tell him I can't speak to him anymore. What's he going to do? It's not like he knows who I really am or where I live. For all I know, he lives in New York City.

A fluffy paw bats at my head, and Stella starts to purr as she nuzzles herself into me. I roll over and pull her in.

"I've made life a complicated mess again, pretty girl. What am I going to do?"

She meows, then purrs before nibbling gently on my finger. The radio suddenly draws my focus as a metal song slams loudly through the quiet of my apartment. I should turn it off and get into bed, but before I can convince myself to get up, half the song is over and my foot taps along to the double bass beat of the drums.

"That was Carnal Sins's hit, 'Firebird,'" the radio host announces.

"Carnal Sins?" I whisper to myself, and Stella perks up. "That's Joel's band! I can't believe I didn't tell you. He's on the radio."

She meows softly as if to confirm to me that she understands I'm sort of, kind of, dating the bass player of the band we just heard.

"It's metal music. I know it's not really our thing," I say as I softly pet her head, "but I kind of like it. And I like *him*. Maybe— I don't know. Maybe that'll be *our* new thing? We don't have many, you know, things."

I frown and let myself wallow in a little self-pity, if just for a minute. There's just nothing going on with me. No passions. No hobbies. Movies are really the only thing that gives me any kind of joy. Acting used to do that, but . . . well, look where that got me.

Stella bites me hard, and I yank my hand away with a gasp. "Hey!" I examine the mark, which thankfully seems to have just been a warning—as though she could hear my own self chastising thoughts. "Okay, I'm sorry," I say. "Let's go to bed."

But as I lie awake, unable to drift off to sleep, the memories of my past break out of their carefully crafted vault to haunt me.

CHAPTER 19

Young Love

KEY

EIGHT YEARS AGO

I don't think I've ever been so bored in my life. All I want is to see Dusty. She said she'd wait for me, and she had a detention after school anyway.

"Keith?"

I blink and sit up straighter in my chair as I look over at Cynthia Redwood, a stuck-up senior who goes to my church. "Pardon?"

She sighs. "I was saying, we should all work together to get signatures for the petition."

My eyebrows rise. "Petition?"

This time she rolls her eyes. "Yes, Prentiss, the petition."

"Remind me what it's for?"

She crosses her arms. "To have that cheating harlot, Dusty Connors, expelled."

I lean forward so fast my chair almost tips. "Wait, what?"

"I heard Mrs. Smith say she's testing at the top of her class. She's obviously cheating."

"So because she's smart she's automatically cheating?" I press.

Cynthia scoots forward on her chair. "She dresses like a street walker, she smokes, and I heard from Emory Radcliffe that she was looking to"—Cynthia looks around then lowers her voice—"score drugs."

My face scrunches. What a load of nonsense. Dusty and I have been secretly dating for months and never once has she mentioned doing drugs. She smokes, yeah, but who doesn't? "Cynthia, that's insane. Also, Radcliffe has never told the truth in his life, so I doubt it. There's nothing wrong with her."

Cynthia huffs, turning to the group. "You see? Even our very own choir boy Keith Prentiss has fallen under her spell."

I roll my eyes. "Spell? She's not a witch."

Another girl, Karen, with headgear and long brunette braids, leans forward. "She may as well be. I've seen the way you look at her. Like you're . . . thinking sinful thoughts."

"It's not a sin to have thoughts, Karen," I retort. "But if that's what you believe, it would explain a lot about you."

She scrunches her nose. "You know that's not what I mean. She's a temptress. And if we don't stop her, how many others are going to follow down that path?"

I scoff. "Oh please. She doesn't even have any friends. She's always alone. Who is she going to influence?"

"Clearly she's influenced you," Matthew says from beside Cynthia.

I narrow my eyes at him. "What?"

"She'll be your carnal sin, Keith," he says, sitting back in his chair looking pleased with himself. "Your fall from grace."

Cynthia and Karen sneer at me. "She's trash, Keith," Cynthia says. "And you know where trash belongs? At the dump. Not our school."

I'm on my feet so fast my chair tumbles backward. "Don't you dare talk about her like that," I yell.

The moment the words leave my lips, I know I fell right into their trap. The girls cling to each other, and Matthew smirks.

"I'm sure Reverend Hollis would be very interested to hear why you've taken such an interest in her. Your parents will be disappointed."

"I haven't taken an interest in her. I just don't think it's right that we judge someone to the point of bullying them out of school. I thought it was god's job to judge us. Since when do you all consider yourselves above the lord?"

I see them squirm in their seats. See Cynthia's eyes move to her clipboard and petition, then tuck it away in her backpack. *Point for Key.*

"Love thy neighbor," I say, doubling down. "Isn't that right? Or have you all forgotten?"

They cast their eyes away, and I grab my bag before heading out of the library, pushing through the doors and into the empty halls. I wipe sweat from my forehead and take a deep breath. That was too close. It still could be. Those narrow-minded jerks could still go to my church—my parents—but at least for now, I think I've stopped them.

A sharp whistle grabs my attention, and there's Dusty, smiling at me from behind a door to my left. I take one last quick glance at the library to make sure no one from Teens for Christ is watching me then jog after her into the room.

When the door snaps shut behind me, it takes me a second to recognize the school auditorium, or rather backstage—the curtains hanging around us block out the lights from the seating. Dusty's hands find me in the dark, weaving through my hair, and I wrap my arms around her waist. Our lips meet and we melt into each other. We take our time, and while I know it's something I shouldn't be doing, I let my hands wander.

Dusty lets me explore her curves, her edges, and everything in between.

"Key?" she whispers.

I nibble on her earlobe and smile as she shivers. "Yeah?"

"When can you get away next? To the cabin."

"Hmm . . . Friday. My parents are taking my brother out of town for some kind of debate tournament."

She looks up at me and her blue eyes sparkle. "So, does that mean you won't have a curfew?"

"Why? Plan on keeping me out late?"

I can just make out her cheeks turning pink. "I just—I thought . . ."

My brow furrows. "What?"

"I thought maybe we could, you know . . . We've been dating for a while now and I thought we could spend the night together."

"I—wait . . . what? You don't mean—"

She offers me a shy kind of smile, like that's exactly what she means.

"We could have sex," she whispers. "If you want."

For a fleeting moment, I think of Cynthia and Karen. Maybe there was some truth there . . . Is Dusty an evil temptress trying to seduce me? But of course it's nonsense. She's my best friend, my girlfriend.

My blood thickens in my veins when I meet her gaze. "Well, I-I mean, of course—I just—" I stumble, take a deep breath. "I just have never, uh—done that before."

She tucks her hair behind her ears. "Me either."

I nearly choke. "You—you've never . . . ?"

"You thought I wasn't a virgin?"

I fear that saying anything will just get me into trouble here, but words tumble out anyway. "I'm just surprised. You're always way ahead of me when it comes to grown-up things."

That must've been the correct choice, because she wraps her

arms around my neck and plays with my hair. "I mean, it's not like I never had the opportunity. Guys tried, but . . . I guess I was saving myself."

The blood whooshes from my head straight to my groin. "You were?"

She nods and kisses the corner of my lips. "I always wanted it to be you."

I cup her face in my hands and look into her starry blue eyes. "You're the only one I've ever wanted," I whisper. "There's no one like you."

MY PALMS ARE SWEATING as I pull my bike up to the abandoned cabin. There's candlelight flickering through the grime-covered windows and I take a deep breath. When I knock quietly and let myself in, Dusty's mouth drops open.

"Oh! Wow, you look so handsome," she says.

I'm an idiot. What kind of guy wears a suit and tie to lose their virginity? "Sorry, I just—I don't know . . . this seemed like a special occasion."

Before my face can get any redder, I hold out the bouquet of flowers I got her. Her face splits into a beautiful, dimpled smile.

"Key, they're so beautiful. Now I wish I dressed up."

"You're always beautiful," I say.

"I didn't know you were such a romantic," she says, taking the flowers and placing them in a large glass with water.

I shrug. "I don't know about that. I guess it's just that the church taught me this is supposed to happen on our wedding night."

An expression I can't pin down crosses her face. "Right."

I sit down awkwardly on the couch, and after a few moments,

she joins me. Neither of us says anything until finally, her fingers lace with mine.

"Key, I . . . if you're not comfortable with this—we don't have to. We could just hang out like we usually do."

I can't hold it in any longer. "Dusty, I love you."

Her eyes widen, those ruby-red lips forming a delicate O.

"I've loved you since we were kids. I don't know why I've never told you, but you're not just my best friend or my girlfriend. You're my everything."

Tears fill her eyes, but I didn't mean to make her cry. "Key . . ."

"We're just two idiots who still haven't finished high school, but when the time is right, I want us to be more than that. I want to drive off into the sunset with you. I want us to follow our dreams together."

I jump up from the couch and walk over to my guitar. I loosen the D string until it comes free, then twist and twist and twist. Triumphantly, I hold up the little wire ring and, as heat pools at my collar, kneel down on one knee before her.

"Dusty Connors," I say, holding up the makeshift ring, "I love you, and I want to be with you always. Will you accept this ring as a token of my promise to love you forever?"

Her gaze bounces between my face and the ring, and my heart has never beat harder. But then she smiles and leans forward, palming the sides of my face.

"Of course I will, Key, because I love you too."

She breathes out a laugh, and I slip the guitar wire ring onto her finger, my cheeks in pain from the smile pulling at them. "It's beautiful," she whispers, twirling it once, twice.

"It's a D string," I confess. "For Dusty."

"Appropriate," she says with a giggle, then she reaches up to the nape of her neck. Her eyes never leave mine but the breath halts in my chest as her necklace comes loose. She holds up the gold chain in front of me then takes my hand. "I know you won't be able to wear it because of your parents, but I want you to have this."

She takes my hand and drops the sun pendant into my scarred palm. "Really? But you . . . You've worn it for as long as I've known you."

With a look down at the necklace she takes a deep breath. "My mother gave it to me the day she left—the day we met. She told me to always look for the sunshine in life. That's why you should have it," she whispers. "Because my world is brighter because of you. And I promise that you'll never have to come back for me again, because I'll never leave your side."

She kisses me, and the candles flicker and burn down to the wick as we spend the night showing each other just how far our love goes.

CHAPTER 20

Separate Ways

JOEL

Al tried his best, but first thing in the morning, that damn article is everywhere. I see it when I drive to the corner store for smokes. When I stop and grab some pick-me-up donuts for Key. That awful headline follows me everywhere.

When I get home, the phone is hanging off the hook. I set it right, wondering how it got knocked off in the first place, but a second later it starts ringing. And ringing. Reporters and journalists calling for a statement, clogging up the line with their barbed comments.

Key is no help of course. He must have been the one to take the phone off the hook in the first place, but no matter what I try, he refuses to get out of bed. James and Dave manage to get through once to ask if I have any new information from Key, and I feel sick to my stomach when I have to admit I have nothing new to tell them. I'm exhausted. Whatever Al is working on, I hope he comes up with something fast.

By eight the next morning the phone is already ringing again. I yank it off the hook, ready to scream at the motherfuckers to leave us alone, when a familiar voice speaks first.

"Joel, honey?"

My eyes widen. "Ma?"

"How's my boy doing?" she asks.

I chuckle and shake my head. "Considering I almost told you to fuck off, not too great."

A thoughtful hum vibrates through the phone. "I read the article. Nonsense, all of it. How could people think such a thing is true?"

I open and shut the fridge door for something to do with my hands. "People always want a scandal."

"Yes, I suppose you're right. How is Keith doing?" she asks.

I glance over my shoulder toward his deserted hallway. "Not good."

"I figured as much. I sent you boys a care package this morning," she says with some pep in her voice. While my mom knows she can't solve every one of my problems, she'll always make sure there's snacks to figure it out with.

"Thanks, Ma."

"So, other than the world falling apart around you," she continues, "anything new going on in your life?"

I shrug. "No, not really."

"Nothing at all?"

Hair the color of flames, that devastating kiss, and the smell of strawberries pull at my thoughts. "Actually, I met someone."

"A new manager? You know I always thought that Simpson fellow wasn't doing everything he could for you. The band still doesn't even have a music video," she criticizes. "How am I supposed to brag to my friends that my baby boy is a rockstar without showing them a tape of you on the television?"

I smile. "Mom, Al is great. And the reason we're not on MTV isn't because of him. It's because of MTV. What I meant was—" I clear my throat. "I *met* someone."

There's a long stretch of silence. I check the phone jack,

thinking maybe we've been disconnected. There's a funny click over the line, but then my mom's voice trills again.

"What do you mean, you met someone?" she finally asks.

"You know, like . . . a girl."

"You met a girl?"

"Yeah."

"Wow, that's . . . wow, Joel. I'm happy for you. What's she like?"

"She beautiful and funny. A redhead."

"A redhead, huh?" The smirk apparent in her tone.

I roll my eyes. I can all but see her wiggling her brows. "Yeah, yeah, go ahead and say it."

"Say what, dear?"

I sigh and wait.

"Oh, you're no fun," she chastises. "But I definitely told you so." *There it is.* "I always knew a redhead would steal your heart."

"Well, it's hardly serious, Mom. She took a hell of a lot of convincing to go out with me, but I think I've turned a corner there."

"Well, how could she not like you? You're a famous rockstar! Albeit, one who's in a bit of a sticky situation right now, but—"

"I haven't told her yet about the . . . uh, problem."

"Oh, well . . . I would tell her straight away. You don't want to start a relationship with any big secrets like that. Besides, women are great problem solvers—maybe she'll have ideas of how to help."

"You're right, but I have to tread carefully. Like I said, she's hard to get."

She laughs. "She's really making you work for it, huh? Good for her. She's a stronger woman than me. When your father appeared in my life one day, it took everything in me not to—"

"Okay okay, I get the point, no further explanation is needed, thanks." I press my fist into my eyes and try to block out the mental image of my parents in any unwholesome situation. "So, that's all you've got for advice, then?"

"The best advice I can give you is to be yourself. Be fun. If this girl managed to grab your attention, I doubt she's a stick in the mud."

Visions of the first time I saw Dusty spinning on that pole swarm my vision. Yeah . . . a stick in the mud is definitely not how I would describe her.

"Show her who you are. If you fake it now, it'll never last," she says. "And if she doesn't fall head over heels for you, then she's crazy."

I smile. "Thanks, Mom."

She hums again through the phone.

"What? I know that tone."

"No, it's nothing. I just—" She takes a breath. "She must be some girl."

I frown. "What do you mean?"

"I mean, you've never mentioned anyone to me before. What's changed?"

I shrug and tap my fingers on the counter. "I don't know. I mean, life has been great. Amazing, actually, up until all this recent bullshit. I never really gave dating any real thought . . . but there's just something about her. I feel like I need to know her."

"And what about Keith?"

My stomach drops. "I haven't told him."

"He'll be the only one without someone."

"But that's what he wants," I say a bit harshly. "He told me himself. He doesn't even believe in love."

A long pause, and then, "That sounds like someone who's had his heart broken before."

I—could she be on to something here? "Nah, you didn't hear him." I shake my head. "He definitely doesn't want any kind of serious relationship."

"If you say so."

I run a hand down the back of my head. "I have to go, but thanks for the care package. I'll call you when I get it."

"Okay, dearie." But before I can hang up, she says, "Everything's going to work out for the best. You'll see."

"Thanks."

I hang up the phone and stand, staring at the clock on the stove for fifteen minutes. My ma's crazy. Key's never been in a relationship before, let alone had his heart broken. We know each other better than anything. I'm sure if there had been a girl at some point, he would've told me.

Or is my mom right like she so often is? What if there *was* a girl? What if something happened and she broke his heart? Does he not trust me enough to share that part of himself? I open a cupboard with no real goal in mind, needing some way to occupy my hands. I need to stop before I get carried away, I know this, but I'm too far gone now because . . . what if I don't know Key as well as I think I do? And if that's the case, what about the songs?

I'm heading down the hall in a heartbeat, ready to shake him awake and demand he provides me with an entire play-by-play of his childhood so that we can figure out how to prove he wrote those songs. But when I open his bedroom door, he's gone.

"Key?" I call, the floor creaking as I step into the empty room. I check a few more places, but he's not there either. It's not till I hear the sound of gravel that I think to check the driveway.

"Son of a bitch," I shout, watching my car's headlights bounce off our garage and disappear down the street. Turning on my heel, I head to the kitchen and lift the phone back off the receiver.

It rings and rings and rings, until finally someone answers.

"If you're calling to ask about the article, you can fu—"

"James, it's me."

"Oh." His voice softens. "Sorry, man, I thought you were—"

"He's gone."

"Who's gone?"

"Key!" I shout. "I just watched him take off in my fucking car."

A pause. "Where's he going?"

"Oh, I dunno, the store? We're out of milk," I mutter into the phone. "Does it sound like I fucking know where he went?"

"Okay, okay. Jesus Christ. Maybe he went to get smokes?"

I shake my head. "I don't know. I have a bad feeling about this."

James sighs. "What do you need me to do?"

There's nothing else I can do, so I grind my teeth and say, "Can you come get me? Drive me around and see if we can find him?"

"Yeah, man, sure. I'll be there in twenty."

I hang up and get dressed, my stomach tumbling like a dryer. As I pass by the kitchen, I glance at the phone again. I wanted to call Dusty today. Maybe arrange to take her out on another date. But now I have all this to deal with. Hopefully she doesn't think I've forgotten about her.

James crunches into the driveway and I head out, climbing up into the front seat of his black van, and put all thoughts of Dusty on hold.

"Right, which way did he go?" James asks without missing a beat.

I glance out his driver's side window and point. "That way."

"Maybe he went to the studio? Or to see Al? They're both that way."

Something makes me doubt that's where he's gone, but at least it's a start because my brain is too jumbled and anxious for much else. "Yeah, okay. Let's check."

James pulls out and drives, going a touch over the speed limit.

I press my head back, digging my fingers into the leather bench seat.

"I'm sure he didn't go far," James says, glancing at me out of the corner of his eye.

I shake my head. "I just have a bad feeling."

We're quiet for a while, scanning side roads and parking lots for any sign of my Honda.

"Nothing down that way," I mutter after an hour of aimless driving.

"Are you guys okay?" James asks.

I narrow my eyes. "Okay? What do you mean?"

James's cheeks flush. "Well, I know you guys sometimes . . ." He rubs the back of his neck. Is he blushing? "Oh Jesus, don't make me say it."

"What?"

His face scrunches. "You know! You and Key and the girls—"

"Oh!"

"I can't believe you made me say it, you asshole." He flicks his turn signal harder than necessary.

I try to smile. "No, I mean. I think we're fine. I talked about it with him like two weeks ago. It's got to be the songwriting shit."

James lifts an eyebrow. "Yeah, of course. I'm sure it is. Just wanted to check in case something had happened, and you needed to talk about it."

"Like I'd talk about it with you, whittle baby Jamesey," I tease. "You couldn't even ask me without blushing."

I ruffle his hair and he punches me in the arm. "Fuck off, dude."

"You know, I didn't realize you were so vanilla. From what I've heard of you and Becks going at it, I didn't think you'd blush at the idea of a threesome."

"All right, all right." He waves me off, but I don't miss the way his cheeks turn maroon. "And Becks and I are hardly vanilla."

I grin. "Sure, kiddo. Sure."

The sun begins to set as we reach the edge of the city, officially run out of options, and turn around. "I need to get gas and get home. But if he's not home in the morning, I'll come back and we can go out looking again, okay?"

"What if he's not back by Thursday, James? That gig we have lined up in Concord—"

"Canceled," he interrupts.

I turn so fast my seat belt locks. "Canceled? Why?"

"Why do you think?"

"The article?" I ask.

He nods. "Yeah, man."

"Shit."

James takes a deep breath. "Listen, I don't want to seem like a bummer when shit is already bad but . . . this little lawsuit problem? It might end up being a really *big* problem."

"It's just one show—"

"But it'll be more. The band's tied to this shit now. Even if the lawsuit goes away, we might never be able to recover in terms of public opinion unless we can prove publicly that it's bullshit."

I chew on the inside of my mouth. "Yeah, I get what you're saying."

"Do you?"

Is he for real? "Yeah, James, I do. What the fuck?"

He lifts his hands in surrender. "Sorry, I just—you two never take anything seriously and this is serious."

"I got it—"

"I just need to make sure that—"

"I got it!"

He presses his lips together and sighs. "Sorry."

My shoulders tense, and my stomach is in knots. I glare out

the window and catch the last rays of the sun reflect off the windows of The Sapphire, the theater Dusty and I broke into, as it blurs past. I'm not too far from her place. Maybe she would let me hide out there for a while to get away from the press. Can I really go back to that empty house? Maybe Key isn't coming back. What if this is over?

"Can you just drop me off here?" I ask when we stop at a red light.

James's face crumples. "Dude, I'm sorry. I shouldn't have said—"

"No, it's fine. You should have. But I think I'm going to just walk around for a bit. I can grab a cab home."

"You're sure? Can't be sending out a search party for you too."

I smile. "Don't worry, man. I'm not going anywhere."

He nods and claps my outstretched hand. "Okay."

Jumping down out of the van, I wait on the sidewalk as his taillights turn a corner down the road. I love the guy, but it felt like I couldn't breathe in there. I know he means well, and he isn't trying to blame me, but I know he secretly blames Key. And right at this moment? So do I. Not for the songs. I don't think I could ever believe One-Punch Logan is telling the truth. But for taking off? Where the hell did that fucker go?

And why did he feel the need to run from *me*?

CHAPTER 21

Maneater

DUSTY

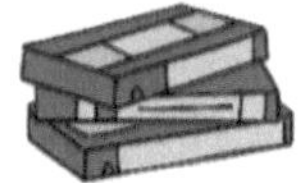

I hip-check my apartment door closed, the carton of eggs at the top of my grocery bag nearly tumbling to the linoleum floor. I'm exhausted. I had to go shopping after work or I'd have nothing to eat, and now I'd rather just hole up in my apartment with Stella and recharge. I'm unloading a loaf of bread out of the brown paper bag and setting it on the counter when there's a knock on my door. Who the hell is here?

"Hello?" I call, thinking maybe I misheard, but a croaky voice answers.

"Hey darlin', it's Doris."

Laundromat Doris?

I cross the room to find Doris, the change lady from downstairs, in front of my door. "Oh, hello."

"Good, you're home. Now come collect your boyfriend."

I blink and let out a nervous laugh. "Wh-what?"

She shuffles toward the stairs. "Your boyfriend. He's been here all night and it's starting to affect my business."

What the hell is she talking about? I reluctantly follow her, asking, "Are you saying Joel is downstairs? Why's he here?"

We reach the landing and she opens the side door into the laundromat. "Maybe you should ask him that."

I follow her gaze to the man in question, asleep and curled up on one of the plastic chairs in the waiting area. His black boots are under him, his arms wrapped around his knees, which are tucked up under his chin. As I walk over, a sense of dread fills my empty stomach.

"Joel?" I ask, placing my hand gently on his shoulder.

He startles awake, body jerked upright, and he has to slam his booted feet onto the floor to steady himself. Wide-eyed, he looks up at me, then squints against the lights. "Dusty?"

"What are you doing here?"

He gives his head a little shake, then stands. "I, uh . . ."

"Ahem."

The two of us turn to see Doris frowning, then with one neon blue–tipped finger nail, she gestures to the door. I roll my eyes, grab Joel by the hand, and pull him behind me. "Come on," I say.

"She's quite possibly the most unpleasant person I've ever met," Joel mutters.

"You should see her if she catches you using fake coins in her machines," I say.

We stop on the landing outside of my apartment and Joel raises an eyebrow. "People do that?"

"Yeah." I sigh. "Me."

The classical music I left on before I went to work last night is still playing softly when we cross the threshold.

"Don't take this the wrong way, but you look terrible. Are you okay?" I ask, cocking my head. He seems tired. And sad.

He closes his eyes and rests his head back against my door. "Not really."

Apparently both of the men in my life are going through a tough time. What are the odds?

"Do you want a drink? I think I have some vodka in my freezer—"

He grasps my hand and stops me from moving away, then with a look of utter anguish, he pulls me against him. Arms wrap around me, squeezing, and I feel him shudder.

My fingers trail up the back of his shirt, skimming gently along to calm him down. "Oh . . . Joel—"

"It's all just such a mess," he whispers into my hair.

He buries his face in my neck for a long moment until I release him, sliding my hands down to grasp his face. At first he won't look at me. Merely stands with his eyes closed, his mouth turned down in the first real frown I've ever seen on him.

"Joel? Listen," I whisper.

His eyes open to meet mine.

"Everything will be okay. You'll see. Whatever has got you down . . . we can figure it out."

"We?"

Something tumbles in my stomach as his gaze darts over my face, and it's like I've missed a step going downstairs. "I mean . . . I just thought—but if you don't—"

His smile comes back. It's still haunted, but it's there. "No, I *do* think . . . I just wasn't sure if *you* did."

I lick my lips, tamping down the excitement rushing through me. "Well, I don't want to rush into anything—" I grasp his hand when he raises a questioning eyebrow. "I'm not seeing anyone else. What I mean is . . . I need time to sort out all these *feelings*. Does that make sense?"

His eyes soften and he tilts his head. "Yeah. It does."

I let out a huge breath. "Okay, good. Because I do want to try this. *Us.* I mean, it's not like you gave me much choice," I tease. "You wouldn't leave."

He chuckles, then his face becomes serious again. "It's okay if you need time. If you need your freedom while you figure things out. But I need you to know—I'm all in."

Can a heart burst? "Really?"

His lip pulls up at the side slowly. "Yeah, but I'll wait for you to be ready. I'm not in a rush."

The kindness in his eyes almost brings a tear to mine. "You sure you want to gamble your heart on me?" I ask.

"Abso-fucking-lutely."

His kiss this time is slow, sensual, and sparks something in my core that I'm not sure I can contain. I want him. I've wanted him and his body for two fucking years, and right now, in this moment, it's mine. He said so himself. So why am I still nervous? As if sensing my hesitation, Joel pulls back to whisper against the corner of my mouth. "We don't have to do anything. I'm happy to just hang out and talk."

I smile. "We could talk on the bed and see where things go?"

That devilish grin is back, and next thing I know, he's scooping me up, his large hands under my thighs, and I'm wrapping my legs around his hips like it's the most natural thing in the world. Our journey to the bed is clumsy and sweet; my shirt gets caught in the doorjamb, and Joel stubs his toe on a chair, but we make it, falling onto my bed in a pile of limbs.

His heat and weight next to me is exhilarating. It's been so long since I've had this kind of contact, and I'm starved for it. He squeezes me to him and kisses my forehead. "I swear I didn't come here with the intention of hooking up. I really just didn't know where else to go, and . . ."

Trailing off, he gently plays with my hair, a look of despair returning to his eyes. "Do you want to talk about it?"

He sighs. "Someone has come forward and accused the band of stealing songs."

I frown. "What?"

"I'm not sure if you've watched the news recently but—"

"Joel," I say, gesturing around my bare-bones apartment. "I don't own a TV, can hardly afford to subscribe to a newspaper."

He shakes his head. "It feels like it's been all over the place. It's ridiculous. The guy is a scab. He was involved in a very early version of the band but never contributed anything except a massive headache. A complete waste of space. But now he's coming out and accusing us of stealing his songs."

I prop my head on my hand so I can meet him at eye level. "But how can he do that if he didn't write them?"

"He says he has proof, but what that is, I have no idea. It's a legal nightmare. Basically, we need to show that we did in fact write those songs and . . . well, it's not exactly an easy process. Plus, because it broke in the news, even if we can prove he's lying, the damage is done. We might never be able to repair our reputation. Venues are already canceling shows . . . It's a mess."

"I'm so sorry, Joel. That sounds awful."

His eyes flick away from mine. "I don't mean to dump on you. This isn't exactly the second date I had in mind."

I skim my fingertips along his creased brow. "Your troubles are important to me."

"Really?" he asks.

"I may not be able to offer any legal advice, but I'll try and support you, whatever comes your way."

He nods then falls silent for a few minutes, his fingers absentmindedly tracing the curve of my hip.

"I'm mad at my best friend."

I blink, and our eyes meet briefly.

"I've never been mad at him before but—he took off. He's been my best friend since I was seventeen years old. We've been through everything together. Forming the band, finding a studio exec to sign us, touring together, recording," he says low. "All of that and"—he avoids my gaze for a moment—"much *much* more, and he just takes off when we need him the most?"

"Where did he go?" I ask.

But Joel shakes his head. "No idea. We live together. He took my car and drove off. I spent all of yesterday looking for him. Then I didn't want to go home and be alone—"

"You've been downstairs with Doris all night?" I ask.

He shrugs. "Seemed like a good idea at the time."

I frown. "And you don't know where he went?"

Joel rolls onto his back and stares at my ceiling. "That's the worst part. It's making me think that maybe I didn't know him as well as I thought. What if our whole friendship has been a lie?"

I wrap my arm around his torso and squeeze, laying my head on his chest. "I don't think that's true. He's probably as overwhelmed as you and scared. He'll be back."

"Being in the band . . . It's been a dream come true. I'm so incredibly lucky, and I can't help but feel like I'm being punished. Like maybe because I was a jerk as a teenager, this is all just the universe's way of balancing itself out."

"I understand what you mean. I feel like I'm always waiting for the other shoe to drop. That any moment everything's just going to go to hell."

He grasps my chin and forces me to look up at him. "Is that why you pushed me away?"

I shrug. "A lifetime of experience has taught me that I'm not worth the trouble. That I'm not worth anything."

His beautiful brown eyes hold mine. "That's not true. You are worth *everything*."

"You hardly know me," I whisper.

"That doesn't mean you don't have worth or dreams."

"I haven't had dreams in a long time."

He bites his lip. "What was your dream? What did you want to do when you were sixteen?"

A smile tugs at my lips. "I wanted to be an actress. I was desperate to be Grace Kelly. Everything seemed so romantic and extravagant."

His lips split into a grin. "I could see you up on the big screen."

Now that I've said it, it seems to pour out of me. "I guess I thought that if I was a big Hollywood star, someone, somewhere, would love me."

His brow creases. "You've *never* had someone—"

I shake my head. "I thought I had someone once . . . but I was wrong."

"Dusty," he says softly, "it might not be love yet, but you mean a lot to me. More than any woman ever has before."

"Just promise me that you won't disappear if you decide you can't love me. Just tell me the truth."

"I would never do that to you. I promise."

He kisses me, pushing himself up over me, and his touch starts to chase away at all the fear. My body burns for him and as he kisses down my throat, I can't stop myself from tearing at his jacket. Long, dark hair hangs around my face like a curtain, the smell of him racing my hormones into overdrive.

He shrugs out of his jacket and I scramble to lift his shirt, but his hands wrap around my wrists.

"We don't have to rush," he says.

"Maybe I want to rush," I whine.

He chuckles, and my core throbs as his teeth pull on my earlobe. "I've waited two years to touch you the way I want," he whispers. "I'll be damned if I blow this."

Slow hands skim up my sides, his touch feather-light and scorching. My brain is fuzzy, drunk on the anticipation. Every inch of my skin is extra sensitive, and my nipples harden to the point of pain.

He pushes my shirt up to just below my breasts and kisses from my sternum to my waist. "Joel—" I pant as his hair tickles my exposed skin.

"How do you like to be touched?" he asks before his tongue circles my belly button.

My pussy throbs, and I'm suddenly speechless. I'm not sure how to answer. "All I know is I want more of this."

"Do you have condoms?"

My eyes fly open. *Shit.* "You don't?"

There's a small drop in his face, then he shakes his head. "I didn't think . . ."

I close my eyes and sigh, my head falling back on the bed, defeated. Figures. This would be just my luck. Here's my chance, and now it can't happen because of something I should've prepared for. But I'm not a stupid girl anymore, I'm not willing to chance unprotected sex, even if I am crazy about him.

He kisses along my jaw again and it feels so good it's almost cruel. "Joel, we can't."

"You're right," he says, his lips everywhere. "We can't have sex . . . but that doesn't mean I can't make you come."

And then he's descending upon my mouth with ravenous hunger. His tongue explores mine as I pull his shirt higher and higher until he breaks away, ripping it off and sending it to the floor with his jacket. He leans toward me, but I push him back. I want to stare at his body. *Need* to. His torso is covered in tattoos. Every kind of devilish ghoul and monstrous demon inked into his beautiful tanned skin. How paradoxical, that this sweet and gentle man is covered in such nightmares. But then I guess we all are— mine are just invisible.

"You're so beautiful," I say as my fingers trail down the image of a cobra on his ribs.

A wide grin spreads across his face, and the next thing I know he's rolling us over so I'm on top of him, my legs straddling his waist and my hair falling haphazardly around us.

"Your turn," he says with the rise of an eyebrow. He pulls my shirt up and up, and I bite my lip as the fabric is tossed somewhere across my small apartment. My breasts are heavy and sensitive as his thumbs brush along the underside of my lacy bra cups.

"They're even better than I remember," he admits, his eyes wide and glued to my chest.

I reach around and unhook my bra with a snap, letting the straps fall as my breasts are slowly revealed. He groans, his eyes squinting shut before he wraps his arms around me and smothers his face in my chest.

A memory of the first time we met comes back to me. How he buried his face then, how it seemed to bring him some kind of peace. I gently trace his shoulder blades, feeling it now like I did then—the tension easing off of him.

"Feel better?" I ask.

He nods against me. "Much. Fuck, you're so perfect." He looks up and grasps my face, pulling me into another earth-shattering kiss. As my hips settle, I can feel him. Unmistakable hardness that has my stomach clenching and my pulse throbbing between my legs.

I might not be able to have it all today . . . but maybe I could have a taste.

He releases my face to take a breath, and I push him back against the bed, taking my time to kiss along his jaw. He reaches for me, but I push his hands down into the sheets, the rumble of his groan vibrating through me as I suck on his neck.

Slowly, slowly, slowly I begin to kiss a path down, along his collarbone, his chest, taking my time to revel in the hard muscles. His body tenses as my tongue wets the skin of his abs.

"Shit," he whispers.

"Is this okay?" I ask, my fingers finding the button of his jeans.

He props himself up on his elbows as I kneel between his legs.

"I think you tricked me," he says with a grin. "Pretty sure I intended to get in your pants first."

I laugh and pop the button on his jeans. "You can take care of me after I suck your cock."

Suddenly, he's sitting up, grabbing me by the arms and flipping me over onto my back again. "Not acceptable. It's you first or us together."

My eyes widen, and a flash of mischief streaks through his eyes when I catch his meaning. Heat floods my cheeks and he smirks devilishly before snagging my bottom lip with his teeth.

A sharp gasp escapes my lips and I'm so keyed up it won't take much to get me off right now. His fingers hook into my shorts, making quick work of pulling them down along with my underwear. I wait in breathless anticipation as he sits on his heels to finish undoing his pants, his gaze heavy.

"You look so good underneath me," he says.

"Damn, Joel, maybe you should get a job with me," I tease.

He laughs and kicks off his pants, pushing his boxers down to release his perfect cock, standing hard and dripping before me. We're still for a moment before he slowly strokes himself up and down. I swallow hard, then crawl up to my hands and knees to look up at him.

"I want to taste you in the back of my throat."

With a visible shudder, his eyes darken and a hunger I've yet to see takes over.

"You can choke on my cock, Dusty, but not unless you're riding my face."

In a flash he's turning and lying down, his head next to my knees before he lifts one of my legs over him, my pussy hovering an inch from his mouth. Without any warning, he grasps my thighs and pulls me down.

"Oh god," I cry as his tongue finds my clit, impressed by not only this man's desire to go down on me, but for doing it so enthusiastically. His tongue swirls and swirls, and I'm sure I'm so wet right now that I'm dripping on his face. The sounds he makes with his mouth are sinful, and I suddenly worry he might not be able to breathe. I move to lift myself up, but he only grabs me tighter.

"Just worried you might suffocate," I say through moans of delicious pleasure.

A smack comes down on my ass. Not hard enough to hurt but sharp enough to make my whole body clench.

"If that's how I go," he murmurs, each word spoken into my most sensitive spot, "then I've truly lived up to my rockstar potential. Now sit on my fucking face, gorgeous."

He pulls me again, and I can't fight it. I need his tongue on me. I need to feel him in my mouth. Bending forward, I grasp his dripping cock and tease the tip with my tongue. His leg twitches as I swirl around the head, my brain trying to focus as pleasure rips through me. I continue, and his tongue halts, a deep moan radiating through him as I swallow him down to the base.

"Fuck." He pauses, gives the flesh at my thigh a punishing squeeze. "Your mouth is so goddamn hot. I knew it would be. Knew it would be the best I've ever had."

With a hiss, he smacks my ass again, this time a little harder, and it stings so good as his tongue finds my clit again, mixing the pleasure and pain together.

I hum around his cock, bobbing up and down as his hips start to gently rock us back and forth. Fuck, this is so hot. My pussy throbs and clenches desperately, and I almost miss the intimate pressure against my back entrance.

I lift myself up, his cock making a loud *pop* as I try to identify the strange feeling.

"Tell me to stop if you need to," he says, and it finally clicks together. He's pressing his thumb against my asshole.

"I—ahh . . . umm," I mumble, but the pressure of his finger and the skill of his tongue together has my thighs shaking on either side of his head. "No," I breathe. "Don't—don't stop."

He pulls me back tight to his face and I can't concentrate anymore. I absently stroke his cock as his tongue flicks and swirls, his thumb pressing gently inside of me. My hips rock and I realize I'm riding his face like a mechanical bull. My legs go numb all the way to my toes, and an animalistic moan erupts from my throat as I come.

I'm still trying to catch my breath as Joel's hips rock into my hand with a sudden frenzy, and a moment later, he groans, cum spilling over my hand and his stomach. My body is limp as I roll off of him, and I stare up at the ceiling as I try to catch my breath. His hand reaches for mine over the sheets and I smile from the contact.

"You okay?" he rasps, thumb gently rubbing over my knuckles.

I close my eyes and nod. "Yes, I—yeah . . ."

He chuckles deeply, then the bed shifts as he stands. "Be right back," he says.

I place my hand over my racing heart and can't help but giggle. Holy shit, that was insane. I haven't come like that . . . maybe ever. After a few minutes, Joel reappears and sits down on the edge of my bed, gently wiping up my thighs with a warm washcloth. He's pulled his hair up in a knot on top of his head. When he's done, he discards the cloth and lies down naked in the bed next to me.

"I didn't push you too far, did I?" he asks, pulling my head to rest on his arm while he plays with my hair.

I shake my head. "No, that was incredible. If the foreplay is that good, then the sex might kill me."

His laugh is breathless. "I don't know if you're ready for the full extent of what I can do to you."

I turn onto my stomach and smirk. "That sounds like a challenge."

"Not really, it's just that some find my preferences a little outside of their wheelhouse."

"Oh?" My heart starts to race. "You're not about to tell me you're into feet or pee, are you?"

He chuckles. "Oh no, although you do have gorgeous feet and if you asked me to, I'd happily suck on them."

I shiver as his hand trails down over my hip, then over my ass to grip under my thigh as he pulls it over himself.

"I just prefer having anal sex."

I blink, my lips parting, and my stomach clenches as I remember him pressing his thumb inside me. "Oh."

He continues to gently rub circles on my butt cheek. "Don't get me wrong, I like having sex the normal way too. I don't know, there's just something about it. Making you come earlier with my finger in your ass—it's just so fucking hot. I came with you barely even touching me."

"I've never experimented back there before," I admit, "but considering I came all over your face, you may have convinced me to consider it."

He laughs. "I know mostly people are afraid of it because they think it'll hurt, but I promise that if you're willing to try, I'll go slow and make it feel incredible."

My eyes search his face, something in me knowing that he's being totally serious. I trust that he'd make it worth my time.

"But if you don't want to. I'm okay with that too."

I take a deep breath and offer my coyest smile. "I'll think about it."

He raises his eyebrows. "Really? You will?"

"Yeah. But you best believe I'll expect the biggest morning-after breakfast as a thank-you."

His laugh echoes through my apartment and fills me with joy. "You got it." He squeezes me to him and kisses my forehead, pulling the sheets up overtop of us. And there, wrapped in his arms, I feel like someone who's unafraid to be myself.

CHAPTER 22

(It Looks Like) I'll Never Fall in Love Again

KEY

EIGHT YEARS AGO

"Hey, Dusty, so I was thinking that maybe I—Dusty?"

When I enter our cabin in the woods it takes me less than ten seconds to realize something's wrong. Dusty sits on the couch staring straight ahead. In the years I've known her, I would think she's maybe watching a movie, but the TV is only static and her face isn't alight like it is when she's watching something special.

"Hey," I say again, dropping my bag on the floor and stepping toward her. "Are you okay?"

As I get closer, I can see the tear tracks that stain her face.

I drop to my haunches, grasping her hands between mine. "What's wrong?"

She doesn't look at me, and my brain trips over itself. Did her dad get out of prison? Did her mom come back? Is she leaving me again?

"Dusty, please," I beg.

She blinks, tears falling over her dark lashes. "Key," she whispers.

"I'm here," I say. "What happened? Why are you crying?"

Finally, she turns, and there's pure anguish behind her normally brilliant blue eyes. Her lips part for a moment, then she closes them. I watch impatiently as she collects herself.

"I—I just got back from the doctor," she says. "I haven't been feeling well, and . . ."

My stomach sinks. Is she sick? What if she has cancer? She's been a touch paler recently. More tired. Not eating as much.

My lips are as dry as the dessert when I ask, "What did the doctor say?"

She looks up at the ceiling then, takes a deep breath and looks away. "I'm pregnant."

There's a buzzing in my ears. The ground I'm kneeling on seems to tip sideways, and I have to grasp onto the couch so I don't fall over. "You're . . . you're what?"

She reaches next to her and produces a white envelope torn open at the top. Handing it to me, I remove the letter from inside and read, but the words and numbers jumble on the page and I can't make sense of it.

"Dusty, I don't know what this means."

She sniffles loudly, then traces her finger down to the bottom. "See there? This means positive. I'm pregnant."

That's when the tears really start, as if she's only just convinced herself of the truth by explaining it to me. She sobs and sobs, and I toss the letter aside to avoid the onslaught of tears destroying it. On instinct I scoot between her knees and pull her against me. She buries her face in the crook of my neck and grips my shirt—the fabric soaking through. And all I can do is try to comfort her. I stroke her hair and shush her, all the while my brain is spinning like a hurricane, unable to comprehend anything.

After a while, her sobs start to subside and my brain slows.

Anger floods me. Not with her, but at myself. How stupid could I have been not to realize what we were doing could result in this? I remember that one time in health class when they talked to us about birth control. I should have known this would happen. I probably would have, if I'd waited until marriage like I was supposed to. Then I would've been old enough to know.

"Key," Dusty finally whispers. "What am I going to do?

I frown. "You?"

She blinks up at me. "I—"

"We're in this together," I tell her. "I'm not leaving you alone."

She holds my gaze for a moment, then nods. "Okay, what are *we* going to do?"

I know I should be terrified and angry and sad, and I am, but I bury those things deep down because I don't want to scare her. My biggest concern is taking care of her, like I always do. Her and . . . our baby.

"I'm going to take care of you. Both of you."

She shakes her head. "No, they'll never support it. Your parents hate me, and I have no one . . . They'll force me to give up the baby, I know it. They'll send me away or I'll end up on the streets with nothing."

I clench my jaw at the unfairness of it all, because I know she's right.

"Then we'll run away."

She frowns. "What?"

"We'll go. We'll just get on a bus and never look back. We always planned to do it anyway, it'll just be earlier than expected. We can go to California and we can get jobs to save money until the baby comes. We can find a place to live, we can even get married when we turn eighteen. I'll take care of you, Dusty."

She presses her lips together and looks away, shaking her head. "But what about music? And acting? What about our plan?"

she asks. "There was so much we wanted to do, and now? It's ruined. It'll be so hard. Life will be impossible. And your parents . . . if they find out about the baby, they'll never let you see me again."

I shake my head. "To hell with my parents!"

Her fingers fly to her mouth, and it hits us both that I've just cursed for the first time in my life. It's freeing, like an anvil has been lifted off my chest.

"To hell with my parents and everyone else in this god-forsaken town. You're the only one I care about—the only reason I have dreams in the first place is because of you. You're the only one I love."

"Really?"

I nod. "Really. We can start our own family. We can make it work."

A shy smile pulls at her lips. "I'm going to get huge."

I shrug. "Just more of you to love."

"The baby is going to cry all the time," she counters.

"Maybe it will like my music and your movies."

"We're going to have to grow up."

I kiss the tip of her nose. "If that means spending the rest of my life with you and our child, then I'm ready."

She laughs breathlessly, but more tears leak from the corners of her eyes anyway. "But what about our plans?"

I cup her face. "We'll just have to make new plans. One day, we'll get what we want. We'll just have to take a little detour first." I'm sure of this, sure of *her*. "It's going to be okay. I'm going to take care of us."

She wipes her nose and I'm relieved to see the tiniest hint of a smile. "You'll save me, Key?"

I smile back. "We'll save each other."

"DID YOU GET A BUS SCHEDULE?" Dusty whispers through the phone.

I nod, even though she can't see me. "Yeah, I got it today. The earlier bus to California is on Thursday," I whisper back. My neck is sore from constantly looking over my shoulder for my parents. It's after midnight now—the only safe time I could call Dusty to finalize our plan. But if my parents overhear me . . .

"Are you sure you want to do this?" she asks.

"Dusty, I've already told you—"

"I know you have." She sighs. "I also don't think you understand what you're agreeing to."

I frown and lean against the wall. "What do you mean? Of course I understand."

"Your whole life is going to change because of this."

"Maybe that's what I want," I insist, pressing my lips into the receiver. "Plus, I'll finally be able to wear the necklace you gave me."

"Key," she says into the phone. "It's okay to admit you're scared. I'm scared too. Actually, I'm terrified. You can tell me."

She's always known me better than I know myself. It's true. *Terrified* is the word. And panicked and anxious and guilty and so many others. But I'm also excited. This baby is a chance to escape the cycle of what I've grown up in. What she's grown up in. "We're going to be amazing parents, Dusty. You'll see. We can do it."

"Right."

Her voice sounds far away. Unsure. Is she having doubts?

"So, Thursday at seven," I say, double-checking the schedule again. "My father has a church elder meeting that night and my mom is supposed to go to her bible study group a few blocks away. My brother will be home, but he won't even notice I'm gone."

There's silence on the other end. I push aside the stack of bills on the counter, making sure the phone didn't get disconnected. "Dusty?"

"Yes. Sorry. I'm here."

"I'll see you soon. Okay?"

"Okay."

"I love you." My voice is louder when I say it. Not intentionally, but because I never want to love her quietly. I never want to whisper it, unless it's in her ear while she's wrapped up in my arms. I never want her to think it's not real.

I'VE STUFFED as much as I possibly can inside this bag. Shirts, underwear, my church suit for job interviews—I can barely get the zipper closed. My parents are out so I know it's the best time to leave. They'll notice eventually that I'm gone, then find the note on my desk explaining why I had to leave; the last thing I want is for them to send out a search party.

But once they know it's because Dusty's pregnant, they won't say anything. I'm sure of it. It would be too shameful. Next to the letter is the test results from Dusty's doctor. She finally explained to me what everything meant and even though it's just a piece of paper, I feel as if my entire future is connected to its existence. How could such an inconsequential thing like words on paper change my whole life? I stare at it again, and can't help but imagine where I'll be nine months from now.

Dusty will be a mother. I'll be a father. And we'll have a beautiful baby girl, or maybe a boy. Will they have her red hair? Her freckles? Will they get my hazel eyes or her sapphire blue ones? One thing is for sure though, I won't raise them how Dusty and I were. We may have nothing, no money, no house, no car— but this baby will know love. Real love. Just like Dusty has always wished for.

I fold up the test paper and put it in the back pocket of my jeans. I hoist the heavy duffel over my shoulder and grab my guitar case. Opening the top drawer of my desk, I reach for Dusty's sun necklace but it's not there. My hand rifles through papers and old textbooks and pencils, but . . . *Where is it?* I drop my bag and guitar case and open the rest of the drawers. Panic starts to rise in my throat. No, I can't have lost it. It has to be here. I put it here, making sure it was covered so no one would find it.

I check the clock on my wall—6:34. I'm running out of time; I need to make a decision. If I unpack my whole bag I'll be late. If I don't . . . No. I must have packed it and forgotten. Where else could it possibly be? Short of tipping the drawers upside down, I do one last sweep of the desk, and with one final look around my bedroom, I grab my things and shut the door behind me, taking each stair down slowly, careful not to make a sound.

Only, the living room isn't quiet like I expected it to be. I stash my guitar case behind the clock in the hallway as my mother comes into view.

"Keith, good, I need help with getting those folding chairs from the basement."

My mouth opens then shuts, as if my brain can't compute this hiccup in my plan. I look past her at the dozen or so ladies standing around in our living room. Oh no. They were supposed to be down the street. What's going on?

"Keith!" my mother says with thinly veiled irritation. "The chairs, Keith." She claps her hands then pushes me along the hallway toward the basement. I glance back longingly at the door, my bags just out of sight. The basement door opens and I robotically step down into the darkness. Okay. Okay, this is fine. I'll do this quickly, then when my mom is distracted by her friends, I'll sneak out the front door.

Of course, though, it's not just the chairs. She needs my help escorting Mrs. Mason to the bathroom. Needs me to serve drinks. Needs me to put the meatballs on a platter.

How can I possibly get out of here? I can't say no or it'll tip her off. But my mother seems to have something else for me to do before I've even finished the last job. And all the while, the minutes tick by on the clock by the front door. Twenty, thirty, fifty minutes.

I'm sweating. Surely Dusty will wait for me. She'll know I've been held up. It's almost eight o'clock now, and my heart is filled with so much dread. We were going to catch the seven o'clock bus but it'll be gone now. *Breathe, Key.* It's not a lost cause. We can take another bus. Any bus. Just somewhere away from here and figure it out later. I can't stay another minute. This has to work!

"Thank you, dear," my mother says with a smile. "You must have homework to do now, isn't that right?"

Her friends are watching me intently. "I . . . yes, but . . . you know, I think I'm going to get some fresh air first. Just for a few minutes."

She holds my gaze for a long moment and something sharp turns in my stomach. Does she know? How could she? But then she turns back to her friends with a grin. "Ladies, shall we get started on that fifth passage? Salvation waits for no one."

I sigh, my shoulders dropping from my ears for the first time all night, and once I'm sure she's occupied, I grab my bag and guitar case, and I *run*. My limbs burn from the exertion the whole way there, but imagining Dusty waiting in the terminal only makes me move faster.

I drop everything by the ticket house when I arrive, my breath coming out in great white puffs on the window. "Excuse me? Hello?"

When the ticket girl approaches, she eyes me nervously. "Can I help you?"

"Yes, was there a red-haired girl here? Freckles. Long legs?"

She shrugs and pops her gum. "I'm not sure."

Okay, Key, keep it together. You can find her. You can do this. Just stay calm. "Are you sure you can't remember?"

"Sorry, I was printing tickets in the back. No one's rung the bell until you showed up. Maybe she got a taxi?"

I suck in a shuddering breath. "Okay. Okay . . . thanks."

She didn't leave. There's no way. Yeah, I'm late, but she must know I'd have an excuse. I'm only an hour past our meeting time. I circle the terminal, but there's hardly anyone here. Maybe she went to get some food, or use the bathroom. But after three laps and twenty minutes have passed, I confirm she's not here.

Where would she have gone? What if something happened? What if something's wrong with the baby, and she went to the hospital? What if—what if she left to come find me? Part of me wants to head back home, intercept her . . . but maybe it's better I stay here. She'll realize I left home late and head right back here and everything will be okay.

So, I wait, glancing at the clock every few minutes, my eyes trained on the glass doors just as often, waiting for the fiery girl I love so much to appear there. An insurmountable anxiousness spreads through me with every minute that passes me by. Other buses come, the previous passengers disembarking, and I keep my eyes peeled.

But she's not here.

An hour of panic feels like a lifetime, and before my very eyes, the dream of escaping grows smaller and smaller. Something bad must have happened. What if she got in an accident? What if she's sick?

But there's a worse reason pushing its way forward: What if she truly believed I wasn't coming?

A flash of headlights blinds me, and my heart jumps as I think maybe it's her, that maybe she got a ride. But then my stomach turns to lead as my parent's car pulls up in front of me.

"Keith," my mother calls through the passenger window. "Get in the car."

I cross my arms and shake my head. "No."

"Keith, get in the car," my father yells.

Does he not understand that it won't work? I'm not afraid of them anymore. The thought of that tiny life growing in the woman I love gives me more strength than I ever thought possible.

"I'm leaving with Dusty," I say. "And we're never coming back."

To my surprise, they don't yell anymore, in fact, they look . . . sad. Is it possible that my leaving has finally prompted them to be loving parents? The engine shuts off and my mother opens her door.

"Come home, dear. She's not coming."

I back away, fighting against the dread of the past hour. "No! No, she's coming. I was late but she knows I'd never leave her . . . she'll be here."

"Darling . . ." my mother says in a voice I've never heard before. Then she holds out a white envelope to me and my heart thuds in my chest. "She dropped this off at the house for you."

The envelope isn't sealed, and for one horrible moment I realize my parents know all my darkest secrets, but they're here anyway to bring me home. To bring me this. I snatch it from my mother's hand, pausing at its weight. I upturn the envelope and something small tumbles out onto my palm.

The guitar string ring I made her.

The ring I gave her with the promise to love her forever.

The ring she returned because she couldn't accept that promise.

And as it sits heavy in my hand, it's as if the weight of the world collapses on top of me. The envelope shakes in my hands and my vision blurs—so obscured by tears that I can't see. I cry, like a newborn baby, sobbing at the bus station, until my mother's arms wrap around me. I take a breath, hanging on to her, and squeeze her tight, as though she's the only thing keeping me from falling apart completely.

She strokes my hair and shushes me, her voice unnaturally gentle. "Come on, dearest. Come home."

And because I don't know what else to do, I nod and get in the back seat while my father grabs my bags and tosses them in the trunk.

The car ride home is silent. My brain is whirring, throbbing against my temples. There is nothing but pain in my chest. My lungs. Every square inch of me. As if my heart has shattered into a thousand tiny pieces. I thought she wanted me. I thought we were going to be a family. And the baby . . . But she had doubts. Didn't I hear it in her voice over the phone two nights ago? She wasn't sure. She tried to talk me out of it. Was I more ready than her? I thought she loved me. Loved us. But maybe I've just ignored a truth that's been there all along and I chose never to see. That I always loved her more. It's why she never stayed. Why she didn't fight to be with me.

She loves me less.

She loves me only a little.

She doesn't love me at all.

Tears spill down my cheeks so intensely that I barely register the black van in the driveway when we get home. Nor do I notice the men in white uniforms that approach me until they've grasped my arms so tight I instinctively try to fight them off. I frantically look to my parents, to my brother's horrified face as he watches from his bedroom window upstairs.

"Mom! Dad!" I cry out.

But they simply stand and watch as I'm dragged into the back of the windowless van.

"It's for your own good, dear," my mother says.

Their faces have lost the compassion I saw fleetingly at the bus station. It was all an act, and I was stupid enough to fall for it. Apparently, everyone in my life is an award-winning actor. My parents. Dusty. How could I have been so stupid not to see through it all?

The doors of the van slam shut, then everything is black. I hardly care what happens to me anymore. This van could take me to my death and I would welcome it, because she left me behind again.

She left me behind knowing that I loved her more than anything.

CHAPTER 23

Goodbye Stranger

DUSTY

"I've missed you so much, sweetheart. Come here. Baby will make you feel so much better."

My eyes shoot open when my alarm goes off, the sky outside my window is pink and orange, the sun setting behind wispy purple clouds. I groan, dreading having to go to work, wishing I could just stay in bed. The subtle weight of an arm around my body anchors me, the breath against my neck comforting, and I sink a little deeper under the sheets. The warm sheets . . .

Oh god.

Joel stirs beside me, and I'm sick with guilt. After everything he's said and done for me, I'm still dreaming of my faceless stranger?

I squeeze my eyes shut trying to erase the way Baby's voice makes me feel. I focus on my feelings for Joel, and after a few minutes it works. Joel is the one for me—my infatuation with Baby is just that. *Infatuation.* And I need to be rid of it.

I roll over to face Joel, and I watch his face perfectly at peace before I disturb him.

"Joel?" I say. "Joel, wake up."

He groans and squeezes me tighter.

"Joel," I repeat with a laugh. "Come on, I have to get ready for work."

"Take the day off," he says against my skin.

"You know I can't do that. I have bills to pay."

He finally opens his eyes, focusing on my face. "I can help you with that. If you're struggling to make ends meet, I can—"

"Shhh," I say, pressing my finger to his lips. "I'm not a damsel in distress, and while I don't particularly love working, it's life. I'm more than capable of surviving on my own."

He nods. "I know. I know you are. All I'm saying is that if you ever need help—"

"I don't need your help!"

He freezes, his hands lifting off of me. Overcome with shame, I bite my lip. *Don't screw this up, Dusty. Get a hold of yourself.*

"I'm sorry," I whisper. "I don't . . . I just mean that I can take care of myself."

I close my eyes and turn away, waiting for him to stand, get dressed, and leave—never to darken my doorway again. But he gently caresses my neck, presses a kiss there.

"I know you can," he whispers against my skin. "I shouldn't have suggested it. I just didn't want to let you go."

I look up, and our eyes meet over my bare, freckled shoulder. "I know," I whisper. "I'm sorry."

He shakes his head. "Don't be. You have nothing to be sorry for."

We smile at each other, and with a kiss to my nose, he sits up in bed and stands to locate his clothes from this morning. I watch him dress, my eyes glued to his gorgeous, toned body. I pull on a satin robe from a nearby chair and drink a glass of water as he gathers up his things to leave.

"When can I see you next?" he asks as I meet him at my door.

I shrug. "How soon do you want to?"

"Tomorrow?"

I grin. "How about I call you when I know when I'm working next. I'd hate for our time to get cut short again."

He nods. "Yeah, okay. I need to talk to the guys anyway. Things are—well, they might get more complicated before they get better."

"Okay."

He grasps my face and plants a kiss on my lips that warms me deep into my bones.

"I'll see you soon," he says, opening the door.

I smile and nod. "See you soon."

He disappears down the stairs, and I close the door behind me, sinking back against it. An ear-splitting grin pulls at my cheeks. There are butterflies in my stomach, and I am *giddy*. Should I call him now? Leave him a message for when he gets home? Will he think I'm crazy?

Stella meows from the floor and winds herself between my legs. "Hey, pretty girl. Hope you didn't mind that we had a visitor." I pick her up and snuggle her in my arms. "He's amazing, right? Tell me you like him too." She meows, and I kiss the top of her head before dropping her on the floor and grabbing her a can of food for dinner.

"This might be it," I whisper. "Tell me I'm not crazy for giving this a shot."

She stares pointedly at my hand until I tip her food onto a plate.

"You're no help," I mutter.

I turn on the radio so I can listen to music while I shower. The voice of Eartha Kitt fills my apartment as I strip down then step into the hot water. There's instantaneous relief as the water cascades over me. The music is dull in the background, but it's gentle and calming. Even though I said—or rather insisted—that I could take care of myself, I imagine what my life might be like a month from now. A year. Ten years.

I haven't had the luxury of that in so long. Not since I was seventeen and thought I had my whole future planned out. An old wound in my heart smarts, and I clutch at my chest as I stand still under the water. Perhaps it'll finally wash away the hurt—it's been duller lately. Maybe that's because of Joel. Because he's given me a reason to believe in second chances.

A strange sound comes from the stereo, and over the noise of the water it's hard to make out. I strain my ears for a minute, the melody oddly familiar. It's metal music again. Did Stella change the radio station? I'm going to have to get that cat a spiked leather collar if she keeps this up. Even though it isn't my first choice, I listen to the rock melody as I finish washing my hair, the song ending when I turn off the water.

"—from Carnal Sins," the radio host says, and I nearly trip over the towel as I race to open the door. Running out into the living room, I halt in front of the speakers. "The band's found themselves in a little hot water lately with an impending copyright infringement lawsuit. Hopefully everything gets sorted out for them soon."

Another song begins to play and I stab at the off button with my finger.

"Do they really have to say that on the radio for everyone to hear?" I ask Stella, who is guiltily sitting on top of the stereo. But the song from earlier is stuck in my head. Like déjà vu . . . or a lullaby a parent would sing to their sleeping child. Only, my parents never did that, so what's this odd feeling?

A boy with hazel eyes and brown hair smiles back at me out of the dark pool of memories in my mind. My eyes blur, and it takes a few moments to realize I'm crying. Salty tears drip down my cheeks, landing on my lips and dripping off my chin. As if surfacing from underwater, I inhale a gigantic breath, the exhale shuddering out of me.

Glancing over at the mirror, I take in my swollen face and red eyes. I poke at the inflamed skin, then my eyes land on my left hand. On the empty space of my ring finger. It's always felt strange. Like phantom pains after an amputation. I touch the spot with my other hand, and a shiver races up my spine. To think that at one point in my life a ring sat here. A ring that meant everything. The promise of a happier future where I would have a home and a family of my own to love—where they would love me back.

But promises are broken all the time.

I shake out my hands. It's time to move on. Joel has shown me such care, affection, and patience that I'm sure, given the time it needs, will grow into love. If I'm honest with myself, I'm already halfway there. Maybe he will give me a ring one day with a better promise. So I need to give him everything I can of myself, which means letting go of my past.

"Time to let you go," I whisper, imagining those hazel eyes receding into the darkness. This time when I look up into the mirror, I feel lighter—free. "Enough," I say to the empty room. "Enough."

I WALK into the nondescript building for work tonight, determined. I need to let Baby know that he can't call me again. That there are a dozen other women I work with who would happily take his calls. In fact, they may even give him a better service than me, since they're more experienced. But after nine phone calls and several cups of coffee, Baby still hasn't called.

To be fair, I don't know his schedule—it's possible he's busy, or working, or, hell, at two in the morning, he's probably sleeping.

Yet something in my bones makes me sure he'll call. Call it intuition or instinct, but when line seven lights up red, I know it's him even before I pick up the phone.

"Hi, this is Cherry, who do I have the pleasure of speaking with tonight?"

"Hey, sweetheart."

My entire body breaks out in goose bumps. "Hi, Baby," I say, and relax into my chair.

"I've missed the sound of your voice," he says.

"You have?"

"I dream about it," he admits.

"I dream about you too," I say. "And . . ." It's now or never. "Therein lies the problem."

There's a pause on the other end of the line. "The problem?"

I look over my shoulder, ensuring I won't be overheard. If management found out I was turning away paying customers, I'd definitely get fired. "I can't take your calls anymore."

"Oh," he says, "Are you . . . quitting?"

"No . . . yes . . . I don't know," I confess, biting into my lip. "It's complicated."

"Complicated," he states. It's not a question.

"I'm sorry," I say.

Another pause. "Did I do something wrong? Did I . . . make you feel uncomfortable?"

"No! No, you didn't. It's not that. Actually it's the opposite."

"What do you mean?"

I take a big breath. "You're not like the others. There's something about you, when you call. Like I've known you my whole life."

There's silence on the other end of the line.

"And that's a problem, because I'm falling in love with someone in real life. With any other caller it's just work, but with you—it's emotional. It's real. And I can't . . . It feels like cheating."

Another long silence fills the space between us. Have I've misread everything that's happened between us?

"Your voice . . ." he says quietly. "It sounds like music."

For the second time today, tears fill my eyes. I look up to try to keep them contained.

"It reminds me of someone I knew a long, long time ago."

I drop my forehead onto my desk, fighting the urge to sob. I *do* mean something to him. Whatever this is between us, I'm not alone—he wanted to love me too.

"This person," I ask. "Were they someone you lost?"

He sighs into the speaker and my heart aches. "It feels as though I lose her every day. Every time I wake up and realize she's not here, I feel like it's happening all over again."

I bite my lip. "I'm so sorry."

"I used to be able to drown it out. Drinking, drugs, girls, partying . . . but lately, I just can't. The only thing that's helped . . . is you."

I'm an awful person. Here is this poor broken-hearted man who simply wants to talk to me because I remind him of his long-lost love, and I'm about to make him lose someone else as well.

"Listen, Baby, I—" I take a deep breath.

"We can't talk anymore," he cuts me off.

"No."

"I'm sorry."

I shake my head. "No, no, don't be sorry. It's my fault, not yours."

"You know, it's funny. I called the first time for fun, trying to take the edge off of being alone. I didn't realize how quickly I'd fall for a stranger," he admits. "I guess it just goes to show how desperate I was for an honest conversation with someone. Maybe

. . . maybe I need to have more honest conversations with the people who are already in my life."

"I know it doesn't help, but I looked forward to our calls. I . . . if my life was different, I would've one day asked to meet you in person. Maybe this would've transcended the phone lines."

"Yeah," he whispers.

"But I can't live like this anymore. Can't be stuck between two half lives. Not when I deserve to live one that's whole. Complete. Do you understand what I mean?"

I can practically see him nodding. "Yes. I do . . . more than you think."

"I hope you find what you're looking for," I say gently.

He hums into the phone and the vibration shoots through me.

"And I hope you've found the kind of love worth risking everything for."

The phone disconnects, and I place the receiver back on the holder as though lost in time. Then I gather the few personal items I've kept at my desk, throw them in my bag, and walk out the door with no plan to ever come back.

CHAPTER 24

Bad to the Bone

JOEL

"What the fuck is taking so long?" Dave mutters from the leather seat in the waiting area.

James shrugs. "Lawyers charge by the hour. Probably make us sit here for longer than necessary just to bill us for it later."

My nail picks at the cording on the leather chair I'm sitting in. Part of me is back in that apartment above The Sudsy Dream and the other is terrified that One-Punch Logan is going to win this case.

"And there's been no word from him? Nothing?" Dave asks, leaning forward in his chair to stare at me.

"Oh, how silly of me. Yes, Dave, I forgot to mention that he called this morning." Dave frowns. "Told me he was . . .what did he say? Oh right, he was taking over production at Willy Wonka's Chocolate Factory."

Dave rolls his eyes. "Oh, fuck off."

James looks over. "Is that necessary?"

My fingers abandon the chair, and I start picking at the nail bed of my left hand. "Seemed it was to me. Or have you both forgotten that I've spent the better part of forty-eight hours searching for him?"

"You're the one who knows him the best," Dave stresses. "And you mean to tell me that you have no idea where he would have run away to?"

The idea that I don't know my best friend as well as I thought I did stings. Like suffering a deep papercut only to squeeze lemon juice on it. Biting and sharp.

"Look," James interjects before I can tell Dave to fuck off, "for all we know, he knows exactly how to prove the songs are his. He'll waltz in here, and this will be over in an hour."

As if to prove him dead wrong, a young woman in a skirt and blazer approaches us in the lobby. "Excuse me, gentlemen, we're ready for you now."

The three of us jump to our feet and adjust our awkward suits. Al insisted we dress appropriately and while everything inside of me is screaming of discomfort, I know it's for the best. We've spent too much of our lives being treated like deadbeat losers for how we look at first glance. The tattoos on James and I alone usually have women like this pretty brunette clutching their pearls.

We follow along down the wide wood-paneled hallway until we reach a large door. The woman pushes it open and gestures for us to go inside. One step in the door and my body is rigid with anger. One-Punch Logan sits, looking unfortunately suave, in a tailored suit flanked on either side by who I assume are his overpriced lawyers.

"Gentlemen, please come in," says an older man with shockingly white hair. He sits at the end of a long conference table next to Al, who's wearing a grim look on his face. His lawyer, who we've met on several different occasions throughout our music career, gives us a nod from where he sits at our manager's side.

We take our seats in the leather swivel chairs, and I make the conscious choice not to look at the traitor across the table. His eyes are on me, I can feel it. I know he hates me. Hated me from the first moment we met. Hated how Key became closer to me and cut him out of the band.

Good. Because I hate him too.

Not because he ever did anything specifically awful to me directly, but because of how he hurt my friend. He was always a jealous leech and I saw right through him. And now, sitting across from me, he's determined to suck the life out of all of us because he knows he'd never become anything without it.

"Right," says the man with white hair. "I'm Judge Horowath and we're here today to discuss the claim of one Mr. Samuels against the members of musical talent, Carnal Sins, for copyright infringement on seven songs, as outlined below."

He lists off the songs—the only songs on both our EP and LP albums that Key was the sole songwriter.

"Are all the members of Carnal Sins present?" Judge Horowath asks.

Al stares down at me with disappointment etched on his face as I shake my head. "No, sir. Keith Prentiss is not here today."

The judge frowns and looks down at the list again. "Mr. Prentiss is the sole songwriter listed on the tracks in question, is that correct?"

One of the lawyers next to Logan speaks up. "Yes, that's correct."

"I see," he says, then turns back to us. "Is there any particular reason that Mr. Prentiss has chosen not to attend today's hearing?"

Dave and James give me a look like *Take the wheel, man*, and I clear my throat. "It would seem he has gone missing."

"Missing?"

I nod. "We've tried to locate him, but even after searching far and wide, we haven't been—"

"What I think my client means to say," Al's lawyer jumps in, "is that the stress of these proceedings has caused significant impacts to my client's mental state. It is possible that he has put himself in danger because he is distraught over the betrayal of a past friend."

"More like he's drinking himself stupid in an alley somewhere," Logan stage-whispers.

At this, I look up, my eyes meeting Logan's, and my whole body crackles with fury. He sits back, a smirk on his lips. He wanted everyone to hear that—*wants* the judge to think Key's a liar and an addict.

"Well, we shall have to proceed without him for the time being," the judge says, opening up the file in front of him. "Mr. Samuels, I apologize, but since I am unfamiliar with this kind of music, and your relationship with the band and its members, could you provide me with your account of your involvement with the band and the creation of these songs."

"Wait," Logan starts, glancing around the table. "We're not doing this in a courtroom? With, like, a jury?"

The judge sighs and lowers his glasses. "Mr. Samuels, this is simply a preliminary inquiry to determine if there is enough evidence to take this to trial. We don't roll out a whole grand jury for such simple matters unless necessary." He gives him a hard stare. "Shall we continue?"

My lips twitch with the urge to smile. It delights me seeing Logan so beautifully chastised by this judge. I'm further comforted when the judge turns to our side of the table and says, "Don't worry. You'll get your chance too."

Logan whispers something to his lawyer behind his hand, and only once he gets a nod does he sit up straighter.

"Okay, fine. I first met Keith Prentiss at the Samson Academy for Boys. I was a troubled teenager. My parents couldn't control me and after a run-in with the law, they gave me an ultimatum: go to juvenile prison, or go to military school. But it wasn't truly a military school, more like a cult. Religious zealots who would beat us if we didn't recite memorized bible verses and stay in line —follow orders. They didn't want to teach us. They wanted to brainwash us."

I can't help but sneak a look at him as he tells his story. To be honest, I hadn't even known why Logan ended up at Samson Academy. I guess I never bothered to ask and he was never willing to share. Not many of us were.

"While I was constantly getting punished for not following the rules, this other boy wasn't. He was clean cut and quiet. He never said a word back against any of the drill sergeants. Just followed every order, every rule to a tee. At first, I thought he had been there before and was already brainwashed. But then I realized that if I did what he did, I wouldn't get punished. So I started following him around, copying his mannerisms and such, and miraculously, my time at the Academy became easier— tolerable.

"When he caught on that he was helping me, we became friends. He kept me out of trouble and I helped him with school. He had terrible grades, which was surprising because with the way he talked, you'd never suspect he was stupid. So we started helping each other. He gave me advice on how to best make the beds and stay out of trouble and I helped him write out his homework. He would dictate and I'd write. From then on, it was like finally having a friend.

"One day he told me he wanted to be a musician. He told me he planned to get out of there when he turned eighteen, and head to California. That he wanted to start a band and make metal music. Well, that sounded exactly like the kind of thing I wanted too. We worked really hard over the next few months to gain enough favor with the sergeants to let us use the guitars they had stashed in the staff house. During our free time, we sat in the bunkhouse together and jammed for as long as we could. This was how the band was formed. We didn't have a name yet, but he played rhythm guitar and I played lead. And those seven songs are what came out of those jam sessions."

I narrow my eyes at him. While I know he's lying, I do actually believe that the first part of his story is true. That this is the way they really met. After all, I was the third wheel who broke them up. But what's bullshit is how Key and Logan created the songs together. That, right there, is the first lie.

"I see," Judge Horowath says thoughtfully. "How was the creative process split between you and Mr. Prentiss?"

At this Logan shrugs. "It's hard to say, really. When you're being creative like we were, it's difficult to determine where his ideas ended and mine started. It was a fairly organic creative collaboration. He would say a line, then I would say a line, or he'd suggest a different word. I'd write everything down, so . . . fifty-fifty, I'd say."

I can't help the scoff that escapes my throat, and for a moment all eyes are on me. I roll my lips inward and slouch down in my seat a little.

"Right. So where do the other members present fit into the narrative?"

Logan looks at me. "Joel Thanger was another punk who showed up at the Academy. They dumped him in our bunkhouse in the middle of the night. He reminded me a lot of myself, actually. Didn't think he belonged there. Refused to obey orders. Thought he could be a smart-ass and get away with it."

Again . . . true.

"I found out from one of the officers that Mr. Thanger had brought a bass with him. That it was locked up in the staff house with everything else you had to earn back. I was beside myself with excitement. I thought he could round out the band. It seemed that Keith had the same idea. He was quick to show Mr. Thanger that his efforts were misplaced, and shortly after that, we had our bass player."

"However, it became very apparent, very quickly, that they were becoming closer than I thought they would. I'd find them huddled together whispering, or playing their instruments together without me. They were even writing their own songs together. I'll admit, it hurt."

His eyes are on me and, when I glance up at him, I can see it. There, deep down beneath the betrayal and the lies, he felt cut out —pushed aside. Hurt. Even though that's never how we meant it —it's what he felt.

"They even decided on the name for the band without me. I was sure they were going to cut me out. So, one afternoon, I decided to confront Keith about it. Told him that if they didn't want me in the band anymore, it was fine, but that I wouldn't let him keep the songs we wrote together. There was a scuffle, and he tore open my trunk of belongings where I kept the pages of written songs. He tried to take them. He said he was going to burn them. He even managed to set fire to a few I had been working on solo. We got into a fight, and next thing I know, Mr. Thanger was there. He attacked me, and I can't remember much after that besides waking up in the infirmary."

My hands and teeth are clenched so hard I fear they might break. I remember the smell of paper burning, the curling charred scraps smoking on the floor as I leapt across the bunks to tackle Logan. I remember Key with tears streaming down his face as he clutched at the ashes.

This is at least partially true. But also all wrong.

"I didn't go back to the Academy after that. When my parents visited me in the hospital and learned about the abuse I had suffered, they took me home. For a long time, I chose to forget about it all. I knew about the success of the band, of course. How could I not? It was devastating to learn that Keith had taken the songs we'd written together and pawned them off as his own. But I had nothing. No proof except my word against his.

"Until . . . I visited my parents a few months ago, and came across the songs buried in the bottom of a box in their garage. I thought they had been lost between moving apartments over the years, but there they were, and I finally had hope."

His lawyer speaks up from his right. "It's not just that Mr. Samuels's songs were recorded, but there was no songwriting credit given, no royalty share, no mention of his contribution to the band in the acknowledgements. It's as if the rest of them simply tried to erase his existence. That is why we are here today. To make right a terrible injustice."

"A terrible injustice?" It bursts out of my mouth without thought.

Logan sneers at me from across the table. "I have as much right to those songs as Keith does and I'll be damned if you push me out again, Joel."

Judge Horowath turns to me with a solemn expression. "Mr. Thanger, since Mr. Prentiss is not here to explain his version of the events and the other two members of your band were not present at the time in question, I will now ask for your perspective."

I release the tension in my hands, and after a nod from our lawyer, I start.

CHAPTER 25

Battery

KEY

EIGHT YEARS AGO

Logan wanted to know my secret. Wanted to know how I made it look so easy. How I could survive here in this hell. The truth is that I'm hardly even here. I've switched off. Tuned out. If I don't think, it can't hurt. If I don't think, they can't hurt *me*. So I turned back into Keith—the boy I was at eleven before I ever met Dusty. Before she bulldozed into my life and opened my eyes to a world of Technicolor.

Now, I'm in black and white, like when Dorothy wakes up back in Kansas. Maybe it never really happened. Maybe I never really knew her. Never met my best friend. Never fell in love. Never proposed. Never thought I was going to have a baby. Maybe it was just a dream.

Maybe I'll wake up and I'll be eleven years old again, and I just fell asleep in a stifling hot church pew.

There's a crash of doors, and I jolt in my bunk as officers escort a boy into the room with tan skin and a fresh black buzz cut. The boy tries to fight, and I want to tell him it's no use. That fighting back here will only make your life hell, and that you'll eventually give in anyway, so why not skip ahead so you don't suffer. But I suppose that's part of why so many of us are here. We enjoy suffering on some level.

"Get off me!" he shouts, and I keep still even as I can tell the rest of the bunkhouse is up and watching the scene.

The bunk next to me is empty, the last one in the row, and I know that's where he's headed. I hear the squeak of the rusty springs as he's tossed on the bed.

"You're expected to be dressed and ready at oh-six hundred hours," the officer says.

"Fuck you." The words are followed by the sound of him spitting on the floor.

There's a sharp smack, and the sound of skin slapping something wet, followed by a grunt of pain. "Don't be late," the officer continues. "Or there'll be worse than that tomorrow."

He's quiet this time, and after a long moment of heavy breathing, the door locks behind the officers.

"Shit," the boy murmurs, and I open my eyes again, turning to see him dabbing at his lip, which is split open and bloody. He collects himself and looks around. His jaw is sharp, but there's still some baby fat in his cheeks and his dark eyes are alight—even after being beaten. Even after being sent here.

Then the most miraculous thing happens—he smiles. It's not a full one, but it pulls at the corner of his mouth as he shakes his head, as though he thinks this is all a joke. Or maybe he's smiling because he knows it's not. That he can only cope with the reality of this through laughter, and that smile lights him up, even in the darkened room.

I stare up at the ceiling and take a deep breath. My eyes have been dead since that night at the bus station four months ago. The light they once carried died that day, and I haven't been able to look at myself since. But this boy, he's not broken, and I'm not sure why, but something makes me want to protect him.

Logan never had that light. He was still fighting when I came, but even then, he didn't have this spirit. Maybe if I can keep this boy's light alive, it'll keep me alive too.

I look over at him again. He's wrapped his arms around his knees protectively but I can still see the remnants of that smile on his face. For a few minutes, we're quiet, and the rest of the guys seem to have gone back to sleep.

Finally, he looks over, and our eyes meet. It feels like forever that he holds my gaze, even as his eyes turn glassy with unshed tears.

"What the fuck are you staring at?" he asks, springing to his feet, his fists clenched at his sides.

I don't say anything. I can't. I also can't look away.

He steps closer this time. "Knock it off, asshole," he says, his voice rising.

My eyes widen as he closes the distance between us. I don't move when he grabs my shirt and yanks me out of my bed. I don't even flinch when he raises his fist over his head and stares down at me with wild, tear-filled eyes.

"Stop looking at me!" he shouts, then punches me in the face —his knuckles slamming into my right cheek bone. Searing hot pain flares across my face, but I relish it. It's the only time I feel anything.

I stare up at the boy who snarls back at me like a bull readying itself for attack. He shakes me and raises his fist again. "Do something! Fight back!" he screams.

I shake my head. "No."

He blinks at me, his fist lowering an inch at a time. "Wh-why not?"

"I've already lost everything. I have nothing left to fight for."

There's a silence that descends upon us as his erratic breathing settles. He lowers his fist completely, releases his grip on my collar. I fall back against my bunk with a squeak but never take my eyes off him.

He stands then glances around the room at all the others who by now have sat up in their beds. "What the fuck are you all staring at?" he asks the room at large.

No one says anything. No one gets up. And after a moment, they all lose interest. His eyes shine in the darkness, holding my gaze, and that's when the tears finally fall. His lips tremble as he cries, his face fighting against the urge to sob. Still he watches me —and I watch him. It's as though he needed this. Needed someone to see his pain. Finally, after a time, he wipes the wetness from his face and walks over to his bunk at the end of the row.

"This is such bullshit," I hear him mutter.

He sniffs loudly, climbs into bed, then rolls over facing away from me. I turn onto my back and stare at the ceiling once again.

I need to help him. I need to protect him.

Because I need him to save me.

"YOU'RE DOING THAT WRONG," I whisper the next morning as we're awoken by reveille.

The boy's cheeks darken and I suspect he must feel embarrassed about last night. He doesn't need to, though. We've all been there. "Fuck off," he says back, and continues to butcher his technique.

"Fold the corners, then tuck them under. Like mine," I whisper again.

"Dude, did I fucking ask for your help?"

I sigh. "No, but they'll beat you until you learn how to do it right."

He stops and stares at his messy sheets.

I lean over. "Maybe you're into pain, but I don't exactly want your blood all over my stuff."

For a moment he seems like he'll continue to argue with me, but I'm pleased when he crouches down to fold and tuck the corners. He glances at my bed for reference and adjusts his own, then fixes his uniform before joining the rest of us at the end of our bunks.

When the lieutenant bursts through the doors he heads straight for the back like I knew he would. He wants to make an example of the new guy. He always does. It's how they break us. Jokes on them, though. I'm already broken.

He stops at the boy's bunk next to me and inspects the bed. I watch out of the corner of my eye and inwardly cheer when all he gives is a rough grunt of approval. The lieutenant steps right into the boy's face and narrows his eyes.

"Wipe that smirk off your face, Thanger," he says, then turns to the rest of the bunkhouse. "*Move out, ladies!*"

We make two straight lines and head out the door into the sunlight, our hands coming up to shield against it. I feel a tap on my back and look over my shoulder.

"Thanks," the boy mutters. "And sorry about last night."

"Don't worry about it."

"I'm Joel, by the way," he says.

"Keith Prentiss," I answer. "And if you want to keep your face from being smashed in? You'll listen to me."

I expect him to laugh, to scoff even. Instead he says nothing and simply follows behind me. Throughout the first day they test him. I know all their tricks by this point, and at every opportunity I fix whatever Joel does incorrectly enough that by nightfall, the officers haven't been able to find a single thing to punish him for. They beat the shit out of him anyway, and that evening, he goes to bed with a smile under his bloody nose.

But in the middle of the night I hear him crying, and the little

I have left of my heart aches for him. I still can't fully explain why. I've never cared about the others. Not like this.

After that, he joins Logan and me at meals and during study time but doesn't say anything for the first week, other than tell us to fuck off when we try to initiate conversation, until that fades too.

One afternoon, around week three, when Logan and I are messing around with our guitars, I spot Joel watching us from the bunkhouse door.

"I heard he brought a bass guitar with him," Logan whispers to me. "Maybe when he gets it back, he could fill out the band."

Like the Grinch, my heart expands at this new information. A bass guitarist would really be something. Don't get me wrong, Logan is a fairly decent guitar player, but he's terrible at improvising. The guy doesn't have a creative bone in his body, so all we do is play covers of our favorite songs. I never feel like I want to share my original music with him. Maybe it's because I'm still broken, and I can't bring myself to open up the floodgates that might come from playing the music I wrote for Dusty. Logan wouldn't understand it—he wouldn't understand me.

But maybe Joel would.

A few weeks pass and still, I see the aftermath of Joel's silent tears in the mornings. The red puffy eyes and the raw nose. If only I could do something to make him feel better. Then, while we're scrubbing the showers one day, it hits me. A radical idea that will probably prove to be something I have to suffer the consequences for, but it's been a long time since I cared about anything.

The next afternoon, I find Joel sitting on his bed in the bunkhouse alone. I knew he would be. He always comes in here after classes to read the comic books he borrows from the library on campus.

"Hey, Joel," I call, and I'm pleased at the way his face lights up when he sees me. "I, uh," I stammer. Why am I nervous? "I got something for you."

His eyebrows pull together, but when I reveal his electric bass guitar from behind my back he jumps to his feet, a look of complete disbelief on his face.

"Holy shit!" He bounds over to take it from my hands. "I—how did you—I thought for sure they chucked it," he rushes out.

I sit on the edge of my bed and watch him pull the strap over his shoulder. I'm mesmerized by the way he so deftly handles the body of the guitar. How nimbly his fingers move, quickly and precisely. The way he slaps and plucks the strings while his other hand dances down the frets catches me off guard and for the first time in months, I smile.

"Damn, Prentiss, didn't know you had teeth," he says, grinning.

I shrug. "It's been a while since I've smiled."

He sits down opposite me, the guitar pulled into him as though he's afraid at any moment it might disappear. "Where did you get this?" he asks.

"The officer's quarters," I admit. "Logan heard they had your guitar held hostage there and . . . well, we thought if you got yours back, you could play with us—you know, if you wanted."

"Really?" he asks, leaning forward.

I get to my feet and lift the mattress, revealing the electric guitar I managed to score for good behavior.

"Radical," Joel says meekly. "Hey, let's play something."

I raise my eyebrows. "Now?"

Joel laughs. "Well, shit, yeah now."

Taking a deep breath, I say, "Okay . . . what were you just playing? I don't recognize it."

"Oh, nothing. I was just fucking around, it's not a real song."

I stare at him and he shrugs.

"What? Was it that bad?"

I roll my jaw, tamping down my rising excitement. "No, the opposite actually. It was awesome."

He jerks his chin at me. "Okay, Prentiss, show me what you got. I'll play along."

My stomach twists. "Right, um, this is one I wrote," I say, and adjust the tuning knobs.

I strum once, my fingers pressing into the frets. It starts slow —like a trickle of water from a crack in a dam. He watches with rapt attention, barely blinking as he follows the movement of my hands. He props his bass on his knee and starts to slap his strings. The sound gives new life to the song. The way he adds depth and feeling to each line—I've never experienced it before. Not on my own. Not with Logan. Never. The music speeds up and just like the dam, it's as if my heart is cracking open and everything I've been repressing starts to gush out. I press the strings until my fingers hurt and when I sing the words I wrote for her, that's when the tears begin to fall.

I let them run down my face. I don't hide from it, and I don't wipe them away. And he watches me. Just like I did for him that first night.

When the song ends, I'm panting. My voice feels hoarse and my face is swollen. "Sorry," I mutter as I place my guitar on the bed so I can wipe my cheeks with my shirt. Joel sets his guitar down and for a split second I wonder if he regrets playing with me. I'm half expecting him to tell me my song is garbage and he never wants to jam again. But he doesn't. He does something I never would have guessed.

He hugs me. Really hugs me.

Who knew a hug could bring someone back to life?

When he pulls away, his smile is small. "You wrote that?" he asks.

I huff out a laugh. "Uh, yeah. What'd you think?"

He shoves my shoulder. "Fucking killer, man. Seriously, that shit was rad. You got more?"

I grin. "A lot more," I say, leaning forward to kick a box under my foot for a better playing position.

"Where'd you get that?"

His eyes are trained on the necklace that has come loose from my collar.

"Is that a ring made from guitar string?"

"Oh, uh . . . yeah." I quickly tuck the chain back inside my shirt.

"Epic. Did someone give it to you?"

I fight against the urge to flinch. The memory of her like a knife slicing across my skin. "No, I umm . . . I made it. It's just —" *Say something.* "It's just a reminder of someone special, that's all."

Joel glances at the hidden spot on my chest, his lips parting like he's going to ask more questions, when a whistle sounds in the courtyard outside. I jump to my feet, nearly knocking him over. "Quick, hide your guitar under your mattress."

He follows my lead, but as we stand straight at the ends of our beds for the approaching officers, he whispers, "What the hell is going on?"

"I may have done something stupid to get the guitar back."

His face falls. "What? Are you crazy?"

"Prentiss!" Officer Pettey shouts as he stomps toward me. "You've got some explaining to do, you little shit."

"Is there a problem, sir?" I ask, aware that Joel is watching intently.

"Yeah, you fucking locked us in the latrine."

"That was a latrine?" I ask, innocently. "My bad, I thought it was your bunkhouse. Smelled just like you."

Joel snorts out a laugh and I smile wide . . . right before I'm punched squarely in the face.

IT TOOK a few days to recover from the brutal beating I got for locking the officers in the toilets. It was all worth it though when Joel stopped crying in the night. It's surprisingly easy to be friends with the kid. By some miracle the higher ups didn't notice his guitar was missing and at every opportunity, we jam together. Even more surprising, I share more of my own music with him and even Logan. Once the floodgates were open it seemed I couldn't stop it.

I show him the chord progressions, and he develops the bass melody, but Logan struggles to keep up. The two of us sound like magic. Like *real* music. And maybe it's cruel, but it's easier to be creative when Logan isn't there. It's like Joel is the power source, and I'm a dead battery slowly being charged back to life. Joel is my other half, so when Logan pulls away to spend more time on his own, I let it happen. I'm actually *relieved* that maybe this trio will break apart naturally.

That is, until the unthinkable happens.

Walking into the barracks I've lived in for almost a year, I stop as a chill races down my spine. At the end of the row of bunks, where Joel and my beds are, sits Logan.

"Hey, what are you doing here? You know you were supposed to report to the mess hall ten minutes ago," I say.

For a second he blinks stupidly at me, but then something hard crosses over his face, and with a quick look past me at the door, he sets his jaw and stands. "You're cutting me out, aren't you?"

I pull back, confused, before looking around for some context. "Uh, what?" I step closer and realize my trunk is open.

"Carnal Sins?" he asks, a piece of paper crunched in his hand. "Really?"

I shrug and glance down at the crude logo Joel drew during

class after we thought of the name together. "Joel and I came up with it. Killer, right?"

He scoffs, his fingers tightening around it. "I can't believe this. You and your fucking boyfriend are doing everything without me. I see the two of you together. You're cutting me out of the band. You're cutting me out of *Carnal Sins*." He spits out the last two words like they're poison on his tongue.

I cross my arms. "Hardly in a position to cut anyone out of anything here," I say with a laugh, gesturing around us. "Not like I can hold auditions for another guitarist."

His face reddens. "You see? You *see*? That. Right fucking there, Prentiss, you asshole." He steps toward me with his finger outstretched. "You think you're so goddamn superior than the rest of us. But you're just an arrogant prick who wants to take away the only thing I have going for me."

I hold up my hands, stunned. "Dude, what the hell are you talking about?"

"The band? The songs? Everything we worked on together? You can't just take that from me," he says, his voice rising. "I won't let you."

But my head is trying to piece broken information together. "We haven't kicked you out of the band, Logan."

"And what about everything else?"

My eyes narrow. "What else?"

"The songs, Prentiss. The songs!" he shouts, his face turning redder and redder. "They're mine!"

In what world does he think he has any ownership over songs that *I* wrote? Then it clicks together and my eyes widen. "Wait," I say, stepping toward him. "Wait, wait, wait. You don't think you co-wrote those with me, do you?"

"I sure as hell do," he spits.

I do something that I know, even in that moment, I'll regret one day. I laugh. I laugh so hard that I clutch at my stomach, the muscles aching while he seethes in anger. "Samuels, are you out of your mind? Since when does you writing down lyrics as I dictate them to you make you a cowriter? That's like saying you co-wrote *Romeo and Juliet* because you copied a verse line by line in your notebook."

I laugh some more, but as it dies out, I understand he's serious. "Logan, you can't think that's what that was," I insist, stepping forward again. "I mean, I appreciate you helping me get them on paper, but *I* wrote them. I composed them. Me. All by myself."

The reality of what he's suggesting starts to eat away at me, the fragile friendship we've had for months fraying rapidly. Was it ever real? Did he just use me? And while he wouldn't be my pick for my best friend now that I've met Joel, he's still my friend. At least, I thought he was. The betrayal stings like the prick of a hundred wasps.

"I thought you just wanted to help me," I say, so close now I can feel his rage radiating. "You know I have problems writing. You told me it shouldn't stop me from becoming a real musician. A real songwriter." I push him hard in the chest. "But this whole time, you wanted them for yourself? Was everything you've ever said bullshit?" I push again and he stumbles, his face hardening before he strikes back and lunges for me.

We go down hard. A tangled mass of limbs and fists and boots. I try to get up but he grabs me by my belt to pull me down again. He kicks the back of my knee hard and I cry out as he gets to his feet. He steps over me, but I dummy sweep his legs out from underneath him and he falls like a sack of bricks into my open trunk.

As he tries to scramble away, I shoot to my feet and fall against the support beam in the center of the room, between the rows of beds. My leg kills, and my cheek and arms are tender to the touch as I try to catch my breath.

"What's this?"

I roll my eyes, thinking maybe he's trying to distract me, but when I see what he's holding my throat tightens.

"Who the hell is Dusty Connors?"

"Give that to me," I say, reaching for it, but he rips it away at the last second, and I know now he's got me—I gave too much away.

His head tilts. "Is this . . ." His eyes focus on the letter and my stomach sinks.

"Give me that," I say through gritted teeth.

His smile is malicious. "All this time, I could never figure out why you were sent here," he says. "Mister do-gooder who always follows the rules. But it finally makes sense. You were never the perfect little church boy after all, were you? Never in a million years did I think you were sent here because you knocked up some slut."

My hands are fisted in his shirt the next second, slamming him into the wall behind Joel's bed. But he manages to raise the test result over my head. The only proof I have left that there ever was a baby. My baby. *Our* baby.

"Where's your bastard baby now, Prentiss? Huh? Where's your whore?"

The anger seems to boil me alive, and something inside me snaps. I wrap my hands around his throat, his eyes bulging as I squeeze. It's a strange feeling. It hardly takes any effort at all for his face to turn red. I've never considered killing someone before, and it frightens me how quickly I make the decision to do it. It's only the sound of something clicking above that pulls me out of the bizarre rage.

He has my letter in one hand and a lighter in the other. I have no idea where it came from, but the lighter bursts to life and he holds it close to my letter.

"No, don't!" I beg, releasing him with a shove, but I see it in his eyes as he gasps for breath. See the hurt he feels. The hurt he wants *me* to feel. I sink to my knees before him, silently begging him not to do this. But he shakes his head as he coughs and walks toward me, still holding the letter hostage.

"It . . . didn't have . . . to be like this," he gasps out, standing over me. "We could've been . . . a great team. All three of us. But you had to go and . . . fuck that up."

I'm vibrating with rage and sorrow when I look up at him. "You better watch your back," I say in a low voice. "There's only so many places in this godforsaken hellhole you can hide."

He tilts his head. "You think I'm staying? Oh, Keith, you're stupider than I thought."

My eyes narrow. What the hell is he talking about?

He kneels so we're level. "You think I'd go through all this just to stick around? No. I'm getting the fuck out of here."

At my confusion his eyes lock on something over my shoulder.

"There's my ticket out of here," he says, that sick smile appearing again, and before I can move, he sets the letter ablaze.

The air around me is silent. All I can hear is the crackling of paper. I reach for it, crying out as I desperately try to stem the flames. But it's no use, and as I watch the remnants turn to ash, a part of me dies. I can't breathe. I can't think. I must be drowning. I don't know what to do. Do I fight him, or try to repair something I know is futile? My body is locked into an internal turmoil that seems to both happen over a millennia and in a fraction of a second.

Joel's voice pierces my consciousness, raised and shouting at Logan. His fist makes contact just once and he's down, the spray of blood arching into the air.

Time passes like sand through an hourglass as the officers stomp into the bunkhouse. As they take in the scene and wail on us with closed fists. As they scream at us about *insubordination* and *discipline* and *choices*.

The ashes of the letter rain down on my scarred hands and face, the pain so incredible I think it'll drag me under, but through all of it, I can see Joel. His light keeping me from sinking beyond all hope into a never-ending darkness.

"It's going to be alright, Key," he shouts at me over the commotion. The name acts like a defibrillator. Restarting my heart and keeping me alive. "I'm here, Key. Stay with me."

CHAPTER 26

Head Over Heels

JOEL

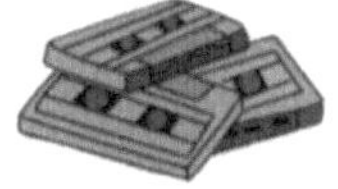

I look around the conference room, avoiding the eyes of James and Dave. They've never heard this story before, and I know they probably have a million questions, but it'll have to wait until later.

"I realize I acted like a barbarian," I admit. "But I was seventeen and already troubled and I saw that my best friend was in pain. I did—I did what I thought I had to do at the time."

Everyone is quiet and the air is thick with discomfort.

"Do you know what it was that led to the final conflict between Mr. Prentiss and Mr. Samuels?" Judge Horowath asks.

I shake my head. "No, he never told me. And I never asked. I just knew it was important. Life-altering. I've never seen him more distressed than at that moment."

He twists his mouth thoughtfully. "You mentioned in your testimony here today, Mr. Thanger, that you believe Mr. Samuels had never heard these songs prior to when you yourself heard them? What makes you think that's true?"

I shrug. "Mr. Samuels seemed confused. Unable to follow along. Didn't know when the verses would end—the lyrics, or the chords. Either he's an exceptionally bad and forgetful guitarist, or he had never heard those songs before."

I'm delighted when Logan's face turns a delicious shade of crimson.

The judge nods. "I see."

"We have evidence to present for our client," one of Logan's lawyers interjects.

My heart sinks. So they really have something.

"I'd like to see it, please," the judge says.

From out of a file folder, the lawyer pulls a small stack of crinkled paper. As Horowath looks it over, the room spins. I glance over at James and Dave, who nervously rock in their oversized leather chairs. When the judge looks up, he's staring straight at me.

"Mr. Thanger," he says, passing one of the pages to Al's lawyer. "Could you please tell me the title of the song on this paper."

I crack my knuckles as it's passed over, and my blood runs cold when I see the words at the top of the page.

"It's, uh—it's 'Neon Crush,'" I say breathlessly.

"That is one of the songs in contention, is it not?"

"Yes."

"And the letterhead at the top of the paper. Can you read that as well, please."

I try to swallow but it feels like nails. "'Samson Academy for Troubled Boys.'"

"One would assume, then, that this creative work was written during a stay at the aforementioned place."

No words come out. My heart's being cleaved in two.

"Mr. Thanger, can you identify the signatures at the bottom of the page?"

I want to lie. I want to sit here and explain to everyone that Key's name isn't on this page. I suppose it isn't until this very moment that the horrifying truth becomes impossible to ignore.

And it will change *everything*.

"There appears to be two people's names here," I say, my voice sounding far away. "Logan Samuels and . . .." I hang my head. "Keith Prentiss."

"Joel. Joel!"

I storm across the lobby and stab at the button for the elevator. I need to punch something and it can't be one of these fancy office walls. Wouldn't want to get stuck with another massive bill.

As the elevator rises and the lights above the doors light up, Dave and James are there, blocking my way.

"Dude," Dave says. "We need to talk."

"What's there to say?"

He pushes against me, and steam is nearly pouring out of my ears. "How about what the fuck are we going to do now?"

"Dave," James interrupts. "Maybe we take a minute to—"

"It's bullshit," I whisper.

"What?"

"It's fucking bullshit!" I yell, and it echoes down the tiled hallway.

"Joel—" James reaches out and touches my shoulder, but I shrug him off.

"No, James. It's not true. Don't you dare fucking believe it."

He holds up his ring-covered fingers and backs up. "I don't. Joel, I swear I don't."

"He must have done something," I say. "Logan . . . he forged those papers, or—" I pull at the roots of my hair. "Or he forced him to write out those songs."

Dave and James both bow their heads. "What do you mean?"

"Key's brain is like a safe. He's always been like that. Even stuff that we wrote at that fucking Academy after Logan was gone. It was never on paper. He always just remembered. It's like he has a photographic memory."

"What's your point?" Dave sighs.

I groan. "My point, assholes, is that you've never seen him write a song or chord or lyric down, but this douchebag is trying to convince everyone else that there are seven perfectly written copies of songs he happened to write at seventeen years old while at an extremist Christian military academy?"

Dave shakes his head. "It doesn't matter."

My jaw drops. "How can you say that?" I hiss.

"Because," Dave continues on quietly. "We can believe him all we want, but that means nothing unless we can *prove* Key's side of the story is true. And we don't even know what that is, because he's not here to tell us! He ran away and left us to clean up his mess and I for one am fucking pissed."

James shrugs and adds, "He shouldn't have left, man. He's fucked us over."

I close my eyes and try to take a deep calming breath but I can't help it. I'm pissed too. In fact, I'm fucking furious. I've never been madder at Key and more desperate to see him in the eight years I've known him. What the hell was he thinking?

"The judge said we have two weeks," I say, looking at them again. "Two weeks to prove those papers are fakes. Two weeks for Key to come back and tell us what really happened. To make this right."

There's an echo of laughter, and the three of us turn to see Logan and his two lawyers exiting out of the conference room, massive grins plastered on their faces. My body tenses, my knuckles cracking as I ball them into fists.

"Joel, don't," James whispers as he steps in front of me. "It's not worth it."

His eyes meet mine, those dark brown eyes begging me to be sensible. How did the youngest of our group become the wisest?

"Yeah, man," Dave says, joining James. "He's got lawyers with him. You do anything, they'll use it against us."

But I don't care, and all I want to do at this moment is finish the job I started at seventeen.

"All right, Thanger?" Logan says with a grin as he and the lawyers stride up to the elevator next to us. "Sorry it had to go this way. I was really hoping we could have handled this without the suits," he says, gesturing to the high-priced lawyers at his side.

My jaw clenches, and it takes all of my willpower not to push Dave and James aside to smash his face into the wall.

"Oh, and no hard feelings about that mess at Samson. After all, you putting me in the infirmary is what got me out of there."

His lips twitch up into the barest hint of a smirk, and I'm shaking with restrained violence.

"When you see Keith, tell him I say thanks."

The elevator dings, then the doors open, and the group disappears from sight.

"You okay?" James asks.

"No," I reply honestly.

"Yeah," Dave admits. "I don't think any of us are."

"HERE, Joel, I made you some coffee," Izzy says, pushing the steaming cup into my hands.

I try to smile at her, if only to ease the worry from her brown eyes. But I can't manage it.

"Thanks," I say, instead.

Izzy sinks into the couch next to Becks, who wraps her arms around her friend.

"I feel so useless," Becks says.

"I think we all do," Dave adds.

"I'm just so worried about him," she continues. "What if—" Her mouth hangs open, and she looks across at me.

I frown. "What if what?"

Her posture straightens. "I just—as someone who's been to some really dark places in my head," she admits, and I don't miss the way that James reaches across and places his hand on her knee. "What if he's really not okay? He's all alone without anyone or anything to pull him out."

The room is pin-drop silent.

"No, I—he wouldn't . . ." I start to argue, but after everything that's happened in the past few weeks, how can I be so sure I really know the man? His signature was on those pages. Why did he never tell me what happened with Logan? Why did I never ask? What else is he not telling me? "No, he wouldn't do anything to hurt himself. Maybe he's just gone back to Iowa. Maybe there's proof there that he needs to make this all go away. It has to be or —no. This can't be over."

It's the thing we've all been thinking since the accusations came out. That this might be the end. The end of the band. Venues won't host us. Our music video project with MTV is on hold indefinitely, and as of this afternoon, Al called to tell us the radio won't be playing any of our songs until the case is settled. And just like Dave said, it doesn't matter if we know Key is innocent in all of this, we need proof. No one wants to support a band they think is guilty of plagiarizing songs.

I watch as James and Becks, then Izzy and Dave, fall into their respective pairings. If this really is the end, I'm just glad that the four of them have each other. That they've been smart with their money, and while they might not make big bucks from music for a while, they've got enough under their feet to keep themselves afloat. Most of all, I'm glad they found love.

"Guys, I need to tell you something," I say.

I nearly laugh as they all collectively hold their breath.

"No, not about the songs. Something else."

They visibly relax and I sit up a little straighter. Run a hand down my face.

"I, uh . . . I met someone."

Becks's mouth drops open, and James blinks at me.

"You . . . wait, what?" Izzy asks. "You met someone? What does that mean?"

I roll my eyes. "It means what it always means, Iz. I met someone. A girl—or, well, a woman."

It's possible that Dave's eyebrows have disappeared. "A woman?"

I nod. "Yeah. Her name's Dusty and she's . . . incredible."

Something small but soft barrels into me, squeezing me into a tight hug. Becks squeals into my ear, "Oh, Joel!"

I hug her back tightly, then she sits next to me on the couch, her arm entwining with mine.

"What's she like? Where did you meet?"

After the aching sadness that has sat heavy on my chest all day, the thought of Dusty lightens everything just enough. "She's the most beautiful woman I've ever seen. Red hair, blue eyes . . . legs for days. But she's more than that too. I don't know how to describe it."

James grins.

"And funnily enough, I met her for the first time the night of your wedding," I say to Becks and James.

Becks taps a finger to her cheeks while James scratches his head, and I can even see Izzy and Dave trying to figure it out.

"Wait," Dave says, "you met her in Vegas?"

"Really?" Becks asks. "How serendipitous is that?"

"But you were—" James cuts himself off. "Holy shit, Joel, is she a . . . stripper?"

The girls' heads whip around to look at me, but I'm not ashamed. "She was."

"Oh my god," Izzy says, rising to her feet. "I met her!"

"You what?"

"The morning after the wedding, when we all met up for breakfast. You told us you spent the night with this gorgeous redhead. When I went to the bathroom there was a long-legged redhead in there. She had a Texas accent and gave me a tam—a tampon," she finishes shyly.

"But, wait," Becks says. "Does that mean she lives here now?"

I nod. "Yeah, we ran into each other at a laundromat of all places. It's crazy."

"So if she's not a stripper anymore . . ." Becks turns bright pink "What does she do now?"

"She's a phone sex operator."

I was completely honest with Dusty when I said it doesn't bother me what she does for work. But from the look of the slack jaws and wide eyes in front of me, I should've eased my friends into this detail. Not because I'm embarrassed, but because I want her to meet them someday and they're not giving me much confidence they won't make things awkward.

"Oh," Dave says, glancing sideways at James. "That's . . . interesting."

Izzy opens her mouth to speak twice, but both times closes it, then crosses her arms and looks away.

Becks though . . . she tightens her grip on my arm and she rests her head on my shoulder. "I'm glad you found someone. She must be so special. I can't wait to meet her."

My head drops on top of hers, and I need to blink quickly to keep myself from getting emotional. I sigh. "There's one problem though," I admit. "Key doesn't know."

"You haven't told him?" Izzy asks.

I shake my head. "I was going to, but he's been in such a shitty mood the past few weeks and he—well, in not as many words, he told me that love sucks. That relationships aren't real and he wants both of us to stay single for the rest of our lives."

James gives a low whistle. "Yup, someone hurt that guy. Knew it."

I frown. "What?"

He shrugs. "Come on. You can't tell me you've been playing those songs of his for how many years now and have never clued in that they're all about *one* girl."

"No . . . no that's—"

"Joel . . . 'Firebird'? 'Neon Crush'? 'Sunshine Mind'?" James counts off his fingers. "Obviously written about a girl he was nuts for. Trust me, I know." He winks at Becks, and she giggles.

"And considering he wrote them before he even turned eighteen?" James continues. "It must have been one brutal breakup."

I shake my head and wave my hands. "You're wrong. Sure, he might have written songs about a girl. A muse, maybe, but—I've been his best friend for almost eight years. Never once has he mentioned being in love with a girl."

Dave sighs. "That's actually what makes it more believable. He can't even talk about it."

The idea percolates in my brain, swirling around like tea leaves in water. Key was in love? Did Key lose the person he loved? But why keep that big of a secret from me? Why not tell me?

"I'm sure he'll be happy for you," Becks encourages. "Just because he was heartbroken once doesn't mean he'd deprive his friend of finding someone. It's not like he had a problem with either of our relationships."

I glance up at James and Dave for a brief moment, who seem to understand the silent communication between us. Because we're a package. Because loving someone else might change what makes Key's and my friendship so special. Reaching over to touch Becks's hand, I nod. "You're probably right, but now's not the right time. It might never be the right time if he doesn't come back."

"He will," Izzy states, brooking no argument. "He has to."

LATER, when I'm alone in the house, I sit for hours with my bass guitar across my lap. As I pluck the tune to Key's songs and the lyrics run through my head, I let myself break down. Because I must be the biggest fucking idiot on planet Earth not to realize these songs are about a girl. Other than terribly in the shower, I don't sing. Key is the songbird and James and Dave are the backups. I've never really had to fit my mouth around each individual word before. But now I can't unhear it. Can practically see the events of this tragic love story play out in front of me. The pining, the longing, the betrayal, the heartbreak . . .

The sun peaks over the horizon to shine through the patio windows, and I'm exhausted, having only gotten bouts of sleep no longer than fifteen minutes all night. I need Dusty. I *need* her. I need her in my arms. To fall asleep next to me. She's probably just getting home after a long night of work, but maybe she'll come.

I push myself off the couch and walk over to the kitchen, slipping the phone off the hook. My palms sweat as I dial her number, but picturing Stella yowling at the sound filling their apartment has a smile tugging at my lips.

"Hello?"

Butterflies roam loose in my chest. "Hey, it's me."

"Oh, Joel, hi. Are you—is everything okay? It's really early."

I press my fist to my forehead. "I've been up all night. It's been the shittiest day."

"I'm so sorry," she says.

"Listen, I know you probably just got in from work—"

"Actually," she interrupts. "I quit."

I blink. "You what?"

She sighs. "I just couldn't do it anymore, and to be honest, even though you said it doesn't bother you—"

"It doesn't," I insist.

"I know. But it bothers *me*. If this thing between us is going to work . . . I want to give myself over completely, and that means getting away from all the confusing emotions that come with my job."

I smile and twirl my finger in the phone cord. She wants to be mine. "You're incredible," I say reverently.

She gives a small laugh. "It's terrifying, but I think the change will be good. I've . . . I've never really known anything else."

"I know it upset you when I offered before—"

"Joel—"

"So I won't offer," I insist. "But, I will support you however you need, whether that's reading over your résumé or circling the wanted ads. I'll be there."

"Thank you," she whispers.

"I need to see you," I say. "I know you're probably tired and want to just go to sleep but . . . would you maybe come over here?"

There's a brief pause. "I . . . sure, of course. But, uh—"

"I get it. You're tired. I'm sorry I asked."

"No!" she says a little forcefully. "No, it's not that, it's just—"

"What?"

She groans. "I don't know the bus schedule for that side of town."

I frown. "The bus?"

She laughs humorlessly. "Are you forgetting I don't have a car?"

"Oh!" Shit, I'm such a fucking doofus. "Dusty, don't be ridiculous. I'll come and get you."

She hums. "Is your friend back? I thought he took off in your car?"

Fuck. "Yes, right. Umm . . . I'll send a cab."

"A cab?"

"Yeah. Be downstairs in ten minutes."

CHAPTER 27

Love is the Drug

DUSTY

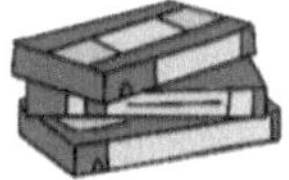

I watch the sun rise over the San Francisco hills, relaxing into the plush seat and feeling relaxed for the first time in weeks. Months? Joel must have given the cab driver his address, because without me having to utter a word, we sped off toward one of the nicer areas of town. Seeing the houses over here, with their pristine lawns and fancy cars, uncertainty encroaches on my sense of peace.

Maybe I never really thought about it before, but . . . Joel must have money. I mean, obviously, he has money. He's a rockstar whose songs are on the radio, and that hardly pays pennies, but as I gaze out the window, I start to think that maybe I underestimated just how many more pennies he makes than me.

Me. With my studio apartment over a laundromat in one of the roughest areas of town, who talks dirty to men on the phone and gets paid by the minute. I sigh and let my head rest against the glass. For all of our class differences though, Joel has never made me feel lower than him. It's rare for a man who finally makes his fortune to not treat people like dirt. Especially women. But Joel is just sweet.

I wonder what his bandmates are like. Do they have

girlfriends too? *Girlfriend.* It's such a foreign word, it feels surreal saying it in my head. And what about his best friend? The one with the song problem? The one who's missing. The one who is so important to Joel that it seems like his whole world revolves around him. And with him missing, that world is falling apart.

Does he know about me? If he does, then does he know the truth about what I do? Did? And if he doesn't . . . why not?

The cab driver turns down a sunlit street. The houses are low and long out here. Bungalows with garages and wide lots. It's so strange to think that a rockstar lives here, but what did I think? That he was living in a gilded mansion with a giant wrought iron fence? We pull into a driveway, and a grin tugs at my lips at the sight of Joel sitting on a chair beside the front door. He grins at me and jogs over to open my door.

"Hey, gorgeous," he says, and without missing a beat, kisses me full on the lips. When he pulls away I nearly whine at the loss. It wasn't enough. I need more.

He closes the door behind me and turns to the driver. "Thanks, man," he says, palming him a few bills. "Have a good one."

The cab backs out and drives off down the street and I turn toward Joel, but a moment later I'm scooped up, a face buried in my chest. Even though I'm tired, I'm energized by his touch. And he needs me. He's going through a hard time, and I meant what I said. His hardships are mine too.

When he sets me down in the entryway and shuts the door behind us, I crane my neck to get a better look at his place. "This is your house?"

He shrugs. "It's a rental. Got a few more months on the lease, then we'll have to find something else."

"Oh."

"I'll be sad to go, though," he admits, wrapping his arms around me and drawing his nose along my cheek. "This was the first house we all rented together when we came out west."

I perk up at this. "You all lived together? That's adorable."

He rests his chin on my shoulder. "Not much that's adorable about four guys and one girl living together."

"One girl?"

He chuckles. "Yeah, Becks. James's wife."

My eyes nearly bulge out of their sockets. "One of your bandmates is married? How old is he?"

His face scrunches as he thinks. "Almost twenty-one. She's twenty."

"Twenty-one . . . That's so young!"

He laughs. "Not for them. I guess when you know, you know, right?"

I nod, and my stomach twists unpleasantly. Wasn't I younger than that when I got engaged? Didn't I think I'd be married and starting a family at eighteen? But now that I'm twenty-five . . . it seems so impulsively *stupid*. What had I been thinking? What had *he* been thinking? Maybe it was better it didn't work out, or we'd hate each other now. A phantom pain hits me, and I rub at the skin on my ring finger.

"You okay?" Joel asks.

I nod. "Yes, sorry."

"Anyway, Becks, she took good care of us. Still does. You know, you and I actually met on their wedding night."

This does shock me. "That's whose wedding you were in Vegas for?"

He grins and nods.

"Wow. Well, I hope to meet them someday."

He pulls me closer and presses a firm palm into my backside. "You will. Soon. I already told them about you."

"You did?"

"Mhm."

"So, this—us, I mean. You're serious."

He frowns. "Did you think I wasn't?"

I gnaw at my bottom lip. "Yes, but I—sorry, I just have a hard time trusting people, that's all. But you keep surprising me, Joel Thanger."

"It bodes well for me that you like surprises."

I wrap my arms around his neck and kiss his jaw. "You've been my favorite surprise."

His hands slowly wind up my waist, over the curve of my hips, up and over my shoulder blades to grasp my face. Eyes locking on mine he leans forward and kisses me. Deep and slow and passionate, my knees already buckling beneath me at their intensity. My body is pliant, ready to give him whatever he wants. He pulls me this way, pushes me that way, angles my head or tugs it back to expose my throat. I allow my brain to turn off and simply *be* for him.

"I haven't stopped thinking about you," he whispers breathlessly. "It's like I'm addicted to you."

"You make me feel," I say, my body growing hot as I try to find his eyes again and when I do, I say it again. "You make me *feel*."

His smile is soft this time. "Do you want a tour of the rest of the house?"

Slowly, I shake my head, then grab the neck of his shirt. "Only if you show me your bedroom first."

His lips tease mine again as he picks me up and carries me down one hallway. The door opens, and I break away to take in my surroundings. His room is dark but cozy. Thick, lush curtains keep out most of the early morning daylight. A large bed with black sheets and walls covered in music posters. There are a few bass guitars on stands in one corner, as well as an amp and pair of headphones.

"Will you play me some of your music?" I ask as he sets me back down on my feet and kisses my neck.

He blinks. "Right now?"

I smirk. I can't wait either. "Later."

He nods. "Later. Definitely. But right now, I need you naked."

"That can be arranged," I tease, swaying my hips toward his bed. Keeping my back to him, I pull off my shirt, the fabric inching up my stomach until it slides over my arms and head. My hair cascades down, tickling my back, and goose bumps prickle up my spine.

A glance over my shoulder exposes his hungry stare. My pulse throbs between my legs at that look. It's like he wants to devour me and I'm getting his meal ready. I reach behind and unclasp my bra, letting it spring apart, then in a way I learned at the strip club all those years ago, make a show of sliding the straps down both arms before holding the garment out to the side and allowing it to fall.

I can practically hear him swallow as he takes a few steps toward me, brushing aside my hair before trailing his fingers down my spine. His lips press gently to my shoulder blade, and I close my eyes against the cacophony of sensations shooting through me.

"I could kiss every freckle on your skin," he whispers, winding his hands around to splay across my stomach.

With a smile, I reach back and tangle my fingers in his silky hair. "That might take a long time."

He nips the skin of my neck, the sting eliciting a small gasp from my throat before he licks gently over the same spot, and I think I might melt into a puddle on the shag carpet. "I've got nowhere else to be."

I turn in his arms, my breasts brushing against his chest. "I thought about what you said. Last time, I mean," I say, forcing my chin up and my shoulders back.

"You have?" he asks. "About—"

I nod and swallow. "If it's what you like, then I want to give it a shot."

Eyes tracking mine, he holds my face. "Are you sure?"

"Yes," I say. "You'll make it feel good?"

"Oh, baby, I'll make you feel so fucking good you won't want anything else."

I cock an eyebrow. "You're mighty confident."

He kisses me again. "I have a few tools up my sleeve."

I'm not quite sure what he means by "tools," but color me intrigued. "Okay then." I drag my fingers against his abdomen, his muscles contracting as I pull his shirt up and over his head, and he takes my nipple in his mouth before it even has a chance to land on the carpet with a soft *thump*. I throw my head back as his tongue swirls and flicks, and I close my eyes as a groan escapes my mouth.

His lips worship my other nipple, and I start to sweat, the room becoming so warm so quickly that I feel like putty in his arms.

"Turn around for me," he says.

I nod and do as I'm told, standing before the bed to face our reflection in the mirrored closet doors. I've always enjoyed looking at my body. I grew up knowing it was my best asset. Perhaps that's why it never fazed me to let others look at it too. However, the sight that I behold of Joel kissing my spine as he bends to pull down my jeans will be something I remember forever.

His fingers nimbly undo the button and zipper as he kisses down the base of my spine, then over my hip, slowly pulling down my jeans and underwear before helping me free my legs.

"Bend over on the bed," he rasps, and my stomach flips with both excitement and nerves.

I step forward until my knees sink into the mattress, and with everything completely bare, I bend forward, placing my hands on the sheets. My aching breasts hang heavily, and for a moment, I'm reminded of my phone call with Baby. How he told me to get on my knees and crawl. A knot forms in my stomach and I clamp my eyes closed, trying to block the thought.

Joel. *Joel.* You're here with Joel. He's here and he's real. Stop thinking about what could have been.

Joel steps up behind me, his jean-clad hips hitting the backs of my thighs. My hands grasp behind me for any of him I can get. I need to focus. He's crazy about me and I've fallen for him.

"Fuck, sweetheart," he mutters, "you smell so good."

I swallow hard, the knot tightening before I discreetly pinch my stomach to rid Baby from my mind. "Can I ask one favor?" I whisper.

He traces the shell of my ear with his lips and I shudder. "Anything."

"Don't call me sweetheart."

Without any hesitation he kisses the spot where my earlobe meets my neck and my knees nearly buckle. "Princess it is."

I let out a breath, the guilt that had built up so quickly dissipating as his fingers explore my body. He presses between my shoulder blades, pushing my chest down further, my ass up in the air in front of him. "Do you have any idea how goddamn gorgeous you are?"

My chest flutters, and he palms my ass tenderly. For a moment I think he might smack it—I want him to smack it—but I shudder hard when his tongue licks up my slit from my clit until it sinks into my pussy.

"Oh fuck," I whine, my words muffled by the sheets. Then he's feasting on me, licking and teasing and I grab on to anything I can, my fists grappling with the black sheets.

It feels so fucking good that I spread my legs wider for him, pushing my hips back for more. Fuck, his mouth is a masterpiece, and he endlessly works at my clit as my breathing grows ragged.

"Oh god, Joel," I moan, my thighs beginning to shake as I careen toward an orgasm. The position he has me in, coupled with his miraculous mouth, has my belly poised to burst, toes scrunching. "Fuck, I'm going to come."

His tongue is gone in an instant and my eyes fly open as the coil starts to decompress, my impending orgasm fading away little by little.

"Wait—" I say, pushing myself up off the bed. "What are you doing?"

Joel stands behind me, his face slick with my juices, smirking down at me. "Not yet, princess."

I open my mouth but can't seem to find the words. "But—but . . . I was so close."

He walks around me to the other side of the bed, unbuckling his pants as he goes, and I realize what's coming. I can't fucking wait.

"You'll be close a lot," he says, dropping his pants and reaching forward to grab my neck so I have to crawl across the bed toward him. "You'll be so desperate to come that you'll do anything for it."

His stiff cock springs forward, the tip glistening in the low light.

"And you'll come, I promise you that," he says, pulling my face up toward his. "But only while I'm fucking you in the ass."

I can taste myself on his tongue when he kisses me next and it's heady and hot. My pussy throbs, my swollen clit desperate for more of his touch. He pulls away though, releases his grasp on the back of my neck, and my body drops back down until his cock is inches from my face.

"Now," he says in a tone I've never heard from him before. "Does this pretty mouth want to be filled with my cock?"

I stare up at him, mesmerized by his eyes. "Yes, please."

He nods, and then his cock is pressing at my lips. "That's my good girl."

Do That to Me One More Time

JOEL

This woman will be the death of me, I know it. Her gorgeous, responsive body spread bare for me, but more importantly, that beautiful fucking mind of hers. She's sex appeal and humor and kindness all wrapped up in one redheaded freckled package, and I can't get enough. Then to top it all off, she wants to do this for me, wants to be adventurous and trusts me to make it good. If I died tomorrow, that would be okay.

But if I'm still alive and this stunning creature is still in my bed, well, I'm going to do everything in my power to make sure she never leaves my side.

"Open up," I say, her pretty eyes laser focused on mine.

She gives me a sultry smile as she wraps her lips around my tip. I tangle my hands in her curls, gathering them up over her head as she licks and sucks. Fuck, her mouth is so good, but I'm going to have more than her mouth, tonight. She lifts one hand to wrap around my cock, the wet sound of her mouth and hand making my balls tighten and my muscles tense.

"Your mouth is exquisite."

She moans, her eyes fluttering as she takes me as far as she can, drool dripping down her chin over my balls. Shit, if I keep this up any longer, I'm going to come, and I have plans for her that will take a while. I pull her off me, her lips giving a wet *pop* before she wipes her mouth.

"Come here, princess," I groan. "Lie on your back for me."

She rolls her lips, then does as I ask. Her red hair fans out around her head like a goddess of the sea, and I lean over her to lavish some more attention on her perfect tits. Back arching, her fingers trail down my arms, nails grazing my skin.

"Joel," she whispers.

I love the way her voice gets deep—raspy. Like she's letting her carnal side take over. I see why men call and jack off to her voice, but there's no pretending here. Not with me. Sinking to my knees at the edge of the bed, I cup the soft skin under her thighs and push them back, spreading her wide open.

Now this is a sight to see. Her eyes closed, head rolling back and forth, fists tangling in my sheets. It happens quicker this time. She comes close to her release, but when her toes curl, I back off, grinning as she voices her displeasure.

"No," she whimpers.

I kiss up the inside of her thighs, giving her a moment for the impending orgasm to recede. Her breasts heave and her pussy drips. Fuck, her wet hole clenches before me, and I'm lost. With my middle finger I gently swipe across her entrance. She jolts, legs twitching at my touch.

"Oh god," she cries.

Fuck, she's so sensitive. With the same finger, I trace her entrance, rimming the opening but never dipping inside. Her hips buck as I tease her over and over, her head lolling to the side.

"Please," she whines. "Joel, please."

I know what she *wants*—but what she needs is not for me to fuck her pretty little pussy tonight. So my finger slides down, the skin slippery as I press against her ass.

She gasps, her head shooting up and her eyes finding mine.

"Tell me to stop and we do, no questions asked," I reassure her.

She shakes her head and before she can tell me to continue, I'm sucking her clit back into my mouth while my finger breaches that tight ring of muscle.

"Relax, princess," I say as I feel her clench. "You hold all the power here. I'm at your mercy."

I hear her breathe out a laugh, but when my tongue licks up her pussy again, she relaxes, my finger sliding deeper. I let her get used to the unusual sensation, with just the first half of my finger inside her. After a minute or two with my mouth on her clit and finger in her ass, her legs begin to shake again and goddamn, I'm hard as steel watching this. I pull back and she cries out, grumbling something that sounds a lot like *not fair*.

"Joel, I'm going to kill you," she threatens.

I chuckle and reach for the nightstand drawer for my secret weapons. "No, I don't think you will."

Her eyes widen. "Uh, what's that?"

I raise an eyebrow. "The lube?"

"No," she says, rolling her eyes. "*That*."

I smirk. "Oh, this?" I hold up the toy, and she studies it. "Never seen one before?"

Tentatively, she shakes her head.

As I drip some of the lube onto her ass and my fingers, I smile. "It's a vibrator."

"A what?"

"A vibrator," I say again, leaning over and kissing her. "And trust me, it's about to be your new best friend."

I hold the wand up next to our faces and turn it on, the machine vibrating with an unmistakable buzzing noise. I trail it down her chest, her breath catching as I caress her nipples with it.

She sighs, her eyes closing again.

"Hold your legs back," I instruct, and she complies

immediately, grabbing behind her knees and spreading herself. My finger breaches her ass again as I glide the vibrator over her clit.

"Oh god!" she cries.

"See?" I smirk.

I take my time, working my finger in and out of her as the vibrator keeps her on the very edge of orgasm. It doesn't take too long before I can easily fit two fingers inside of her.

"Such a good girl. You're doing so well," I praise. "How about another one?"

"I feel . . . so full," she whispers between panting gasps.

"Do you need me to stop?" I ask.

"No! No—it's good. Strange but . . . oh shit," she says as I tease her again with the vibrator, "so good."

With three fingers inside her, I start to pump in and out, in and out. Her tits bounce from the movement. She shudders and my cock twitches impatiently as she rocks her hips—chasing my fingers.

"Joel, oh god, please—please let me come."

"You need to come, don't you?" I ask. "It's driving you crazy. Look at this," I say, swiping my thumb across her entrance. She jumps, her muscles clenching around my fingers, sucking them further inside her. "You're fucking soaked, princess. Making a puddle on my bed."

"I-I, *ah*!"

"But you're loving it aren't you?"

She pants out a desperate *"Yes."*

I pull my fingers out of her slowly, then crowd her space. "Good, because I'm about to fuck this perfect little asshole of yours," I murmur against her cheek, her eyes widening. "And when you come, don't be shy. I want to hear how much you love it."

I kiss her deeply, passionately, our tongues both fighting for dominance in each other's mouths. I love when sex gets like this, rough and messy and without inhibitions. When you can let how you feel carry you away. Does she understand how she makes me feel? Does what we're doing together communicate how much I feel for her?

I release her lips, grab a condom from the nightstand and sheathe myself, then slather a healthy amount of lube over my aching cock. To be honest, I'll be lucky to fit all the way inside her before blowing my load. But damn, just being here is worth it.

"You ready?" I ask.

Fuck she looks so gorgeous right now. Her skin flush, pussy dripping and swollen with need, eyes glazed . . . she's stunning. A galaxy of shining stars pulling me in with her gravity. She nods, and I guide my cock to her ass, pushing forward gently. And . . . holy shit, she feels better than I could've imagined. I'll do anything for her. Feed her, clothe her, fuck her, worship her, as long as she's mine.

CHAPTER 29

Every Rose Has It's Thorn

DUSTY

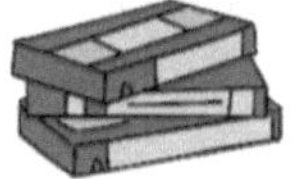

"Eyes on me when I fuck you, princess."

It's so much. It's overwhelming. Oh god, how does it feel so good? He stretches me further than he has yet and it's as if my whole nervous system gets a restart. The pleasure isn't localized, but everywhere. All I want to do is close my eyes and ride out this wave blindly, but he wants to see my eyes so I force them open.

"Fuck, Dusty, you're doing so good," he grunts. Fuck, he's so gorgeous. Glistening with sweat, his face twisting with self-restraint. I can tell he wants to just let go—to use me for himself —but he's making sure I enjoy it and fuck, I can't believe it, but I do.

"Joel," I say, my voice hoarse, my brain fuzzy. "Make me come."

He kisses me hard, his cock sinking into me deeper, and I gasp against his lips. When he leans back, I hear the buzzing from that beautiful toy, and he touches it to my clit. I fight against rolling my eyes back in my skull, unsure whether anything will ever feel this good again. Then he starts thrusting and, oh my god, it's so good and I'm on the *very* edge.

"Fuck . . . fuck," I cry. "Oh god, Joel, just like that—"

"I'm so close," he grits out. "Come with me."

Wave after wave, it builds inside me. He touches a finger to my empty wet hole, and I cry out. He slips two fingers inside as he fucks my ass, and I'm gone.

"Oh Joel! Oh god, I'm coming so hard. Fuck!"

And I do. My vision blurs with it, and bright lights pop in my eyes as fluid gushes from my pussy. Joel's thrusts speed up, then falter as he groans and gasps. He doesn't collapse on top of me like I imagined he would. No, instead he peppers my face with tiny kisses. Like he knows anything more right now would be too much.

I can feel every twitch and movement as he pulls out of me, and I suddenly feel empty. As he moves off of me, I roll over, tucking my knees up as I try to calm down. It's like every emotion is heightened—the world suddenly being thrust into hypervision. Tears fill my eyes and silently spill down my cheeks.

"Shhh," Joel soothes.

"I—I'm not sad . . . I promise," I blurt.

He nods and kisses my forehead, wrapping himself around me. "I know. It's intense. Just take your time. You did amazing."

I nod and pull in a deep, shaky breath, exhaling a short laugh. "I didn't expect *that*."

His forehead creases. "I didn't hurt you, did I?"

"No. Not at all. That was—"

But I don't have the words. Brand-new? Unprecedented? Earth-shattering?

"I suppose you truly lived up to your promise," I say, opening one eye to peek up at him.

He chuckles softly. "I'm glad you aren't disappointed. I've never done that before."

I gasp. "You—what?"

Then he throws his leg over me. "I'm just fucking with you."

I laugh. He can always make me laugh. The light he holds in his heart and smile is the most beautiful thing I've ever seen. If it were pitch-black, I could still find it.

"Do you want some water?" he asks as he brushes my hair back.

"Yes, please. Then I believe you have some showing off to do."

He cocks an eyebrow. "Didn't I just do that?"

I roll my eyes and place my hand on his chest. "You said you'd play me some of your music. I haven't heard it yet."

He grins. "I guess that's true. How about I get us some water and when you're ready, come out to the living room and I'll put on the stereo."

"Okay." He goes to get up, but I grab his arm. "Wait."

"What's wrong?" he asks.

I scan his face, fingers running down his exposed neck. "I just —I want you to know that I feel *something* . . ."

He raises his eyebrows. "Oh?"

"In here," I say, placing his hand on my heart. "I know I shouldn't say the words . . ."

He holds his breath. Waiting to hear what I have to say. Desperate for me to say it.

"So I won't say it. Not yet. But I do—feel them, I mean."

He kisses me so tenderly my heart might actually burst. "I do too."

I watch from the bed as he gets up, throws on a pair of sweatpants, then walks out the door. My muscles are sore and stiff, and for a while, I simply lie on the bed, staring at the ceiling and thinking about nothing. I was tired before, but now? I'm both exhausted and wide awake, brain buzzing.

Finally, I peel myself off the sheets and try to stretch out my limbs. I grab Joel's sleeveless shirt from the floor and pull it on over myself, then find my panties, which somehow landed on the lampshade. As I walk toward the door, I catch sight of myself in the mirror above Joel's dresser. My hair is utterly wild. My lips are swollen, my eyes bright. I'm glowing, but disheveled, and it might be the prettiest I've ever felt.

I fluff my hair and smile, then head out the door and down the hallway. When I enter the living room, the gas fireplace is on and Joel is standing in front of a wall unit housing a complicated-looking stereo system.

I sidle up to him and wrap my arms around his stomach. "I thought you were going to play your guitar for me."

He rubs his hands along my arms. "I would, but my fingers are dead tired. I promise I'll give you the live version another time. Besides, I don't sing or play the melody, so you should hear the full versions first."

"Okay," I say, and after he sets the needle on the album with a gorgeous blond girl on the front looking positively scandalous, he pulls me over onto the couch.

The music starts harsh and fast, and compared to my own old-fashioned tastes, it takes a moment to adjust—to appreciate it and let myself hear the melodies. Joel can barely sit still next to me—his fingers, which don't look tired in the slightest, play an invisible rhythm on his thigh—and I smile softly at just how fucking cute he is. His face lights up like a kid on Christmas morning and I can't take my eyes off him.

"What do you think?" he asks.

"I like it," I admit. True, it's not my preferred genre, but I can feel him shine through the music.

His head starts to bob. "Oh, I love this part, listen . . ."

There's a complicated guitar solo that plays at breakneck speed, and I can't help but be impressed that someone has managed to put so many notes together so seamlessly.

"James absolutely kills that riff live," he says.

"James plays the guitar?" I ask. He's never actually told me the names of his bandmates.

"Yeah, James on lead, Dave on drums and—" He nods, then stands abruptly as something in the music changes. "Here comes Key with the lyrics."

The music warbles in the distance as if I've suddenly been plunged into an icy cold river. My body shivers, and I can't hear anything past the ringing in my ears. Nausea rolls in my stomach, and the pleasant ache I felt throughout my body a moment ago turns every inch to agony.

"Wha—what did you just say?"

My voice is far away. I'm having an out-of-body experience. I can see myself frozen in fear on the couch as Joel plays air guitar in front of me, no idea he just said the one thing that could completely shatter me.

"Key," he says, none the wiser. "He plays rhythm guitar and is the lead singer. Can you believe this guy started out as a do-gooder church boy from Iowa?"

Joel grabs a picture frame off the shelf above the stereo and hands it to me. There are four men. A tall blond with long hair holds a pair of drumsticks in the air above him. He stands next to a young man with long, curly black hair and dark eyes—their free arms wrapped around each other with the kind of carefree smiles that must come from doing what you love. But what stops my heart in my chest are the two boys next to them.

With his silky dark hair and million-dollar smile is Joel. But the fourth one. The final one—his eyes are more than familiar. How many times have I dreamt about his eyes, that face? How many nights have I stayed up filled with anger and regret and overthinking so many things? How much have I mourned what we had together?

Joel points his finger to the man. "He's the one who's missing. My best friend—Key."

And with those words, my world is ripped apart.

CHAPTER 30

Love Bites

KEY

TWO YEARS AGO

I wonder what my parents would say if they could see me right now? Half drunk and wandering the Las Vegas Strip with my friends for a wedding that didn't take place in a church. My mom would probably have a heart attack. My dad would remain stoic and disapproving, his palm itching to reach for his belt to lay more welts across my palms. But me? All I can do is think about how happy James and Becks are. While most people wouldn't understand the desire to get married so young . . . I get it. Sometimes you just *know* and don't want anything to get in the way of building your own family—especially when the one you were given is so shitty.

The smile falls from my face as I think of what feels like another life. My life before the band, before military school. Before San Francisco. Back in Iowa, when I sat at a bus station waiting to run away with the woman I loved. But she left. She left me, and every day since I've thought about why I wasn't enough. Why didn't she want me? And our baby . . . oh god, to this day I sit and wonder if there even is a baby. Do I have a child walking and talking out there somewhere? Or did she end it as quickly as that last night?

I finger the ring she so unceremoniously returned, trying to imagine her happy. That it was worth it. That she's living the life she always dreamed for herself. That all that heartbreak and pain wasn't for nothing.

An arm wraps around my shoulders, pulls me back, and I smile as Joel leans in close. "Hey, man, I have a feeling James and Becks are going to ditch us soon."

I look over to find our friend wrapped around his new bride, who yawns widely. "Yeah, you're probably right." I glance over at Dave, who's watching Izzy with a kind of feral obsession. He looks like he's about two seconds away from throwing her drunk ass over his shoulder and taking her somewhere she can lie down before puking.

"There's a strip club across the street," Joel suggests with a smirk.

"Perfect," I reply. What an excellent way to get the thought of lost love off my mind.

"Hey, guys," James calls. "Becks and I, we're going to get a room at the Flamingo for the night. You know, wedding night and all." He grins. "How about we meet up at that diner by the chapel in the morning for breakfast?"

"Told you," Joel whispers.

I chuckle and wrap my arm around James and squeeze. "Aww, Jamesey's got to go take care of his wifey," I say, making an obscene kissing gesture as he pushes me away.

"That's cool," Joel says. "We were thinking about hitting up the strip club anyway."

"Yeah, well, don't blow all your money," James warns.

What else am I supposed to spend my money on? The woman I want is gone. The family I would've worked hard to support doesn't exist. And my best friend? He enjoys watching the girls, therefore I do too. Because what's the alternative? Sitting in a quiet corner to brood?

"There's no greater purpose for hard earned cash than spending it on tits and ass," I say to deflect, then pull Joel along with me. I wave at Dave, but he's following along after Isabella like a lost puppy, and I start to see it happen. Them—together. Will they start dating? What if they end up married? What if Joel is next? What if they all end up happy and I'm left alone?

"So what are we thinking," Joel says, clapping his hands together eagerly. "You feeling a Vegas team-up if it's an option? Or you want to go solo tonight?"

I remember the exact moment that Joel and I figured out we like to share girls. We've always had the same taste in women. Or rather I could always find something in the women he liked that reminded me of Dusty. The first night it happened we were playing at some shitty bar in downtown Iowa before James joined the band.

We were both hammered and Joel was flirting with a pretty brunette. When I saw her, I thought about how her freckles were just like Dusty's and how I wanted her simply so I could imagine I was with the one I lost. When Joel brought her over to tell me he was taking her back to our one-bedroom apartment, I couldn't help myself. I kissed her right in front of him at that bar. Shocked by my own jerk move, I apologized immediately, blaming it on the alcohol. To my shock she wasn't upset, just grabbed my hand, then Joel's, and before I knew it we were all in bed together.

Deep down I know the reason I insert myself into Joel's relationships. I know it's really because I'm worried he'll fall in love. That he'll find his soulmate and it won't be me. And that's terrifying. I don't want to be alone, because that's when I'm crushed by the memories of what could've been.

I shrug. "Vegas team-up sounds fun. You sure you want to waste the motel voucher though?"

He laughs. "Who says it'll go to waste? After we're done, I plan on going to my own room. You can snuggle with the girl while I get some uninterrupted shut-eye. You snore like a freight train when you're drunk."

I grin, and the two of us walk up to the velvet rope walkway in front of the club. Thankfully, there isn't much of a line, and within ten minutes, we're being ushered inside. The speakers are blaring Whitesnake, and before we get far, there's half a dozen nearly naked girls within a twelve-foot radius.

"I'm going to go get us some drinks," Joel says in my ear, and I nod before watching him walk away toward the back of the club where a neon bar stretches the length of the place.

I love these places because the haze in the air and the music help to keep the memories away. It works like a charm. Naked women and loud music plus alcohol equals burying my feelings. Not exactly healthy, but it's not like I care. I find a pair of chairs and a table off to the side of the stage and sit down as I wait for Joel. There's a dancer on the pole before me. A blond with thick thighs, and I groan as I think about what it would be like to have my face between those legs while Joel fucks her ass. But she's not looking at me. She's trying to get the guy in the fancy suit to choose her and . . . yup, she's got him. Lucky bastard.

Sometimes, it takes a few tries to get the girls to look our way. Strippers tend to pick the guys who dress expensive, likely assuming they have the most money, and ninety-five percent of the time they'd be right. But not with us. No, we have money to burn. Just waiting for the—

"Hiya, handsome. What brings you in here tonight?"

I turn toward the voice and there she is. I jolt forward, my hand coming to my chest. Did I die? Am I in heaven? Or is this hell? What other reason would there be for gazing upon that gorgeous freckled face? Those eyes as blue as the sky? It seems to hit her too and she freezes in place.

I don't know what to do or say or think. How is she here? How is she in Vegas at a strip club of all places?

"Dusty?"

Her unblinking eyes dart over my face so fast they nearly blur. "Key."

She straightens, her mouth gaping like she can't string together any words. I don't blame her. Neither can I. She blinks, then spins and walks away.

My legs move on instinct, following as she weaves through a crowd of people, and I have to dodge them to keep up. I can see where she's headed, and my heart, which is already sprinting, starts to constrict.

"Dusty, wait! Please," I call over the noise.

A waitress with a tray full of drinks slows her down and I reach forward to grasp her wrist. Finally she stops, but pulls out of my grasp, her eyes panicked and scanning our surroundings.

"Don't grab me," she says frantically, "or they'll throw you out."

I hold my hands up in surrender. "I'm sorry, I'm sorry, I just . . . I needed you to stop."

She bites her lip, and I'm flooded by memories of us as teens when she would get anxious and do this exact same thing. It feels like I'm back there, in that humid, dank cabin in the woods.

"You're . . ." I start, but I hardly know where to begin. "I can't believe you're here."

She drops her head and crosses her arms. "Yeah, well—"

"What are you—"

I take in her clothes. How she's wearing quite possibly the smallest black bikini I've ever seen with a neon green fishnet dress overtop, leaving nothing to the imagination.

"Wait, you're working here?"

Her jaw tenses. "No, I just came for the free buffet. Of course I work here."

"But," I start, licking my lips that have turned to sandpaper. "Why?"

"Why do you think?" she grits out. "It pays money. I have bills that require money. Therefore this place pays the bills."

"Oh, well, sure. Yeah."

Her nails tap rhythmically on her arm as the silence stretches on between us, punctuated by some awful disco song in the background.

"Look, are we done here?"

My mouth drops open at the hostility. Why is she acting like this? *She* left *me*. "Did I say something wrong?"

She closes her eyes and sighs. "No, just—I'm working and I can't be doing *this* right now."

It hits me like a truck. She works here. She *works* here.

"Dusty, tell me you're not—" She avoids my eye so I push on. "You're a stripper?"

None of this makes sense. She left me to make something better of herself. She wanted to be an actress. Or work with movies. And while I would never shame the girls who *do* choose this life, did she seriously leave me at that bus station to spend her nights working as a stripper?

She doesn't say anything, and the anger that builds in my chest is suddenly bubbling over.

"You—this is what you left for? Working as a stripper in some sleazy, bullshit club in Vegas?"

Her eyes narrow and it's as if the electricity in the room flickers. "Yes, Key! I'm a stripper at a sleazy, bullshit club in Vegas. Why the fuck do you care anyway?"

"Why do I—why do I fucking care?"

But she just stares at me hard. Waiting for my answer.

"Because we were supposed to be together. We were going to be a family and make something of ourselves and instead you left me to do this shit? And the b-baby?" My voice cracks and her face crumbles. "For fuck's sake, was there ever even a baby to begin with?"

She stumbles back half a step. "How dare you!"

"What am I supposed to fucking think? It seems like I never really knew you at all."

"Don't!" she yells over the music. "Don't you dare come in here and judge what I do with my life." Her entire body is vibrating with fury and her lips tremble with every syllable. "Of course there was a baby. But it's gone now. I never had it. Happy?"

Some of the rage subsides, replaced by the unsatisfied feeling of a long-awaited question not being answered the way you wish. I never realized until this moment how much I wished our baby was born. How the finality of its existence hurts me deeper than I ever thought it could.

I'm going about this all wrong. Why am I so angry with her? I reach out for her again and gently touch her arm, the familiar feel of her skin like a drug relapse after being sober for years. I shouldn't be angry. It's not her fault—it's mine. "Dusty, please—I couldn't take care of you properly then, but I can now."

"Key, don't—"

"I'm sorry I yelled. Just—" I shake my head. "Come home with me. You don't have to stay here," I say, moving toward her, my hands tracing up her shoulders until I'm cupping her face. "You don't have to do this anymore. I can take care of you. Let me save you."

The moment the words leave my lips I wish I could take them back. Tell her I didn't mean it the way it came out, but there's fire in her gaze and she pushes me hard in the chest.

"Save me?"

She laughs. An unrestrained, maniacal sound that sends a chill down my spine.

"That's all this ever was, wasn't it?" she says, wiping the

mirth from her eyes. "It was always about saving me. Saving me from my trashy parents, from my abusive dad, from myself, from our *mistake*."

My heart splits in half. "Our mistake?"

"I suppose I can't be mad about it. It's how you were brought up. Jesus saves Mary Magdalene too, right? The good boy who saves the whore."

I can barely breathe. "No! No, that's not—it was never like that for me," I say desperately. Pleadingly.

She shakes her head and backs away, and I see the tears trickle down her freckled cheeks. "Don't feel bad for me, Keith. I never wanted your pity."

"But how could you choose this?" I ask, throwing my arms out wide. "How could you end up here instead of . . ."

With me. Just say it. *Say it.*

"I won't apologize for the choices I made, because they were mine. And whether they were good or bad, I won't stand here while you make me feel guilty about them."

"Dusty . . ." I reach out for her and touch her arm, and for a moment I can see the way it calms her. The tension easing in her muscles.

"Hey, man, hands off!"

A thick, muscled bouncer grasps my arm and twists it behind my back. I grunt in pain, and my knees buckle as I'm hauled away from her. I fight against the man, but another one joins in and soon I'm being dragged away. Surely she won't let them take me. Surely she won't . . . but she's backing away, shaking her head.

"No! Stop, I need to tell her," I beg.

The bouncer turns to her. "This guy bothering you?"

And with a coldness I never believed she was capable of, she nods. "Yes."

The breath is knocked out of me with that one word.

"All right, pal. You're done here," he says, pulling me away.

There's still so much I have to say. "No," I whisper. It can't be over like this.

I reach out for her again but she's gone, disappearing through a black door where I can't follow. My chest feels like it's caving in, the pain so excruciating that for a moment I worry I might be having a heart attack. It feels like that awful night all over again. Her choosing to leave me behind. Then the panic sets in as I'm carried out into the gutter behind the club, and as I'm tossed into the street, I search around for men in white uniforms who might pop up out of nowhere to take me back to Samson Academy.

They don't come. I'm safe from that at least. The tears start next and everything hits me at once. She never really loved me. It's the only explanation. How else can someone be so unfeeling and cold? I brace my hands on my knees and throw up into a sewer grate.

Forever passes before I pull myself up. Part of me hoped Joel would come find me, but he must have met a distraction, and I can't fault him for that. All I want to do is curl up in my bed at the motel and cry, so I stumble back down the Strip toward the chapel where our night started so happily. I suppose part of me always thought that maybe if I ever saw Dusty again it would be like it is in my dreams. That she would realize we were meant to be together. That she hadn't really meant it when she left me. That there's a better explanation.

Our history says differently though. She was always leaving me and I was always too stupid to think she might finally stay. That she only ever left because she had to. And is she right? Was I only ever in love with her because she was someone for me to fix? So I could play the hero because I couldn't even save myself from my own life?

I've swallowed a hard truth tonight: She's no damsel. And I'm no hero.

CHAPTER 31

Love Will Tear Us Apart

JOEL

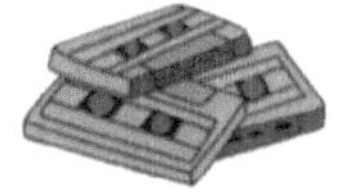

"Dusty, are you okay?" I ask. "Hey, you—you look like you've seen a ghost."

Her chest rises and falls rapidly. Is she hyperventilating? Eyes wide and terrified, she's trembling like a leaf. Maybe she's dehydrated from earlier.

"I'll get you some water, okay? Actually, maybe I'll grab you some juice," I correct myself, thinking maybe her blood sugar is low. We were in the bedroom for quite a long time and I was so excited to finally have her in my bed that I didn't ask her when she last ate.

She doesn't respond, but gives a kind of shaky nod of her head, so I take that as a yes. Shit, I shouldn't have pushed her so hard. Why did I insist we do that for our first time together? I'm such a selfish idiot. I walk toward the fridge and grab the bottle of apple juice and a glass from the cupboard. Mid-pour, I'm startled by the sound of the door opening.

"Joel?"

I look up and feel the most intense relief of my life. Key's here. He's back. I look him up and down, making sure he's okay, my heartbeat galloping in my chest as I fight back tears. I thought

I lost him for good. But it's short-lived by the rage that follows. Maybe I need some juice too, because I'm suddenly lightheaded.

"Key?"

He's really here. What the fuck has he been doing?

"Joel," he says, shaking his head. "Listen man, I'm so fucking sorry. I'm so—I can't even begin to tell you how sorry I am for just taking off like that."

"You're *sorry*? Are you fucking kidding me right now? Do you have any idea what's been going on?"

He runs a hand through his tangled curls. "I know, I know, I'm sorry."

I lean forward over the counter and lower my voice. "We've been looking everywhere! I called hospitals. We thought that you might have . . ."

His eyebrows lift. "Might have what?"

"We thought you might have tried to kill yourself," I finally rush out.

For a moment he looks like he's going to argue with me. Like he's upset we could ever think that. That the situation wasn't that serious. However, he must see the look on my face. Must understand that it's exactly that serious.

"Oh, god," he murmurs. "I didn't . . . I would never—"

"That means nothing! It's what we all thought," I say, my voice rising. "Where the fuck have you been anyway if not dead in a fucking ditch?"

He flinches, but I don't care. I'm furious with him. Relieved, yes, but mostly furious.

"Look, I had to do something," he says softly. "I couldn't just sit around and wait for shit to hit the fan."

"Shit already hit the fan, you asshole!"

"Will you just fucking listen to me?"

"No," I say, blood pounding in my ears. "We needed you here. I had to sit across from Logan in that fucking lawyer's office and listen to him *lie* about you. Say that you wrote those songs with him."

"That's not true."

"Then help me prove him wrong! He had the songs written on paper with both your signatures on them! Please tell me you have *something*."

Key closes his eyes and sighs. "Joel, look, I'll tell you everything, okay? I—"

A shuffling noise from the living room draws his attention.

"Wait, is . . . is someone here?" he asks.

Fuck, I forgot about Dusty. "Uh, yeah, actually . . . wait—"

"Who is it?"

Shit . . . I was hoping this conversation would come at a better time, but I can't avoid it now. "It's my girlfriend."

He blinks at me and the muscles in his face spasm. "Your—?"

"My girlfriend," I repeat. "I didn't tell you because . . . because you were so adamant on us staying single. Then everything else started to fall apart, you left . . . then she happened and, well—"

"I know, Joel." He taps at the wonky cupboard door with his shoe, looking everywhere but at me. "I-I overheard you on the phone," he says, and I'm relieved at least by the flags of color on his cheeks. "When you were talking to your mom on the phone, I was—fuck, I was listening, okay?"

My mouth drops open. "What the hell, man?"

"It was an accident!" he insists. "Those reporters were calling morning and night and I picked up the phone to tell them to fuck off but it was your mom and . . . look, I'm sorry. And," he continues, "I'm sorry I made you feel like you had to hide it from me."

He looks hurt, and my insides twist. "I was going to tell you. I was just waiting for the right time. Then you left, and I've been so worried—"

"Guess you weren't *that* worried about me," he says, rolling his eyes. "You still had time to get your cock wet."

"Watch it, man," I say, pointing my finger at his chest. "You left us to deal with this shit storm. It's been hell. Plus, you listen to my private conversations then insult my girlfriend the moment you're back?" I shake my head. "And, this is *not* just some girl, okay?" I admit. "I have real feelings for her."

"*Feelings?*"

"I . . . I love her."

I can't believe I just said that. But now it's out there, and it's the truth. That I love that fiery redhead. My heart has been sprinting ahead while my brain was lagging behind and they only just now decided to catch up to each other.

"Wow." Key places his hands on his hips and looks down at the floor. "I'm sorry, man. Seriously. I—I don't know why I said that." He grabs a fistful of his hair, his brows pinching together. "I feel like I'm going crazy lately, but I shouldn't be taking it out on you. I'm sorry."

"I didn't expect it to happen," I say truthfully. "It just . . . kind of did."

Key nods but says nothing. He doesn't look at me, and I suspect he needs a few minutes to process the information. We stand together in silence until finally he looks up, sniffs loudly and says, "Okay, well, you going to introduce me to your . . . girlfriend?"

"Key," I start.

He raises his hands in surrender. "Just introduce me, will you?"

He offers the barest of smiles, and right there, I know the worst of it is over. That it'll take some getting used to, but that ultimately my best friend is happy for me, so I smile back. "Fine, but we have a lot more to talk about and I'm not the only one who deserves an explanation and an apology. Not while she's here, though."

Key nods. "Okay."

"Come on," I say. "She's in the living room."

I grab the cup of juice for Dusty, and Key follows behind as we walk down the hall and turn into the living room.

Something's wrong.

Dusty is standing in the middle of the room, her hands clasped around that framed picture of the four of us. Her knuckles are white and her face is pale and streaked with tears. What the fuck?

"Dusty?"

I cross the room and place my hands on her shoulders when something uncomfortable clunks into place. It wasn't me who said her name. I look back over my shoulder where Key is standing—his face wrought with a dozen different emotions—and something knocks around in my brain like a loose puzzle piece. No . . . it can't be. That's impossible.

They *know* each other.

An eternity seems to pass as the three of us stand around looking at one another. No one seems to want to speak first. Perhaps no one can. I certainly can't, even though there's a million questions circulating in my head. Finally, Key takes a step forward.

"What the fuck is she doing here?" he asks bitterly.

I see Dusty shudder, her skin pebbling beneath my shirt. She looks terrified.

"Key, this is Dusty," I get out. "My girlfriend."

Her eyes flick to me, wide and horrified.

"No," Key says. "No. Absolutely not. I'm fucking hallucinating. Tell me that isn't Dusty Connors."

"Key," she whispers, her voice breaking.

But he shakes his head. "No, no—"

"Will someone explain to me what the fuck is going on?" I say.

"Are you here to hurt me again?" Key yells across the room. "You couldn't stomp on my heart enough, huh?"

She shakes her head, tears trickling down her cheeks.

It's as if I'm watching a tennis match. My head whips back and forth, not daring to miss a thing. "Someone please—"

Key steps forward until he's only feet away. "In all the years I knew you"—his voice is calm, lethal—"I never thought you were a vindictive bitch. But this? This is fucking next level."

My palms make contact with his chest and he stumbles back. He looks at me, his eyes stunned. "Don't call her that!" I yell.

Key's face twists. "So you found me here and decided to trick my best friend into loving you to get back at me. Is that it?"

She flinches as he shouts, stepping back, and I instinctively step in front of her. Key looks crazed, and it worries me.

"What more could you possibly take from me?" he shouts at her.

"N-nothing," she whispers.

But Key is crying now too, and I'm reminded of that day all those years ago at Samson Academy.

"All I ever did was love you," he chokes out, and my stomach swoops violently. "All I did was love you too much."

Everything suddenly makes sense. And my world that was just moments ago full of bright lights and music, is now dark and silent.

"The songs," I whisper. "They're about you."

She's sobbing now. "I didn't—I didn't know you were . . . friends. I s-swear."

My ears are ringing. "You loved her," I say, the truth of it like a tidal wave.

"She was my entire fucking world!" Key cries, suddenly turning and walking away. "We were supposed to run away together," he continues. "We were going to get married. Have a baby."

My breath halts in my chest. "What?"

"Then when the time came?" he spits venomously. "She left. She left me at a bus station. Gave me back my ring and disappeared from my life. She didn't want a life with me. Is she making you the same promises? Well, you should run far away, Joel, because she's a *liar*."

Dusty wraps her arms around herself and sobs.

"And all that bullshit you told me in Vegas," Key mutters. "How all I ever wanted was to save you. Be the big hero. Well, news flash for you, Dusty. You needed fucking *saving*!"

She closes her eyes and trembles. So do I.

"You were being abused. Getting into trouble. You got pregnant at seventeen because we were too fucking stupid to know any better."

Key takes a long breath, his face wet with tears.

"I never wanted to change you. I just wanted to be with you wherever you were. Whatever you were doing. I was ready to spend forever with you, but you couldn't even wait an hour for me? Did you even show up at all?"

I can hardly breathe. Key loved her. Loved her so much he was going to marry her. Loves her still.

"The ring," I whisper.

Key and Dusty both turn to look at me. "The ring you wear on that necklace. You told me once it was a reminder of someone special. You didn't tell me it was an engagement ring."

"Joel . . ."

"And a baby? You were—"

"She was," Key says with disgust. "But she didn't want that either. She got rid of it."

"No!" she screams. "I didn't get *rid* of it." Her face looks haunted, her chest rising and falling at an alarming speed, cheeks turning pink. "I didn't get rid of it," she repeats.

Key's expression loses its hardness. Its anger. "You—you didn't . . ."

She tries to take several deep breaths. Then her face turns a deep red, and there's rage and fire in those blue eyes.

"I waited for you! I waited and you didn't come!" she yells. "How do you think it felt? Standing at that bus station, pregnant, knowing I was completely alone. That the one person who said he loved me more than anything wasn't there? Then when your dad told me you weren't coming—that you'd changed your mind—"

"What?" he asks.

"It confirmed what I had worried about for weeks. That it wasn't really me you wanted. It was everything else."

Key's face looks like it's aged years. His eyes are weary as he steps closer, his chin wobbling. "Dusty. *No.* How could you believe *him?* He lied!"

"He had my necklace. Told me you wanted to give it back. That's when I knew I lost you." She cries and covers her face with her hands. "I lost it, Key. I lost our baby."

He moves, and for the briefest of seconds, I panic, thinking I might have to hurt my best friend. But he wraps his arms around her and she dissolves into horrible, wrenching sobs. My heart aches from the sound of it. From the terrible tragedy of it all.

I look between the two of them. How she fits so perfectly in his arms. How his head rests naturally on top of hers. How they move in such a way— god. They're so familiar with one another. They were going to be a *family*.

And with a horrible, nauseating realization, I see it. *I'm* the odd one out. They have history. They were always meant to be, but the timing wasn't right. Me? I'm just the placeholder. The one to bring them back together.

She's not mine.

"I need to get the fuck out of here."

"Wait, Joel!" Dusty rushes out of Key's grip and grabs my arm, her eyes pleading. "This doesn't change the way I feel about you," she says. "Please believe me. I-I still have those *feelings* for you, just like I said."

The first tears leak from the corners of my eyes. "But you'll always be his, won't you?"

Her eyes flit over my face, her cheeks shining in the low light. And that moment of hesitation is all I need, so I turn and go. I can hear them both following after me as I grab my keys off the counter where Key left them.

"Joel, wait," Key says.

The rage begins to bubble up again. Not at her, but at him. "You lied to me," I say, heart aching. "All these years, and you never told me about her? I told you everything about myself," I yell. "All these secrets. Did I ever really know you?"

I'm yanking open the door, not waiting to hear his pathetic response, and walking down the stone path toward the driveway. They're calling after me but I can't stay. I won't. They don't want me. They have each other now, and the band has gone to shit. Here I was worried Key would be the one left behind—who knew I would be so wrong? Who knew it would be me?

The engine roars to life and I back out of the driveway. I don't even know where I'm going. All I want to do is drive. At least it's something to do. I don't know how long I'm on the road for but finally my tears dry, and as I wipe my face, I almost don't notice the red light before slamming on the brakes.

"Shit," I curse, bouncing back against the headrest.

A car horn blasts on my right, jolting me further, and I watch two gigantic headlights barrel toward me.

CHAPTER 32

Baby Can I Hold You

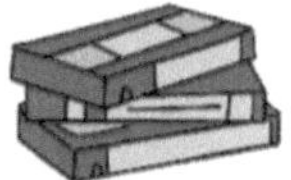

Everything is a mess. My life always is. Why did I think it would ever work out for me? I was right to push Joel away. I only end up hurting the people I love. And I do love him. And Key . . .

Is it possible to love two people at the same time?

Because the truth is I never stopped loving him. I've pushed that love down into the deepest darkest parts of me, but when he hugged me it was like a dam broke, and everything I've kept hidden for all these years burst over the shore like the waves of a tsunami.

But I ruined it again. I hurt Joel and possibly broke the friendship that he's held so dear for so many years. I'll never forgive myself for it.

Key stands in the open doorway staring out at the street as if willing Joel to come back. I don't know what to do, but I'm freezing. Shivers cover my body even on this summer day, but perhaps they're not because I'm cold.

"Key?"

He turns around to look at me, and his tear-streaked face will haunt my dreams. "I . . . I . . ." he tries, but he can't seem to get the words out.

Should I comfort him? I want to. It feels natural that I would, but he was so mad at me. He must hate me. He hugged me, yes, but that was only because I told him about the miscarriage. Maybe he wants me to leave.

"Can I use your phone?" I ask.

He blinks for a moment, then his brow furrows. "My phone?"

I nod and wrap my arms around myself, realizing I'm still in Joel's shirt and nothing else. "I'll leave. I can call a cab and go."

"You're . . ." he starts. "You're not going to wait for him to come back?"

I shrug. "I don't think he wants me to be here when he comes back."

Key closes the front door, crossing his arms over his chest. "Yes, he does."

"No. I didn't tell him the truth about . . . I didn't tell him about my past. He won't want to speak to me now."

"Yes, he will. He loves you."

More tears sting my eyes but I wipe them away. I need to pull myself together. "He can call me if he wants to talk," I say. "I'll get dressed, then I'll be gone. You won't have to see me again."

I head for Joel's bedroom hallway but Key stops me, his warm hand wrapping around my wrist. "Wait."

He can't even make eye contact with me. I'm a horrible person. If only we had talked in Vegas. If only I wasn't so stubborn, so proud, so guarded. If only I trusted the boy who said he loved me more than anything over the man I knew spent the majority of his life hurting his son. If only, if only, *if only*—there's too many to count.

"Maybe . . ." he whispers, staring at my bare feet. "Maybe you could stay. Maybe we could talk?"

His gaze finally meets mine and *god* how I've missed those

hazel eyes. For a moment, it's like we're teenagers again, when he was the only good thing in my life.

I need to say yes. This could be my only chance for us to clear the air, and we both need closure, so I nod. No more *if onlys* . . . especially if I want to fix things with Joel.

"Okay," I whisper back. "I'll get dressed and be right back . . . then we can talk."

He nods, and I wind my way back to Joel's bedroom. When I enter, it's like a punch in the gut. The room smells of sex. The sheets on the bed are everywhere and my body can't help but remember the ghost of Joel's touch. How he made me feel.

I gather up my underwear and clothes, and I nearly get dressed, but the faster that happens, the sooner I'll have to talk to Key. *Take a shower, Dusty.* I meet my reflection in the wardrobe mirrors and nod to myself, shaking out my hands. The spray of warm water will clear my head if nothing else. Besides, the idea of Key smelling it on me is too much to bear.

The water runs hot and I climb in, letting it soak my hair and ease the tension off my swollen face and sore neck. Yes, this was a good idea. Things are starting to seem less impossible. But even though my brain doesn't feel befuddled anymore, I still have no idea what to do. The bravest decision would be to leave. To tell Key and Joel that they deserve better than me. That I don't care about them and they're better off without me in their lives.

But I'm so tired of lying. So tired of having to be brave. Key was right. Sometimes I just need to be fucking saved. For someone to make the decision. But what if they make the wrong one? What if Joel never calls me and that's the end? What if Key can't forgive me? What if this is all just . . . tragedy? Can I survive any more?

When I find myself back in the living room, skin raw and wearing the clothes I arrived in this morning, Key is sitting on the couch, looking at the picture I held in my hand an hour ago. He looks exhausted but so undeniably handsome.

These past few years have turned him into a gorgeous man. His wavy brown hair is slightly too long. Just long enough to piss off the parents of his fans, I'm sure. He's filled out. His upper body is lean and strong, the muscles in his neck defined.

"Hey," I say, announcing myself.

He looks up. "Hey."

"Sorry, I just . . . I figured I should shower."

"It's fine."

I join him on the edge of the sofa, unsure where to start. For a long moment, we sit in silence, the tension building between us.

"What a mess, huh?" he says, the faintest hint of a smile on his lips.

I breathe out a laugh and nod. "You could say that."

He presses his head into his hands, ruffles his hair and sighs. "I'm sorry about earlier." He twists his mouth before taking a deep breath. "I shouldn't have said what I said. I was just . . . shocked and angry and everything that happened between us just came rushing back."

I shake my head. "It's fine. A shock is putting it mildly." His mouth twitches at the side into a half-hearted smile, and my stomach flutters. It's been so long, and I thought I'd done a good enough job of burying my feelings for him, but apparently not enough, because here they are. Like a shot of adrenaline to the heart, my body is vibrating. Overwhelmed by so many conflicting emotions.

But here's my chance. It's now or never.

"Why didn't you come?" I whisper.

Our eyes meet, and he doesn't need to ask what I'm talking about. He knows. "I did." His answer hits me in the gut, and I have to gulp down air. He did come. He did. How can two words make everything better and more painful all at once?

"You did?" I ask, my voice shaky.

"I tried to get away," he explains, "but my mom had her friends over and she kept . . ." Another deep breath. "It doesn't matter. What matters is I was there, and you weren't. Why didn't you stay?"

I blow out a breath. "When your dad came to the bus station, I was terrified. Panicking. I thought something had happened to you. I thought your parents found out. But when your dad gave me back the necklace . . ."

He closes his eyes. "I should've known they found it—"

"I was stupid and scared. When he told me you didn't want to do this anymore—that you were afraid of ruining your life—I believed him. How could I not? I was terrified too, but I couldn't get away from the mess we were in like you could. So I gave your dad the ring you made me, got on the bus, and left."

"I thought you changed your mind," he says, almost to himself. "It just confirmed all of the doubts I was already having. God, and my parents? How did they even know? Fuck, I'm so stupid!"

"We were both stupid," I admit. "We were seventeen trying to act like grownups. It was foolish to think we could make that work."

He looks at me then. "I would've tried."

My lip trembles as I smile. "I know. I know you would have."

He nods, clears his throat. "Can I ask what happened? With the baby?"

My chest aches at the thought of it. "When the bus stopped in Nevada, the bleeding started," I say through a shaky breath. "There was so much, I knew something was wrong. I left the bus station and went to the hospital and that's where they told me . . . it just went away."

His face contorts with anguish, and I hate that I've spent all these years feeling alone in my devastation. Of course Key would feel it too. It was never just my baby.

"They told me it happens sometimes," I continue. "More often than you'd think. That it wasn't anything I did. But I've always thought it was punishment for every bad choice I made in my life."

He leans toward me. "It wasn't your fault. It's mine. If I had been there, maybe it wouldn't have happened. Maybe I could've stopped it—"

I shake my head. "Neither of us could've stopped this. It wasn't meant to be."

"Just like us."

I look to the floor to avoid his eyes now. There it is. The uncomfortable thing that I've been avoiding for years. That maybe it was doomed from the start. How can the universe be so cruel as to make you love someone so much only to rip them away from you? How can that love still be so strong after so much?

He glances sidelong at the front door. "Does he make you happy?"

I wipe away the tear that trickles down my cheek and look up at him. "He makes me so happy."

He nods and fidgets with his hands. The scars look worse than I remember.

"I'm glad," he says. "I'm glad you found someone to love you. Even if that someone couldn't be me."

I wanted it to be you for so long. "What about you?"

"Me?"

I open my hands toward him. "Yeah. It's been a long time. Has there been anyone who you—"

"No. It's always been you."

Sucking my lip into my mouth, I chew nervously.

"I mean," he continues. "There've been girls, but they were

just distractions. It never meant anything. It wasn't until recently that anyone ever came close to you. Or at least she reminded me of you. I never even met her . . ." he finishes to himself.

At my raised eyebrow he continues.

"A fantasy phone girl, if you can believe it." He huffs a short laugh but my heart may have stopped beating. "Pathetic, huh?"

My watery eyes search his face. For a trace, for any hint that this is a joke. There's no way. It's *impossible*.

"What's wrong?" he asks.

My hands shake, my head following along as though my physical body can't accept any more. "Baby?"

Then he freezes too. The two of us stuck, frozen in time. The world is simultaneously crumbling around me, and yet everything makes sense. The connection through the phone line. The way the sound of his voice made me feel. How he was watching my favorite movie. How he came to me for comfort. How he continues to enter my life and make me fall in love with him over and over and over again. Every. Damn. Time.

He drops off the couch onto his knees before me. "Cherry?"

The truth of it is in my eyes. He can see it. Then with the desperation of a man grasping for a life raft, he wraps his arms around my waist, his grip unyielding. "It's impossible," he whispers against my ribcage.

It is. It truly is. We both crossed an entire country only to find each other again and again. Even over the phone?

Looking up at me, he grabs my face in his hands. His eyes scan mine and I watch the words form in his mind. How he showed me how he really felt for the first time at thirteen, and that pure-hearted innocence is still there. How he said them to me at seventeen, when we expressed that feeling physically. He's about to say them, but all I know is the undeniable guilt at wanting to say them back, after almost saying them to Joel.

"Dusty, I—"

Ring rrrrring.

We look at the phone, then at each other. Neither of us moves. It rings again, again, again. We drift as one to the kitchen and the spiral corded phone on the wall. I know Key's thinking the same thing: Joel is calling.

Key reaches it first. "Hello?"

My body is vibrating with adrenaline, nerves peaking when Key's face scrunches. Is it not Joel? Who would be calling now?

"No, I'm—I'm his roommate," he says into the speaker. Then he turns ghostly white. "What do you mean?"

Key looks up at me, his eyes wide and terrified.

"Is he okay?" he asks through the phone.

My stomach turns to stone and I have to grip the counter to keep from falling over.

"Yes, I-I'll be right there. Yes. Thank you."

He hangs up and it's like I already know the answer. "Who was that?"

Key is shaking, but he swallows hard and turns to me. "That was the hospital," he says, and I can't breathe. "Joel was in a car accident."

CHAPTER 33

The Waiting

KEY

The ER is buzzing when the cab drops us off at the
hospital. I feel so helpless as we wander inside the
automatic doors, looking around for anyone who might
be able to help. My stomach is in knots. If Joel isn't okay, I'll
never forgive myself. I'm the reason he left—he was only in that
car because of me. And here I am with no idea where to go
because I can't read the fucking signs.

"Key, this way," Dusty says, pulling me down the hall.

I follow along behind her blindly past the gurneys and
orderlies, aware my hand is still in hers. I don't want to like it but
it's familiar, and right now, it's my life raft. Finally, we end up at
a large round desk.

"Excuse me," Dusty says to the older woman sitting at the
desk. "Can you help us? We're looking for Joel Thanger? He was
in a car accident."

The lady looks between us, smacking on a piece of gum.
Finally, reluctantly, she picks up the phone. "Let me see what I
can find out for you."

We nod and step back while she dials a few numbers. I can't

stand still and my legs dance from side to side as we wait. I try to focus on the pattern of the floor, the rhythmic timing of monitors, the gritty texture of the walls, but nothing helps. After another few minutes, the lady hangs up the phone and beckons us both forward.

"He's still in surgery," she says, and I have to bite back the vomit rising up my throat.

"Surgery?" I cry.

She raises her eyebrows. "Yes. When he's done they'll be taking him to recovery. You can wait there. Just go all the way down that hall there and turn left." She motions with a manicured hand. "There's another desk, tell them who you're there to see."

"Thank you," Dusty says, and then we're bolting down the hall.

Horrible images start to play out in my mind. Images of Joel cut up and bleeding, of legs torn off, of his body broken and bruised. I'm starting to get lightheaded—nauseous. Dusty arrives at the nurses' station first, which is just fine because I can't form a single thought around the blood pounding in my ears.

"And what is your relation to Mr. Thanger?" the nurse asks.

"I—well, I . . ." Dusty says.

"We can't let anyone who isn't an immediate family member through," she says.

"She's his wife." The words come out louder than I intended. I hadn't intended to say them at all. But if I understand what they're saying, they won't let either of us in unless we lie.

"Oh," the nurse says, "right, he's still in surgery but if you have a seat in that waiting room over there, we'll inform you when he's moved to recovery."

The nurse walks away and Dusty turns to me, her eyes bloodshot and watery. "Key?"

"Put this on."

"What?"

I reach around the back of my neck and unclasp the chain once we're tucked inside the waiting area. "Wear the ring. If they believe you're married they'll let you see him. His parents live too far away, you need to be there."

I slide the ring on her finger, the one I made all those years ago. The one I never believed I'd see on her hand again. She tenses, like she's remembering it too. That vulnerable moment all those years ago. But I shake it off. This is important; I can't get bogged down with memories.

"But what if they ask me questions I can't answer," she whispers.

"He's twenty-five, birthday is September eighteenth, allergic to pineapple and his blood type is B+."

A strange look overtakes her face.

"What?"

She blinks and smiles sadly. "You really know him, don't you?"

I sigh. "He was always the honest one. The better one. I'm the one who kept myself hidden away."

"It should be you," she says. "It should be you who goes."

"Yeah, well," I say, sniffing my nose. "I think they're more likely to buy you for the wife than me."

She frowns and looks at the floor, the sound of a crackling announcement overhead and shoes squeaking on the terrazzo flooring the only noise. She takes a deep breath, and I realize she's quivering.

"Dusty," I say gently. "It's going to be okay."

She presses her lips together before looking up at me with tears in her eyes. "He has to be," she whispers. "I love him."

That small balloon that had been secretly filling with hope inside my chest bursts. Part of me expected it. How could anyone not love Joel? But the smaller part of me also hoped against hope that maybe it was fleeting. A way back together. For fuck's sake, we even fell in love as strangers over the phone. How many coincidences can a person experience before it becomes fate? Or maybe the universe has a cruel sense of humor.

I try to smile as I reach forward and brush away the tears from her face. "I know."

She crumples in my hands. "I'm sorry," she squeaks out.

"You don't have to apologize to me," I say. "Love means you don't have to feel bad about feeling it."

Her eyes dart over my face, her lips parting before—

"Mrs. Thanger?"

We both look up at a somewhat confused-looking nurse. I take in the scene from her eyes—the intimate closeness of our bubble. I drop my hands and take a step back.

"I can take you to him now."

Dusty nods and tucks some of her wild hair behind her ear. "You'll stay?" she asks.

I nod. "For as long as it takes."

She swallows. "I'll talk to you soon."

Then her red hair disappears down the hallway, a flash of her blue eyes finding mine before she turns the corner.

"Excuse me, sir," a paramedic brushes past me pulling a stretcher and I press into the wall. My head falls back against the cool tile and I close my eyes. How has life gone from bad to the worst thing imaginable? I thought the universe was supposed to be about balance, but what kind of bullshit is this?

I glance down the hall and see a payphone. I should probably call James and Dave. They'll want to be here. I walk over, rooting around in my pocket for some quarters, but before I can put one in, I stop.

They don't know I'm back. They don't know what's happened. They're going to hate me. I'm the one who took off and abandoned them. Made them all think . . . Then for me to come back without a solution only to have caused more damage? This is all my fault—all of it. They'll never forgive me. How can they, when I know I'll never forgive myself?

But none of that stops me from dialing the number.

Joel would want them here and that's the only thing that matters.

CHAPTER 34

Alone

JOEL

CHAPTER 35

Live to Tell

DUSTY

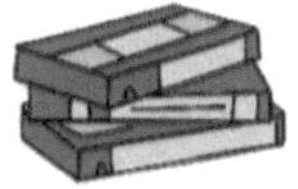

Key is Baby.
Baby is Key.
And I'm fucked.

Rooms blur past my periphery as I follow the nurse down several corridors. Some with their doors open, some shut tight. I can't help but look into each one I pass, my heart pounding harder and harder. What if he isn't in a room at all? What if he's not in recovery and they're taking me to the morgue?

We push through one last set of doors. It's quieter here, and finally the nurse turns into the first room on the right. I follow, but stop in the doorway. I can smell the blood. The bandages. That overwhelming sterile smell. It hits me viscerally, freezing me in place, and my throat closes up.

"Mrs. Thanger?"

The kind nurse takes my hand. She must see the fear in my eyes. How could she not? I must look like an utter mess.

"He's right over here," she says.

I give her a shaky nod, but I still can't move.

"Were you in the accident as well?" she asks, and gives me a careful once-over.

"No, I . . . the smell." Why is it so strong? "I lost a baby once . . . in a hospital."

She understands immediately. Clasping both of my hands, she says gently, "I'm sorry. That must have been awful. Here . . ."

She reaches into the pocket on her scrubs, beneath the name badge that reads *Nancy*, and reveals a tiny bottle of liquid.

"Peppermint oil," the nurse—Nancy—explains. "Just a little under the nose and—"

Like a miracle, the smell is gone. Or at least the wrong smell is gone, replaced by one that clears the fog and loosens my muscles.

"Better?" she asks.

"Yes. Much. Thank you." My feet are still stuck to the floor, like there's Elmer's glue on the bottom of my shoes. With a tug to my hands, Nancy pulls me into the room toward the curtained off bed.

"I should warn you," she says quietly, "he probably looks worse than he is. It might be frightening for you."

I stop and squeeze her hand. "I—I . . ." I whisper. "Please, I—"

"You can do this," she says gently. "He needs you."

Blinking furiously, I nod once, then take a shaky breath and follow her behind the curtain. I let out a choked sob at the sight that greets me. Joel lies on the bed, his hair shaved off one third of his head, giving him a kind of one-sided mohawk. There's a long, angry scar and black stitches. The tattoos on his chest peek out from behind white bandages, and one of his arms is in a cast up to his shoulder.

"Oh god," I breathe, stumbling forward. My hips hit the side of the bed in my rush to grasp his free hand. "Joel, oh my god!"

His face is so bruised he's barely recognizable. Ugly black and blue lumps on his face. Bloody and swollen lips. How was it only hours ago that I kissed those delicious lips without a care in the world? What if we can never go back? The tears pour out of me as I feel a hand on my shoulder.

"Oh dear, Mrs. Thanger, you're freezing," Nancy says. "Let me get you a warm blanket. I'll be right back."

I wait until her steps retreat down the hall before breaking down completely. I sink to the floor, the strength it takes to hold myself up vanishing. I'm too terrified, too exhausted, too out of my mind.

"Joel, I'm so sorry. Please," I whisper. "Please don't leave me."

The only response is the slow, steady beeping on the heart monitor. I lift my head and stare at his face.

"I know I couldn't say it before, but I love you. Please, I love you so much. Come back to me so I can tell you. Even if you never want to see me again, I need to say it. I need you to know. Please . . . please!"

But the beeping just continues its sad march. I kiss his knuckles, rubbing my thumb over the calluses on his hand.

A bald man with green scrubs appears across from me with a chart in his hands. His words sound like something from the bottom of a well. Words like *fractured clavicle* and *broken ribs*. *Scalp laceration* and *probable concussion*. That there doesn't seem to be any internal bleeding at this point, and I simply need to wait until he wakes up. But how can I wait? How can I sit here and do nothing?

Mid-spiral, a soft blanket is draped over my shoulders. The doctor is gone, but the scraping noise of furniture moving registers and I'm being eased off the floor and into a chair next to the bed.

"Thank you," I whisper, hastily wiping my face.

"You poor thing," Nancy says. "You must be exhausted. Try to get some rest."

"I can't. Not when he's like this. I need to do something."

"He needs you to be strong for him. Can't do that if you don't sleep. Here," she says and passes me an extra pillow, "try to rest. I'm sure he can sense that you're here."

Offering her a shaky smile, I take the pillow and nod. "Thank you."

"Just ring the bell if you need anything, okay?"

"Actually," I say. "The man I came in here with—"

The nurse cocks a brow at me. "Yes?"

"Keith Prentiss. Could you update him for me? He's his best friend. I'm sure he's going out of his mind with worry."

She presses her lips together for a moment and glances at the ring on my finger. "He's *his* best friend?"

There's a tone to her voice, and I recognize it immediately. She saw how we were together in the hallway. How friends don't embrace like that. Perhaps she thinks I'm cheating on Joel with him.

"Yes, his friend. They—I mean, we . . . we all live together."

She rolls her lips, her face softening, and smiles. "Of course, I'll let him know."

Then I'm left alone. Alone with my thoughts and my grief. I pull my legs up under myself and hug the pillow, never letting go of Joel's hand.

"I'm so sorry," I whisper. "This is all my fault."

He doesn't move, and eventually, my eyes slip closed. But in the darkness is where the guilt thrives. I can hear Key's voice, and all of those phone conversations replay on a loop. I'm such an idiot. How could I possibly not have recognized his voice? It's been years, yes, and his voice has changed from the seventeen-year-old who asked me to marry him, but it's still him. The same inflection, the same comfort. Maybe deep down I did recognize him. Maybe that's why I so easily fell for a stranger despite that never happening to me before with the hundreds of other callers I've taken—because I was already in love with him.

But I love Joel too.

Fuck, it's all such a disaster. Key and I have such a long and complicated history. I've been so angry at him—at myself—for so long. I've spent years thinking I was unwanted and worthless because of a terrible misunderstanding. But those vulnerable telephone calls, and the hot ones too . . . God, it's almost unfathomable how good his words and his voice made me feel. It's frightening. I was right to put a stop to it when I did. Because Joel is real, and everything I've ever needed in a man. Someone who is willing to fight for me while letting me be myself. He cares for me despite everything. If I'd had the courage to tell him about my past, I'm certain it wouldn't have mattered any more than my present.

He just needs to wake up.

And I need to make an impossible choice.

CHAPTER 36

I'll Be Loving You (Forever)

KEY

Two broken ribs.

Fourteen stitches.

Fractured collarbone.

Concussion.

"All we can do is wait until he wakes up, then we can go from there."

It's been two hours since the nurse came to update me on Joel. Two hours since I watched Dusty disappear down the hall to sit with my best friend while he fights for his life. Two hours and two million times I've gone over that list of injuries.

Two broken ribs.

Fourteen stitches.

Fractured collarbone.

Concussion.

I've already thrown up once in the waiting room bathroom, and from the looks I've been getting from other visitors, I probably need a shower. I can't imagine Dusty is doing any better, and I wish I could see her—talk to her. But she's where she needs to be. Somewhere I can't go.

"Key?"

I glance up from my spot on the bench and spot Dave walking hand in hand with a frazzled-looking Isabella.

"Dave," I manage to say before his arms wrap around me. Then I can't stop it. Tears spill down my cheeks and I cling on to him as if he's a buoy in the middle of the North Sea. "It's all my fault," I cry. "It's all my fault."

"Key, stop," Dave says, pulling back and running his hand down his face. He looks pale, his eyes red. "Just . . . just tell me what happened."

I shake my head; I don't even know where to start.

"Joel got into a car accident. He's unconscious but stable. He's pretty banged up. Broken ribs, collarbone, fourteen stitches . . ."

Isabella's hand raises over her mouth and tears form in her eyes. "Oh god—"

But Dave is staring at me hard. "If he got in an accident, why is that your fault?"

I close my eyes. "Because I'm the reason he was out driving in the first place."

"You're going to need to explain this to me, Key. In fact, you're going to need to explain where the fuck you've been for the past two weeks as well. Do you have any idea how fucking worried we've all been? How fucked up it is that you just left without a word?"

"I know," I say, "I know. It was shitty of me. I'm sorry."

Dave frowns and glances at Isabella, and I take the opening. "I left to try and get some proof that I wrote those songs long before I ever met Logan. I only ever wrote them down one time . . ." I take a deep breath. "Because it's hard for me to read and nearly impossible for me to write."

Isabella blinks at me. "Really?"

I shrug. "I could never figure it out. My parents and teachers always made me feel stupid because letters just never made sense to me. But I did write the songs down once."

Dave sits up straighter. "Key, that's amazing! We can take that to the lawyers. They'll prove to the judge—"

I shake my head. "I don't have them."

"What do you mean, you don't have them?"

"I wrote them down . . . to give to a girl."

"Oh, Key . . ." Isabella sighs.

"We used to hang out at this abandoned cabin back home. I thought maybe if I went I'd find them . . . but they weren't there."

Dave lets out an exasperated sigh. "What about this girl? Is it possible she still has them? How can we get in touch with her?"

I close my eyes again, the image of Dusty standing in my living room burned into the back of my retinas.

"That's just it . . . I went to Vegas after Iowa. That's the last place I knew she was."

"And?"

I laugh darkly. "I guess I never needed to go anywhere. She's here."

"Here?" Isabella asks. "Like in San Francisco?"

"Like in the hospital."

"*This* hospital?" Dave and Isabella ask in unison.

I nod.

"But . . . how did she know to come?"

"She didn't. She . . ." I glance up at the ceiling. "She and Joel are dating, and I had no fucking idea."

Their silence about sums up how I've been feeling since I walked into my house earlier today.

"Wait," Isabella says, holding up her hand. "The girl you were in love with as a kid . . . is dating Joel? How—what are the odds of that?"

I shrug. "To be honest, it's like a bad joke."

Dave's brows furrow. "But . . . you're not still in love with her, are you?"

I haven't prayed in a long time. Not since Dusty left me waiting for her at that bus station. Not even when I was forced into prayer at the academy. But at this moment, I pray. I pray for strength because it kills me to think it, let alone say it out loud.

"I'm so in love with her."

CHAPTER 37

This Woman's Work

DUSTY

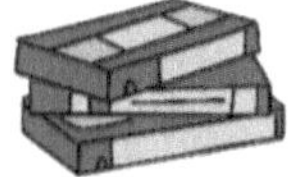

My hand is frozen to the wall when I hear those words. I hadn't meant to eavesdrop. I came out here to check on Key, to let him know that Joel is still asleep—that I'm more terrified than ever before.

I'm so in love with her.

He can't. He can't do this to me. I can't do this.

"You know," a woman's voice says, "Becks and I have had this theory for a while that you were desperately in love with some girl. That you hated relationships because someone broke your heart."

"It's complicated," Key says quietly.

"But do you think she still has the songs?" another man's voice asks.

Songs?

"Dave, this isn't the time," the woman says.

"Izzy." Dave sighs. "Of course it's the time. She's here. She might have them on her. We could clear our band's name. *Today.*"

"If you haven't noticed," she huffs, "we have a bigger problem right now."

"Joel is going to be fine," Dave says. "Key said he's stable, he just needs time to recover."

"That could take months! Plus, it's only been a few hours. What if something happens and he gets worse?"

Enough.

I turn the corner into the waiting room where I see a tall blond man, his hair pulled back in a ponytail, and a pretty dark-haired girl with bangles on her wrists. Key sits on the plastic bench attached to the wall behind them. They all notice me at once, and there's an overwhelming sensation of shame that descends on me. This Dave and Izzy—what they must think about me? What will they think of me when I have to break someone's heart?

Key is on his feet then and rushing over to me, scooping me up in a tight hug, and I want to just float away in it. To sink into his arms and finally fall asleep. Instead, I push away and he sets me down on my feet.

"Hey—Joel . . . has he woken up?" Key asks.

That voice. It's so obvious now, and for a brief, sleep-deprived moment, I imagine us having this conversation through the phone back in my cubicle at work.

"No," I whisper. "No, he hasn't." I swallow hard as three pairs of eyes wait for me to deliver the news. "I just came out here to check and see if you're okay."

It feels like I should be crying, but there are no more tears. I've run out, or perhaps I'm just too dehydrated. When was the last time I ate or drank anything? My knees falter beneath me but Key is there. He's always been there. Why did I ever get so mad at him for it?

"I . . . I have them."

Key shakes his head. "You . . . have what?"

"The songs you wrote. I have them."

He extends his arms to get a better look at me. "You do?"

"Of course I do." I sigh. "How could I not?"

He stares at me, and I don't understand the expression. I thought maybe he'd look relieved. Or happy? Instead, he seems confused. I turn to his blond friend.

"I'll go get them," I whisper. "Your band's name with be cleared by this time tomorrow."

His mouth drops open. "No!" he nearly shouts. "No, I didn't —that's not what I meant."

"Dave, you complete asshole." Izzy shakes her head and smacks him on the chest.

"No, he's not," I say. "This is important. It's important to Joel. And rather than have me stand around uselessly at the hospital waiting for . . ." I pause, reminding myself that Joel might not want to see me when he wakes up. Maybe it's better if I'm not here. That way I can't do any more damage. "Please, let me help."

Izzy steps forward and grasps my hand. "Come for a walk with me."

I blink at her, taken aback. I don't even know her. Why does she want to take a walk with me?

"Come on, let's go outside. I think you need some fresh air."

Her eyes widen imperceptibly and I understand what she's really trying to say. That she wants to talk to me out of earshot of the others. About what, I don't know, but I nod. "Yes, actually— that's a good idea."

"Perfect," she says with a smile, then links her arm with mine. "Boys, we'll be right back."

Izzy escorts me through the maze of hallways toward the emergency bay doors until we step out into the cloudy afternoon air. It hits my face, and I'm instantly relieved. I close my eyes and breathe. The peppermint oil the nurse gave me was helping but this is so much better.

"Thank you," I say as her arm drops and she turns to face me.

"No problem. Smoke?" She holds up a pack of cigarettes.

I laugh, relieved. "Actually, yes. Thank you, again."

"I'm Isabella," she says, lighting her smoke and taking a long puff. "Or Izzy, as everyone calls me. I realize we weren't properly introduced."

"Dusty," I say. "It's nice to meet you."

"I don't know if you remember, but we've actually met before."

I choke on the smoke. "We have?"

She nods. "In Vegas, at the diner? You gave me a tampon in the bathroom."

My brain is too tired. Too scattered. But it does come back to me. "Oh my god, yes of course! That was the morning after I met Joel."

She smiles. "He talked about this amazing girl he'd met for hours," she says, exhaling deeply. "It was a long ride home."

A warmth spreads through my chest. "He . . . he is very sweet."

"Key was quiet and distracted. I don't even think he registered that Joel had spent the night with you, he was so caught up in his own world. I thought at the time that he was just really, *really* hung over."

I chew my cheek and look down. "I-I may have seen him earlier in the night—before I met Joel." Then I realize why she's talking to me about this. She's trying to determine whose heart I'm going to break.

"Listen," I start, "you have to believe me, I didn't know they were friends. I was—"

"I get it."

My eyebrows rise. "Wait, get what?"

"Why they're both attracted to you."

My lips part, but I don't know what to say.

"You're exactly their type," she says with a laugh. "Believe me I've seen them with their fair share of women, and you're like, their perfect choice all rolled into one. They've always had the same taste. I think that's why they're so close."

I close my eyes. "I never meant for this to happen," I say into the wind. "I don't deserve either of them. Key and I—there's so much history and feelings there, but also so much hurt. And Joel? He's too wonderful to ever consider breaking his heart. If I was a braver woman, I'd leave now. I don't know what happens next, but if their friendship ended because of me? I'd never forgive myself."

Izzy smiles and touches my arm. "And now I understand why they're both in love with you."

I thought I had no more tears left to cry, but one slips down my cheek as I take a final drag of my cigarette. "What am I going to do?"

"You're going to go back in there and be by Joel's side until he wakes up. The songs can wait. I know it feels like you need something to do, or maybe you're thinking about a worst-case scenario of him waking up and not wanting you there. But I promise you, he does. Just be with him. Maybe try to sleep a little. I'm sure you're exhausted."

With a nod, I sniff. Is she right? "And after?"

She smiles. "I can't see the future, but something tells me everything is going to work out for all of you. You'll see."

What does she mean by that? In what world does this work out and we all end up happy?

"Come on," she says. "I'll deal with Dave, and Key will understand."

I reach out and grab her arm as she turns for the doors. "Thank you," I say. "I, uh . . . I don't really have any girlfriends or . . ." I trail off, chuckling nervously. "Or friends at all, so I appreciate you being so nice."

"We're a family," she says simply. "That's what we do."

CHAPTER 38

The Things We Do for Love

JOEL

Everything hurts.

My face, my chest, my arms and legs. Where am I? The last thing I remember . . . wasn't I at home? No, I was driving. I try to move but there's something warm tucked into me. When I open my eyes sage green walls stare back at me and some kind of beeping sound bounces around in my brain.

Fuck. Am I in the hospital? How did I—

The car.

I stopped, but that truck went right through a red light and . . . why was I driving? I hear a gentle sigh and look down, my heart rocketing into my throat at Dusty's curled-up form.

It's all it takes to remember. The way her body responded to mine in my bed. How Key returned home and I introduced her as my girlfriend. How it all went completely sideways because it turns out they know each other. Not only that, they were in love. Engaged. About to have a baby. How I was just the stand-in. A temporary fix for her one true love. I roll my head to look away and blow out a breath through cracked lips.

Why is she here? Why is she clinging to me as though I'm the most precious thing to her?

And Key. I know he's here. I can feel his anxious presence pacing the halls. For a moment, it feels as though he's standing just outside the door. I wish he would come in. There's so much I didn't know—didn't understand.

Dusty snores quietly as she nuzzles her chin into me. I adjust the blanket over her and kiss her forehead. She sighs contentedly then continues her rhythmic breathing. There's a scuffle at the door and I glance up to catch Key slipping out of the room.

"Key," I whisper.

Nothing.

"Key?" I ask again.

Finally he steps into view, his hair a mess over his forehead and his face a picture of worry. "Oh, hey, you're awake," he whispers as he enters the room.

I fight the urge to roll my eyes. I know he's been lurking around out there. "Yeah."

"I . . . I didn't want to interrupt," he says sheepishly, glancing at Dusty.

"She's asleep," I say.

"Not for lack of trying," he says, taking a step forward. "She hasn't left your side for over twenty-four hours."

My brow creases. Have I really been out that long? Looking back at Key, his eyes are glassy and his lip trembles. "Hey, man, you okay?"

"I thought—I thought you were gone," he whispers. "I thought you were going to leave us and I'd forever know it was my fault."

"Key, don't—"

"I just need to say," he cuts in, "that I'm sorry. For everything."

I try to offer a smile. "It's already forgiven."

His lips pull at the side and he nods. "Right." We're quiet for a long moment, then he takes a deep breath. "She has the songs."

"What?"

"She kept them," he admits. "After all this time. She kept my songs."

My heart sinks. "Oh."

"It's great, right?" he asks. "She can testify on our behalf. Logan's case will be thrown out and everything will go back to normal."

"Normal," I whisper. "Right."

How can it go back to normal? I glance down at Dusty and frown. She kept his songs? Someone she never thought she'd see again and who— wait, what the fuck is this. I lift her left hand into the light and voice the question to my best friend.

Key's face pales. "It's—well . . . it's a ring."

My stomach ties itself into knots. "You mean it's *your* ring."

He treads into the room on uncertain feet, stopping only when he's at the side of my hospital bed. "We had to. They wouldn't let anyone who wasn't immediate family back to see you. It was my idea," he admits, and I'm pleased to see he looks ashamed. "I told her to wear it. To say she was your wife so they'd let her be by your side." He gestures around the room. "It clearly worked."

I try to shake it away. The unpleasant feeling of seeing Key's ring on her finger. My thumb brushes against it, feeling the individual grooves of the string wound around and around.

"You don't have to worry, Joel," he finally says. "You won."

I clear my throat. "Won?"

"You won her," he admits with a shrug. "She loves you. She told me herself. She hasn't left your side since we got here. So, you don't have to worry. She made her choice—and it's you."

I chew on my split bottom lip. "Key . . . it was never supposed to be a competition. I didn't even know—"

"I know," he says. "I had so much time with her. Time that . . . while it was the happiest I've ever been, it was also the most difficult. But now she can have her perfect ending."

A tear slips from the corner of his eye.

"She deserves that."

He reaches forward to brush a stray curl away from her face, tucking it ever so gently behind her ear. Her breathing slows, a subtle sigh reverberating somewhere down deep. Key looks up at me and smiles, then turns to head for the door.

The knots tighten in my stomach. I don't want him to leave. I only ever thought about how Key and my relationship might change with me being in a relationship. But being with the girl he's still clearly in love with? And her with him? That scenario never crossed my mind, and now that it's playing out, there's a sudden peaceful clarity that takes over.

Why do I *have* to choose? The two most important people in my life are here. Will I just let one of them walk away? Besides, I know something Key doesn't seem to be able to see.

"Key, wait."

He stops and brushes at his cheeks before angling his body my way. "Yeah?"

"She loves you too."

His lips part, and for a moment his eyes flick between Dusty and me. "No. No . . . she just—I realize what it looked like when we hugged at the house, but that's because of—"

"She loves you, idiot," I say around a laugh. "She always has and, well, she probably always will."

"She said that?"

"She doesn't need to. I can see it. It's in the way she looks at you. The way she touched you. Key, she kept your songs. How much more proof do you need?"

"It doesn't matter," he says, pressing his hand to his face. "She may still have feelings for me, but she made her choice."

I take a deep breath. "What if she didn't know there was another option?"

He frowns. "What do you mean?"

I almost roll my eyes at how obtuse he's being but restrain myself. "What I mean is, we hardly live a normal lifestyle."

"What—"

"We could both have her. Share her. Love her, together."

Something eases in my chest when comprehension dawns in his hazel eyes. He takes a few tentative steps toward us.

"You would—you'd be okay with that?"

I nod. "Yeah, I would."

He sniffs, tension locking up his shoulders. "She might not want that," he whispers.

"No, she might not. But maybe she feels the same way I do."

He tilts his head. "And how's that?"

I smile. "Like having to choose between either of you might kill me."

The Search Is Over

DUSTY

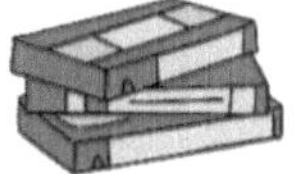

"Hey there, gorgeous."

I open my eyes and nearly squeak when they lock on Joel. I wrap my arms around him and squeeze. He grunts, and I scramble off him.

"Oh my god," I say, checking him over. "I'm so sorry."

But that smile . . . oh, that smile will be the death of me. "Don't be. Best thing I've ever felt is that hug."

I'm all aflutter. There's so much I want to say, but before I can even begin, his finger touches my lips.

"It's okay," he says softly. "You don't need to explain yourself."

I shake my head. "No! No, I do. You have to let me tell you why—"

"Key told me."

My heart sinks. "He—what did he say?"

"That you love me."

My eyes flutter closed. I don't know why I thought Key would try to keep us apart. A part of me will always jump to the worst possible conclusion. But he loves his friend like a brother. He'd never hurt him. He'd never hurt me.

"And," he continues, "that you've been here since the accident—"

"I couldn't leave—"

"And you haven't eaten anything for fear you'd miss my waking up."

"It's been a rough twenty-four hours."

He chuckles, the dimples I love so much appearing in his cheeks. I reach forward and press my hand to his warm face.

"I thought I might never see you again," I croak.

He turns his face to kiss my palm. "I'm okay now, but you also need to take care of yourself."

"I love you."

I prayed for the chance to tell him, and I'll be damned if I don't follow through now. I'll tell him every minute of every day from here on out until life pulls us apart forever.

"I love you too," he says back. His voice is clear, like there's no chance of him changing his mind.

My muscles ache, but I let the smile split my face anyway, burying myself against him as he does his best to hold me. And for one spectacular moment, everything is perfect.

"Dusty?"

"Hmm?"

"I need to tell you something important, okay?"

My throat tightens. Oh god. All this time I've been worried about choosing between them. But what if they don't choose *me*?

He takes a shallow breath. "My whole life I've been waiting for you and I didn't even know it. Key was waiting for you but didn't want to admit it. The two of us, we love each other in a way that transcends friendship, in a soulmate kind of way. And you know what I realized? I don't want you to choose. He doesn't want you to, and I don't think you do either. I think you want to be with both of us, and we want to be with you. We want to keep being soulmates, except you're here now, and neither of us has to wait anymore."

My heart might be exploding. I don't even know if I can speak through the blubbering mess I've become.

"You know, we've done it before. I don't think either of us has mentioned it, but in the past, we've been with the same woman at the same time. Nothing like this, of course. It was just a hookup preference we both enjoyed . . . Who knew we were just getting ready to welcome you into our lives?"

I blink. Then blink again. Maybe I was in the accident too, because what Joel is saying right now doesn't make sense. ". . . at the same time?"

"Do you understand what I mean?"

"I—"

"It was just for sex, but for you it would be everything. I'm telling you this because you could live in a world where you don't have to choose." He takes a deep breath. "The three of us could be together," he says. "If that's something you want."

"The three of us . . ."

"Together."

What does he mean, the three of us? As in . . . be with both of them together? Us all living together in the one house? Where would we sleep? Would I have my own room? Would I sleep with Joel one night and Key the next? Odd versus even days? Or do they mean . . .

"So, Key and I would date, and you and I would date—but at the same time?"

He smiles gently. "Well, yeah—"

"Would we keep a schedule?"

He chuckles. "I—"

"Would we draw straws on whose turn it is to . . . oh god, how would sex work?"

He clears his throat. "It would be up to you. It could be you and Key or you and me or . . . all three of us at once."

I think I'm starting to finally understand. "Oh."

"I know it's not natural for most people to think about—"

"You wouldn't be jealous of me sleeping with another man?"

He grins. "I thought we already established that I'm not the jealous type."

"But me talking dirty on the phone is a bit different than sleeping with your best friend down the hall," I argue, then remember the revelation of Baby. "Speaking of, I guess if we're laying everything out on the table . . . Key is the reason I quit the fantasy phone job."

He frowns. "What?"

"Turns out Key and my connection even transcends the phone lines," I admit with a shake of my head. "I swear I didn't realize it was him. He didn't recognize me either. But there was something between us there too."

He smiles and pushes back my hair. "That must have been hard. That you had to lose him all over again."

Tears spring to my eyes, but I hold them back. "I was getting too deep with someone over the phone, but you . . . you were real. I had to leave that behind to give this a real chance. I wanted to give all of myself to you."

Joel chuckles and shakes his head. "Just another reason why you should give this a chance. He is destined to be in your life. One way or another."

I play with a loose thread on his pillow. "And if we—" Now it's my turn to blush. "If we were all together?"

With a gentle touch of his hand, the heat from my face spreads to my chest then down to my belly. "If you were with Key and me, well, I'm already imagining you pinned between both of us."

My pussy clenches hard at the visual.

"Dusty," he whispers, gently pulling my attention back to him.

"I want to have you in my life, and the thought of Key having you in his doesn't make me jealous. It makes me ecstatic. He's the best person I know, and he deserves to love and be loved by a woman like you. And I do too. And you deserve more love than you can handle, which we would both give you. You're not mine and you're not his. You're ours."

While the prospect of being the redheaded filling of this man-sandwich makes my insides squirm delectably, there's something even more powerful going on in my chest.

"You know, that's the one thing I wished for as a kid. Over and over again. To be loved," I whisper. "And now that it's here, I'm not sure how to accept it. It's been this unattainable thing and now it's in my hands like a gift. I love you both," I admit. "So very, very much, and I desperately want to live in a world where all of us can be happy together."

Joel nods with a small smile. "You don't need to decide anything right now, take as much time as you need."

I brush back the hair from his forehead. "Are you tired?"

"A bit."

"You need to sleep. I'll still be here when you wake up."

"No, you should go home."

"Don't be stupid, I'll—"

"Dusty," he says sternly. "You haven't been home. You need to sleep and eat and shower and none of those things are fun to do at a hospital. Please." He dips low to catch my eye. "I'll be fine. It would make me feel better if you went home and made yourself feel better too."

I want to argue, but it's hard when he's making sense.

"I suppose Stella must be wondering where the hell I am. She'll probably claw my legs apart desperate for food when I get home."

He smiles. "See? I've got to look out for my girl, Stella."

I nod. "Okay, but I'll be back as soon as I can."

The corner of his mouth twitches.

"I love you," I murmur.

He peeks through a squinting eyelid. "I love you too."

I smile and push myself off the hospital bed.

"Do me a favor?" Joel adds.

"Anything."

"Take Key with you."

"Are you sure?"

He nods. "He's been through a lot and—" He looks up at me through his eyelashes. "I know he's beating himself up over everything. Besides, I think he needs to know for sure how you feel about him."

Joel doesn't say anything else. He closes his eyes and lays his head back against his pillow, and I stand lost in thought by his side until he drifts off.

For so many years I thought me leaving was what Key wanted —what he needed. But if what he said is true, then everything changes. How did my leaving affect him? I imagine that scared boy sitting with a single bag and his guitar at that empty bus station. The panic on his face growing more and more pronounced as he wondered why I wasn't there. Why I didn't I wait for him. How he must have thought his life was over.

I shuffle out into the hallway. I'm feeling better, but I'm also craving a shower and my own bed. Joel isn't wrong; I need to go home.

"Dusty?"

Framed in the doorway is Key's silhouette.

"Hey," I reply, biting my cheek.

"Feeling better?" he asks.

I nod. "Yeah, much. But, umm . . . I'm going to duck over to my place for a bit. Joel's insisting."

"Oh, right. Of course," he mumbles.

"Only," I start, peering up at him. "I don't have a ride. Do you think—?"

"Oh! Yep, right . . . umm, let me just check with Dave and I'll be right back."

In a moment of panic, I reach forward and grab his arm. "Wait, Dave?"

"Yeah, he has a car. I don't think he'd mind driving you home."

"Oh."

"Is that okay?" he asks.

"Uh, yeah—yes. Only . . ."

Take Key with you.

"Only, I was wondering if you could drive me home."

He tilts his head, angling his ear toward me like he didn't catch what I said. "You want *me* to?"

I nod. "Do you think that would be okay?"

His mouth works for a few moments until finally, "I—yes. I mean, let me ask Dave if I can borrow the car. Just . . . hang on, okay?"

"Sure." This feels so awkward but, I suppose it can't be helped. How can we act like ourselves when there's this huge decision weighing over both of us?

Before I know it, Key's back, keys in hand.

"We're good. James and Becks just got here so they can drive Dave and Izzy. You ready?"

My eyes flutter closed. "I'm more than ready."

A quiet peace washes over me as the two of us walk side by side toward the parking lot and I think that elusive, hard-to-accept reality finally cements in my heart. Joel wants this. Key wants this. All I need to do is show them I want it too. Both of them. Forever.

CHAPTER 40

Love to Love You Baby

KEY

"Just pull up here by the curb," she says, pointing to an open space in front of a laundromat.

"Sure." I look through the window and read out the neon sign. "*The Sudsy Dream*?"

Her cheeks turn pink in the light. "Yeah, I . . . my apartment is upstairs."

"Oh," I say, glancing up at the dark windows above. "Right."

We're quiet for a few moments, and I rake my brain trying to think of something to say. This drive has been torture. I know she and Joel talked. I made myself scarce so they could have their time, plus I didn't want to pressure her. I know her too well, even after all these years apart—the last thing she needs is to feel backed into a corner.

But her decision is looming, and I'm itching to know it.

I wish I could tell her I'll live with whatever she decides. That I'll always love her and that if she doesn't want me, I'll stay away so she can be happy. But that honorable part of me is dwindling by the second. My chest gets tighter the longer my mind spins without real answers and . . . shit, what if I lose her again?

"Do you want to come up?" she asks.

My stomach tumbles. "What?"

"I can give you the songs," she continues, waving her hand.

Right. The songs. "Uh, yeah. Sure." But this isn't just about the songs. She's inviting me inside because we need to talk.

Meowing starts from the other side of her door when we make it up the stairs, and there's soft scratching against the wood.

"Yes, I'm home!" she calls.

The door opens to reveal a perturbed-looking orange cat.

"Oh, Stella, I'm so sorry, I didn't mean to leave you so long but—you would not believe what happened."

Dusty heads into the apartment and disappears around a corner, but Stella glares up at me. I'm genuinely concerned this cat is going to attack me. "Heyyy, kitty cat," I draw out, stooping low and offering her my hand to smell.

The cat doesn't move, and for ten agonizing seconds I feel like a complete idiot. Of course this cat hates me. She probably thinks I'm here to ruin Dusty's life.

"I promise I won't hurt her," I whisper.

The cat tilts her head, then with a quiet meow, rubs her head against my hand. Something lifts in my chest. I never thought that I'd need to ask for the approval of a cat, but here we are. I chuckle softly, then stand as Stella scampers off back into the apartment.

Dusty pops her head out from around the door. "You can come in."

"Right," I say, stepping across the threshold before shutting the door behind me.

"I'm just going to turn on the shower, then I'll grab those songs for you."

The apartment is one big room. Her bed is still unmade and there are a few dirty dishes in the sink, but it's clean and tidy. It smells like peppermint and roses. I remove my shoes and feel the textured carpet against my feet. The sun shines in through the open curtains, flickers of light bouncing off dust particles that Stella kicks up as she hops onto the windowsill. It's beautiful.

Dusty crosses the room and opens the top drawer of a vanity. For a moment she searches through it, then pulls out an old folder. She opens it, rifles through the pages, then looks up at me and smiles.

"Here they are," she says, walking over to me. "I never could get rid of them. No matter how many times I moved around they were always the first thing I packed. I don't know why—"

"Thank you," I whisper. My voice is gone. It has no strength left.

"I—" She pauses. "I didn't realize you only ever wrote them down this once."

I shrug, my insides buzzing. "They were about you. Seemed only right that you had the only copies."

She hands me the folder and I open it, staring at the crumpled, aged paper within. The horrendous handwriting staring back at me.

"Are you okay?" she asks.

I nod. "Yeah. It's just—"

"What?"

Tears well in my eyes and my nose begins to run. "Sorry." I sniff. "I just . . . it's this place. It's this." I gesture to the folder. "It's you."

Her eyes bounce between mine and I stretch out a hand, gesturing to the apartment.

"This could've been ours."

She tenses. "What?"

"This life," I continue. "This apartment."

There's a nervous kind of chuckle that leaves her lips. "Key, don't be silly. It's not the Ritz, it's a studio apartment—"

"And yet it's the most incredible place I've ever been."

She's quiet.

"You were always like that. Turning the ugliest, most unfortunate, sad thing into something beautiful. The scars on my hands, the cabin . . . me."

Tears spill down my cheeks.

She steps closer to me and presses her palm to my heated cheek. "Why are you crying?"

I hold her hand to me, closing my eyes as I take a deep breath. "This could've been our life." I can feel her step toward me, and a shiver races up my spine. If this is the day she decides, she needs to know everything. "You know, I thought I saw you six months ago," I admit, wiping my face on the back of my hand. "We went to this award ceremony for Izzy—all of us, together. We were in this big fancy theatre when I saw this woman with curly red hair."

Her eyes flit over my face.

"Every time I saw hair like that it felt like having a heart attack—I was going out of my mind. All I wanted was to go back in time and take back all the awful things I said to you in Vegas. Then a few weeks ago, it was the anniversary of the day you left. The day my family betrayed me. The worst day of my life, and I just . . . I needed someone to talk to. I flipped through the phone book and I saw this ad. What are the odds that you were the one who answered my call? The one person I wanted to talk to more than anything, and I had no idea."

She presses her hand over my heart and it pounds against her palm, as if it's trying to tell her exactly what I want to say but can't.

"I love you, Key."

My eyes open and she is smiling at me.

"I've loved you my whole life. I think that's why I kept your music. You had my heart . . . so I held tight to your soul."

In a flurry of movement, I grasp her face. "I love you, Dusty, and I always will. Through the years, the loneliness and frustration. Through thinking I wasn't enough for you. Through knowing you also love my best friend . . ." I swallow hard against the lump in my throat. "And now, I love you even more for it. Of course you love him and of course he would love you. It makes so much sense now, and I'll continue to love you through everything that has yet to come our way because when the love is real, it will always find a way back."

She smiles. "I did promise I'd come back for you."

I kiss her then, and it's like finally breathing clean air when everything has always been smoke. My head is light and dizzy; my lungs expand and my mind revels in the first real bout of clarity to hit me in years. Her kiss ignites nostalgia and reminds me of stolen time and joy and wonder. She tangles her fingers in my shirt as she kisses me back. It's not the same as I remember it being all those years ago—it's better. It's grown-up. *We're* grown-up, and I can't believe she's back in my life after all this time.

She pulls back, her face flushed, and whispers breathlessly, "I should shower."

I let go of her face. "Right."

When she looks at me again, her blue diamond–eyes sparkle. "You should come with me."

She grasps my hand and with a subtle smile pulls me toward her bathroom. I go with her, because where else could I possibly be but with her. The room fills with steam, the heat caressing my sore bones. In truth, I'm exhausted. I've been awake for more hours than I can count, but as she turns to me and pulls her shirt over her head, I'm shot with adrenaline.

"Dusty—"

Her blue eyes flick up, her gaze hooded and dark. She turns away, facing the mirror. "Will you help me take it off?"

My cock twitches, all of the blood rushing downward with unprecedented speed. It makes me light-headed. "Sure."

I glide the backs of my fingers up her spine and I watch with fascination as her eyes flutter. I snap her bra clasp and it comes undone in one swift motion. Dusty gives an audible gasp then giggles.

"Your technique has improved," she teases.

I chuckle, then turn her toward me, allowing the bra to fall to the tile floor. Her breasts are larger than I recall. Fuller—with the tiniest pink nipples. They're so goddamn perfect. She hooks her thumbs into her jeans and shimmies them down her legs and I follow suit.

"What's that?" she asks, her finger tips tracing over the sun tattoo on my back.

"My tattoo?"

"It's beautiful," she whispers.

I swallow my fear and tell her, "It's you."

Her forehead creases. "What?"

"You were always the sun, Dusty," I say. "You were the light that gave me life. When you were gone, I had to immortalize that in some way. A reminder to keep me from getting lost in the dark."

She smiles. "Somehow we always come back to each other."

I'm desperate to touch her, but also to feel that hot water on my skin.

She opens the shower door, peering at me over her shoulder, her long red hair skimming the top of her plump ass. "You coming?"

Something sharp hits me in the guts and I think of Joel, alone in that hospital bed. Before I do this, I need to know she's choosing him too. I can't bear to lose either of them.

She frowns. "What's wrong?"

"I just need to make sure—"

With a step toward me, she holds my face in her hands. "You want to know what I figured out on the way here?"

My eyes dart over her face. "What?"

"That I can choose for all of us to be happy. I want both of you. I love both of you. Never in my wildest dreams did I think I could have so much love in my life. It was my greatest wish. Knowing there's a door number three where we can all be together—"

"But if the three of us are going to be together," I push, "you need to be sure. If you're not—"

"I'm sure, Key. I'm still working out all the details of how everything will work. But what I know for sure is that I want to be with you—with him—all of us, *together*."

I pull her toward me by the waist, her back arching, and lean down to capture her mouth with mine. Our bodies press together and I'm overwhelmed by the newness and the familiarity. We part again, and Dusty leads me into the shower. Her hair darkens as the water hits her and my muscles scream with joy at the instantaneous relief.

She slots in next to me and heaves a contented sigh. "Oh god, this feels so good."

I tip my head back and let the showerhead soak my hair. I didn't realize just how awful I felt until now, and it's as though I'm being baptized, only this time it's my choice. I can exit here with a new sense of purpose and love because she loves me back. She's not going anywhere this time.

Dusty grabs a bottle of shampoo and pops the cap. "Here, I'll do it," I say, reaching around her.

"No, I got it. I can do it."

"Dusty," I say, "I know you can do it, but you don't have to. You're the strongest woman I know, you can take a break."

I see it in her eyes. The way she wants to fight. To prove that she can do it all on her own, and I know she can. She's proven over and over again that she can take care of herself. To survive. She's survived so much.

"I'm not trying to be a hero. I just want to take care of you."

For a moment all I can hear is the gentle rushing of the shower until she nods. "Okay."

I smile. "Turn around."

She turns her back to me and I grab the shampoo. I lather up my hands then gently massage her scalp, watching the lather spread and turn sudsy, already seeing the tension rolling off her shoulders. Her head becomes limp in my hands, her neck loose, and the sound of a moan makes me bite my lip as I wash her hair.

"That feels incredible," she says.

The water cleanses away the shampoo, and it feels like she's finally letting go as her doubts and fear wash down the drain. When she turns to face me again, her eyes are bright.

"Kiss me," she whispers, before wrapping her arm around my neck. Her lips are frantic and addictive. I pull her to me tighter and she grabs my bicep with one hand, her fingertips squeezing delectably. Soon I can't get enough of her. I can't get close enough, then we're falling into the shower wall as I try to press our bodies closer than is possible—my cock squeezed between us begging for her touch.

She presses her breasts against my chest, her tight nipples rubbing against my sensitive skin. Like a drug, I crave her and it's not enough. It's been too long. It's been too much to overcome. Too much heartbreak and lies and surprises. She's my destiny and if it took all of our past to get to this point, that's something I can live with.

CHAPTER 41

Time After Time

DUSTY

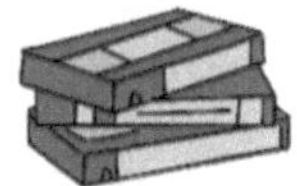

I need him. I need all of him.

In one swift movement he grips beneath my thighs and I instinctively wrap my legs around him. We're simultaneously so close and too far. His kisses cover my face and neck and I gasp when I feel the tip of his cock brush against my pussy.

"Oh god, Key, I need you."

"Not in here," he says, fumbling for the tap, and I plunge into scattered shivers as the heat flies away from me. He wraps his fist in my hair and squeezes out the water before stepping out and carrying me with ease. As if I'm only a doll.

I can't stop touching him, my hands caressing his back and shoulders while my teeth gently snag the edge of his ear. I'm aching for him. Some long and hidden feeling bursting through me like a suppressed and forgotten dream. It's not enough.

"Please," I beg, "I need all of you."

His eyes are dark but hazy, like he's lost in the fog too. "Condoms?"

I nod and point to my nightstand. My heart thunders along as I wait for him to get ready, then he's over top of me, lining himself up and sinking into me so perfectly I cry out louder than I ever have before.

Sex with Joel is incredible and it's different. It's slow and methodical and builds to an insane euphoria—like being high. Sex with Key is desperate, needy and animalistic—it's grounded in the earth. Like two wild animals we ride each other. His body hits and pulses into mine and before I even know it's happening, I'm coming hard and fast, my nails scraping down his back as he grasps a fistful of my hair and groans against my ear.

"*Fuck!*" he cries, holding me tighter against him.

He collapses over me a heartbeat later, but it's not suffocating. It's the opposite. It feels freeing. As if not having him in my life has caused me great strain. My body knows this was always what was needed. Him and me.

"Are you okay?" he asks. "Sorry, I couldn't hold back."

I smile and push the dark curls away from his face. "Me either."

And then the giggles start. My body vibrates with deep, belly laughter. He's confused at first—or concerned, I suppose—but I know he feels it too: this has been a long time coming. I feel like a teenager again, giggling like a schoolgirl who just walked into class and caught the boy I've loved my whole life staring at my underwear.

"I wanted you to look, by the way," I whisper.

He rolls to the side and props up on his elbow. "What do you mean?"

"That day in school when you looked at my underwear," I admit. "It wasn't an accident."

He pinches the skin at my ribs. "What! You had me thinking I was a pervert for weeks."

I lift my hand, my palm facing him. He raises his own, his fingers gently sweeping across my palm before our digits entwine.

"I can't believe we're here," he whispers as though thinking out loud. "It feels like the most beautiful dream."

"We got lost," I say, letting sleep consume me. "Took the long way home."

EVEN THOUGH KEY and everyone else in the boardroom is confident, I can't help but shake a little.

"It's going to be okay," Key whispers in my ear.

I nod stiffly as we wait for the others to arrive. On my left is Key, who holds my hand under the table, and on my right is the band's lawyer. I'm the only woman in the room, and I tried my best to look professional, but with my job history . . . I mean, I don't just have pantsuits hanging in my closet.

My heart is fluttering and my fingers tap nervously on my thigh. Oh god, what if this doesn't work? What if we waited too long and they want more evidence?

The door creaks open and in walks a man with light brown hair and the smuggest smile on his face. That is, until he sees Key.

"Keith," he says, the note of surprise in his tone clear. He takes his seat at the table across from us, rolling his shoulders back and doing his best impression of a man who didn't just have the rug pulled out from under him. He did *not* expect Key to actually show up. "It must be so embarrassing for you and the band to be going through this. I believe even the local radio stations have stopped playing those songs." The two men at his sides—his lawyers, if I had to guess—exchange a look that says *Get this kid under control.*

Heat flares in my face, a rage brewing in my gut, but Key squeezes my hand and simply smiles.

"Logan," he says. "I wish I could say it's nice to see you again . . . but, here we are."

Logan rolls his eyes, and thankfully, an older man in black robes enters.

"Good afternoon, everyone," the judge says as he seats himself at the head of the conference table. "I take it from the several new faces here today that this is the infamous Keith Prentiss."

"Yes, sir."

The judge tilts his head and looks right at me. "And you might be?"

I swallow down the nerves and open my mouth. "I'm Dusty Connors."

"And your purpose in being here today?"

The lawyer on my right clears his throat and leans forward. "Will be introduced in due course."

The judge furrows his grey brows and opens his file. "I see that we've left things a little last-minute. You had fourteen days to provide contradicting evidence for your case and this is the final day. I assume then that either you have nothing, or you have something quite significant."

At this, I feel eyes on me and look across the table to where Logan sits. He is glaring at me. If looks could kill, I'd be dead a hundred times over, but the throbbing pulse in his neck tells me he's also nervous. Good.

"We must apologize," Key says. "One of our bandmates was very gravely injured in a car accident a week ago and it has been a very difficult time."

The judge's eyes widen. "I'm very sorry to hear that and I hope he is doing better. You could have requested an extension."

"Unnecessary." Key smiles. "He's coming home from the hospital tomorrow."

"Very well." He turns to Logan. "Mr. Samuels, you have

already presented your evidence for the songs in question, do you have any further evidence to provide this court?"

Logan chews his lip, then turns to his lawyer who shakes his head. "No, we don't."

"I see. And, Mr. Prentiss, is there new evidence you wish to submit on your behalf?"

Key turns and looks directly at Logan, a smirk pulling at his cheeks. "Yes. There is."

The lawyer leans across the table and passes down a folder I know all too well. The judge grabs it and flips it open. His brows grow tighter the more he reads.

"What is this?" he asks.

"Those are the only original copies of the songs in question. Written before Mr. Prentiss and Mr. Samuels met at military school."

The judge flips through more of the papers. "But half of this is nonsense. It's barely legible. How does this prove anything?"

"Because I have dyslexia, sir."

I blink and look at Key with confusion.

The judge's eyes open wider. "Dyslexia?"

"Yes, sir, it's a neurodevelopmental condition that—"

He raises his hand. "Yes, I know what dyslexia is. My grandson was just diagnosed with it." Something skips in my heart—a connection. "Please, continue."

Key clears his throat. "When I was a kid, no one could figure out why I couldn't read or write. I said all the right words and understood when things were read aloud but the moment I had to read something off paper or write an answer down, it just got all jumbled. My teachers thought I was just stupid, so did my parents, but then I met Dusty. She told me that no one who composed songs the way I did could be stupid. It's very possible that is the day I fell in love with her."

My chest tightens. He's never told me that before.

"I had gotten in the habit of anticipating answers or memorizing things to avoid reading and writing at all costs. And not just school—even when it came to writing songs. However, I always wanted to share my songs with one particular person."

His hand squeezes mine and I smile.

"As you can see, they weren't the most legible, and some of the letters are jumbled, but Dusty was always able to read them and miraculously, kept them after all these years."

The judge looks again at the yellowed paper.

"You mix up your *b*s and *d*s the most," he says. "My grandson does the same. And, young lady, you are willing to testify to the authenticity of these?"

I nod. "Yes, of course I am. They were given to me as a gift. You can see the dates they were written on each of them. It spans years of us knowing each other, as early as nineteen seventy-four."

The judge sits back in his chair and sighs. "We will have to verify the handwriting first . . ."

Key's lawyer stands up and pulls another few papers from his binder. "Actually, I can provide that now. Here is a copy of the contract that Mr. Prentiss signed with Megaloud Records, as well as other official documentation. These are from just a few years ago, all of which have been witnessed. As you can tell, the handwriting is identical, as well as the common spelling errors."

The judge considers them, his brow relaxing as he takes it all in. Then he pulls out another file of paperwork where there are several bundled papers stuck together with a paperclip. "Mr. Samuels, you entered these documents into evidence to prove that you were involved in the writing process; however what Mr. Prentiss and Miss Connors have just brought forward contradicts the timeline in which these songs were written. What do you have to say about that?"

Logan's face is as red as a brick wall. "They—they've obviously manufactured those documents to disprove mine!"

"Or"—Key addresses Logan directly—"you could tell everyone how you wrote down the songs I dictated to you under the pretense that you were helping me overcome my 'challenges,'" he says, his fingers making quotation marks. "That I might need them someday. Only to claim you were a cowriter when you were nothing but a scribe."

"You son of a bitch!" Logan says standing up, spit flying from his mouth. "Those songs are mine!"

"No. You *wish* they were yours and you stooped lower than the lowest sub-species of human being in order to pretend they were," Key says, standing up to face him across the table. "But it ends here. I just wish I had the courage to stop you eight years ago. Face it, you are a mediocre guitarist who saw an opportunity to make money and ran with it thinking because of my disability I'd never have the courage to write down the songs. But you were wrong. My only regret is that Joel isn't here to finish you off this time around."

"Counsel, please control your clients," the judge says over the noise. Logan's nostrils are flaring with every breath like a raging bull as he's wrestled back to his seat. "Very well," he continues, "if Miss Connors is willing to provide a written declaration to the documents' authenticity, then I'd say this matter is closed."

"Closed?" Logan shrieks.

"These documents are clearly written by Mr. Prentiss. With Miss Connors stating they were given to her as a gift prior to you ever having met each other. So yes, I would say they have effectively proven no wrongdoing in this case."

"But—! But . . ." Logan splutters.

"Very well," the judge says. "This matter is settled. May I suggest bringing a claim against Mr. Samuels for defamation. He

said himself that your songs have been taken off of the radio—
I'm assuming due to the false allegations made."

"You can't do that!" Logan yells.

"Something to think about," the judge says, a subtle smirk pulling at his lips.

Logan's hands are fists, and he begins to shake in his seat. Meanwhile the judge hands the lawyer my statement explaining the letters, and the room is silent as I sign them. With a short nod, he takes them and heads through the tall oak doors.

After he's gone, there's a moment where I worry Logan might actually try to hurt one of us. He's convulsing with fury, and after the tense seconds that follow, he abruptly stands from his chair and bursts through the doors into the lobby.

Key squeezes my hand, and I turn to see him give me a gentle smile. "You did amazing," he says.

"No, you did. It's over."

"Congratulations," Key's lawyer says, stretching out his hand to both of us and shaking it. "Miss Connors, you really saved the day with those songs. Thank you."

I smile. "I'm glad they could help after all these years."

"I think celebrations are in order," he says, then pushes out the door.

I turn and wrap my arms around Key for the tightest hug I can manage. "You must feel so relieved."

He lifts my hand and kisses the backs of my fingers. "In a lot of ways. What do you say we meet up with everyone for a drink?"

"I really think we should get back to the hospital. Joel will—"

He squeezes my hand. "Joel will be fine for two more hours. Besides, I want to properly introduce you to our friends."

"I've already met them all at the hospital?"

"That was at the hospital and all we ever spoke about was Joel and how he was doing. I want everyone to get to know *you*."

My stomach jolts. "What if they don't like me?"

"They will," he insists.

He squeezes my hand and together we walk out toward the elevators. The doors ding and we get in, pressing the button for the lobby. Next thing I know, Key has me pressed up against the mirrored walls, his lips locked on mine. That nervous jolt turns into butterflies as my arms snake their way around his neck. His lips are like a drug—my whole body feels alive at their caress, my nerves tingling.

The elevator dings again and we walk outside into the cool early evening air. Only it's anything but peaceful as we notice Logan waiting for us with a menacing stare.

"This isn't over, Prentiss," he half shouts. Several onlookers on their way home from work slow down to watch.

Key sighs. "Samuels, enough. You lost. Deal with it; you're never going to get any money out of this."

He steps closer and the hairs on my arms raise in alarm. "Money? That was only half of it." Logan begins to laugh wildly and I grasp Key's arm tighter.

"Then what?" Key shouts. "What else could you possibly have wanted from all this?"

"To destroy you and that piece of shit you call a bass player."

"That's what this is all about? You're jealous of him?"

Logan is right in his face now, only a few inches separating Key's straight nose from Logan's crooked one. "How do you think it felt to hear those songs on the radio over and over again and know that should've been me?"

My whole body is rigid, certain that at any moment one of them is going to swing at the other. Then I feel Key sigh and the tension in his back eases.

"Logan, I'm sorry. I never meant to hurt you."

My eyes widen, and Logan blinks as though not sure he heard him right.

"I was in a really bad place when we were at Samson Academy, we all were, but I can't help that I connected more with Joel than with you. And if you recall, we never actually kicked you out of the band."

There's a long moment that presses down on all three of us—as though the very breeze dares not to blow. For a minute, I think that Logan will apologize as well, but then his face contorts into a fierce rage.

"You're such a pretentious piece of shit. And your apology is fucking worthless, just like you. Just like you've always been."

"He's a better man than you'll ever be," I say, pulling Logan's focus.

His eyes narrow and his lip curls as he looks me up and down. "This is her, isn't it?"

Key tenses. "What are you talking about?"

"She's the slut you knocked up. Isn't she?"

"Enough," he says with a deadly calm. "You lost. Deal with it. You thought you could take everything away from me and win? You're a liar who, rather than do any real work for yourself, has to steal it from others."

"At least I'm not a dumbfuck who had to cheat off me in school just to pass your exams." Then he turns to me with a cruel smile. "This is the father of your baby? A fucking retar—"

I'm not sure where it comes from, but suddenly my hand is stinging, a bright-red palm print blistering over Logan's cheek as he stumbles back. My vision blurs as my eyes fill with tears. There's a sudden silence that comes over the space. Perhaps it's because everyone has stopped breathing, unlike me who is gulping down air to try and keep upright.

Logan's cupping his reddening cheek, looking stunned. "You bitch!" he shouts, his hands whipping out to push me back. His force hits me and I stumble, but before I can even right myself, a loud crack echoes down the street and I watch as Logan falls like a sack of potatoes to the ground. Key is shaking as he stands over Logan's unconscious body, his fist bloody where the skin on his knuckles is torn open.

"Key," I whisper. He turns to me, checking me over with trembling hands.

"Are you okay?" he asks.

I nod. "I'm fine, I—I'm sorry, I shouldn't have—"

"No, you definitely should have. He crossed a line on so many levels."

We both stare down at the limp pile of limbs. "We should call an ambulance," I say begrudgingly.

"Don't worry, I'll tell my secretary to make the call."

Both Key and I turn to find the judge, still in his black robe, smoking a cigarette and eating a hotdog from a street cart. My jaw hits the floor. Has he been there the whole time?

"Sir," Key says, panicked. "I didn't mean—he pushed her and—"

The judge takes another bite of his hot dog and looks down at Logan. "Oh, don't worry. You were clearly defending the young lady here from this riff raff. Purely defensive. I'll make sure the police know what really happened when they arrive."

"I . . . really?" I ask. "But I slapped—"

He holds up his hand. "Afraid I didn't catch anything before the push. I would suggest that both of you leave now before anything else happens."

The judge bites into his hotdog and we, dazed, head toward the parked car. Once out of earshot, Key begins to laugh. He laughs so hard he falls against the brick of a nearby building.

"Key, what are you—"

He wipes the mirth from his eyes. "I thought the first one was a fluke. But nope." He pops the P. "He's still One-Punch Logan."

He laughs again and this time I can't help but join. "You okay?" I ask Key as his chuckles fizzle out.

"Better than okay," he says with a grin. "I've wanted to do that for years."

Under Pressure

DUSTY

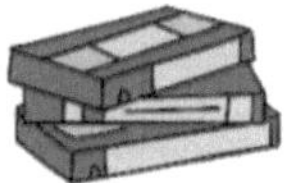

As we pull up to the bar there's a different kind of nervousness that jumbles my belly. The outside is nondescript. Brick with dark wood trim. The windows don't give much away and the inside is dimly lit by the occasional neon sign. I slow down when we near the door, pulling Key to a stop.

"What's wrong?" he asks.

"What if they *really* don't like me?" I ask. "Or worse, what if . . . what if they don't approve of, well, our situation?"

He kisses my knuckles again. "They're a lot more open-minded than you would think. I know they're going to love you. Come on."

He pulls me gently and after a moment's hesitation I relent, taking deep breaths as we pass over the threshold. It's not overly busy inside. There are a few people sitting at the bar and several around a pool table in the corner, but then I see . . .

"Joel?" I whisper.

From the far side of the room, he smiles at me, flanked on either side by the two other couples. His hair is starting to grow back in and his face is still bruised, but he's up and he's out. He's out of the hospital a day early.

Every worry I have flies out of my head as I run across the bar. That gorgeous grin spreads across his face as he stands and opens his arms so I can throw myself into him. He lets out a little *oomf* as we collide, and I realize maybe I shouldn't have been so forceful, but when I try to loosen my grip on his shoulders he buries his face in my neck. Maybe he needed this as much as I did.

"Hey gorgeous," he whispers in my ear.

I nearly sob on the spot but all I can do is hold fast to him. To take him in. His smell, his energy, his touch, it's like the other half of me. Finally, I pull back to face him and he pushes the curls away from my face.

I lean forward to kiss him and feel him tighten his grip on my hips. An intoxicating rush of adrenaline rushes up through my toes all the way to the top of my hair. Key is all calm familiarity —Joel is electric spontaneity.

When our lips part I murmur against his cheek. "I love you so much."

His nose nuzzles with mine. "I love you too."

"Ahem."

A throat clears and I'm startled to remember that we're not alone. In fact, there's a whole crowd of people I need to like me watching on. I jump away from Joel but he grasps my hand to keep me close by as he chuckles.

"Dusty Connors," he says happily. "Officially, I'd like you to meet James, Becks, Dave, and Izzy."

My cheeks burn as I wave and smile at the two couples in front of me. "Hi," I say, my voice cracking. "It's so nice to meet you all . . . officially and under happier circumstances."

I see it. The looks in their eyes as they bounce between Joel, Key and me. The slightly forced smile on everyone's face, except

. . . the blond's. She walks right up to me, her green eyes bright and her short hair swinging, and hugs me tight. My muscles relax as I sink into her hug before she pulls back and grabs my free hand.

"Dusty," she says breathlessly. "You're every bit as wonderful as I knew you would be. We're going to be great friends."

My heart swells. Friends?

"I'm Becks, James's wife," she says, tucking herself into my side so she can introduce the others more thoroughly. "That dark-haired stud muffin there." She points and giggles, and I smile at the way James blushes.

He reaches out his hand and I have to let go of Joel to take it.

"It's nice to meet you," James says, and while a moment ago there had been judgement in his eyes, there's nothing but kindness now.

"And this is Isabella, or . . . we call her Izzy," Becks explains, pulling me away from Key and Joel.

I nod. "Yes, we . . . uh, we talked briefly already," I admit. "At the hospital. And prior to that, apparently."

"Oh! That's right," Becks says.

"To be fair," Izzy intercedes, "at the hospital, it was a crazy night. I'd totally understand if you've blocked all memory of me."

My jaw twitches as I recall what I can of that night. How horrible it all was. I must have looked like a lunatic to them.

"And this is Dave," Izzy continues.

The blond man looks at me with piercing blue eyes. Eyes that aren't judgmental but aren't friendly. He nods almost imperceptibly, then stands up straighter. "I'm going to go outside for a smoke," he says, then turns toward the door, the sunlight cascading across the floor for a moment as the door swings shut behind him.

I blink. Did he—does he not like me? My suspicions are confirmed when I see the look that transpires between Becks and

Izzy. Well . . . I guess as far as success goes, three out of four isn't bad. Maybe he just needs time to warm up to me. Or, maybe he'll be the person to remind everyone I'm trash and that I'm not worthy of being part of their group. Their band. Their family.

"I think I need a drink," I say, and pull my arm away from Becks. "I'll be right back."

I weave my way toward the bar and take a deep breath, trying to will the blood out of my cheeks. As I wait for my whiskey and soda, warm fingers slide along the back of my neck.

"Why so tense, sweetheart," Key whispers in my ear as he comes around to face me and leans on the bar. "I told you everyone was going to love you."

My fingernails click on the bar surface. "Not sure everyone does," I mutter.

I see Key frown out of the corner of my eye. "What do you mean?"

"It's nothing."

I grasp my drink and take a long sip, nearly draining it down. When I try to walk away, Key grabs my wrist. "It's not nothing. Did someone say something?"

My eyes flick to the window where I can see Dave standing outside smoking alone. I shrug. "I just don't think some people are as excited for me to be here as you think."

Key glances at the window and I can tell he's fighting the urge to roll his eyes. "So it's a Dave problem."

I open my mouth to say no, but there's only four of them. He would've figured it out eventually. "Maybe."

"Just talk to him," Key says with a soft smile. "If there's one thing I know about you, it's that you can talk anyone into doing whatever you want."

"There's a big difference between getting a guy off over the phone and trying to get this guy to be my friend. Or at the very least, not my enemy."

Key leans forward to kiss my temple. "I'm sure you can figure it out." He pats me on the bum then heads back over to his friends. Rolling my shoulders back, I take the last sip of my drink then head outside to find Dave smoking his cigarette and staring out at the road.

"Hey," I say, trying to sound casual and failing.

He glances over at me, then back out to the road. "Hey."

"Think I could bum one of those?" I ask.

I watch as he hesitates. Yup, really doesn't like me. Miraculously, he decides to hand me one, probably knowing he'll be a complete asshole if he doesn't and wants to save face. I'm even surprised when he holds out his lighter for me.

The smoke pleasantly burns my lungs and I try to focus on it to make it less awkward that we're standing in silence outside together. But his cigarette is almost burned down and if I want to try and fix anything, I need to do it now.

"You know," I start, and he looks over surprised. "I should probably mention that I quit my job—at the phone sex line."

His eyebrows rise spectacularly high on his forehead.

"It paid well but it made life too complicated, and I realized I wanted more for myself than that. Is that really something you'd judge me for enough to hate me?"

Dave's mouth goes a little crooked. Is he confused? I take another drag on my cigarette to mask the nervous tremor in my hand.

"I know it's not as refined as award-winning journalist or trend-setting fashion designer like the other girls, but this kind of work has been all I've known. All I ever thought I was good enough for. And even through that, I was never ashamed of it. The only problem I had was jerks who judged *me* for it. And really . . . who are *you* to judge me? You don't even know me!"

"No, I—"

"I'm going to make something of myself, but because I want to. Not because I have to."

"Wait—"

"And if you think I'm with them for the money, you're dead wrong. I haven't taken or asked for a cent of their money, ever."

"Dusty, stop," Dave begs, holding his hands up in front of him. "Stop. Your job was never the problem. Nor did I ever think you were a gold digger."

I swallow and it feels like barbed wire. If it isn't my job or the money, then it really is about the three of us together. I rub my lips together. "I understand that three people in a relationship together isn't exactly normal—"

He shakes his head and steps toward me. "No, no . . . it isn't that either."

I frown. "Then what? What is it about me you don't like?"

He looks down and crosses his arms over his chest. For a long moment he's quiet, as though putting together what he wants to say. Finally, he looks up at me.

"You almost broke up the band."

My immediate reaction is to argue, but I stop. The words wash over me. Ones I hadn't even considered. "I—what?"

Dave flicks away his cigarette and lights another. "You and Joel. You and Key. I don't know what the odds are on it all but fuck, the universe really likes to mess around doesn't it?"

Now it's my turn to look shocked. "Sorry?"

Dave takes another step toward me. "Listen, you're perfectly lovely. You're beautiful and I couldn't care less about what you do for a job . . . but those guys in there are my brothers," he says, pointing with his cigarette back at the door. "What do you think would've happened if they weren't the type of guys who like to share their girl?"

I press my lips together and think about it, but Dave continues voicing my thoughts out loud.

"They would've had to choose. *You* would've had to choose. And do you really think their friendship would've ever been the same if you picked one over the other? They're more than friends. They're brothers. Closer than brothers. In truth, it's actually even a little weird sometimes how close they are. They're like soulmates. And the only time there's ever been any drama between them is when you showed up."

There's an edge to his voice and it's clear to me now that he isn't angry. He's worried about his friends.

"Would they have been able to stay together in the band if one of them was left out? Do you know what it's like having to choose between your dream career in music and the love of your life?"

He sounds as though he knows exactly what that feels like. "No. I suppose I don't."

"Don't get me wrong, I'm unbelievably grateful you knew Key all those years. Some of our best songs are about you. Then when that lawsuit happened and you had them . . . You really saved us," he says with a half-hearted smile. "But you also almost destroyed us."

My heart is pounding.

"I know that's not what you meant to do and I apologize for being standoffish, but I guess I'm just worried that this whole thing you three have arranged is going to blow up in your faces and it'll ruin everything all of us have worked so hard to achieve. Sacrificed so much for. We're just at a really vulnerable point right now." He scoffs. "I don't even know if we'll ever be able to get the public back on our side after everything either."

I look at the ground, shuffling from foot to foot as I take another drag on my cigarette, but it tastes bitter now.

"I get it," I say quietly. "I understand, and while I can't predict the future, I'll tell you, truly, that I am in love with them. Both of them."

When I glance up, he's watching me. His blue eyes meeting my own.

"Key was always the best thing in my life. I've always loved him, ever since I was a little girl. It seems like some kind of predestined miracle we keep finding each other. The universe's way of trying to make up for all the horrible shitty things we both had to endure growing up. And even though I thought he was lost to me for good, I never stopped loving him. In fact, I was sure there'd never be anyone else. No one could ever replace the space he took up in my heart."

I lick my lips and swallow.

"But then I met Joel. And meeting him changed my life. Not only that but also changed how I felt about myself. Just in the short time I've known him, I've fallen head over heels in love with both him and myself. Something I've never been able to do. He's seen something valuable in me besides my looks that no one but Key ever has."

Dave nods.

"So, I know our arrangement is unusual, but I can't choose, and I shouldn't have to. I can't choose between two halves of my own heart. Can you at least understand that?"

His eyes bounce between mine for a moment then relief washes over me as a smile tugs at the corner of his mouth. "Yeah, I think I can."

A sigh rushes out of me and I close my eyes in relief. "Thank you."

He steps closer to me. "No, I'm sorry. This has been a really stressful few weeks and . . . well, it was wrong of me to take it out on you."

"So . . . you really didn't care about what I did for my job?" I hedge.

He shrugs. "Dusty, we're in a metal band. If you think any of us would judge you for making a living, then you definitely need to get to know us better."

I smile as he tips his head toward the door.

"Come on, I'll buy you a drink for winning us the case."

"Actually, I might be able to do better than win you the case."

His blond brows scrunch. "What do you mean?"

"That public opinion problem? Do you think it would be easier to get your fans to believe your side if you had Logan's confession that he lied?"

His lips part. "I—I mean, shit, yeah . . . but we don't have that. And I doubt he'll publicly take back what he said without a huge payout."

I smirk and pull my purse across my body onto my hip. I dig into it only to retrieve the cassette recorder I stashed there this morning and hold it out to him. "What if I happened to record a little encounter Key and Logan had outside the courthouse?"

Dave takes the recorder from my hands as if it were a fragile baby bird. "You did what?"

"I'm about to save Carnal Sins."

CHAPTER 43

Need You Tonight

JOEL

Even though my ribs are killing me and my face is sore from smiling through the bruises all afternoon, when Key, Dusty, and I walk up the stone path toward the house, I couldn't be happier. While we've all had a few drinks, none of us is drunk, and we share a smile as the door opens and the smell of home engulfs us.

"Welcome home," Key says, slapping me on the shoulder.

I try not to wince but Dusty catches it, and she mouths to me, *Are you okay?*

I nod and brush it off. "Thanks, it feels good to be home."

"Are you tired?" she asks.

I shake my head and find the soft skin of her waist. "Not even a little bit."

I pull her to me and she comes freely. I tilt her chin up and press my mouth to hers. Her kisses have always been the sweetest. Those juicy red lips are so agonizingly plump that I'm semi-hard after just a single touch of them. I pull her against me so she can feel it and the warmth of her fills me with excitement. My hands go into her hair, her curls sliding between my fingers as I keep her to me. She traces her hands up my arms, memorizing the muscles there and making it hard not to want to pick her up and throw her over my shoulder, but I'm supposed to "take it easy." Doctor's orders. But this—her—can't wait.

"Come to bed with me," I say against her lips.

Her eyes widen, that gorgeous blue ocean staring back at me. "You should be resting," she says.

"I can rest later. Right now, I want you."

Her cheeks turn pink under her freckles but a devilish smile plays upon her lips. "I'll be gentle," she says.

I chuckle and she shivers in my hands as I drag my nose along her cheek to whisper in her ear. "Fuck, I hope not."

"Joel, you're supposed to be in recovery," Key says abruptly.

I watch Dusty's face as she steps back from me. It's almost like she's embarrassed? That simply won't do. I want her to feel comfortable in all of this and that education starts now.

"I guess you'll have to join us then. Make sure I don't pull something," I say with a smirk.

Key's eyes flare and Dusty's face flushes deeper.

"Is that something you might want?" I ask her.

"I—I . . ." she stammers.

Key walks up and cups her cheeks. "Remember, you don't have to say yes if you're uncomfortable. This is new and it's a lot. Just know you don't have to be embarrassed. I've thought of nothing for days except for how much I want the two of us to fuck you into oblivion."

She gasps and Key captures her mouth with his. A heady haze washes over me as I watch them kiss. The way her body responds to his touch is mesmerizing. Her fingertips reach out to grasp the front of my shirt and tug. I step forward, sliding my arm around her back waiting for my moment and as if he can read my mind, he pulls away.

Her heavy eyes latch onto me for just a moment before I'm smothering her with my own kiss. I feel the moment her knees give out. A tiny tremble in her self-consciousness that has her hooked on feeling this much all at once. When I pull back her eyes remain closed and her pulse flutters in her neck. Key's hand gently caresses her stomach and she sighs as her fist closes in the fabric at my chest.

"Yes," she whispers, her eyes softly opening. Her teeth snag her luscious bottom lip. "Yes, I want this."

Key's eyes meet mine and a slow grin spreads across his face. Next thing, he's throwing her over his shoulder and heading toward my bedroom. My chest swells as I realize he's quietly making a gesture of respect. His actions tell me that once this is done for the night, that it'll end on my terms. That we'll sleep in my bed. That if I want her and I to be alone, I can simply ask for him to leave. I won't—but the offer means a lot.

When we enter, I'm surprised that my bed has been made. The sheets have been changed and the room is tidy. One of them must have cleaned up for me while I was in the hospital. Key sets Dusty down on the floor and she looks up at the two of us through her long eyelashes and her chest rises and falls rapidly.

"You can say stop at any time, remember?" I remind her gently. "If it gets too much, or you don't like something . . . just tell us. You're in control, okay?"

Adorably, she raises her chin and nods. "Okay."

I step forward and drag my fingers across the skin of her shoulder, pulling down the strap of her shirt. "You're going to be a good girl for us, aren't you?"

She shivers, goose bumps prickling her chest and arms. She draws in a sharp breath before nodding. "Yes."

I reach for her neck, the pad of my thumb swiping across her lips. "Don't be nervous. We're going to make you feel so fucking good."

"I trust you. I trust you *both*."

With another kiss, my hands roam over the familiar curves of her body. Her body is absolutely unmatched—I swear, god broke the mold when he made her. Even if that's what attracted me to her so long ago in that dark Vegas strip club, she proved that very night that there was so much more beauty to her than that.

She hesitates at first but as if she's finally switched off her brain, she kisses me back. She wraps her arms around my neck and she pushes her chest into me. I waste no time in finding the hem of her shirt and pull it up. My fingers swipe against Key's, his hand back to gently caressing her side.

As I break our kiss to pull her shirt off, I feel pressure on my cock and peer down where I find her hand gently cupping me. I'm pleasantly surprised. It usually takes girls longer to get involved and a lot of them participate in a way where they don't have to do much. She must really want this. Want me. Want us—together.

She unclasps the button of my jeans and now it's my turn to take a breath. I leave her mouth, trailing kisses down her neck to the top of her breast still confined inside her lacy green bra. I reach behind her to unhook the contraption and it springs open. As the bra falls away, my tongue finds her nipple. Small but hard on her large breasts and as my lips close around it, I look up at her to see her head fall back, right onto Key's chest.

I can hear the thundering of her heart as I flick and tease her nipple, my fingers gently tugging at her other breast. Key has a hand gripped to her waist, the other sliding down her stomach to the top of her skirt.

"You're doing so good for him," I hear Key say. "But what will I find if I touch you here," he continues, and his hand disappears between her legs. Her whole body jumps and she cries out, her grip on my shirt tightening. "I knew you'd be soaked," he says. "But how much of that is for him and how much for me?"

I watch enraptured as her eyes roll back in her head, meanwhile she's trying to form a coherent thought. Fuck, she's a sight to behold.

"I—ah, for both . . . for both of you!" she finally cries out.

I meet Key's eyes and he raises his brow at me before pulling his hand from between her legs. I let go of her breast, the skin glistening in the low light from where I just worked my mouth over her.

Key leans in until their faces are only inches apart. "Prove it. Get on your knees and show us just how hot you are for two cocks."

I can't see her face but I hear the tiny squeak that escapes her lips. Key unbuckles his belt, pulling it from the loops of his jeans, and I follow. Dusty looks between us and like a fallen angel sinks to her knees.

"At least there's one thing that came out of going to church," Key says with a smirk. "All that practice made you look goddamn gorgeous on your knees."

He pulls his cock from his pants, the jeans slipping down his hips, and without breaking eye contact she wraps her red lips around him. He hisses, his eyes closing briefly before returning to watch her with fascination and adoration. I'm so fucking hard that I nearly pop the button of my fly as I try to get my pants undone. Without even looking over, she brushes my hand away to fiddle with the enclosure until it opens. I sigh with relief as the pressure eases but it's only momentary because then I feel her soft fingers pulling me out into the open.

Key's fist winds its way into her hair as his hips gently sway forward. "Damn, your mouth is fucking sacred."

Her eyelids flutter and she moans around him, her pace increasing ever so slightly. And I watch them. They're so fucking beautiful together. Key pulls her head back, not hard but enough to know he means business and he leans down in front of her.

"I thought you were going to show how much you wanted us both, meanwhile the only dick you're sucking is mine."

Dusty's wide blue eyes find mine and she looks up pleadingly at me. "Yes, sorry—I," she starts, but Key pushes her face toward me then crouches down to whisper in her ear.

"Now open wide for him. Let him fuck this gorgeous face until you're a mess."

She nods then grips me tight and swallows me down. My stomach contracts and my balls tighten hard and fast and I have to tangle my fist in her hair to stay upright. Key's right. Her mouth was made to worship.

I'll worship all of her, forever.

CHAPTER 44

Nasty Girl

KEY

Never in a million years did I think I'd be here. It's crazy enough to think that Dusty would be back in my life and that it would be in a way where I get to love her. But this? I remember what she said to me the first day I ever met her. That her greatest wish was to be loved. I've always loved her but she needs more, and now she has it. She deserves it. The universe sure has a dark sense of humor, because surely this was all meant to be—life was always meant to end up this way. What else could explain the astronomical odds of my best friend falling in love with the love of my life?

Dusty slides her tongue up the underside of my dick and I groan. Her hand works Joel while she sucks me off. Then, as if to prove to me she does love us both equally, she strokes me while sucking him. I watch, fascinated, as she switches between us. Her lips are swollen and her chest shines from the drool that has spilled down her mouth and neck. Years of fantasies are coming true in this moment.

"What do you think, Joel? Is she messy enough for you yet?" I ask.

She sits back on her heels and swallows. The muscles of her throat working so beautifully.

"I think she's done a pretty good job," he says, humming softly.

Joel, Joel, Joel. Always with the praise. Guy doesn't have a mean bone in his body and while I'm hardly a bully, there's something about leaving behind the religiously traumatized boy to become this version of myself that turns me on. Dusty was always the one in control of our narrative. It was her who came and went in and out of my life. Now? I'm taking that power back. And while I wasn't sure if she could handle it at first, that look in her eye right now tells me she loves it.

"If you're satisfied," I say with a careless drawl. "But I think she needs to prove herself a little more to me."

Joel smirks. "I think I know exactly what you mean. Lie on the bed, princess," he says.

She wipes her mouth and moves to obey, but I grasp her wrist as she passes me. Her eyes crease at the corners as she looks back questioningly.

"Lose the bottoms," I say, gesturing to the skirt and underwear she's still wearing.

"Oh," she whispers, "right—"

"I got you, princess," Joel says, stepping behind her. He hooks his thumbs into the belt loops of that devastating mini skirt and pulls down. Her matching green thong sits delectably on her hips and when she steps out of the skirt, I spot where the fabric is damp and my mouth waters.

Joel leans down to kiss her hip, and her eyes close for a moment as he sinks his teeth into the soft skin of her thigh. He pulls the fabric down exposing her and I'm not sure how it's possible but I get harder seeing all of her bare like this.

"Lay her down, head off the edge of the bed here," I say, pointing in front of me.

Joel guides Dusty over, her eyes dark and wild as they linger. She shuffles her way to the edge of the bed where I stand over her. I reach forward and pinch her tiny nipples and she sucks in a breath but it has the desired effect and distracts her from Joel. He kneels between her legs and with a quick push forward, buries his face in her pussy.

"Oh my god!" Dusty cries out, and I watch for a minute as she squirms, her hands twisting in the bed sheets. Joel wraps his arms around her hips to pin her to the bed as she begins to thrust and I gently tap her cheek. Her eyes fly open and she looks straight up at me, her gaze darting between me and my cock.

"Tap my leg if it gets too much," I say. "Open up."

She does, and I begin to fuck her mouth. Hot, sweet warmth envelops me. Bliss, absolute bliss. I can tell she's trying to concentrate, but Joel's tongue brings her closer and closer to the edge and her rhythm starts to falter. I love the way I can feel her losing control. My cock hits the back of her throat, her saliva coating every inch of me. I can't wait to sink myself into her but these things take time.

Her toes start to flex and her legs shake and while I could keep fucking her mouth, I want to see her come for him. I pull myself free and sink to my knees next to her head.

"Come for him," I whisper. "Show him how much you love his tongue in your cunt."

She looks at me and tries to lift her head but I pin her to the bed, watching as her eyes roll back and a great trembling takes over her body.

"Oh fuck!" she cries. "Fuck! I'm coming!"

Her whole body shakes. She breathes hot in my ear, her pants sharp. Then she does something I'm not expecting. She grabs hold of my neck and kisses me. Moaning against my lips she devours me and I return the favor. My hands wind through her hair, our tongues clashing beautifully as I reach down to caress her chest. This is where we want her. That place where your brain turns off and you simply do what feels good.

Society and its "rules" don't have a place in here with what we're doing. And while I may call her a slut and a whore behind closed doors, I'll kill any motherfucker who attempts the same. Those names are from my lips only because only then will she know that she can be whatever version of herself she wants to be. If she wants to play the good girl/innocent angel, I'll love her. But if she wants to be the wanton, sex-crazed nympho who fucks two guys at once? I'll encourage that all day long.

"You're so filthy," I say against her lips. "I love you so fucking much."

I kiss her again and she gasps out loud, her body contorting before we both look down at Joel whose smirking like it's his birthday. At my quizzical glance, he shrugs. "Just getting the backdoor ready."

I look back down at Dusty and give her another passionate kiss. "You hear that, sweetheart? You're about to feel so good you forget your own name."

Sexual Healing

DUSTY

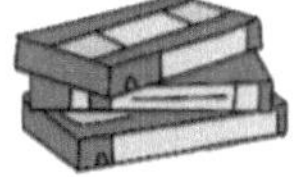

I hardly know which way is up or down anymore. All I know is that I'm lifted and tossed around. Caressed and touched in the most beautiful and pleasurable ways. Key's filthy degradation and Joel's praise take me to levels I never even knew existed. All I want is to be good for them. To let them do whatever they want with me because there is a single truth that I know: I trust them with my entire being.

I trust them with my heart. My body. My mind. And I would do anything for them. My gorgeous men.

"Time to show me how wet your pussy is after it's been thoroughly licked," Key says, and I shiver.

He grabs me, gentler than I expect, and rolls me on top of him. My legs straddle his waist and I sigh at the touch of my soaked pussy on his stomach. He maneuvers me a bit then he holds both sides of my face.

"I'm going to fuck you now," he says, his eyes intent on mine.

I nearly sob with desire. "Yes," I whisper. "Please . . . please!"

I sink onto him and nearly come from that alone. It's as if the universe knew exactly what I needed because he fits inside me so perfectly I wonder how I ever survived without him. Our desperate quickie after years apart was intense, but this is different. So intentional and thorough that I hardly know how it could possibly get better.

Until I feel the pressure of Joel's fingers on my ass.

"Relax for me, doll," Joel whispers in my ear. His digits push into me and combined with everything else, I hardly know how to speak anymore. "That's right," he coos. "You're doing so good."

The feeling is so strange. Not bad in any way, but new. It's slow and rhythmic and I find myself thrusting in a groove that seems to work for everyone. Then I'm not sure if Joel or Key is responsible but something changes and suddenly Key's cock is hitting my g spot and I know I'm about to orgasm.

"Oh god!" I cry. "Right there, please. I've been so good!"

There's a momentary pause where I sense a silent exchange, and then Key thrusts just a little faster. With Joel's fingers inside me and Key in my pussy I shake and tremble as I come for so long it feels like it goes on forever.

Key lifts himself to kiss me and it's as if I've sunk into oblivion. I'm floating and can feel nothing except bliss. Then there's even more pressure against me from behind and Joel's breath is in my ear.

"You can take us both, gorgeous," he says, wrapping his hand gently around my throat. "Just float here and relax."

"Okay," I whisper, the sound barely audible.

He pushes into me easier than before but it's so tight. The space I have for Key shrinks as it's taken up by Joel and my heart pounds from the intensity.

"Oh shit, oh shit, oh shit," I say, falling forward onto Key's chest. "Oh god, it's so much," I say.

"Dusty," Key calls as if from some far-off place. "Dusty, look at me."

It takes me a few seconds to find the strength to open my eyes but when I do, his hazel gaze is the comfort I need.

"You were made for this, Dusty. You were made for us."

And when they both move inside of me, I gasp out loud with the knowledge that yes, I was made for them. Both of them.

It begins slowly then pace is quickened. Rhythm alternating, spots I didn't even know I had lighting up inside of me, but when Joel turns my head so he can kiss me—that's when I fall apart. Everything contracts and my vision darkens as the most earth-shattering orgasm of my life rips through me. Complete and utter euphoria.

I think Key and Joel were holding back and waiting for me because I hear their twin groans just behind my own and the calm serenity that follows when you're completely physically satisfied.

I don't know how I've lived so long without enjoying this particular aspect of physical love but I don't think I'll ever be able to exist without needing it all the time. I'm gently rolled onto my side, my skin resting on the sheets for just a moment before Joel pulls me into his warm body. I shiver and tremble, my adrenaline dropping after being kept so high for so long. Key disappears into the next room but I hardly worry. Joel has me and his thumb gently strokes the wispy curls at the edge of my face.

"I love you so much," he whispers, his nose grazing mine.

The muscles of my face are sore and exhausted but I manage a small smile. "I love you too."

"Let me clean you up, sweetheart," Key says gently before I feel the warm damp cloth on my tender skin.

He takes his time and is thorough in his task before I find myself missing him terribly. I want his chest against my back as I fall asleep nuzzled into Joel's neck.

"Key?" I whisper.

The bed dips and I feel him curl around me. "I'm here."

"I love you," I whisper, my fingers entwining with his on my hip.

He gently kisses the back of my neck and runs his nose along my hairline. "I love you, Dusty. I'll never stop."

It's not long before I drift off into the most peaceful sleep of my life, wrapped in all the love I've ever wished for.

ONE MONTH LATER

JOEL

"Right, well I think that's the last of the boxes," I say, setting them down on the kitchen counter then wiping the sweat from my forehead.

"Beer?" Key asks, opening the fridge behind me.

I nod. "Definitely."

He grins and grabs two bottles, which clack together as we sit at the kitchen bar. We crack them open as we take stock of all the boxes that are officially moved in from Dusty's laundromat apartment. I'm tired just thinking about unpacking them all. Maybe that can wait until tomorrow.

"Can't believe we made it," Key says as he peels at the label on the bottle.

I smile and use my shoulder to give him a little shove. "I know. It's great."

"I don't think I've ever been this happy," he says.

"Me either."

"Who would've thought, huh?" Key says again.

"Well, it wasn't for lack of convincing," I remind him.

He grins. "She's a stubborn woman. But she couldn't stay

there. Her quitting her job aside, I don't think I could stand another week not being under the same roof."

I take another sip, then ask a question I've wondered since I found out about Dusty and Key's past. "Why didn't you ever tell me?"

Key's brows furrow. "Tell you what?"

"About her. About what happened."

He chews on his lip. "I don't know," he starts. "It just hurt too much. I didn't just lose her, I lost the baby too. I lost the home and family I always wanted. It was finally within my reach and cruelly got torn away from me. Then, just when I thought my own parents might have finally found some compassion for me, they sent me to that academy like a damn prisoner. If I had any idea that they had told her I didn't want her . . ."

The muscles in his jaw grow taut, and he drags his bottle through the ring of condensation on the counter. I wait, careful not to rush him.

"I don't know what I would've done."

I nod. "I understand. I'm sorry. About everything."

"I can't help thinking maybe it was always meant to happen this way. After all," he says, turning to me and grinning, "how else was I to become a tortured artist?"

I smile back and the two of us take a long drink.

The door opens behind us and Dusty walks in wearing the shortest shorts I've ever seen and a loose shirt that covers a neon purple bra and tumbles off one shoulder. Stella, upon her arrival, slinks through her ankles then runs off down the hall, meowing loudly as if to claim her territory. "Hey! I thought you guys were supposed to be helping," she says, setting the bag of clothes down and walking over to us with a deliberate sway in her hips. "And here you both are, drinking without me." She pouts dramatically.

My hand squeezes her hip and she smiles at me. "These are the last of your boxes, princess. I think we're done for today.

Besides, we're going to have to start getting ready soon," I say. "Can't be late. The show is sold out thanks to you."

"Thanks to me?" she asks.

"Of course," Key adds. "You're the one who got Logan on tape confessing his claims were bogus. All Izzy had to do was give it to her friend at the *Chronicle*."

"I'm just glad that's all over." She sighs. "I'm so excited for tonight. I can't wait to finally see you all play for real," she says, doing a little dance where she stands.

"Yes, but first . . . I think we have time for a quick shower. If we all go together, that is."

Her smile turns into a sultry grin. She backs up, pushes down her shorts, takes off her shirt and walks toward the bathroom. Both Key and I stare after her, that gorgeous freckled body perfectly at home with us in this house.

She turns back and raises an eyebrow. "Well, aren't you boys coming?"

We give each other a look, clink our bottles, then drain the beer before tripping over ourselves to follow her down the hall.

Epilogue
DUSTY

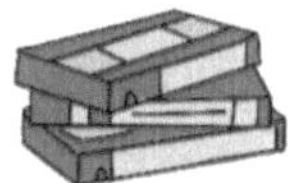

"Are you excited?" Key asks.

I tear my gaze from the limo window to look at him. "Excited? I've only been waiting for this day for half of my life!"

He smiles, his whole face lighting up like that boy I first met in that stinking hot church. "Who would've thought we'd actually get here, huh?" he says.

I squeeze his fingers between mine. "It still feels like a dream."

"We're here," Joel says, a huge grin overtaking his face.

My heart flutters. I've listened to Joel and Key's music on repeat. I know every lyric by heart—but I have yet to see them perform live with the rest of the band.

Joel opens the limo door and climbs out, reaching back for my hand. "M'lady," he says.

I grin and step out onto the sidewalk, feeling Key exit the limo right behind me. I glance up at the huge lit marquee, *Carnal Sins* displayed in giant black letters. There's a warmth from the lights on my face that's familiar and comforting. Then I see the chip in the molding on the corner, then the faded black paint on the front doors and I forget how to breathe.

"This . . . this is . . ." I whisper, my jaw dropping open. "This is The Sapphire!" My stomach is doing a mambo. "The first performance I get to see of your band and it's at The Sapphire?"

"That's right," Joel says, placing his hand on the small of my back.

"But," I mumble. "How? How is this even possible? The theater is abandoned."

I turn toward the two of them with a million questions. What are the odds?

"Actually, not quite abandoned. Just neglected," Joel corrects me.

My brow creases. "What?"

Key shrugs. "It actually had an owner, but they didn't have any interest in doing anything with it. So . . ." he says with a look at Joel, "they were willing to let it go to someone who had big ideas to make it into a space where a lot of great things can happen."

"We thought you should have it."

I blink. Once. Twice. Three times. What is happening? Then Key holds up an old ring of keys in front of me and my pulse is racing like the rapids. "We bought it. For you."

"You . . . you what?" I squeak out, barely lucid enough to clutch on to the ring that Key places in my hand.

"It's all yours to do with how you said," Joel says, stepping closer. "To show old movies, host performers, and run art and acting classes for kids so they can stay out of trouble. Maybe if kids have a safe place to explore art, they won't end up in trouble and get sent off to horrible places like we were."

"You can work your magic," Key continues, "and bring out the beauty you always knew it could have."

The tears begin to trickle down my face and for once I have

no shame in standing on the street and openly sobbing with joy at this incredible gift.

"I don't know what to say. I'm . . . is this real life?"

"It's real," Joel says, wiping at my cheeks with his thumbs. "You can have all of your dreams come true, too, you know."

A burst of pure joy radiates out of me in a contagious giggle. I'm crying and laughing and feel like I'm floating. "I don't think I've ever been more surprised or happy in my whole life!"

Key takes my hand and kisses my knuckles. "We know you can take care of yourself. You've been surviving for twenty-five years. But now, we want you to live."

I close my eyes and pull Key into my side, my head falling on Joel's shoulder.

"I will. I can. Because we're together."

Epilogue
KEY

"Hey, Key?"

I turn my head to look over at Dusty. Her wild hair is in two knots on top of her head. Her father's attempt at parenting after he couldn't be bothered to brush it, she told me. "Yeah?"

She continues to stare up at the blue sky, her chin rising over the long blades of grass we lie in side by side. "Hmmm . . . never mind."

"No," I say, lifting myself up on one elbow to see her face better. Her freckles seem to have multiplied by the summer sun and I often catch myself counting them, thinking one day I'll finally know exactly how many are there. "Tell me."

She sighs. A sad sound. One that makes my heart twist. She gets like this sometimes, and I can't always bring her back right away. Back to that smiling, shining person she deserves to be.

"I just had a thought . . ." she says as she bites her lip. "Do you think we'll ever be truly happy?"

That twisting feeling gets tighter. What a thought for a thirteen-year-old to have. Then I think about it for a minute. Am I really happy? I'm happy now. I'm happier than I've been in weeks . . . months—but only when I'm with her. Being at home is like torture. A prison. A specially crafted hell made by my parents and, if I'm really to believe everything they teach me in church, God too. I swallow hard. "Are you not happy right now?"

Her sapphire eyes find mine. "I think so."

I blink. *Ouch.* Sensing my hurt, she sits up, a few tiny white flowers stuck in her hair from lying in the grass. "I don't mean that you don't make me happy. Actually—" Her cheeks turn pink. "You're probably the only thing that does make me feel happy."

A nervous smile tugs at one side of my mouth. "You too."

The tiniest laugh escapes her before she frowns again. "I just mean . . . let's say we both achieve everything we've ever dreamed of, do you think we'll be completely happy then?"

I shrug. "I don't think achieving your dreams is the only thing that makes you happy. I think maybe, it takes a lot of things. And maybe they're not all perfect at the same time so you know to be grateful and recognize the things that truly make you happy when they do."

She nods, plucks some grass and lets the breeze take it away off her palm. "I always knew you were smart," she says with a grin. "I think I know if I'm happy or not now."

I raise an eyebrow. "You do?"

"When we're *not* together I'm unhappy . . . maybe it's so I can recognize how to feel when we're together. Like the universe is shining a huge flashlight to show me the good part of my life."

Now it's my turn to blush. "Surely I'm not the only good thing in your life."

"But you just said I'm the only one in yours?"

My mouth opens but it's true. I did say that. "Dusty," I say, grabbing her hand. "You're my best friend."

She smiles. "You're mine."

"Let's promise that no matter what happens, no matter how

long we're apart, or how old we get . . . we'll always try to make each other happy. That's what best friends do, right?"

"Right," she says, lying back down and closing her eyes to bask in the sunshine. "I think that's what love feels like."

THE END

Acknowledgments

I can't believe we're here. The final book in the Carnal Sins series is complete and in the hands of readers. A Ballad of Betrayal and Beauty may be the most difficult challenge I've faced as a writer. Three different points of view, three different voices, two time periods, secrets and deception. When I told friends of my plans for how I wanted to approach the writing for this book, we all agreed it would be incredibly difficult. And while that is certainly true, this may also be my favourite book to date. I love how this story came together and I love these characters and I hope above all else that you love them too.

Thank you as always to my amazing family who love me unconditionally. Please grammy, do me a favour and don't read this one. Mom . . . maybe you too.

As a base for so much of the Carnal Sins lore, a big thank you has to go to Metallica. In particular the devastating tragedy and death of bassist Cliff Burton in 1986. While Joel was headed toward the same fate at one point, I owed it to Cliff to give him a happily ever after. A huge shout out as well has to go to Charles Berthoud who has given me an incredible new appreciation for bass players. You should really check him out. I learned so much.

Music has always been an inspiring part of the writing process but for this book, it was hard to nail down a particular song or album that helped get me in the right headspace. However, Novo Amor's *State Lines* was probably the top runner for most repeated on the playlist.

Thank you to Luisa for my incredible cover. It is everything I hoped it would be and more. You were such a pleasure to work with and I hope there are more projects in our future together.

To my editor, Britt, your insight and critiques are always thoughtful and in the best interest of the story and prose. You continually make me a better writer and your comments make me laugh out loud.

To all my amazing beta readers: Melanie, Ashley, Emily, Gaby, Kate, Lacey, Madison, Taylor, Erin and Marissa. Your feedback was so incredibly valuable and I appreciate all the time you took out of your busy lives to give this story your attention. Thank you so much.

As always there's the IG writing crew that is always available to discuss the current gossip, politics, relationship issues and, of course, writing. Becky, WH and Heather, I know we don't always chat on the daily but the support you've offered over the years has truly made all the difference in my life and career as a writer.

To the one and only, Lety. Thank you for your constant friendship and love. Where would I be without you? Probably weeping in the corner without a completed novel. I will forever cherish you and I cannot wait to visit you this summer!

Finally, to the readers. Thank you. Thank you for picking up this book. Thank you for supporting indie authors like myself when there are thousands of options for you out there. I hope these characters and their story spoke to you. If this is your last journey with Carnal Sins then I hope you enjoyed the ride. If you're only discovering them now, I hope this encourages you to go back and discover the other stories. Finally, to all the strong, independent women who have tirelessly fought to stay afloat and survive, I hope you find the love you deserve. Because you *do* deserve it.

About the Author

L.H. Blake is a full time high school teacher living in rural Ontario, Canada. An avid reader and creative writer since childhood, Blake has always loved fantasy and romance stories. This is her fourth full length published novel with many more works in progress. Outside of books, Blake has been involved in the arts her whole life with passions for dance, musical theatre, crafting, embroidery and backyard astronomy. She currently lives with her three little boys, husband, kitten and massive dog in total chaos 24/7.

instagram.com/lhblake.author
tiktok.com/@lhblake.author